Also by Ann Rich Duncan

Travel With Johnny Vic Through The Metals of Time
(A Johnny Vic adventure series *for young adults*)
ISBN 0-7414-2315-4

And
ask about the exciting action game
"Johnny Vic's BIG DIG"

Kathy – It was so
great to see you again!
We have so many memories.
It's an honor to sign this
for you.

Annie

THE SEED

By
Ann Rich Duncan

ISBN 0-7414-3072-X

Published by:

INFIΏITY
PUBLISHING.COM

1094 New DeHaven Street, Suite 100
West Conshohocken, PA 19428-2713
Info@buybooksontheweb.com
www.buybooksontheweb.com
Toll-free (877) BUY BOOK
Local Phone (610) 941-9999
Fax (610) 941-9959

Printed in the United States of America

Printed on Recycled Paper

Published June 2006

ACKNOWLEDGMENTS

Many thanks to all those who made this first book in the John Victor adventure series happen, including: James King, Brigadier General, USMC, retired, who helped get the military characters on track; Merry Lee Corwin, local "critic of kindliness," who set me straight at the very start; Karen Elliott, first reader extraordinaire; Jim and Liz Edwards, special second readers; free-lance editor, Roberta Buland, who put me on the right path with the first draft; Linda Nye Barbaro, co-founder of the Horace Greeley Foundation, friend and writerly mentor; Tom Stearns, lecturer, heirloom seed grower & purveyor of planty wisdom; Jackie Becker, MNA, wise medical practitioner, for sharing her expertise; Elizabeth Marie Rich, for her editorial skills and suggestions for bringing more action to the story; my husband, Donald William Duncan, Jr., whose concerns about hybrid seeds and genetically engineered foods inspired this story; Jeffrey Smith, author of *Seeds of Deception,* a book that rekindled the desire to publish this story and is a must-read for those who are interested in scientific information regarding the dangers of genetically modified foods; the staff at Pember Library and the Poultney Public Library, for their patience and assistance; and finally special creative kudos to the 'real' John Victor—my eldest brother, John Victor Pulling—who lives a life that confirms Thoreau's message: "Our truest life is when we are in our dreams, awake."

***

This book is dedicated
to the memory of my parents,
Robert L. Pulling,
WWII hero, man of honor & integrity
&
Ruth Madeline Powell Pulling,
purveyor of wisdom & peace

Introduction

*But people who long to be rich fall into temptation
and are trapped by many foolish & harmful desires
that plunge them into ruin and destruction.*

I Timothy 6:9

For many years, my husband, Don, has felt uneasy about unchecked applications of biotechnology, the glut of hybrid seeds in the marketplace and the dependence of our farmers upon them. He asked me to write about his concerns, and that's how *The Seed*, this fictional novel, sprouted within my imagination. But I had to do some research first, and the more I learned about the subject, the more concerned I became about the path we are following on this planet. To be competitive, many farmers have abandoned the use of heirlooms—embracing the use of hybrids and quickly finding themselves <u>dependent</u> upon suppliers of seeds that cannot sustain their enhanced characteristics for future crops. *Dependent!* We've gone from hundreds of heirloom seed companies to a handful. I can't help but wonder, *what if* someone gets control of *all of them?* And then, there's our government. Legislation has already been written that mandates stiff penalties regarding a farmer's use of seeds that have been patented. Even, as I understand the issue, the seeds from fruit that he's grown from his own harvest! How far will it go? I even heard a farm professional talk on the radio—real life radio—about satellite surveillance of farmlands to make sure they're growing the 'proper' acreage of crops. I can't help but wonder, what are our politicians thinking when they write some of this stuff and why do they allow these patents before long-term testing can be done? Shouldn't we wonder, just who they are protecting? Who are they helping? I'm not against science—I'm all for it. But, God's creations—our fruit and vegetables—are now being patented and when I think <u>patent</u>, I think <u>money</u>. *Big money!* The phrase, 'follow the money, honey,' echoed through my brain as I wrote this story.

1

A generation ago, people were a lot more self reliant. They knew how to grow their own food. They knew how to save seeds for future harvests. But, with each decade, we seem to know less and less about the land. About survival. About the very sustenance of life! We're growing too dependent upon industrial agriculture and less knowledgeable about our own needs for survival. That is a very dangerous circumstance if someone gains power over the production of food. They could use that power to control people. *Us*! And so, I talked with professors, scientists, seed producers, politicians and a host of other people. I acquired information from organizations like NOFA, MNL and Rural Vermont, and with each interview, the need for a story like *The Seed,* seemed to grow within my mind..

I'll never forget one conversation with a professor of horticulture. He spoke of a terminator technology that shuts off the growth capabilities of a plant. He said it could be a great thing for golf courses and apple orchards—and lawns. After all, who wouldn't love to throw away their lawnmower? When I told Don about it and said that I wanted my 'bad guys' to use the terminator technology but I wasn't sure how, he glanced upwards at a grid of contrails crisscrossing the sky and his imaginative brain proclaimed, *that's it!* Thus, 'The Terminator' formula that my character Julia would create quickly sprouted within our fruitful imaginations. In *The Seed,* Julia would take it a step further—to inhibit the growth of weeds—and SanFidel's people would bring it to a frightening level. Far fetched? At first, I worried that, yes, it was too farfetched, but then came September 11.

A.R.D.

***

I've sprinkled a few of my favorite well-known authors and some of the grassroots organizations that I've learned about throughout this story, and have listed them at the back of this book. (For more information you can can search for them on the web or at your local library or your favorite book store.):

Prologue

*T*he memory of Colonel Mitchem's eager eyes clung to Julia Mahoney's brain with the intensity of a raw, red canker sore. She realized he'd kill her if Alexander ordered him to do it. *He'd probably take pleasure in it.* She sat at the edge of her bed in the West Wing of Alexander Graham Rossweild's Tennessee mansion in a mindless, autistic-like state until a noise from the hallway snapped her out of it.

Somebody's coming! She leaned forward and strained to listen, her eyes darting from the ornate glass doorknob to the sliver of light below. Shadows flickered under the door and then they were gone. "Good." she crooned. "They're not coming for me—at least not yet." She believed that Alexander wanted her dead. *Why else would Mitchem lock me in?* she reasoned.

A door slammed from somewhere above and more footsteps came her way. It seemed to go on forever—this endless marathon of muffled voices and shuffling footsteps. She returned to her mindless rocking and moaned as she snugged the thick coverlet tightly around her. She was exhausted. Eventually, the convulsive shivers ended and Julia was lulled into the blissful oblivion of a deep sleep. She began to dream then, and found herself cradled within the protective embrace of a benevolent giant who was saving her from her enemy's clutches. Unfortunately, Julia Mahoney, the scientist, could never completely surrender to a dream.

The only giant she knew was Alexander's pride and joy, SanFidel, Incorporated, and he *definitely* was *not* kindly toward anyone even remotely perceived as a threat to it.

JULIA WOKE UP SOBBING. She wondered if she would be killed and dumped on some remote hillside in Tennessee like useless residue from one of SanFidel's failed experiments, but luckily, that thought provoked a burst of anger. *Useless residue? I'm not useless . . . my formula worked! It's going to make them millions!*

Julia crawled out of her warm cocoon. She *would* escape but her only chance would be tonight. She thought, *They'll settle down sooner or later.* She looked around, thinking, *I need a tool or a weapon or something—but what?* She peeked under the bed. *Nothing darnit. Well, maybe there's something in the closet.* She stopped to listen for activity in the hall, then eased the closet door open. A quick glance revealed a tidy space—almost empty, but not quite. At her feet was a neatly stacked pile of metal. *A fire ladder? Perfect!* She picked it up, momentarily surprised by the weight of it, and tiptoed toward the window. She felt almost giddy as her slender fingers tore at the plastic ties that bound the rungs together. *Thank God for Alexander's morbid fear of fire! I bet all of the rooms have one of these tucked away somewhere!*

Julia's excitement almost dissolved when she peered out of the window. *Oh, God. It's so far down—I can't do this!* A tear trickled down her cheek and she turned away, ready to slink back to the bed, but the sudden unbidden memory of Mitchem's cold eyes quickly renewed her determination. She just couldn't let him win.

AT 3:00 AM JULIA TUGGED AT THE WINDOW. It seemed as if it would never budge, but it finally did open—with a vengeance. When she lowered the ladder, it clattered dully against the thick granite exterior of the mansion. Her mind shrieked, *Oh no! What if somebody heard that!* She peered out of the window, but she could not

4

see a thing. The patio was virtually swallowed by the shadow of the West Wing. Paralyzed by fear, Julia clung to the rungs of the ladder. She forced herself to take deep, rhythmic breaths. It helped, but a guilty barrage of questions echoed through her brain. *Why didn't I tell Martin about this when he called the other day? Why didn't I tell him to watch for the package I sent? Why didn't I?*

Julia felt sickened at the thought of Alexander's un-ethical team and what they might do with her formula. *Ruthless pigs! Why couldn't they be more like Martin?* Sobs of regret gurgled in her throat and the ladder renewed its jittery dance as she forced herself to continue the treacherous climb downward.

Julia dropped to the patio after one last attempt to look around, unaware of the opal button that had pulled loose to settle between the milky white slabs at her feet. She pressed herself against the abutting stonewall as she struggled to catch her breath. She felt glad she had finally sent her reports to Dr. Martin Bascomb. The thick manila envelope that she had mailed to the world-renowned botanist contained enough evidence to stop Alexander and all of SanFidel's schemers. *Martin will know how to expose these miserable criminals. Martin always does the right thing.*

JULIA EMERGED FROM THE SHADOWS, com-forted by the belief that her report was in the right hands, excited to realize she had escaped unharmed. Without a single glance backwards, she galloped gracelessly toward her car, across the damp expanse of grass . . . right into full view of surveillance camera number four.

#

MARTIN BASCOMB STILL looked grim when Millicent bustled into his study. *My goodness,* she thought. *I've got to cheer him up!* Millicent was a trusted housekeeper and friend. She was fiercely loyal to her employer and extremely proud of his reputation as one of the world's leading botanists.

"Well now, Martin . . . I have the mail." She waited, her own frown deepening when he did not answer. She tried again. "There's quite a lot of it today—wouldn't you like to look through it right now?"

"No, Millie. Just set it over there." He gestured toward the Victorian library table that was snugged against the window. Millicent's narrowing gaze leaped from Martin's fluttering fingers to the table and the expanse of heavy floral drapes behind it. Her eyes widened with inspiration. *Some sunshine might help!* She zoomed closer and tossed the mail toward yesterday's stack. It hit its mark, but one thick manila envelope slid between the table and the colorful swirl of damask peonies and flowing, golden leaves.

MILLICENT PROCLAIMED, "Well, it's dark as a witch's cauldron in here, Martin. I'll just brighten things up a bit." He paid no attention, so she raised her plump arms to tug at the drapes. She turned to speak once again, unmindful that Julia's evidence had sunk noiselessly behind the table.

"Now . . . isn't this better? Don't you just love the sunshine?" Millicent's expectant grin was as bright as the sunlight that filtered into the room, but she failed to dispel Martin's gloom. He grunted absentmindedly. With a sad little sigh, she slipped out of the study. It was almost lunchtime. She would fix one of his favorite dishes.

That'll do the trick!

***

Chapter 1

"Wisdom is often nearer when we stop than when we soar."
WILLIAM WORDSWORTH

*J*ohn Victor stopped to enjoy the view. He loved this section of Tournagain Pass. To his left, the Chugach Mountain Range cut its jagged course across the bright Alaskan sky. In the valley below him an immense forest of snow-covered evergreens mimicked the vertical reach of the white-tipped peaks. There were no sounds except the crunch of snow under his skis and the sharp chafing of his stiffened jacket—Mother Nature had muffled the region with an unexpected, late-night coverlet of snow. "Absoluuuuuutely magnificent!" John crooned. "But cold." He snugged his cap tighter against a frigid gust of wind and took a deep breath, reveling in the panoramic scenery. He just knew the air could not be crisper, cleaner or brighter anywhere else on earth. For John Victor this rugged Alaskan landscape was picture perfect, but even more importantly, it was inspirational.

AS USUAL, JOHN FOUND THAT today's foray into the wilderness helped to clear his mind. His uneasiness stemmed from a meeting that he had recently attended. The leader, who called himself Colonel Mitchem, described it as a citizen's action meeting, but after just one session with them, John was afraid of the type of action they might take. *It's a wonder they didn't blindfold me, spin me around and drive me all over creation so I wouldn't be able to find them again,* he thought. *That's what a group like that would do in the movies.*

WHEN HE WASN'T LOOKING for hidden treasure or family heirlooms for his clients, John worked as a fire crew coordinator for the State of Alaska. Manny, a guy he had recently met on patrol had invited him to the meeting. He believed that Manny and most of the people were motivated by the desire to improve their lives. However, he was convinced that the group's leader had ulterior motives. John thought scornfully, *if Mitchem's a real colonel, then I'm a naked monkey's Dutch uncle—his eyes sent shivers up my spine. Oh well,* he thought, *I'd better get going so I can work on my plan.*

John's skis cut into the icy crust, propelling him across the snow like a diminutive schooner at high wind. Each turn of the winding hillside trail brought him closer to the cozy lodge that he shared with his wife, Betty, on the outskirts of Upper Summit, Alaska. She'd be returning home by nightfall and he wanted to be finished by then.

As he sped along, John acknowledged gratefully that once again Alfie's theory had worked. He now felt refreshed and ready to solve his problems. He wished he could find the old coot and thank him. Alfie, a hermit-like prospector who once lived nearby, spent many decades panning for gold and avoiding human contact, but during a rare contemplative moment, the secretive old prospector had told John, "Nature has an answer for everything if you just take the time to listen."

Alfie said it had come to him unexpectedly one day when he was feeling alone and desolate. An inner voice said to look beyond himself, to witness the beauty of nature and to appreciate its miracles. In that fleeting moment Alfie had discovered the richness that could be found in the balance of nature. His newfound theory was simple; for every need there is fulfillment, but too many wants can cause things to come unbalanced. Perhaps Alfie had heard the voice of God. Or perhaps it had been guardian angels. Whatever the source, the message had a profound effect, and from that day forward Alfie's wants were few and he relinquished his dreams of striking it rich.

While John was not ready to stop his own quest for riches, he did think there was a lot of truth to Alfie's 'balance theory' that always seemed to unleash an inner wealth of wisdom. So whenever he did not have the answers, he returned to nature—to stop, to listen and to find the road to balance.

JOHN REALIZED SOMEWHAT ruefully that he never even knew Alfie's last name. Soon after that remarkable visit, he found the grizzled old man's cabin stripped of all of his personal belongings. He had left without a single goodbye.

JOHN'S THOUGHTS RETURNED to the citizen's meeting as he came within sight of his front entrance. He was afraid that the leader's motives were not good. He'd be willing to bet his biggest gold nugget on that. After all, he was no stranger to the criminal mind—as an accomplished treasure investigator and gold miner, John Victor had seen more than his share of unsavory characters and the chaos they could create and an inner alarm rang loud and clear as he watched Mitchem that night. He knew he had to stop the guy before someone got hurt. *Damned fool—his eyes practically sparkled. I bet he was hoping they'd get violent!*

John came to a quick, snow-spraying stop. He un-hitched his boot-locks, scraped the icy clumps off his canary yellow Rosignols and burst through the door. He couldn't wait to get started, and as he stripped off his wet outer clothing, he decided there were a lot of good people at that meeting—good people seeking positive changes. Unfortunately, the good people had a bad leader. *No balance there,* he thought, and he realized he'd have to find them a good one.

Reassured by his own determination, John Victor slung his soggy jeans onto the towel bar before pulling on his favorite gray and navy sweats.

***

Chapter 2

*J*ohn sat down to think. First, he needed a leader—someone he could trust who would recognize that most of these people had the right intentions. *Somebody charismatic—a regular George Washington or Martin Luther King would be good!*

Well, there ya go! John thought. *C.D. would be perfect!* C.D. was a long-time army friend who was currently stationed with the Research and Development Unit near Washington. *Heck,* he mused, *C.D.'s even a dead ringer for Morgan Freeman—the ultimate box-office good guy. I always think of him when I watch Freeman's movies.*

Affectionately called C.D., Colonel Lucas Everett Davidson had been a First Lieutenant in John's regiment. C.D. had proven himself on the battlefield in Viet Nam and again as a Lieutenant Colonel during Operation Desert Storm. The two men had kept in touch throughout the years despite their differing lifestyles and John always looked him up when his travels brought him near C.D.'s headquarters.

JOHN SMILED. C.D. was willing to attend the next meeting. *If anyone can bring them around, C.D. can.*

"I did good," John said to himself.

He decided to reward that good self with a generous helping of Betty's apple pie, a hot toddy and a long soak in the tub. He figured she'd be home well after he attacked her delectable pastry.

***

Chapter 3

Liquid gold

*T*hree stars were visible in the misty moonlit sky and the peepers and crickets were in full voice. Their high-pitched chirps created an unworldly atmosphere as a shadowy figure listened for movement within the six-plane hanger. Melvin wondered how such tiny creatures could be so loud. It was as if they were trying to squeal on him. To make matters worse, hungry mosquitoes buzzed around his head and vague fears of the West Nile Virus made him wish he'd brought bug repellent. "Darn-it!" he groused, his eyes following one of the buzzing creatures.

There were no security guards in sight, but Melvin didn't really expect anyone to be there. That's what he liked about small, state-owned airports—easy access. He figured luck was finally on his side with this job. *Yup . . . I feel lucky tonight! Ricardo's client must be a real chump to pay so much money. All I haf'ta do is add that stuff to the holdin' tanks. They say it won't hurt nuthin' . . . the stupid gover'ment was stoppin' them from testin' it.*

As he turned from the hanger, a new thought occurred to Melvin. *Gee . . . it might even make the planes fly better!* He decided this was his chance to do some good in the world, and earning two thousand clams certainly made it worth his effort.

And, they'll give me another two to do the next airport—not too shabby! Melvin felt a sudden surge of pride.

AT THE SOUTHWEST END of the field, Melvin stared at the two fuel tanks. They looked like big white grain silos. *Boy them things is tall!* He did not relish the idea of climbing that high.

The nearby crickets stopped chirping when Melvin got close enough to read the lettering. The first silo held AVGAS, the fuel used for the small piston airplanes. He shook his head. *Nope. I don't want that one.* He read the lettering on the other tank. JET FUEL. *Yup . . . that's the one.* He snipped his way through the barbed wire fence, climbed to the top of the silo and pried open the hatch. Already tired from the exertion, Melvin slowly backed down, tightly clutching the vertical supports on the narrow metal ladder. His flabby belly bounced from rung to rung until he reached the bottom and hopped to the ground. After catching his breath, he scuttled across the parking lot to his rusted VW van and trudged back with a large black case.

"This thing weighs more than my buddy Ritchie's ol' lady when she's on a bender . . . nuthin' but dead weight," he grumbled as he struggled through the opening in the fence. "Darned skeeters don't help neither." After stopping to give the buzzing insects a futile swat, Melvin dragged the large coffin-like case the rest of the way and opened it up. Inside was a heavy agitator assemblage that would blend the liquids. It had three lightweight tubes that had to be connected as a single unit, then eased into the silo.

AFTER MOUNTING the tubes, Melvin bounced back down for the agitator. According to the instructions, the thing had to run for two hours to adequately mix the solution into the fuel. *It's nuthin' but an oversized 'lectric mixer,* he thought. *Thinka' the dough this baby could stir up. And, man . . . it's stirrin' up mucho dough for me!* Melvin cackled merrily. He continued to grin at his own joke as he fetched the two five-gallon buckets.

It was a struggle to get them to the top, but he was determined to make just one trip. He had to stop three times to rest and swat at the relentless mosquitoes. By the time he reached the agitator, the veins pulsed in his neck and his chest heaved with hard, raspy breaths and as he emptied the buckets, both the mysterious golden brew and his sweaty face glistened in the moonlight.

***

Chapter 4

*J*ohn Victor was still in the tub when Betty arrived. She called to him as she struggled through the house with her luggage. "Hello, sweetie . . . where are you?"

John's mellow reply prompted her to call out again.

"Of course . . . you're in the hot tub. Do you look like a prune yet?" She bounced into the bathroom playfully wielding a gaily-wrapped package. "I've got something for you. When Mary and I went shopping I heard a little voice say, '*Buy me for John! Buy me for John!*' . . . so I did!" She waved it back and forth, hoping to coax her husband out of his tranquil soak.

John reached for a towel and tried to snap her with it.

"What a brat!" she exclaimed as she skittered out of reach. "You better be good, Johnny Victor, or I'll ask Jonathan to take you back!" Jonathan, the pastor of their church and a close friend, had presided over their marriage ceremony four years ago. It was the second marriage for both of them.

"I tell you what, brat . . . I'll put on the coffee and you can open your present later . . . when you're dry and civilized!"

JOHN PEERED INTO the steamy bathroom mirror as he toweled off. Lively blue eyes stared back. *Pretty darned good for an old fart. Maybe a little on the short side, but all muscle. Not necessarily handsome, either . . . but as*

15

Betty says, I'm definitely adorable. Yup, ah-DOR-able! His image nodded in vainglorious agreement.

John called out, "How's everyone in Anchorage? Mary must be ready to pop any minute." Mary was soon due to give birth and Betty had spent the past few days helping her daughter-in-law in her efforts to furnish the nursery.

Betty poked her head through the doorway. "Mary's so cute. She positively glows . . ."

John's heart skipped a beat as he stared at his wife. *She can't be glowing any more than you are,* he thought. He decided that Betty looked more like an aunt than a grandmother.

Betty continued her report as she seated herself at the head of their maple dinette set.

". . . and Jonas is all thumbs. I swear that boy's going to have a heart attack before the baby's even born." She smiled brightly. "It was so much fun!"

John bent down to give her a welcoming kiss. "You better watch out, sweetheart, dearest love-of-my-life . . . you're gonna spoil that kid. And then Mary and Jonas'll find a way to get even."

"Nosirrreee," she countered. "I never spoiled any of my boys and I won't spoil this one either—at least not too much." She twisted in her seat to look at him. "So, how about that coffee? And, by the way . . . is there any pie left?" Her arched brows wriggled, but before he could respond, she said, "Let's check the mail, too. I stopped at the post office on my way home and there's a *big* pile of it."

"Sounds like a plan." John chose to ignore her accusing tone—he had not checked the mail since she left and he'd eaten the entire pie.

She was about to stand up when John stated in his finest British tone, "Stay where you are my lady—I'll pour." He gallantly placed a checkered dishtowel across his forearm and reached for the coffeepot. As he padded back to the table, he breathed in the steamy aroma. "Beans of excellent vintage, madam, but I'm afraid we're all out of pie. The establishment has been exceedingly . . . umh . . . busy of late, you see."

Betty exploded with a hearty giggle as she pulled two mugs from the moose shaped mug rack that hung near the table. "Ate it all, didn't you?"

John quickly shed his proper British persona. "Yup."

"I thought as much." She knew the pie would be gone. After all, she *had* left him alone with it.

John reached for the sugar and cream and said, "I'm glad the kids are doing okay. By the way, I have some news, too." He dumped three heaping spoons of sugar into his coffee and told her about Manny and the meeting and how he had contacted C.D. His spoon bumped the ceramic mug with a muffled clunk as he stirred a generous helping of cream into his coffee.

Betty reached across the table and gave his hair an affectionate toss as she said, "You're such a Boy Scout . . . but I'm glad you called him. Sounds like that bunch needs some good leadership."

"That's for sure. *Yuck!* This coffee's definitely strong enough!" He splashed more cream into the offensive liquid, then looked up to ask, "Now that we've got all the news out of the way, let's move on to the important stuff, like . . . where's my present?"

Betty reached for the box.

"Here you go, Johnny."

He tore into the garish gift wrap like a child on Christmas morning.

"Terrific! A book on treasure hunting."

With a bright smile, John happily thumbed through the pages, his coffee already forgotten.

Betty reached for a letter and murmured, "Glad you like it, sweetie."

***

Chapter 5

Gold—from the Civil War!

*A*mong the bills and junk mail was a letter to John from Ingrid and Donald Dickerson, a couple from Tennessee. They were asking him to search for a hidden chest of gold, and when he saw a reference to the Civil War, his heart danced. It was his favorite era.

John's work was seasonal and allowed him to be free for at least three months each year to pursue his favorite activity—treasure hunting. For the past six years, his partnership with Jason brought him on searches throughout the country to find family heirlooms and lost artifacts for their clients.

The partnership gained a great deal of attention during its second year when John found a thick wad of municipal bonds for a woman in Idaho. The stories about her family's missing fortune were thought to be just rumors until John uncovered the bundle that made her seven million dollars richer. And, just four months later, he and Jason unearthed a trunk filled with gold coins from a century-old bank robbery. The news coverage of both stories quickly spread and their reputation was launched. John enjoyed the thrill of the hunt even more than the thought of becoming rich. Jason was already wealthy, and while he liked the excitement, his responsibilities often kept him away from the field excursions. He usually just funded the initial cost of the projects, much to John's delight.

ENCLOSED WITH THE LETTER from the Dickersons were a handwritten note and a crude map that had been discovered during renovations of their home. The letter, dated February 14, 1862, was written by Jeremy Tuttle, a Union soldier. John thought, *Wow, a soldier from the Civil War!* He tingled with excitement and tried to imagine the man who penned the note. *Was he in uniform, gazing across a snowy field with fingers that ached on a frigid February morning? Was he enthusiastic about his cause? Did he have any idea how important his struggles were to his nation?*

The note said they were encamped at Fort Donelson and were proud to have taken control of it for the Union.

In addition to the usual personal endearments, Tuttle mentioned his buddy, Sergeant John Hays, and wrote that a trunk of Rebel gold was buried at a neighboring hillside.

"Hey, Bet . . . sorry to interrupt your total absorption in that piece of junk mail . . . but this looks like an interesting project." John explained the details and as he knew she would, Betty encouraged him to take it on. Thus encouraged, he reached for the telephone.

JASON SAID HE could not get away, but he agreed to fund the research if John thought the Dickerson's request was worth the time and expense. "Why don't you check out the Fort Donelson thing—maybe head down to the Library of Congress. If it checks out, I say go for it."

"Sure thing, Jas. I'll get right on it."

John gave the table a happy tap. "Jason said to go for it. This is perfect timing because I don't have to check in at work for another month or two."

Betty recognized the gleam in her husband's eye. She knew that he'd soon be off, pursuing his passion.

***

Chapter 6

Melvin's dream

*M*elvin screamed. A giant mosquito was hurtling toward him, its razor sharp beak thirsting for his blood—*all of it.* And as the horrific buzzing pounded his eardrums, he screamed again. This time, the sound of his own terror woke him up just as the force of his thrashing knocked him off the couch. His head hit the grimy linoleum and he rolled across the floor, wrapped like a mummy in his beer-stained blanket. Still confused and desperate, Melvin struggled, but he could not get out of the shabby shroud. His sleepy haze faded but the buzz continued its relentless drone, causing anger to replace pangs of fright. "Darned alarm clock!"

Melvin twisted around to give the off button an irate swat. At the same time, he remembered he needed to check in with Ricardo, so with one hand still clutching the blanket, he reached for the telephone. Too late, Melvin realized he was top heavy. He teetered and made a grab to steady himself. Unfortunately, he got a grip on the telephone instead of the table and tottered backwards. The force of the motion knocked him to the floor, rump first, and propelled the instrument—still clutched in his hand—right into his forehead.

"Ouch, ouch, ouch!" he screeched as he kicked at the stubborn blanket. He continued to angrily kick and sputter— until he remembered the trick his mother had taught him as a young child.

Still partially mummified, he stopped and counted to ten—very, very s-l-o-w-l-y.

Counting always helped to calm him down.

Poor Melvin counted a lot.

SEVERAL MINUTES LATER, Melvin dialed Ricardo's number. He scowled. Ricardo was a squirmy fellow with a squeaky little voice, even if he was a big shot with the FDA. Melvin only put up with the man because he often came through with easy jobs that paid good money. *Very good money!*

The ringing stopped and Melvin waited for the beep before leaving his coded message, "The soup's hot—time to eat." He knew Ricardo would be glad to hear that the enhancer had been added to the jet fuel without a hitch. *Smooth as Mom's pumpkin pie,* he murmured as he hung up.

A glance at the clock told Melvin there was still plenty of time for sleep. He yawned and scratched his expansive belly with long, satisfying strokes on his way back to the couch. He hoped Ricardo'd show up with the money before he had to leave for his shift as a security guard at the Miller Building.

As he drifted off to sleep, Melvin smiled. He expected to make a big score there, too.

***

Chapter 7

Is it a bomb?

*W*hen the mail clerk dropped the battered package on his desk, FDA executive Bob Jette had a premonition. *Could this be a bomb? You never know these days—especially when you work in a federal building.* He quickly dismissed the idea. *Heck, there shouldn't be anything to worry about—they take precautions with packages these days . . . even here in the Food and Drug Administration.*

He turned it over. There was no return address, but the postal mark was from Tennessee. He frowned. He did not know anyone from Tennessee and he hadn't been working on any apps from there, either. He tore it open and peered inside. "Hmm. It's a video." The video had a handwritten message on its label. "See that this gets to . . . "

"Hell's bells! The ink's smeared."

The only other part of the message that Bob could make out was the first three letters of the name. He thought it said, 'P-e-r.'

So, who do I know with a last name that starts with p-e-r? He shrugged. *Oh well . . . maybe if I move on to something else, it'll come to me.* As he sorted through the rest of his mail, a name popped into Bob's head—Timothy Perkins. *Of course! Commander Perkins was here last fall, looking into a matter for the Army's R&D Unit. I bet he wants me to pass this on to his people. But, then again—why would he send it to me if he wants THEM to get it?* Bob tried to recall his sessions with Lieutenant Commander Timothy

Perkins. *He works with General Carrey and that Colonel they call C.D. so I guess he's honest—I know they're good guys.* Bob pursed his lips as he pictured the man they called Perkins. He'd been impressed by his sharp mind and his ability to process reams of data. He wondered if Perkins had a photographic memory.

BOB DECIDED TO WATCH the tape before taking any action. He stuffed it into his briefcase, thinking he'd watch it while his wife Carla was at her P-T-O meeting.

The rest of the day dragged along as Bob busied himself with the usual paperwork and confirmation calls. With each hour, he grew more impatient to see what was on the mysterious video. In Bob's estimation, five o'clock did not come soon enough.

AFTER THEY ENJOYED a quiet dinner together, Bob gave Carla a peck on the cheek. He watched intently as she buttoned her jacket, noticed how her hair bounced with each movement. Moments later, he stared nervously as she nosed her car out of the driveway. *It's funny,* he thought, *how you notice the little things when you're scared.*

Scared? Where'd that come from? It's just a video.

Bob frowned at his briefcase and waited until he was certain that Carla was well on her way. With an impatient shake, he picked up the tape, fumbled through the fridge for a can of beer and strode toward the family room.

***

Chapter 8

A formula, huh?

Bob's disbelieving eyes refused to blink as the scene unfolded before him. A group of men were examining something in a bottle. Bob recognized one of them as Perry Jordan, the chief executive officer at SanFidel, Inc. Perry was one of the strongest proponents of the latest GMO legislation, and Bob's boss, Ricardo, was responsible for verifying his supportive documents that outlined SanFidel's research on genetically modified seeds.

Bob scrunched forward to get a closer look. Apparently they did not know they were being taped—they were too outspoken about their unethical plans for the formula. He mused, *A formula, huh? Looks like liquid gold.*

When Perry and his companions turned away from the camera, Bob found himself yelling, "Come on! Speak up you skumbags!" He swatted the air as Perry tucked the bottle into his briefcase. "What the hell is that stuff?"

Bob snatched up the remote and rewound the tape to listen again. They were boasting about their spin on the documentation for the GoMO Bill. The GoMO, named for genetically modified organisms, was aimed at food products that are generally referred to as GM foods, or GMO's. They bragged about how passage of the GoMO would pave the way for unlimited control of the food industry. A cold chill surged up Bob's spine. He knew that it would give them immense power.

"Too much power," he snarled.

The controversial GoMO Bill, GS116-3s42, had been introduced by Senator Miller, a Democrat from Arkansas. If passed, it would allow large chemical conglomerates—*like SanFidel*—to claim greater control over their patented, genetically modified seed crops, fruits and vegetables. *Not to mention the related inventions and formulas.* The video verified his suspicion that SanFidel's data was deliberately misleading. He paced back and forth.

"How the hell did Perkins manage to tape this thing—if it was him—and why did he send it to me . . . and not Ricardo?" Suddenly weary, he sat down and rubbed his eyes.

"What the hell am I supposed to do with it? Well, he obviously didn't want anyone in the military to get it—he'd have sent it through normal channels, whatever they are. He *must* have meant for it to come to someone in the FDA.

"Oh yeah! Ricardo was on vacation when Perkins was doing his investigation. I was probably the only one he spoke to that day."

Bob flung the remote down and rubbed his eyes until they burned. He finally looked up. With a surge of indefinable longing he stared at a carefree family photo that hung on the wall. *Was it only this morning that we were planning our next vacation? What'll happen if these monsters get their way? Will we even be able to have vacations?*

"Good God, where'd those maudlin thoughts come from? I gotta get a grip."

BOB REALIZED HE'D have to be very careful. He suspected that Perry Jordan was a ruthless man and if he knew about the tape, he'd be extremely dangerous. *This thing's too damned sensitive to bring back to the office until I'm absolutely sure of what to do with it.* He decided to hide the evidence and it did not take long to figure out where. Right in front of him was the family's collection of videos. *I know,* he thought. *I'll camouflage it as a Disney tape. The kids don't bother with them anymore. It'll be safe there.*

Bob chose *Snow White*. He copied some of the real cartoon onto the blank beginning of Perkins' tape—*just in case*. After he covered it with the colorful *Snow White* wrapper, he decided to contact Ricardo.

Right from the start, Bob had been frustrated by Ricardo's lax attitude toward SanFidel's reports. He took a final swig of beer after placing the camouflaged video onto the shelf. *I've got you now,* he thought. *There's enough evidence here to bury the GoMO forever—not to mention the indictments that could be made. Ricardo will have to listen to me now!*

* * *

Chapter 9

"Of course, it's Marshmallow gut . . ."

*P*erry Jordan studied the mirror-like finish on his desk with cold eyes. Even when his lips formed a smile and he was dishing out praise, his eyes failed to register warmth.

"That's good news—your friend has done an excellent job."

"Thank you, Mr. Jordan."

"What did you say his name was?"

"His name is Melvin. Melvin Marshall." Ricardo gripped the telephone tighter to his ear. "He is no one that you would care to deal with, I assure you."

Perry tried to remember why the name sounded familiar. *Oh, of course . . . marshmallow gut.*

"So, Ricardo . . . isn't he the rather plump fellow with the sweaty face? Didn't we get him a position at the Miller Building?" Perry sniffed. The first time he had seen Melvin he felt the sudden desire to fumigate the entire 20-story structure.

"Yes, Mr. Jordan. He has proven useful on several occasions."

"Yes, he has at that." Perry's smile almost reached his eyes. *Yes, Ricardo, I do know our Melvin and he'll snitch on you in a heartbeat.* Perry had asked Melvin to keep an eye on Ricardo's activities, just in case the swarthy little man got ideas of his own. His face crinkled into a smug grin as he punched the off button. He was pleased with the news that Melvin had added the terminator formula to the jet fuel at two rural airports. Samples of the crops within those flight paths would soon be collected and analyzed. He knew that if their growth cycle was successfully stunted, he could proceed on a large scale.

Perry thought about the next stage of the scheme and tapped the top of his desk, but as his eyes traveled to its shiny surface he noticed a smudge. *Oops . . . can't have that!* He buzzed his secretary and asked her to bring a dust cloth. As the CEO of one of the top firms on the cutting edge of the biotech industry, he mustn't present a blemished image.

Perry watched with lusty eyes as his busty secretary wiped the hard surface of his desk. Although she was primly dressed, there was no doubt about the ample cleavage that bounced within her softly hued cashmere sweater. *I've got a hard surface you can rub,* he thought wickedly. However, visions of his busy schedule interrupted his erotic musings. *Nah. Not enough time.*

"Thanks, Lillian."

"Your welcome, Sir. Is there anything else I can do?" She smiled, totally unaware of his lascivious thoughts.

"Yes, actually . . . there is one thing."

Lillian waited obediently as he inspected his calendar.

"Call the Lab in Tennessee and tell them I'll be coming for a tour. I'm not sure when, so just tell them to be ready right away. *I'd like to see those test results myself. Gotta stay on top of everything.*

Lillian nodded and said, "Certainly, Mr. Jordan," before turning toward the door. Perry watched with hypnotic interest as she swayed out of the room.

***

Chapter 10

The list

---

*J*ohn and Betty performed their nightly ritual of tidying up the kitchen before she zoomed into the den to watch a rerun of *The Match Game.* He was not ready to settle down, though, because thoughts of the meeting still buzzed in his brain. Instead of joining her on the couch, he offered a peck on the cheek and sauntered toward his desk. It was time to make the list for C.D.

Half an hour later, with a cramp in his hand, John dropped his pen and vowed to learn how to type—in his next life. His list included a variety of worrisome things that came up at the meeting, including mob mentality, military abuse, tax abuse, gun control, and the dangers of genetically modified foods. *They sure had a lot of complaints and that last one was downright weird,* he thought. *Can they really put mosquito genes into tomatoes? Sounds like science fiction to me.*

John got up to get a cold drink and as he reached for a root beer he thought about the young woman who had introduced herself as a member of Mothers for Natural Law. She had explained that her group, the MNL, lobbied for mandatory labeling on genetically modified foods. John pictured the tension-packed room as he popped the top off his root beer. The woman had complained about a big chemical company called SanFidel and the stuff they did with seeds. She claimed that they spliced the ability to

29

produce a pesticide, known as Bt, right into them. *How the hell can they do that?* He sipped his soda absentmindedly.

The young woman claimed that the company held a patent on their seeds and according to a new legislative proposal, the farmers who purchase them will be breaking the law if they save and use seeds from their own harvest. *Sounds like the plot of a bad sci-fi movie if you ask me,* John scoffed. *I can't believe they'd pass a law that makes it a crime for a farmer to use seeds from his own crops.* He sat down and closed his eyes as the memories played through his mind.

ONE MAN SWATTED THE AIR and groused, "Oh, come on. How can that happen if they own the land and they purchased the seed legally, and planted and tended the crops? Seems like they'd have a cut 'n dried case if you ask me."

"I know it doesn't sound fair, but you've got to understand . . . many crops are not thought of as crops anymore—they're inventions!" She emphasized each word. "They're . . . patented . . . inventions."

Angry murmurs filled the room. The young woman shifted her weight from her left foot to her right and squared her shoulders.

"The farmers are forced under contract to purchase seeds each succeeding year. And by the way, they also have to purchase pesticides to combat weeds and diseases . . . pesticides that only the patent holder sells because without the proper chemical composition, other brands might destroy the crops. But each year, the bugs become more and more tolerant. Which means more and more chemicals have to be used. Do you understand what this means? Do you know that, until we succeeded with our lobbying, most Americans have, most likely, eaten potatoes that actually produced a pesticide within their genetic structure? And that until some of the largest fast food companies supported our efforts in England, practically all the French fries and other nationally marketed potato products consumed in America came from potatoes that had the ability to produce a pesticide within their genetic structure? And there haven't been any long-range studies to measure the effects, either!"

"WHY DON'T WE JUST wash the potatoes off and get rid of it?" a thin, elderly woman demanded. Convinced of her own logic, she jabbed a knobby finger into the air.

"You don't understand . . . nothing's been put on them. It's part of their molecular structure. It would be like trying to wash off the color of your skin—and it's being done with some types of corn, and soybeans. They're working on every food crop they can! It's terrible!"

"Why don't somebody tell the gover'ment?" one man demanded. "They'd do somethin' about it."

"Oh, they know all right. Who do you think grants the exclusive patents?" Indignant murmurs could be heard above the creaking chairs as people shifted in their seats.

"What? How could our own government do that? Aren't they suppos'ta be protecting us? What about the Food and Drug Administration?"

"It's the same government that creates unfair gun leg-islation, isn't it? It's the same government that creates unfair tax laws, isn't it?" She raised her arms with frustration. "The same government that you've been complaining about all evening, right?" Her arms fell with a soft plop. "And don't forget . . . that same government controls the FDA."

One man scoffed, "Okay, so what if they are doing this? I don't see anybody dying from it yet, do you?"

"NOT YET—BUT IT MIGHT happen some day."

Heads shifted toward the heavyset man with the booming voice in the back of the room. "That young woman is right on the mark. You'd better believe everything she just said and more. Not only are the chemical giants playing with our lives and the eco-structure of this planet . . . they're methodically gaining a staggering amount of control over the food production in the United States." He swung his arm dramatically and added, "Possibly even the world!

31

"For example. They created hybrid seeds that sound great, right? Bigger plants. Prettier flowers. More fruit, and vegetables. Lots of pluses, right? But think of the negatives. After the first generation, hybrid plants lose their superior qualities. That means poor quality seed crops and poor quality fruits and vegetables. If farmers want to remain competitive, the seed supplier is guaranteed the future sale of their superior hybrids. And think of this . . ." He stopped, waited for their undivided attention. "Will the supplier continue to make them available to individual consumers like you? So you can plant your own vegetable gardens? Maybe not! Not if he knows he can get a higher profit by selling you the food itself. And I believe that it's very possible they'll have the power to create a seed shortage in the near future! Then it'll be easy for them to make us all completely dependent upon *their* crops. In the meantime, they've got a clever campaign going on that gets groups like yours upset and focused on *other* stuff, like taxes and child care . . . so you'll be too busy to pay attention to these issues."

"JUST WHO ARE YOU, ANYWAY? You seem to know an awful lot about this stuff. I ain't seen you here before have I?"

"No you haven't. I'm just visiting the area and I heard about this meeting." He shrugged. "I'm always interested in public opinion. My name is Benjamin Frankel. I publish a weekly in French Lick, Indiana."

Soft snickers erupted.

"*Hey!* French Lick is the proud hometown of Larry Bird, you know! I bet you're familiar with ballplayers like him—even here in Alaska."

Ben offered a modest smile.

"Anyway, one of the people I interviewed recently was an employee of a large seed distributor, and his story was pretty much the same as this young lady's." He turned, swept his arm toward her. "She's right on the money regarding this frightening news about our food supply. It's really happening, folks. Right under our noses. And she's right about another thing . . . some members of our government know about it."

There were no more chuckles. Chairs creaked and people leaned forward, eager to hear more.

"And do you remember the gas lines in the '70's? And the shortages? Remember how prices skyrocketed? Then decades later we heard rumors about how it was staged. Well, a gasoline shortage is bad enough, but what'll happen if there's a food shortage? Chaos? Marshall law? God only knows!"

JOHN SCOWLED AS HE REMEMBERED how one man had shouted, "They wouldn't get away with it if the government wasn't in their pockets! We gotta stop 'em!" Another man yelled, "We should shoot them—that's what we should do!"

The response was deafening.

Shoot whom? John had wondered with alarm. The memory still brought shivers up his spine. He figured they might even get worked up enough to bomb a building or something—especially when they were being led by a guy like Mitchem. He thought about the look on Mitchem's face. It made him fear for the man from French Lick. *Malice,* he thought. *I saw it in his eyes. Pure malice. I hope that pudgy guy's watching his back.* This new fear reinforced John's belief that a competent leader was needed. *Badly.*

John ended his report with the time, date and site of the next meeting and he urged C.D. to attend.

AFTER A FINAL SWIG OF his root beer, John called the Library of Congress to make arrangements to review data on Fort Donelson. Then he decided to look it up in his own reference book. A treasured gift from Jason, it contained hundreds of pages brimming with historical facts, detailed illustrations and sobering photographs depicting the Civil War. He flipped to the Index and slid his finger down through the D's until he found Donelson.

HOW ABOUT THAT? They probably served under the old man himself! John read that in February of 1862, General Ulysses S. Grant had captured Fort Donelson. It was a major victory for the Union, causing the South to lose Tennessee and Kentucky. And it had been an important turning point for General Grant's career, earning him a promotion to Major General of Volunteers. The victory was also apparently where he coined the phrase, "Immediate and unconditional surrender."

During the Fort Donelson battle, 2,000 men died, including 500 Union troops and 1,500 Confederates. John slid back in his seat, sobered by the courage of the men who struggled through the bloodiest war ever fought on American soil.

THE CORROBORATION OF details from the Dickerson's letter convinced John to proceed with the Tennessee project. He dialed his partner's number and left a message.

"Jas . . . I'm going to DC, p.d.q. to visit C.D. and the LOC." He snickered. "In other words, I'm gonna leave soon to do some research on that Civil War project for the people in Tennessee. Oh, and while I'm down there, I'll probably spend a few days with my sister, Evie. She's working for Martin Bascomb, that big-time botanist in Massachusetts. Well, that's it for now. See you soon." He hung up and reached for a pen and paper. *Guess I'll send a note to Evie.*

BY THE TIME John got to the second page of his letter, he realized he'd been venting. He almost tossed it out but changed his mind.

It's better than no letter at all, he muttered as he stuffed it into an envelope. *Besides, Evie's always complaining that we don't confide in her often enough. Trying to protect her or something, I think. Well, she'll get an ear full with this—or should I say an eyeful?*

***

Chapter 11

C.D.was seated at his desk, dictating his last official memo for the day. His broad ebony forehead creased in speculation as he struggled for the right words. He hated doing correspondence and it showed. He fidgeted and jabbed his pen into the snow-white desk blotter, creating a blizzard of dots and jagged dashes.

"Dammit! Where was I?"

It was a rhetorical question and Lenny, his assistant, knew he need not answer. The colonel hated paperwork, but Lenny knew how much the man loved the military and the satisfaction that grew from turning a handful of struggling, undisciplined boys with no real purpose in life, into strong, capable men with ideals and a sense of duty to themselves, their country and the defense of the Constitution. Lenny knew those ideals had never failed to excite the colonel, but the paperwork was another story! Even so, it wasn't like C.D. to struggle with what he had to say.

Lenny did not know that C.D. was concerned about his next memo—one that he intended to write secretly. He did not know that C.D. was afraid that it might cause trouble. *Big trouble.*

C.D. FINALLY GAVE UP. With a shake of his head, he said, "I tell you what, Len. You know the gist of what I want to say here. Why don't you take a stab at it? But first, type what we've already done and have it ready for my signature in time for the afternoon mail."

"Yes, Sir." The young aide saluted, gathered his papers and retreated from the room. C.D. listened for the click of the latch, then pulled a key from his pocket and groped along the side of his huge oak desk. With a twist of the key a narrow compartment opened to reveal three papers—one was John Victor's letter and the other two were anonymous accusations. He pulled out the letter and read it with a frown before scanning the unsigned notes. They were full of claims that C.D. had considered ludicrous—until John Victor's letter arrived bearing similar charges. Worst of all, the notes added a chilling twist—they said the military was involved in some sort of biochemical scheme.

Although C.D. had dismissed the messages as the work of crackpots, something in his gut told him to hold on to them. He glared at them. *There may be something to these unbelievable claims after all.*

It sickened C.D. to think that members of his military, the institution that he had devoted his entire adult life to, might be guilty of such a blatant threat to their own citizens.

C.D. had always been one to face a problem or enemy head on, so he decided to start with a memo to his superior officer, Major General H. Edward Carrey, known through reputation as HarryCarrey. Everyone respected the man, but no one ever relished the thought of coming head on against the infamous HarryCarrey! So, C.D. was unusually nervous about his memo.

It shouldn't be calumnious, he worried. *But, damn! Even the slightest hint of a false accusation against any of Harry's people could send him on the warpath—against me! It could be the end of my career!*

C.D. read the notes again. The first one said, "Watch your back, Colonel Davidson. Don't tell anyone yet, but there's a scheme involving military aircraft. More info will follow. Don't take action until then."

Take action? On what?

The second note came soon after. It mentioned a motive. 'A huge chemical company is involved in an attempt to eliminate competitor's crops—with military aircraft.'

"What!" C.D. roared the first time he read the note, but he quickly decided it was nonsense. *Probably fabricated by one of those anti-military radicals. Crackpot! Numbskull! Not worth my time, that's for sure.* He tossed it in the basket, then decided to hold on to it. *I'll keep my eyes open . . . somebody will tip his hand sooner or later, I'm sure.* He did the same with the second note, but John's letter changed his opinion. He felt he had to take the accusations seriously and his first thought was to alert Harry.

C.D. CRUMPLED HIS FIRST DRAFT, then tried again. *Nope.*

After three tries, his heart lurched. *How can I be sure Harry isn't in on it? It's gotta take someone with a lot of authority to pull a stunt like this. Somebody with the balls to do it,* he thought scornfully. Unfortunately, Harry fit the mold. *Good Lord, now what do I do?*

Moments later, C.D. placed a call to his friend, Senator Thomas Monroe. *Tom might've heard something, but if he hasn't, he might be willing to check it out.*

"IS THIS C.D.?" asked the sultry feminine voice on the other end of the line.

"Yes, Helen. Would you tell Tom we've gotta talk as soon as possible? And, Helen—this is private. Totally private. I don't want anyone to know that I'm trying to reach him. Is that clear?"

"Of course, C.D. Discretion is my middle name . . . you know that. So, are you okay? Is there anything I can do for you?"

"I'm fine, Helen. Just be sure that Tom gets back to me p.d.q." He paused and said, ". . . and Helen,"

"What?"

"I'll owe you one."

"Actually, that'll be ten you owe me, soldier!" With that brash declaration, Senator Thomas Monroe's top administrative assistant sent her lilting laughter through the line before hanging up.

Thank God for assistants like Helen. We sure don't deserve them . . . and boy, do they remind us! C.D. had his first chuckle since receiving John Victor's letter, and despite his inner turmoil, he hung up with a smile.

***

Chapter 12

Oh, oh, what's wrong?

"*H*elen gave me your message, C.D. So, what's up?"

"That was fast, Tom! But, man—am I glad. I really need your help. Can we meet for lunch?" C.D. felt reassured just to hear Tom's friendly, but crisp, tone. *No wonder he's so successful in the Senate. He gets right down to business and yet, he never fails to put you at ease.*

"Lunch? Sure. Just say where and when and I'll juggle my schedule." Tom breathed deeply, then added, "You got Helen mighty worried, chum."

"Yeah? Well, I guess I did sound a bit mysterious. Then again, she can read me like a book." C.D. looked up at his clock. He hoped Tom could meet him right away. "So, how about Dunkin Donuts? The usual? Can it be today?"

"Umh . . . sure. See you then."

TOM SLUMPED IN HIS SEAT. He thought, *This's gotta be serious. We haven't used the Dunkin Donuts code for a long time. C.D. must be afraid he's being bugged . . . or that I am!*

***

Chapter 13

*T*he Dunkin Donuts ploy would alert Tom. C.D. was sure of it. They had worked it out years ago. The suggestion of lunch at Dunkin' Donuts meant they should meet secretly at C.D.'s house at the lake. C.D. grinned—usually it was Tom doing the asking because of his penchant for digging into controversial legislative issues. *Well, this one'll be right up his alley,* he thought.

C.D. WANDERED THROUGH the two-bedroom bungalow, scanning the contents of each room like a restless lion on the prowl. He stopped at his grandmother's beloved Hepplewhite sideboard to stare at a collection of family photos. His finger conjured up fond memories as it gently circled the copper frame that held a cherished picture of his grandfather. He smirked. Grandpa Tyson was always telling poor Gramma T that he hated the Hepplewhite because it reminded him of a giant kidney bean with chicken legs. "That thang is ugly," he'd say. "Ain't nothin' should have chicken legs but a chicken!"

C.D. spoke softly as his gaze lingered on his colorful forebear. "So, Grampa T, what do you think? Do you mind being displayed on this ugly old piece of mahogany?"

In the kitchen bright blue and yellow curtains hung at the windows and Gramma T's collection of teapots still lined the tops of the cabinets. It was what she had proudly called the French colonial look.

C.D. spoke once more.

"I wish you were both with me now, Gram, but you know what? I feel better just being here." He closed his eyes and imagined that she was still bustling about. He could almost smell her culinary trademark—garlic. He was suddenly reminded of his Aunt Theresa, hovering in the background, sniffing with annoyance, her nose as high as her beehive hairdo. She always complained about the pungent odors in her mother's otherwise immaculate kitchen.

She never turned down your cooking, though, did she Gram? Testy Theresa was always the first to gobble down her mother's enticing entrees . . . and the last to leave the table.

Just then C.D. thought he heard Tom's car. He turned on his heel and strode toward the front door. A peek through the window proved him right.

C.D. opened the door. "Thanks for coming, Tom."

"Don't mention it. But, this better be good, old friend. I don't mind telling you I've been on pins and needles, wondering if I'm being tailed or bugged or something . . . wondering what the hell is so important you'd pull our old D & D routine."

"Couldn't be helped, Tom. Something big's up. Involving the military. Could be disastrous if it's true!"

"Good God, slow down, boy—what are you talking about?"

"C'mon, let's grab a seat and I'll tell you all about it." C.D.'s handsome, six-foot frame led the way to the den. An eclectic assortment of rustic furniture and accessories filled the cheery retreat with natural materials that, Grandma T said she loved because they, '. . . celebrate the marriage of man's creativity and the wonders of nature.'

"You're the only person I dare to tell this to, Tom. I don't even know if I can trust Harry!"

Tom tossed a decorative pillow aside and lowered himself into an overstuffed chair without taking his eyes off his harried host.

"So, come on. Give me the details."

C.D. thrust the anonymous notes into the senator's hands. He was not surprised when he scrunched them up.

"C'mon, C.D. These were obviously written by kooks! Look—they didn't even have the nerve to sign their names. Why would you take them seriously?" He gave C.D. a good hard look.

"That's what I thought, too, at first . . . but something made me hold on to them. So, read this one." He tossed John Victor's letter onto the coffee table. It hit the highly varnished pine slab with a soft thud.

Tom squinted at the return address and muttered, "Hmmm. John Victor . . ." Thought lines rippled his forehead as he searched his memory. "Didn't he serve with you in Nam? The eccentric one who was into treasure hunting?"

"Yes, that's the one. He may be eccentric, but I trusted his judgment then, Tom . . . and I trust him now." C.D. clasped his fingers together and scrunched them into his chin. "We still get together now and then when he comes to DC. He lives in Alaska, you know."

"Yeah. Well, I guess if you're sure about him. So, what does he have to do with those crazy notes?"

"Read his letter and see for yourself."

TOM WAS ALREADY pulling John's letter out of the envelope. His eyes scanned the jagged blue script and he mumbled, "Guess he didn't excel at penmanship, hey?" But moments later, he stopped with a gutteral grunt. "Well, I'll be . . . he mentions the same thing!"

***

Chapter 14

What's this about inventions?
I thought we were talking about seeds.

"*Y*ou know, C.D., these biotech supporters do have a lot of people—and a lot of money—on their side. That reminds me . . . I've been trying my darndest to drum up enough opposition to stop Miller's GoMO Bill. Have you heard about it?"

"Yup. I don't know much about it, but if you say it's bad, then I believe it's bad. So, what's wrong with it?"

"It looks harmless on the surface—just one more re-quest for patent rights. But if you read between the lines, it gives the mega-corporations, like SanFidel and Comfood, the power to litigate for compensation even on totally new, untested, even unapproved inventions. It goes way beyond the previous patent laws and it's too ambiguous. I know from experience the harm that this kind of legislation can do and I'm pretty sure it's just a foot in the door to serve their greediest aspirations." Tom's eyes narrowed. "And I won't stand for it!"

"Sounds like you've got quite a fight on your hands. Like you said, they've got the big bucks behind them. But, I thought the GoMO was all about seeds and crops. What's this about inventions?"

"Well, are you familiar with genetic engineering?" When C.D. shook his head, Tom explained, "I wasn't either, 'til I started reviewing the initial proposal for the GoMO.

43

Now I'm beginning to feel like an expert. Next thing, I'll be reciting this stuff in my sleep.

"To begin with, they also call it gene splicing. It involves the addition, deletion or reorganization of the basic structure of life that makes every organism unique—you know, splicing from one organism to another. It's all about the genetic code."

C.D. gave a perfunctory nod, urging Tom to continue.

"Well, as with conventional hybrids, these new life forms can be patented by the corporation producing them—patented, because they're recognized as *inventions!*" He stopped, looked up to see if C.D. was following his explanation.

"So," C.D. pursed his lips before posing his question. "So . . . all the hybrid fruits, like the plump tomatoes we now see, and the huge oversized peaches, are considered to be inventions? That sounds crazy! A peach is a peach . . . is a peach. Last I knew, *God* 'invented' peaches!"

"Right! But the law sees it all differently, and with the new legislation, the farmer who grows them no longer will own them. The chemical company who supplied the genetically modified seeds will own the plants and fruits and their seeds."

"But that doesn't make sense. Doesn't the farmer buy them? In order to grow them? On his own property, for cryin' out loud—to sell in the market place?"

"Technically, yes. But legally . . . *no.*" At C.D.'s quizzical look, Tom threw his arms high above his head. He waggled his hands. "Yeah, I know! I know! But it's complicated as hell . . . and the corporate giants are pushing for more and more legislation to give them more and more say about what happens to the whole shebang." He continued to wag his hands. ". . . including the plants, the fruits, the vegetables—and, more importantly, the seeds. With all of the money backing them, they've been able to lobby hard in the New England states."

TOM CROSSED HIS ARMS. "You know, C.D., there's so much at stake here. You'd be amazed at the lengths to which these people will go. Were you aware that they now use satellite surveillance to monitor the farmlands? They can tell if a farmer plants more seed than he's purchased, and with the GoMO they'll have the right to hang him up in court—with charges that he's used seeds unlawfully—while they search for substantiation. It could take so long the farmer could be ruined before it's over . . . guilty or not! And, if he's at fault, he could be fined heavily. Or put in jail. . . ."

C.D.'s angry scowl deepened. Tom continued.

"The poor members of the Vermont legislature, according to my friend Fred Hanson, are stymied about what to do. On the one hand, they have the big money boys pushing them to enact legislation in their favor, and on the other hand, they've got the farmers . . . a strong and vital local voting constituency, who are losing their autonomy. But, thank God, it's on the wall, as Fred says."

C.D.'s brows jumped. "On the wall?"

"Yes. That's what they do with a piece of legislation they can't get passed, or don't really want to pass, for whatever reason. It gets posted in sort of a not-dead-but-pending status. Could stay there for years, until they gain more ammunition to fight for their cause . . ." Tom's voice changed to a gutteral growl. " . . . or increase their buying power. It's not just Vermont, though. It's happening all over, on both a state and federal level."

Tom sprang to his feet. "My God, C.D., to me and Fred it's as simple a decision as it possibly can be! We don't know the long-term ramifications of genetic engineering or of the power these giant corporations are pushing for, either. So we should just say 'no' until we get it figured out. Trouble is, not all of my colleagues see it that way." He gave his hands another over-the-head waggle.

"Too many dollar signs clouding their vision?"

"It just sickens me, C.D., but you're probably right." Tom bent down to retrieve John's letter. "So, here we have

45

John Victor in Alaska of all places, questioning these very same issues. Now how do you suppose a treasure hunter would hear about this—way up there?"

"Well, if you read further, you'll see he mentions some meeting—sort of a political venting session, I think, with a leader who might have ulterior motives. I was hoping you could help me figure something out. Maybe you could do a little quiet sniffing around. But in regard to John's concerns, I think I'll accept his invitation and attend the next meeting. I'd like to see if we have some legitimately concerned citizens like he thinks, and I'd like to get a first-hand look at their leader. Besides, I do have to check out some land up there—hafta see if it's suitable for testing our new CWT apparatus."

"CWT?" You mean cold weather training? Does this mean your people are on schedule with the new cold weather gear? That Ultraflexiblend—II sounds phenomenal. You know, chum, these breakthroughs in R&D never cease to amaze me. Harry's assembled the finest team of engineers, chemists and mechanical wizards in the country—maybe the whole world, for that matter."

"We're definitely proud of the whole team, but, I'm sure there'll be a few kinks to work out once we're out in the field. There always are."

"Well, nobody's gonna question why you're flying up to Alaska if you have some state-of-the-art cold weather gear to check out. So . . . what exactly do you want me to do?"

"You could sniff around a little? Check out these wacko claims about contrails? Present your questions as feelers for some sort of legislation or something . . . ?" His voice faltered.

"As a matter of fact, I've been putting off the whole issue of contrails for quite awhile—just because I've considered it wacko." Tom's face twisted conspiratorially. "You know, the damned sky *does* look like a jigsaw puzzle sometimes—with all those jet fumes." He grinned. "Consider it done, old chum. I do have a bit of a reputation for 'sniffing around' as you call it."

"Don't I know it." C.D. failed to stifle a snort. He was thinking about the most recent investigation that got a lot of media coverage. Too much, in C.D.'s estimation. "But could you keep it down to a dull roar this time? We don't need the press sticking its nose into this one—at least not yet."

"Gotcha."

"HEY, DIDN'T YOU SUGGEST lunch? Let's go to Dunkin Donuts and make this meeting legit."

C.D.'s face crinkled with mirth.

"Donuts? Man . . . you must have been a police officer in a previous life!" He pointed toward the back of the house before adding, "There's a bag of your favorites in the cupboard. I picked up some sandwiches, too."

***

Chapter 15

A snag in the line . . .

*T*om Monroe had just returned from C.D.'s bungalow. He settled comfortably in his chair and let his mind wander, as it often did when he was puzzled. The bigger the problem, the more it wandered—and this *definitely* was a big one. It was as though his subconscious was scrambling from one object to another, searching for stimuli, gathering information, cataloging and comparing it to judge its usefulness. Eventually, something would click and the answer would come. It was a ritual Tom was not even aware of. His chest heaved with a deep, tired sigh as he stared at the crease in his pants. It produced a straight, crisp line. *Sharp,* he thought. *That's a real sharp crease.*

The ritual continued as he turned his gaze toward the sleek blinds on the window facing the Delaware Street parking lot. *Sharp lines there, too. Rows of them. Parallel lines working together to block the light. Kind of like the forces trying to block the light of truth.*

Tom's pulse quickened. He stared with a growing sense of purpose. His eyes traced the path of the string, noticed how each narrow panel connected to the next, how the string ran back and forth continuously from top to bottom, right down to the plastic pull. *A smooth operation unless there was a snag in the line.* He sat up. *Now there's something . . . a snag in the line. A snag, then lots of light— or the truth—can flow right through it!*

"That's it—all I have to do is create a few snags—just like the blinds! Just like the blinds!"

Helen burst through the door.

"What is it, Tom? Were you just shouting something about the blinds?" She stared at the wall of windows.

"Nothing is wrong with them, Helen—they're *wonderful!*" Tom laughed heartily. "Listen, forget the blinds. I want you to call C.D. right away. Tell him to meet me for lunch at Dunkin' Donuts on Friday. Tell him I know what to do." Her raised brows prompted him to add, "He'll know what I'm talking about." His grin widened.

Helen agreed to make the call, but she could not resist another glance at the blinds. Tom enjoyed her confusion. He hoped his prey would react the same way.

"See?" he croaked merrily. "Aren't they wonderful?" He ushered her through the door before scurrying back to his seat.

Now, all I have to do is make a few phone calls to get those snags started. He felt it all had to be connected to the GoMO Bill. He was sure that John Victor's concern about genetically modified foods and C.D.'s anonymous notes would ultimately be linked to Miller's proposed bill. *Somehow. . . .*

TOM'S FIRST CALL was to Perry Jordan. He instinctively disliked the man. He knew that Perry was tight with Senator Miller and that he was lobbying hard for a vote on the GoMO. He thumbed through his rolodex and hummed happily as he punched the numbers.

Tom told the startled man that he was reconsidering his stance against the GoMO.

He said, "I'd like to meet with you one more time, though, before I publicly rescind my position." He tried to envision Perry's face and thought, *I'd love to be a fly on the wall right now, or Alan Funt's Candid Camera. He's gotta be wondering what changed my mind. Probably wondering what I'll ask for in return.*

Perry played it cool, but Tom thought his voice was a bit too controlled. He knew the guy *had* to be suspicious of his sudden turnaround. He also knew he'd have to be careful—Perry Jordan was shrewd, and if Tom's instinct was correct, he was dangerous. *Extremely dangerous.*

Next, Tom called the FDA and asked for Ricardo. He told *him* that he'd just learned there was some misinformation regarding the GoMO and he'd be investigating the issue more thoroughly.

Tom said, "I want to meet with you next week. By then I'll have what I need."

Ha! Did I hear the little weasel's eyelids pop open? Tom congratulated himself when he heard Ricardo's tremulous voice. *Yup, I'm good—I got him.*

"Of course, Senator Monroe. That will be fine, but couldn't you give me a few details now? I must prepare the proper reports, you know."

"I've gotta roll a few more stones before I reveal any-thing . . . even to you and your associates at the FDA. Sorry, Ricardo . . . you'll just have to wait."

"Very well, then. When can I expect you? I assume you'll want to come here?"

AFTER THEY AGREED UPON a time and place, Tom hung up with a satisfied grin. *I bet he's already trying to reach Perry Jordan—I've had my suspicions about that squirmy little man!*

***

Chapter 16

"Don't give him anything—you got that?"

---

*T*om was right. By the time he'd poured himself a cup of coffee, Ricardo was already dialing Perry Jordan's number— with shaking hands. After all, Perry would hold Ricardo responsible for any slipups at the FDA. *Perry and whomever he's answering to. Must be Rossweild—it certainly isn't that slime ball Miller—he's just an errand boy himself. I wonder if we can reel in the big guy himself on this one?* Tom brightened at the thought. Alexander Graham Rossweild would be a big fish, indeed.

RICARDO SQUIRMED AS A polite monotone answered after the fourth ring. "Good afternoon. Thank you for calling SanFidel. This is Wendy. How may I help you?"

"Get me Mr. Jordan, please. Immediately. Tell him it's Ricardo from the FDA."

"Of course, Mr. Ricardo. And thank you again for calling SanFidel."

Ricardo heard a faint click before the monotonous hum of elevator music flowed through the receiver. He fidgeted as he waited for Perry Jordan's syrupy greeting.

"Ricardo, my friend, how are you?"

He plunged into his explanation. "Mr. Jordan, we have some big problems ahead of us. For one thing, Senator Monroe just called and he says he has found some discrepancies and misleading information that will support his fight against the GoMO."

Perry's head jerked upwards. He squeezed his eyes into slits and cursed explosively.

Ricardo squeaked, "Monroe wants to meet me to review the details." His voice rose even higher. "What should I do? He must be on to us." He was forced to wait, his heart beating erratically, like a frightened bird's, while Perry considered his options.

PERRY FINALLY SPOKE. "Okay. Go ahead with the meeting, but whatever you do, don't tip your hand—Monroe may just be on a fishing expedition." He hardened his tone. "You don't give him *anything* . . . you got that?"

"Yessir. Of course, Mr. Jordan."

"Good. Now, in the meantime, I'll arrange to take care of our good senator."

Ricardo's already skipping heart lurched. "What do you *mean*—take care of him—I won't have any part in it . . . he's a United States senator! There would be investigations!"

"Listen, Ricardo. You should have more fear of Rossweild than the feds. You just act as if you're gonna meet with Monroe, as if you're none the wiser. If he does show, well, you just be as shocked and concerned about his little bomb as he wants you to be. Tell him you'll get right on it." Perry laughed again. "That's if he shows."

"So, what was the other thing you wanted?"

"Other . . . ?" Ricardo's brain floundered, then wrapped itself around another frightening memory. "Oh yes—my assistant, Bob Jette, said he's received something that could blow the lid off the GoMO." Ricardo held his breath, anticipating another explosive curse.

Perry snarled. "So, what does *he* have?"

"He refused to say on the telephone, so I agreed to meet in one of the little-used conference rooms right here in the Miller."

"When?"

Perry's sharp query startled Ricardo.

"Six thirty, tomorrow morning."

PERRY CONSIDERED THE NEWS. He said, "I'll be there, too. I want to see what Jette's got. In the meantime, don't forget about our good friend, Senator Monroe." Perry chortled. "It seems you're going to be a busy boy these next few days, Ricardo." He hung up with a force that startled his queasy accomplice and thought, *If I have my way, we'll take care of Senator Monroe before he gets there.*

PERRY DIALED SENATOR MILLER'S number. As he waited for the secretary to buzz her boss, he twirled his pen. *Hmmm. Perfectly balanced. Should be . . . damned thing costs more than most men pay for their best Sunday suits.*

When the senator finally answered, Perry growled, "So, Miller. Let me cut to the chase. Our friend Tom Monroe seems to be playing games." His eyes narrowed. "Dangerous games. He calls me and says he's changed his mind about the GoMO—wants to add his support. Then, just minutes later, he calls Ricardo—you know, the little weasel at the FDA—and he sets up a meeting. Says he's got some kind of evidence that'll bury the whole damn thing!" He snarled, "And we can't *have* that. You get Monroe over to your back office tomorrow afternoon. I don't care how you do it, just get him there. I'll handle the rest."

Miller whispered, "Now wait a minute, Jordan. I've already done enough. I won't have a part in anything ugly!"

"You're already into ugly, Miller—right up to your neck. And if you want to save that neck of yours, you'll cooperate." After a calculated pause, Perry continued. "And another thing, Miller . . ."

"Yes?"

"Like I told Ricardo. You're better off fearing Rossweild, than the feds."

"I *am* one of the feds," Miller asserted, but he cringed when he heard Perry's soft laughter. He knew he was out of his league this time—and on the wrong side.

PERRY'S NEXT CALL was to an answering machine in a sleazy apartment on the West side of town. He recoiled at the thought of the tenant's protruding belly, but he would have been horrified if he knew that the apartment that Melvin called home had become a target for local teenagers whose greatest bragging point was their urinal prowess. The answering machine that whirred into action sat upon a rickety table in front of a window that opened three feet above the highest of a chain of dark, smelly stains.

After three short rings, Melvin's raspy voice said, "State yer businezz at the beep."

Perry held his receiver at a distance, as if something unpleasant might ooze out of it, before he demanded, "What has our pesky senator been up to?" As the most vocal opponent of the GoMO, Tom Monroe was one person that Perry had been watching. "Report to me at once. And don't forget to keep your eyes open at the Miller every day, but especially tomorrow morning—in the old wing—around six."

WITHIN AN HOUR, Lillian announced the call that Perry had been waiting for. He listened to Melvin's now-familiar voice, thinking, *probably smokes two packs a day, in between several pints of cheap liquor. Probably sweaty, too.*

"Ya called," Melvin announced unnecessarily. "He's been very busy, our boy. I followed him to some top brass military man's place out on the lake. Wasn't no social call, middle of a work day 'n all. Was a Colonel Davidson."

Perry squeezed his cold eyes into angry slits, but his voice gushed, "Good work, my man. Good work. You'll be handsomely rewarded." When he heard the sudden, rattley intake of air on the other end of the line, Perry imagined that Melvin was puffing up like a proud peacock—*a scruffy, lice infested peacock.*

"Now yer talkin' my language! An you c'n bet my eyes'll be peeled 'n wide, every day, at the Miller. Just like

ya want." Melvin happily pictured his ever-increasing bankroll.

"Thank you. But Melvin . . . ."

"Yeah?"

"You don't have to tell Ricardo that I've been in touch. Understand?"

"Gotcha! Mums the word."

***

Chapter 17

*P*erry's lips twisted with anger. He thought, *Davidson's one of the ones I've been concerned about. He's just too chummy with Monroe. Dammit, I can't risk having them snooping around now. NOT NOW!* He decided to contact Rodney Carrousel to see what *he* knew about C.D.'s activities. As Major General Carrey's aide, Rodney was on top of all of the movements at the Research and Development headquarters, and as the embittered son of a Viet Nam MIA, he was a very cooperative addition to Perry's organization.

PERRY'S CONVERSATION with Rodney did not set his mind at ease. While he had not seen any suspicious contact between the general and the two troublemakers, he said that Davidson was becoming a little too nosey.

"I think you'd better have Mitchem's men get on it. I don't care how they do it—as long as they get Colonel Davidson out of the picture." Perry rubbed his temples. *Well now,* he thought. *Things are definitely starting to heat up!*

Too arrogant to be fearful, Perry buzzed Lillian and asked for coffee. He didn't really want any. He just wanted another glimpse of her in that sweater. He knew that if he scooted his chair back far enough, she'd have to lean forward to hand it to him. A delicious zing shot through his pelvis at the thought.

***

56

Chapter 18

*I*t was too early for Ricardo's taste. *Even the commuters haven't come out yet,* he groused. Dampness clung—not yet willing to give in to the heat of the rising sun. A few feet away, bickering sparrows fought over the remains of his donut. Ricardo watched the birds and lit a cigarette. He took several long drags, but the nicotine failed to calm his nerves as he waited for Perry Jordan. They were going to meet with his assistant, Bob Jette, to see what he had against the GoMO bill, and he feared for Bob's life. He hoped he could persuade him to back off.

Ricardo cocked his ear toward the road. He thought he heard the distant drone of a car. When he saw that it was, indeed, Perry's limo, he tossed his half-smoked Winston into a shallow puddle on the damp tarmac. The lit end flickered in protest before releasing a thin ribbon of smoke that danced into oblivion.

The nose of the long black car eased to a stop over the puddle. Ricardo pulled at Perry's door and uttered a polite greeting. "Good morning, Mr. Jordan. Bob's car is here, so he must be waiting for us."

Perry Jordan stepped out of the limo, followed by a tall man in impeccable linen. Ricardo watched curiously as the dapper stranger carefully pinched the crease back into his trousers and surreptitiously scanned his own inexpensive suit with chagrin.

57

Perry introduced the man as his associate, Damian LaSalle.

"We call him Damo," he added as an afterthought.

He gestured impatiently for Ricardo to show them the way to the meeting room. The little man quickly obeyed, but as Perry and Damo strode toward the entrance, he was forced to scuttle behind them.

"GOOD GOD."

Bob Jette swayed involuntarily as he watched from a window overlooking the parking lot. He had feared that Ricardo was involved somehow. It would explain his reluctance to question SanFidel's claims. *Perry Jordan's presence kind of clinches it,* he thought sadly. He wondered who the other guy was. He was sure he'd never seen him before. *That tall guy looks like a thug—a well paid thug.*

Bob stiffly backed away from the window as he pondered this unexpected turn of events. *No sense in being frightened. They won't do anything to me here. Too public. Boy . . . I'm glad I didn't bring the video.* He resolved to be firm, but noncommittal. *I won't mention the evidence right away . . . I've gotta get Ricardo alone and feel him out, just to be sure.*

Bob prayed for Ricardo's innocence. When they reached the conference room, he greeted the other two men with a nod then spoke to his boss.

"Thanks for coming, Ricardo. Look, I need to talk to you right away, but I can't discuss this in front of outsiders."

"Certainly," Perry said. "We'll wait in the hall." Despite his agreeable tone, his expressionless eyes sent a chill up Bob's spine.

BOB TOLD RICARDO he knew the information in SanFidel's report was not valid, and his own worst suspicions were confirmed when he saw the fear in Ricardo's eyes. He knew then that he could not reveal the existence of the tape to him. He shook with anger. Too loudly, he threatened to take his information to the media. Too loudly, he proclaimed that he'd blow the lid off the GoMO. He stormed out of the conference room without even a glance toward Perry or Damo.

DAMO LOOKED AT PERRY with questioning eyes after pointing toward Bob's back, pulling an imaginary trigger and blowing at an imaginary puff of smoke.

From the doorway, Ricardo squeezed his eyes shut and clenched his hands. He had seen Perry's nod of endorsement.

NONE OF THEM had sensed the presence of a witness to the scene—a witness who heard Bob's heated assertions. It was Brickford Little, one of the new executives at the FDA. Brick had been working quietly behind the thin sliding doors that separated the two-part conference room, and while he could not see them or recognize the voice of the man that Bob was arguing with, he had seen the tall man's threatening gesture and the glint of approval in the other man's eyes. Instinct told him that it was not an idle threat.

***

Chapter 19

He's a freaking botanical encyclopedia!

*L*ate the following day, Brick signaled a right-hand turn and eased his rental car onto the unpaved drive at Pleasant Acres. The crunch of tires on gritty stones created a welcome change from the monotonous hum of highway driving. He searched for a parking space, but the lot was crammed with cars. *Darn!* He slapped the steering wheel, then spied a happy couple, their arms laden with chunky brown parcels. Their beaming faces suggested that they were satisfied customers, and Brick thought, *Good—I hope he makes me happy, too.*

As soon as the couple pulled out of their slot, Brick's green Nissan sped into it. Only then did he allow himself to feel the exhaustion. With hands clenching the steering wheel and head resting on forearms, he closed his eyes. His lids felt like sandpaper. He had driven all night on his quest to find Martin Bascomb.

As he sauntered toward the bustling garden center, Brick saw that the affable, award-winning botanist was busy with a long line of chattering customers. He clenched his hands. *Here I am, plunged into a world of murder and bio-technical espionage, and I have to wait for Martin Bascomb to finish doling out advice to half the county—about gardens, at that! The guy's a freaking, walking botanical encyclopedia for cryin' out loud!*

BRICK SHOVED HIS hands into his pockets, then unconsciously ran his thumb along the circumference of a nickel. He found the warm circular shape somehow soothing and as he felt the slight indentations and raised surface on the face of the coin, he marveled at the ability of blind people to read Braille. No matter how hard he tried, no matter how familiar he was with the sight of a nickel, its touch could not conjure up a vision of his hero. When he flipped it over, though, he realized that he *could* feel a straight line. *Must be the base of Monticello.* Brick pulled the coin out of his pocket. *Yup. I was right.* Then he flipped it over and stared at Thomas Jefferson.

Speaking softly, as if addressing the memory of a cherished friend, he said, "How I wish you were here now. We could use good men like you. I only hope that I'm right about Martin Bascomb and that he's a good man, too."

Brick noticed that one table on the porch held a large jug of lemonade. Nestled in a tub of sparkling ice cubes, it beckoned to him. Moments later, he thrust a wrinkly dollar bill into the money jar.

The first few sips of the tangy liquid soothed Brick's parched throat. He closed his eyes and breathed a long, satisfied sigh.

DETERMINED TO BE CASUAL, Brick sat down with the tall glass of lemonade still in hand, resigned to the fact that he would have to wait until every last person had queried the award-winning gardener. *Gardener's an understatement,* he thought.

Martin Bascomb, Ph.D., local gardening guru, was recognized as one of the world's leading botanists. During his fifty-year career, his expertise had been sought by world leaders and scientists that recognized his work to improve food production. As he continued his thoughts about the remarkable accomplishments of Dr. Bascomb, Brick mused, *The most amazing thing is, what he really loves is this place and his work here. He even calls himself the plant man!* Brick sighed. *He must have the patience of a saint! Well, I hope he has the morals of a saint, too.* He sighed again, his brow creased with frown lines.

The grimace emphasized the craggy vertical lines of his rugged, tanned cheeks. His face had suddenly transformed from worried exhaustion to raw determination. *It's a nightmare,* Brick thought. *And here I am, in a garden center in the middle of the Berkshires of Massachusetts, waiting for a self-professed plant man!*

Brick could still feel the horror that had engulfed him when Bob Jette was gunned down on the steps of the Miller Building—*in broad daylight*—and his frustration when the attending law enforcement agencies of Washington, DC had quickly closed the case. *Too quickly,* Brick thought. The motive given was random gang violence. The alleged perpetrators were two teenage boys, said to have taken on a dare in order to join a local gang.

Frosty chips of ice and tangy bits of pulp tickled his lips as Brick downed the last few ounces of the refreshing lemonade. He crunched angrily into the ice and his scowl deepened. *Those boys were not alone in that car!*

BRICK WAS SO LOST in his morbid reflections that he did not notice the lovely blue eyes that opened with amazement as they witnessed his sudden rage. From the first, the eyes admired the grace and power that were evident with every move of the impressive man on the porch. They admired the thick patch of unruly hair, the strong chin and deep set eyes. But Evie Victor's admiration quickly turned to suspicion when she realized that he was watching Martin Bascomb.

Why's he angry with Dr. B.? she wondered. As she continued her covert study of the handsome man, Evie was unaware of the shop patrons who paused to admire *her.* With her heart-shaped face, thick mane of honey blond hair and cheekbones that any woman would die for, Evie rated second looks no matter where she was—even on a scorching day in June, dressed in jeans and an over-sized safari shirt.

AS MARTIN BASCOMB listened to a customer, he saw his young intern, Evie Victor. His mind wandered to the assessment he received from the University of Vermont. They said she was, "top of her class and hardworking, with an amazing analytical mind and a love of plants that sees the long hours and tedious research as fun."

Maria was not exaggerating a bit, he thought. He marveled at how lucky he was to have acquired such an energetic, competent intern. *For the whole summer, too!* He made a mental note to send a special thank you to his old friend, Maria Charbonneau, for sending Evie to him. Maria—from the Career Services Office of the University of Vermont. Maria—a close friend for decades. *Ah . . . Maria.*

THE SUDDEN, HIGH-PITCHED trill of his customer's voice brought Martin back to the present. He blinked, then asked her to repeat the symptoms before rendering advice on the danger of watering one's garden during the peak period of the mid-day sun. He was relieved to see there was no one else in line and the momentary reprieve allowed him to take a deep breath and revel in the sights and smells of Pleasant Acres.

Martin had never married. The garden center was his pride and joy. Built log-cabin style 20 years ago, it was nestled at the base of a hill along a meandering road and was a popular stop for tourists and local gardeners.

Talented hands had cleverly concealed long, moss covered window boxes, replete with carefully selected blooms. They contained delicate mounds of mauve cranesbill geraniums and rich purple clusters of floppy, early rose vervains that were in stark contrast to the perky yellow beards of Johnny jump-ups. And throughout the manicured grounds, bronze statues and wrought iron garden adornments added a mix of whimsy and artistic embellishment.

Martin saw that Evie was staring toward the front steps of the shop. The object of her fascination was a young man who looked out of place in his pinstriped suit, and Martin was surprised to realize that the stranger did not seem to notice her. When he finished his own perusal of the man, he was startled by the intensity of his eyes—eyes that unflinchingly returned his own stare. With a shiver of premonition, Martin decided to see what the intense young man had on his mind. Just then, another customer—a teenage boy, who was probably on a quest for his parents—strode toward him, so he called to Evie. "Would you please come and assist this young fellow?"

MARTIN SAUNTERED toward Brick, happy to find himself on the cooler, shady side of the wrap-around porch. In contrast to his slow, easy movements, Brick jumped up and thrust out his hand.

"Hello, Dr. Bascomb. My name is Brickford Little. I can see that you're very busy, but I've just gotta talk with you. It's important!"

Martin deliberately chose the lighthearted approach. "Well now, have you killed the wife's favorite tea rose? Or do you need a top-notch gift for a special occasion? Don't look so glum—whatever you need, I'm sure I can help."

Brick winced. "Glum is an understatement. And, no, I'm not here on a personal issue. Lives are at stake . . . but we can't talk here. I may have been followed." Brick glanced around furtively until his eyes settled upon the oversized safari shirt. With his gaze riveted toward Evie, he spoke again, his voice suddenly dropping to a monotone—hollow with exhaustion. "This really is a life and death matter."

Martin's brows bounced upward, then plummeted. His premonition had been correct. His fingers fluttered with quick little movements as he called to Evie once again.

"Evie! Come over here, right away, please!" He explained to Brick, "That pretty young thing is my assistant for the summer. We're slowing down a bit now, so I'll ask her to handle the shop alone. I can trust her to close up."

"Thanks." Brick's eyes burned with intensity as he followed Evie's approach.

"WHAT'S THE MATTER, Dr. B.?" Alarmed by his urgency, Evie had rushed to Martin's side. "Is something wrong?" Her eyes settled suspiciously upon the tall stranger.

WORDS ESCAPED HIM as Brick Little stared into the prettiest eyes he had ever seen. An electric current flowed through his body, emitting a pleasant, heated tingle as his eyes held hers. Curious blue eyes, sort of a teal blue, gazed back at him with equal abandonment.

On some unknowable level, a bond was being established, but Martin broke the spell with an embarrassed cough. Brick and Evie turned in unison with self-conscious confusion.

"Evie, this is Brickford Little. Mr. Little, this is Miss Evelyn Victor." He quickly added, "Evie, would you mind closing up the shop when the customers have gone? Mr. Little and I are going to have a little meeting."

"Sure, Dr. B. Whatever you need." She looked at Brick with renewed interest, but his eyes blazed with a confusing mixture of emotions. Finding his scrutiny too intense, she shifted her own gaze toward Martin.

"Are you sure nothing's wrong?"

"Nothing to concern yourself about, my dear." Despite his reassuring words, his eyes darted nervously.

"Well, I'll get to work then. Don't worry about the shop, Dr. B. I can handle it."

"I know." Martin's eyes conveyed fatherly pride. "I know I can count on you, Evie. I'm so glad you're here."

She returned his smile. "Okay, I'll see you later, then." She felt compelled to turn toward Brick. "Nice to, umh . . . to, uh . . . meet you, Mr. Little."

EVIE'S FACE BLAZED as bright as the scarlet geraniums as she scurried up the wide wooden porch steps and slipped into the shop. With pounding heart she leaned against the door. *Nice going, dunderhead . . . you really impressed him with your eloquence!* As she struggled to regain her composure, Evie remembered the fear she had seen in Dr. B.'s eyes. *Maybe it's just as well I didn't impress that guy. He scared Dr. B. I'm sure of it!*

***

Chapter 20

He'll think I'm crazy!

Martin Bascomb's front hall was brimming with fragrant plant life. Edwardian containers and porcelain pots of all shapes and sizes housed an impressive display. Brick found himself wondering how many hours it took to care for it all.

"This is amazing," he said to his host. He reached down to touch a velvety green leaf. "I never imagined that plants could make a home come alive like this."

Martin grinned with satisfaction. "Thank you. Perhaps that's why we coined the phrase, 'plant life?' But, you did not come all this way just to admire my flowers." He pointed toward the end of the hall. "Let's go to my study."

WITHOUT TAKING HIS EYES off his guest, Martin carefully backed into his favorite leather chair. Brick guessed that the deliberate movement was painful. His lids narrowed with appreciation for his host's advancing years.

"Now, I don't mean to be rude, young man, but just what in thunder was that, 'life and death' talk about?"

Brick shook his head. "You're not rude. I didn't mean to alarm you, and I'm really sorry, but, I've stumbled upon a nightmare and, well . . . I'm hoping for your help. I just didn't know where else to go." He breathed heavily and his heart pounded as he slumped deep within his seat. He had rehearsed his story over and over in the car, but now that he was in front of the renown botanist, the whole thing seemed unreal. *Or crazy,* he worried. *Cripes, he's gonna think I'm a freaking lunatic!*

Despite his ruminations, Brick was glad to see that Martin was waiting patiently. The great man's kindly gaze had a calming effect. He decided, *Well, I guess it's now or never!* He scooted to the edge of his seat and began his tale. One by one he hammered home the vital points, making certain that Martin understood the magnitude of the threat to the production and distribution of the nation's food supply. When he finished his story, Brick realized that Martin's eyes had lost their suspicious glint. In fact, he did not appear to be surprised. Brick had not expected this quiet acceptance. It threw him off balance. Drained him. He found himself wishing, *C'mon, Doc . . . tell me I'm crazy. Say something!*

For a long time the two men stared at each other.

Martin's voice finally broke the silence, but he did not extend any words of comfort. He did not invoke any words of wisdom. He simply offered to rustle up a pot of coffee.

***

Chapter 21

*L*eft alone with his thoughts, Brick relived his nightmare.

He had gone to work early that day to finalize his presentation. He was alone in the little-used extension of Conference Room B on the second floor of the Miller Building when he overheard the familiar voice of a colleague through the sliding doors. Normally Brick would have called out to him to signal his presence, but Bob Jette's shaky tone had stopped him.

Thank God for that, he thought as he waited for Dr. Bascomb to return with the coffee. He realized he had been lucky, too, because he had not put in a written request to use the room.

While the other voice was too low to be recognized, Bob's was uncharacteristically loud and angry. He was going to go to the media, he had shouted, to blow the lid. Brick almost jumped out of his skin when he heard why—Bob was going to expose a scheme to destroy the country's food supply.

Brick now realized that with that last remark, Bob had probably sealed his fate. According to his accusations, 'they' had virtually gained control of the seed market already—through the development and sale of hybrids. Brick had also overheard something about genetic engineering and some sort of terminator—and Bob had mentioned the letters G-M-O. *Something to do with genetics?* Brick now realized they were referring to patented GM foods.

Bob's voice had shaken with anger. He shouted, "Don't you realize the implications of this scheme? How can you allow them to continue? They could end up destroying so many of the small independent farmers! And that new breakthrough could be devastating if it gets into the wrong hands. IF? It is already! Why can't you see that?"

Brick knew very little about agriculture, but he did know that hybrid seeds produced great plants and that the fruits and vegetables from these plants, while entirely edible and worthwhile as food, were not capable of passing their superior qualities on to the next generation. Often times, the next generation did not even produce fruit or vegetables— just spindly vegetation. As a result, gardeners with hybrid plants must remain dependent upon the seed companies each year.

The hybrid market had already been around for decades, and on the national level there were very few organic seeds available. Except for scattered pockets of rugged individuals, few others were aware that hybrids had come to dominate the marketplace. Most people failed to recognize the imminent dangers. *Most people just don't seem to care,* Brick lamented. *They trust the government to keep an eye on things. People like me,* he thought sadly, *until now! I do care. I do.*

The availability of heirloom seeds, according to Bob's rantings, would be withering up. Then, anyone controlling the seed supply would control the market. Brick immediately recognized the dangers and the potential profits of such a scheme. But control of gardens wasn't the issue. It was the entire food industry and the trillions of dollars that went with it. *Power beyond belief—the effects could be devastating. These guys are bound to be ruthless with stakes that high,* Brick reasoned.

That was why Bob's next statement had made his blood run cold. He had shouted that he was going to take his story to the Post that night. He had demanded support, but apparently his demands had fallen on deaf ears.

Still hidden behind the partition, Brick had silently urged, *C'mon Bob . . . who the hell are you talking to? Who's involved?* He had fervently prayed that Bob would mention a name—as a newcomer to the organization, he still did not know many of his associates or their bosses. Unfortunately, his prayers were not to be answered. Bob had stomped out of the room, slamming the door behind him. That was when Brick had peered into the hallway just in time to see the tall, dapper man who pretended to shoot Bob in the back.

When he was sure that the men had gone, Brick worked quickly and methodically to eliminate all traces of his early morning use of the conference room. He was glad he had not booked it, having assumed it would not be in use so early in the morning. He also felt fortunate that there were no security cameras monitoring this older portion of the building. Even more lucky for him, in their hasty exit, Bob's companions had not thought to search adjoining rooms for witnesses. *They're awfully cocky—or just stupid, and I doubt that. God, I wonder if they'll have a way of knowing I was here? Spies, maybe. Somebody watching the parking lot. No telling how many people are involved.*

Brick decided he could not trust anyone within the FDA. He snatched up his belongings and crept out the door.

WITH BRIEFCASE IN HAND Brick had raced through the building, unaware of a set of calculating eyes that noticed his haste. The watcher's sweaty face glistened and his eyes gleamed as he thought of the reward he might receive. Melvin was sure that a report on this young executive would be worth a lot of money. He had seen him before, but although he did not know his name, he knew the guy's foxy little secretary. He decided to be extra attentive later and offer to empty her wastebaskets or something.

I'll find out who he is easy enough . . . then I'll call Mr. J. I bet he'll be generous. Real generous! Melvin's belly bounced with happy anticipation as his eyes followed Brick's dash through the building.

BRICK DECIDED NOT TO go near his car. *Somebody's probably watching the parking lot.* He realized that anyone powerful enough to infiltrate a carefully screened government organization like the FDA—and to concoct a scheme that could gain control of the country's food production—probably had the resources to monitor the building and to trace ownership of the vehicles in the parking lot. He hoped he could figure out what to do before they tracked him down.

Several blocks away from the Miller, Brick hailed a cab. "Take me across town," he said. "The long way."

"Sure, bud. Hop in."

While Brick was settling in, the driver gave the finger to a speeding motorist who cut him off. He then growled and gunned the engine until he saw a hole in the traffic. The force of their takeoff knocked Brick's head against the back of the seat. He wondered if he'd have been safer with the dapper thug and his imaginary gun.

Brick watched for signs of a tail as his cab zigzagged across three northbound lanes. When he was satisfied that no one was following, he asked the driver to stop in front of a small diner. Once inside, he found a seat at the back of the room. *This is a real good spot,* he thought. *I can face the door.*

The tantalizing scent of freshly baked bread beckoned, so Brick ordered two slices, lightly toasted—cut extra thick—with his favorite breakfast. *Food,* he thought. *The power of food. Here I am, scared out of my wits, expecting to be hunted down any minute . . . and yet my mouth still waters at the smell of freshly baked bread.* He wondered if his life would ever be normal again. He wondered how Bob Jette could have been so foolhardy as to threaten exposure—and as he spread a thick layer of strawberry jam across a golden slice of toast, he devised a plan.

BRICK STARTED BY canceling all of his appointments for the next few days. Then he called Bob, hoping for a chance to talk. *Oh good,* he thought. *He's answering.*

"Bob. This is Brick Little. How are you? And the Mrs. and those kids of yours?"

"Brick—good to hear from you. Oh, they're fine. They're all fine. And how are you doing? Still happy to be at Feeday?"

Brick grinned at Bob's reference to the FDA. They exchanged a few lighthearted stories about first days on the job—both reluctant to voice their concerns.

After an awkward pause, Bob brought up his family once more.

"Guess what? Jenny got a part in a play put on by a local theatre group. It's a modern rendition of *Snow White.*"

"Exciting stuff for a teenager I guess?"

"Yup." With lightning speed, Bob's thoughts raced through a series of questions about the man on the other end of the line. He decided he had to trust his first impression of Brickford Little. *He seems like a good guy. Maybe he can help.*

"I hear the voice of a proud dad. So, what else is new, Bob?"

"Well, actually Brick, I'm glad you called. There's something I need to talk to you about—it's important."

Oh, boy. Here it comes, Brick thought.

"Sure Bob, what is it?"

"Well, why don't we meet at the Miller this afternoon? I'll explain then."

"Sure. What time?"

"Does four o'clock sound okay?" Bob's mind scrambled for a clue that would put his associate on the alert. Any clue. Uncomfortable silence filled the line as he wondered what to say. *Of course! Perkins' tape in the Snow White wrapper—thank God for Jenny's play!*

"Say, Brick—Jenny's the fourth dwarf in that play. It's a parody on *Snow White.* I have the video, you know.

It's . . . umh . . . very interesting, Brick. Very interesting—especially at the end. Have you seen it? You should."

BOB REALIZED A MAN LIKE BRICK would not be interested in a Disney cartoon. But, at a loss for anything else, he continued. "Umh . . . Jenny would be thrilled if you came over to see it. Look, Brick, I have to run. We can make plans when we meet at four."

Bob prayed that Brick would pick up on the clue, realizing that it would be a long shot. *As if Brick Little would even want to watch a Disney video. Snow White, at that. But what else could I do?*

Judging from Ricardo's actions this morning Bob realized he could not go through normal channels—the corruption could go far beyond Ricardo.

BOB PARKED HIS CAR on a busy city street. He felt alone and vulnerable as the traffic passed him by in jerky starts and stops. Some of the drivers, slouched with angry scowls and clenched hands on steering wheels, felt trapped in the seemingly endless lines of vehicles. Seasoned commuters, though, listened to their favorite morning talk shows and accepted each stop as a chance to sip piping hot coffee from Styrofoam cups or brightly-colored travel mugs.

On the sidewalk, a young mother wheeled her infant past Bob's car with long, purposeful strides. He watched as she slowed to ease the carriage around a heaping basket of bright red apples. He found himself wondering what kind of fruit her baby would eat when it grew up. He also wondered if SanFidel would have complete control of the food supply by then. He hoped that he'd be able to prevent that from happening.

Bob jumped, startled by the discord when three young girls clutching bundles of thick textbooks, shrieked with unfettered mirth. They were pushing their way through a small cluster of shoppers in an effort to catch up with four boys in red and gold letter jackets, who sauntered ahead, full of their own importance. Bob wondered if baseball would be so important to them if they knew what SanFidel was up to. His eyes traveled back to the heaping bins of fruits and vegetables and he took a deep breath. He was suddenly more aware than ever of the tangy scents of the apples, bananas, grapes, and lemons on display at the overflowing sidewalk market. Mingled with the gasoline fumes and flowering trees, the scent of the plump fruits helped to fill the hot city air with its own pungent aroma.

***

Chapter 22

So what are GM foods . . . ?

*B*rick wondered why Bob would think that he'd be interested in a *Snow White* video. He quickly dismissed the thought. *Chock it up to proud parenting,* he reasoned. Realizing he had several hours before their four o'clock meeting, he decided to learn what he could about seeds, food production and genetic engineering. *Maybe I should see what I might learn about GMO's, too. I know it refers to genetically modified foods . . . but I don't know much about that stuff.* He left the diner and took the bus to the Library of Congress.

His search confirmed what he already knew. Most of the seeds available today are hybrids and their superior qualities end with the first generation. Unfortunately, most of the information about genetic engineering was textbook stuff, too technical for the layperson.

Brick did find several references to grassroots organizations. One, called Rural Vermont, was proud of a public endorsement from Willie Nelson, the country music star. They were affiliated with another group called Vermont Gean. There also was a very active national body, called Mothers for Natural Law, or MNL. All of the groups were actively lobbying for mandatory labeling and stricter controls on genetically modified food products, but most of the information was about the MNL. When Brick clicked onto a website featuring news about GM foods, he found a series of articles arguing against the latest proposed legislation. The bill that received the most coverage was called the GoMO Bill. According to the article, it was established to provide the producers of genetically modified food products, including hybrid seeds, more of the rights they were demanding. *Yeah—a monopoly of rights,* Brick grumbled. Senator Miller was the main sponsor.

YOU MIGHT KNOW Miller's involved with this stuff, Brick thought. *I've never liked him or his tactics.* The Miller Machine was highly effective, but Brick believed they were usually on the wrong side when it came to important issues. The article claimed that the GoMO legislation was detrimental to farmers, and elaborated extensively on a long list of the possible dangers of allowing the free reign of untested biotechnology.

Here's where the GMO's come in, Brick noticed. *It stands for genetically modified organisms and can refer to either plants or animals. They also refer to them as GM foods.*

There were also several references to a botanist named Martin Bascomb. He seemed to be in the forefront of scientific discoveries. He had a lot of good ideas about safely increasing food production and had traveled extensively to help people in Third World countries to raise crops such as corn, soy and wheat. Brick read that Dr. Bascomb's methods significantly increased yields wherever they were put into practice. He thought the next piece of information was significant. Bascomb had steadfastly refused to allow commercial use of the genetic technologies that he had developed. Instead, he insisted that they study the long-term results. Brick was not surprised, therefore, to see that Dr. Martin Bascomb had been lauded for his ethics.

With a glimmer of hope, Brick decided to contact the famous botanist right after his meeting with Bob Jette. *Maybe we can both talk to Dr. Bascomb.* He decided that it wouldn't hurt to try.

AROUND FOUR IN THE AFTERNOON, Brick watched from his rental car as Bob Jette sprinted up the steps of the Miller Building. Before he could open his car door, he heard the unmistakable sound of gunfire. To his horror, Bob reeled from the impact of a bullet. Brick was not the only one who heard the gunshot, and although his ears buzzed from the shock of it all, he heard shouts for a doctor above the din of screams, angry horns and squealing brakes. When he twisted around to see who had fired the shot, the image of two frightened teenage boys burned itself into his memory. He stared helplessly as their rusty Chevy Cavalier rattled past him and careened out of sight. He also thought he saw a third person brandishing a gun at the boys from the back seat. A person in white linen. *Oyster white, or ecru,* Brick's aunt Margie would have said.

Good God, he really did it! Brick was sure it was the man he had seen that morning—the dapper finger shooter!

AS ATTENTIVE AS HE WAS, though, Brick missed one detail—Tommy Sykes, a teenage boy with kinky brown hair, a perpetual toothy grin and a sprinkling of freckles across his nose. Tommy had just hoisted one leg onto a bench to tie his hitops, but his too-long and too-tattered pant legs, the acceptable style of the day, kept getting in the way. When he heard the shots, he looked up to see a man make a desperate grab at the sky before collapsing onto the concrete steps in front of the Miller Building. Tommy was also horrified to see the barrel of a gun being yanked back through the rear window of a familiar old car.

The toothy grin disappeared.

"Holy crap! The shooter's in Larry's car! And Benji's there, too—what the heck is goin' on!"

Tommy forgot his dangling laces as Larry's Chevy Cavalier swerved past a long line of confused drivers. He continued to stare until the sound of sirens broke his trance. The two boys were his friends and he was not going to stick around and be questioned by the police. Tommy quickly scrambled across the park. He ran until his side ached and he was far away from the commotion.

***

Chapter 23

Melvin's coffee break

*I*t was break time. Melvin grabbed a chair at the small round table that was set up for the security staff, and plopped down in a snit.

"I shoulda' been more careful, darnit!" He raised one arm and inspected his shirt. "Yup! That's a sweat stain all right. Now I gotta do the laundry—ain't got no more shirts left!" He had hoped to get by for another week or two with this one. After all, it only had one little splotch of mustard on it—until today. *And it's all her fault,* he thought.

Melvin did not often work up a sweat. He was very good at avoiding work. But today there had been no getting out of it. When he went up to that Brick Little guy's office to snoop, the secretary was right in his face, all cute 'n perky, begging for help. She had to clean out their file cabinets because some new ones were going to be delivered—*any minute now*—she had whined.

Melvin figured he would just empty a drawer or two, and while he was at it, he could get some information out of her. But she got stuck on the telephone and he ended up doing it all. *I musta' moved a couple tons of paper . . . and this is what I get for it. Laundry!*

Melvin slammed his fist onto the faux marble table top, then yanked it back with a yelp of pain.

"Darnit! Galldarnitalmighty! That thing's hard! It just ain't fair! First I gotta do the laundry, and now I hurt myself." Melvin scowled at his throbbing hand and muttered,

"Somebody oughtta pay for this." And that's when he got a great idea. *Yeah, that's it—Workman's Comp!*

Melvin scrunched his shoulders with glee. His luck was getting better every day. He was on a roll!

Oh well, I better check in. Mr. Jordan's gonna wanna know who was in the old wing this mornin'. He looked around to see if anyone was watching—not wanting to get caught using his injured hand. Satisfied that he was still alone, Melvin dialed Perry Jordan's number. *It's a good thing that little secretary didn't mind talkin' about her new boss,* he thought. *At least I know how to find the guy.*

When he heard the beep, Melvin relayed what he had learned. He felt like a star in a James Bond movie as he left his message.

"A Feeday guy was there in the old wing this mornin'. He ran away kinda' like he was scared. One of the new hires. Name's Brick Little. Lives with Jerry Johnson, a shrink in DC."

He started to hang up, then remembered something else, "Oh, yeah. The phone's listed under Johnson's name."

***

Chapter 24

*B*rick came out of his nightmarish reverie at the sound of Martin's footsteps. The elderly botanist was carrying a tray of coffee and the makings for thick, meaty sandwiches.

"Well, Mr. Little, I assume you've not had proper nourishment for awhile . . . so please, help yourself." With a flutter of hands, Martin urged him to make a sandwich.

Brick felt like Pavlov's dog when Martin lowered the tray. His mouth watered and he wanted to pounce on the food. Instead, he spread mayo onto a slice of bread, then piled a mound of roast beef on top.

"Thanks, Dr. Bascomb." Brick's eyes traveled from his host to the sandwich, then back again. "You're right—I am famished!" To prove it, he took a big bite.

As he ate his sandwich, Brick watched Martin with friendly eyes. He liked everything he had read about him. Martin Bascomb's unwavering insistence upon monitoring the long-term results of his experiments and his demand for environmentally safe practices had earned him a great deal of respect from all of his peers in the scientific community as well as his customers. Brick instinctively felt that the articles were correct.

Glad that he came, he ate heartily.

BEFORE HIS GUEST finished eating, Martin decided to continue their discussion.

"Well, Mr. Little, I . . ."

Brick interrupted.

"It's Brick. Please call me Brick."

"Yes. Thank you. Well—Brick—I was doing some thinking in the kitchen . . . and as fantastic as your story sounds, I do believe you. I happen to know that a terminator technology exists that has the potential to create disastrous results. I've warned several of my colleagues against it." Martin removed his glasses and pinched the bridge of his nose as he gathered his thoughts.

"Once unleashed, it could create a nightmare of global proportions—and there's no quick fix. An entire crop could be annihilated. Not to mention the health risks when you're dealing with genetics. It's a gamble . . . a veritable crapshoot! Genetic engineering often brings surprises—one never really knows what might be created—new toxins, rampant cancers, debilitating allergies. And I've done my best to warn them, to convince them there simply has not been enough time to examine the effects." He shook his head with a mixture of sadness and bafflement as he pulled out a clean lens cloth.

BRICK WATCHED AND CHEWED as Martin busied himself with his glasses. He finally continued, "We do have one thing to our advantage, however. It will be easy for me to verify the scoundrel—or should I say scoundrels?—behind your assertions." He frowned. "I have a few suspicions—I'm convinced that the terminator is the key to what you've told me, and there simply aren't many people with that capability." He paused to give Brick a hard look. "But I refuse to mention any names at this point."

"What do you mean? We can't just sit here! We can't give them the chance . . ."

Martin held up his hand.

"Hold on young man. We won't lose that much time—I promise. But I won't make any accusations until I've made a few tactful inquiries. Careers could be at stake, you know. And another thing . . . it's not the scientist who poses the threat. You've got to follow the money." He peered at Brick after he pulled on his glasses. "Do you know what I'm saying?"

"Yes, of course. Look, I'm sorry. I guess I'm just edgy."

"Understandable. You've been through a lot, Brick. You've witnessed a tragedy, you feel betrayed and you have information about an alarming scheme. You've got a right to be edgy." Martin smiled cagily. "I'm reminded of a line from the Book of John . . . ' . . . *and the light shineth in darkness, and the darkness comprehended it not'*. In other words, my friend, the good shall prevail—with the element of surprise, perhaps."

"A Bible-quoting scientist? Isn't that a contradiction, or . . ."

Martin interrupted with a hearty chuckle.

"Good heavens, my boy, it's not a contradiction at all! Let me ask you this—have you ever marveled at the perfection of a finely crafted Swiss watch?"

"Sure. Haven't we all?"

"Unfortunately, Brick, most people don't take these musings to the logical conclusion. When you marvel at creation—any creation—by man or God, your thoughts should lead to a series of questions. Wondrous questions—and wondrous answers!"

Brick forgot about the sandwich he had just made. He leaned forward to urge his host. "And they are . . . ?"

Martin's eyes sparkled.

"Question number one: *Could all of the gears of that watch have fallen into place by accident?*"

Brick shook his head.

"Of course not—it wouldn't be logical."

"Right. I can see that, but . . ."

"So what is the logical assumption?" Martin didn't wait for Brick's reply. "It must have been created." Martin could see that Brick was still not following him. "Now—think about our universe! Think about the sun, the moon and the Earth! Think about the other planets—and all of the galaxies in existence. Aren't they spinning through space like the gears of a fine Swiss watch? And doesn't the motion of the moon pull the oceans? As predictably as the gears of a finely tuned Swiss watch—don't you think?"

BRICK'S MIND WAS grappling with the concept. He'd not been a religious man; had looked askance at theology, but Martin's simplistic argument for creation made sense.

"I see your point. The world didn't just happen, there's too much order—it had to be created!"

"Yes, Brick, and doesn't that lead you to the ultimate question?"

Brick jumped to his feet and pointed at Martin. "Who was the Creator? That's the ultimate question isn't it?"

"You've almost got it. But, I daresay you should be asking, who *is* our Creator. And you can find the answer in the Bible." Martin began to quote the Book of John again. "In the beginning was the Word, and the Word was God, and the Word was with God." He looked at his guest. "You know, Brick, just because there's an ultimate Creator, it does not mean we have to stop searching for answers—cannot continue to seek and invent. One *can* be a scientist *and* a Christian, too!"

Brick felt a growing sense of peace—and a growing conviction that, with Martin's help, he'd be able to stop Bob Jette's killers. He took a huge bite out of his sandwich.

"By the way—why did you seek me out?"

The sudden change in topic caught Brick off guard. He had to rearrange a mouth full of roast beef. "Right after I overheard Bob . . ." He finished chewing and swallowed. ". . . I went over to the Library of Congress to learn what I could about biotechnology, GMO's and stuff. And your name seemed to pop up everywhere. You were recognized for your integrity so I decided you wouldn't be involved and it stood to reason you could be helpful on the scientific end. So, here I am!" *Yes, here I am . . . in need of a shower, exhausted and unshaven. I bet Evie wasn't too impressed.*

Martin did not realize that it was thoughts of Evie that created Brick's sudden frown. He tried to be reassuring. "We'll stop them, Brick. I'm sure we'll stop them in time."

Brick nodded doubtfully. He thought, *I may not be beaming as happily as that couple back at the parking lot, but you have eased my mind a bit.*

AS HE HEADED TOWARD HIS CAR, Brick stopped to admire the grounds. He thought he'd love to have a place like this to come home to, with a wife, kids and a big floppy-eared dog. *A wife!* The image of long shapely legs, an oversized safari shirt and honey blonde hair appeared. The mere thought of Evie brought a resurgence of that pleasant tingle. *I'd better get out of here, fast—before I start daydreaming about a wedding!*

Brick jumped into his car and sped off. He whizzed around the first curve, then found himself desperately pumping his brakes. He shouted, "Oh, God, I'm going to hit her!" The tires squealed and for several agonizing seconds he continued to hurtle toward the startled young woman.

The car did finally stop in time, but his heart still lurched at the thought of losing her. *Losing her? I've barely even met the girl!* Unwilling to deal with this sudden rush of feelings, Brick shifted back into drive and sped off, resolving to lecture Miss Evelyn Victor some day on the need to be more mindful of speeding traffic.

When he reached the main road, Brick aimed his car toward Boston. He'd get rid of the car and catch a train to DC.

SEVERAL HOURS LATER, Brick pulled into a vacant motel. It did not take long to check in and make arrangements to return his rental. He was glad to learn that he could leave it right at Union Station which was only minutes away.

"Check out time's 11 AM. You gotta pay up front for each night you wanna keep your room. 16's ready for you— it's around the corner over there, to the left." Brick thought the thin young man resembled a teacher's pointer stick when he aimed the top of his bright orange Mohawk toward the hallway across the room.

"Thanks. I'll just need it for tonight."

"Super." His tone made it quite clear that he did not think anything was super. He accepted Brick's money, handed him the key, and without another word returned to his comic strip. Brick didn't care—he just wanted to get some sleep.

BRICK UNLOCKED THE DOOR and reached for the light switch. Only one bulb in the four-bulb ceiling fixture lit up. *Why am I not surprised,* he thought as he lumbered across the room. He emptied his pockets, tossed his jacket onto the nearest chair and stripped to his briefs, and as he climbed into bed, he wondered idly if plants could improve a shabby motel room. *Probably not,* he thought.

WITH MARTIN BASCOMB'S promise of support and a renewed sense of hope, Brick quickly fell asleep.

AT THE OTHER END OF THE STATE, porch lights illuminated Martin's garden to create a misty, fairy-like atmosphere, but the good scientist was staring with indifference, uncharacteristically blind to the peace and harmony before him. And as he turned away, he realized somewhat ruefully that, for the first time in years, he probably would not sleep well.

***

Chapter 25

Successful scientists care!

---

*A*fter Dr. B. left her in charge of the shop, Evie had seen to the needs of the last customers and had industriously handled the ritual of closing—mindful that as kind as he was, Dr. B. was a stickler for details. She smiled at the thought of her illustrious mentor. Because of his awesome credentials, she had been nervous about applying for the internship, but the woman from the career services office at UVM had said that she'd be perfect for it. At first she thought that Maria had been too insistent that she take this job, but now she was glad. She vowed to send Maria Charbonneau a bouquet of flowers as a special thank you.

EVIE HAD BEEN EAGER to break into the fascinating world of research, but Dr. B. had insisted that she first become competent at running the shop. A love of plant life that people care about and a healthy understanding and respect for the needs of his customers, was, he believed, imperative in order to understand his research and its importance in the world.

'A successful scientist,' Dr. B. was fond of saying, 'cares as much about the impact of his work as he does about the work itself.'

So, with her usual enthusiasm, Evie plunged into the not-quite-so-fascinating world of the retail garden shop. She was proud of the fact that during these two short months at Pleasant Acres, Dr. B. had quickly come to trust her judgment. In his own words she had . . . *Now what did he say? Oh, yes. I have more than adequately fulfilled the quotidian tasks that lay before me.* A quick trip to the dictionary told her that quotidian meant, 'mundane, repetitive, everyday tasks.' *Maybe now he'll agree that I'm ready for the important work,* she decided.

It seemed to Evie that she had spent her whole life trying to prove herself. Her brothers were always saying she was too young, or too small, or too female for the fun stuff. But, despite—or maybe even because of them—she had learned to throw a football, with fingers positioned just so on the stitches, and hurl it, spinning like a top, straight toward its goal. And she could shoot the cans off a fence post with chilling accuracy. Even her brothers were proud of that.

Evie's biggest triumph, however, was in science. Although she was popular, the other girls in school had no interest in her experiments and the boys just laughed at her. But she proved herself there, too, when in the ninth grade she won first prize in the state science competition for demonstrating the growth cycles of the hairy-stemmed daisy, *Leucanthemella serontinum.* She still felt the thrill of that first scientific accomplishment. After all, that early taste of success was the launching pad for future scientific recognition and a full scholarship at the University of Vermont. And here she was today, working on her dissertation and completing a coveted internship with "the" Doctor Martin Bascomb.

EVIE THOUGHT MARTIN WAS wonderful. While he definitely was grandfather material, he reminded her of her brother John. They both had the same integrity and enthusiasm for their calling in life—albeit a different sort of calling. *Very different,* she thought. *Treasure hunters and world-renowned botanists don't travel in the same circles.*

Thoughts of John reminded her of his most recent letter and the fact that he'd be visiting soon. She couldn't wait—she always looked forward to his witty recounts of the world of treasure hunting. He often wrote about his hilarious misadventures, but this last letter had given her a sense of unease and as she locked the door to Pleasant Acres, she resolved to read his letter again.

EVIE STARTED TO JOG UP THE winding path toward the Bascomb residence. Dr. B. had insisted that her salary include room and board at his spacious home. He had welcomed her like a long-lost daughter, and it did not take her long to feel completely at ease—even pampered. And the ever-faithful Millicent was good company as well as a fabulous cook who insisted upon learning Evie's favorite meals. She grinned. Shortly after her first encounter with Millicent, she overheard the plump woman declare to Martin that she would, ". . . put some meat on the bones of that pretty—but skinny—young thing."

JUST BEFORE SHE reached the crest of the big hill, a green sedan burst out of nowhere. As it screeched to a heart-stopping ten inches from her feet, Evie found herself staring into the frightened eyes of its driver. An odd feeling of paralysis swept through her. She couldn't move, but there was nothing sluggish about her brain which kicked into warp speed.

My God his eyes are big . . . I never even heard the engine . . . he shouldn't have been driving so fast! In the middle of her mental tirade, her eyes widened with bewilderment. *Why does he look so angry? I'm the one who almost got killed!*

Evie opened her mouth to speak, but the car backed away from her, then pulled around her and sped away. *Not even an apology or an effort to see if I'm okay?*

"RECKLESS MANIAC!" she screeched.

Tears flowed from Evie's eyes as she watched Brick Little's car disappear around the curve. She decided she'd lecture that man on driving etiquette—if she ever saw him again. *I'll really let him have it,* she vowed. But then, somehow, the vision of his angry face dissolved into a tender stare, and despite her rage, Evie found herself wondering what it would be like to feel his lips softly brushing against her own.

"My God . . . I've lost it!" With an angry snort, she resolved to avoid any more romantic thoughts of Brickford Little. *That maniac!*

Fueled by resentment, Evie stormed over the big hill, oblivious to the exquisite botanical sights before her. It was the first time that she failed to admire the long Palladian house of gray fieldstone. Nestled comfortably in its surroundings, it was flanked by magnificent oaks and sugar maples that proudly flaunted their green summer leaves.

Throughout the grounds, the contrasting foliar effects were further evidence of the owner's skills in working with plant life—from the bursts of tall, waggling grasses to the sheared conical evergreens, every inch had been coaxed alive with the colors and the mingling scents of flowers and herbs. An assortment of climbing roses laden with cream, pink and deep red buds spilled from the tops of stone walls in anticipation of a riotous blooming season.

To Evie's far left, the delicate Japanese honeysuckle vines released their sweet fragrance into the fresh country air to blend with the heady scents of lemon verbena and golden sage. Nearby, a pair of sheared Alberta spruce stood sentry behind a fountain that poured its bubbling contents into a freeform, pebble-lined pool. In the distance, one could see the tower on top of Mount Greylock, touted by locals to be the highest peak in the State of Massachusetts.

***

Chapter 26

Hoopla—it seems to follow John!

*E*vie dashed through the front door and sprinted up the steps toward her rooms. Wanting to forget the close call on the hill, she picked up John's letter and sprawled onto the luxurious featherbed.

John, the eldest of the Victor siblings, captivated everyone who knew him, including prim and proper Aunt Glenna, who would often look him in the eye and call him the family rogue. She delighted in telling his younger brothers and sister about his devilish antics as a 'wee one.' She noisily scoffed at his yen for adventure, and he openly proclaimed her to be a meddlesome old battle-ax. And yet, when he became a treasure investigator, she kept a scrapbook, filled with letters and clippings detailing his lively escapades.

Memories of her brother's entertaining tales brought a smile to Evie's face. As a treasure hunter he had traveled a lot. From coast to coast, and from Alaska to South America, he had gained a reputation for being an astute investigator. Her favorite story involved millions of dollars in gold coins. Of course, there was intrigue and murder, along with an assortment of off-beat characters mixed colorfully into the equation when John told the story. Evie was not sure how many details were the embellishment of a gifted storyteller, or how many were pieces of actual factual information—but it was true that he had returned the loot with a great deal of hoopla. The coins, missing since the early 1800's, were gratefully received by their rightful owner, a bank in West Virginia. Evie chuckled. *Hoopla! It seems to follow my brother wherever he goes* . . . .

EVIE REACHED FOR the bedside lamp and plumped her pillows before settling in to read her brother's letter. Once again, it seemed uncharacteristically sober. He mentioned a new case that he'd be working on involving artifacts from the Civil War. *He'll love that one,* she murmured. But he also wrote about an upsetting meeting and his concerns about the path the people might take. *I hope he doesn't get into trouble with that bunch,* she thought. *More hoopla?* She giggled, then read his puzzling postscript. He asked her not to mention the meeting to anyone. She thought it was odd. *Why would I talk about his meetings, anyway? And to whom?*

***

Chapter 27

*W*hen the alarm rang, Tommy Sykes dragged himself out of bed with the energetic grace of a zombie. The shooting and the death of his friends was hard enough to deal with, but he was also torn between his instinctive urge to seek revenge and his desire to avoid more violence.

Tommy followed the stories in the papers, but the man he saw in Larry's car had somehow vanished. There wasn't even a single reference to him, and to make matters worse, Larry and Benji were blamed for the murder of that Jette guy.

Maybe I should tell Dr. J. about it this afternoon. He's pretty smart . . . I bet he'll know what to do.

Tommy had recently befriended Jerry Johnson, a psychologist who hired him to do odd chores at his home.

TOMMY LEFT FOR WORK before anyone else was up. He had a part-time job at The Westside Journal, a weekly paper where he helped in Circulation. It was boring work, but it gave him some spending money and he was off duty long before any of his friends were even out of bed. It was good that way, Tommy reasoned when he took the job, because the guys might not understand his desire to work. Tommy felt that he had to belong to the gang so they'd protect him and his little brother and his mother. They were basically okay, but sometimes they could be a tough bunch. Sam and Fingers had been fending for themselves since they were very young children, while Rob had been a victim of domestic violence. *Not for long, though,* Tommy thought with a slim grin. *Rob was already almost six feet tall when he was in the sixth grade. He didn't take nothin' from nobody by then.*

Dr. Johnson said Tommy's friends just needed to prove to themselves that they had some sort of control over their lives. *That's why they tried to be tough every now and then,* Tommy concluded.

When the last bundle of newspapers was bagged and tagged, Tommy dutifully started the prep for the next day's mailing. He lugged a bundle of scratchy mailing sacks over to the stuffing station. It took about forty minutes to pile up enough of them, and once the metal zip-code tags were filled, his job was done and he punched out.

TOMMY DASHED ACROSS the busy street and took a deep breath, loving the tangy scents at the fruit stand. He chose a red delicious apple and tossed a crumpled dollar bill at the old man behind the counter. Tommy loved fruit. He thought it was amazing how such tasty food could grow on a tree, but he felt a little guilty eating it, because his mom could barely keep cheap cuts of meat and potatoes on the table. *Some day,* he sighed. *Some day I'll buy her all the fruit she could ever want.* As he worked his way toward the seedy core of his apple, Tommy strolled toward Dr. Johnson's house on George Street.

Tommy met the friendly psychologist at the fruit stand shortly before Larry and Benji were killed. They were both chomping into huge oranges when Tommy accidentally squirted juice on him. Tommy expected an angry tirade, but the man just laughed and joked that Tommy must be an expert marksman. He introduced himself as Jerry Johnson. He said he was a psychologist and lived with his best friend, Brick Little. They talked for a long time that day, and Tommy agreed to do chores for Dr. J. every week.

Each time Tommy arrived at Dr. J's home they talked. Tommy didn't realize how much information the skillful psychologist was getting from him. All of their discussions seemed to flow naturally. He liked the way the man talked *to him* not *at him*—and he always felt better afterward. It was like having his own personal support system.

With that thought in mind, Tommy was glad that he'd decided to tell Dr. J. about the shooting and the death of his friends. *We gotta find the man with the gun,* he decided. *I bet Dr. J. will know what to do.*

***

Chapter 28

Damo's listening

---

*B*rick woke up in a strange bed. He had no idea what time it was or where he was, until his eyes adjusted to the gloomy interior. *Of course! Pointer boy and his dingy motel.* He was in the middle of wondering why anyone would deliberately wear his hair that way when he remembered something else. *Oh no—the train!* He leapt to his feet. *What time is it? I've gotta catch the train to DC!*

Twenty-five minutes later, Brick was shaved, showered, checked out, and on his way. At the train station, he called Jerry and asked to be picked up when his train arrived. "The train gets in at 5:30, Jer. Can you make it?"

"Sure. I'll be there. So what's up? Where's your car? And where the heck are you calling from?"

"It's a long story, Jer. Let's plan to grab a bite to eat down at Peggy Sue's Restaurant. I'll tell you about it then.."

"Okay. See you at 5:30."

"GOOD! IT'S ABOUT TIME we heard from you. And I'll be starvin' by that time, too," sneered a voice that neither Brick nor Jerry could hear. Their telephone had already been tapped. "So . . . how come you don't wanna tell him on the telephone, you creep?"

Damo wondered what Brick had heard at the Miller Building. He also wondered why the guy had gone to Boston so suddenly.

"I'm beginnin' ta think you know too much," he growled, "but I'm glad you're comin' back already."

Damo sighed with relief. He'd been expecting this to be a long, boring week. All that he had heard so far was a few of Johnson's therapy sessions—the guy didn't seem to have many patients. Damo didn't know that the successful counselor was working on his doctorate and had not accepted any new clients for the past year.

Damo stretched his lanky frame. He'd been cooped up in the surveillance vehicle for several hours and had amused himself by listening to the therapy sessions. At one point, when a man was whining to the ever-patient Johnson about his wife's multiple affairs, Damo shouted, "For cryin' out loud, just dump the bitch!" He slapped the dashboard with disbelief. "This is as bad as those talk shows on TV. These people gotta be stupid!" He angrily pinched the crease back into his favorite trousers. Damo loved his linen suits. He wore them all the time—even on a hit.

JUST BEFORE 5 PM, Damo flexed his toes, then slid out of his van. The restaurant was an easy stroll away. He stopped to pinch his crease. *A guy's gotta look good,* he thought. Damo fancied himself a ladies' man—and he did attract the ladies. *Like moths to a flame,* he thought as he strode along. The only trouble was, the flame quickly burned out when the ladies heard him talk—about himself—all the time.

***

Chapter 29

The more level heads, the better

The conference room was buzzing with activity. John Victor scanned the room for familiar faces and noticed that tonight's attendance was almost double that of the last session. A diverse assortment of men and women filled the cramped rows of seats, sitting knee-to-knee, auditorium style, while latecomers leaned against the wall beneath a series of historical photos in cheap, black frames.

Manny sat to John's right, next to a young woman with raven black hair, and at the front of the room, two American flags flanked Colonel Mitchem and his companions. John's eyes narrowed. He did not think the flag should be associated with them. He wondered anew how they could attract such a large following of good people. He decided they must be masters at recruiting and found himself wondering what else they were masters at. "Nothing good," he muttered.

JOHN WAS TOO BUSY sizing up Mitchem's group to notice that C.D. had appeared. He did see his stepsons, Keith and Jonas before scanning the room one more time and was relieved to see C.D. who gave a quick hand signal. John signaled that he understood. The stealthy gestures reminded John of their struggles in Viet Nam when they couldn't always tell who was friend and who was foe. *Kind of like here,* he mused uneasily.

***

Chapter 30

C.D. watched with smoldering anger

---

*T*he expectant crowd hushed at the sound of the gavel and a small, energetic man extended his greetings before asking them to recite the pledge of allegiance.

Nice touch, thought C.D. *I definitely approve of the pledge.* He relaxed in his seat and wondered if John Victor had been 'shouting wolf'. But it did not take long for him to realize that the pledge was about the only thing he *did* like about the proceedings. He watched, with smoldering anger, as Mitchem baited the crowd with a series of lies and accusations aimed at the government. After a young man—*probably a plant,* C.D. thought—told his story about being ruined financially by the IRS, Mitchem seized the opportunity to fuel the anger. *That guy could be cast as an evil preacher in an old western,* C.D. mused.

" . . . THE ALMIGHTY LEGISLATORS who created these unjust laws and who sit around secure with the million-dollar pension plans that they created for themselves! Look at what they did to this poor man's family—why, they should be shot!

With shaking fists, the crowd began to chant, "Yeah, yeah, yeah! Shoot them. Shoot them. Shoot them!" They clapped their hands and stomped their feet, creating a deafening racket that jarred the senses.

John twisted in his seat with a silent plea, but C.D. signaled, "Not yet." He was determined to see where this was leading. Even from the back row, he could see that Mitchem's eyes were shining. *He's loving it*, he thought.

C.D.'s disgust turned to pure astonishment when Mitchem waved a handgun over his head and pulled the trigger. The crowd watched with hypnotic fascination. *Good Lord—are they people or sheep? They're too confused to do anything. And where the hell are the local officials?*

"Don't worry," Mitchem shouted. "I'm not a madman . . . I just wanted to get your attention. These are blanks!"

A few men sniggered. Some people stirred nervously in their seats, but most of them waited to be told what to do.

"I'm telling you now. It's going to be up to us—up to you and me—to stop them once and for all!"

Like the moon with the tide, he drew them in an out of his spell, and each wave brought renewed vigor and shouts. They stomped their feet with a deafening rhythm— until Mitchem blew a shrill whistle—and they became silent once again.

C.D. recognized a conditioning technique that terrorist organizations use to brainwash their most zealous followers. He decided to take advantage of the sudden quiet.

"WHO ARE YOU GOING TO stop? And how?"

Heads turned as curious eyes searched for the owner of the deep, baritone voice.

Mitchem demanded, "Who said that!"

"I did." C.D.'s voice hardened with calm authority. "And I'll ask again. Who are you going to stop, and how? Are you going to look at every government official and assume he's an enemy? Are you going to terrorize voters at the polls who don't agree with you? Are you going to march into Washington and start shooting? Maybe you'll bomb a government building to make a statement. How many innocent children, secretaries and file clerks might you kill with your violent protest?"

Mitchem glared. "It was just a figure of speech. But if you're so smart, what's your solution? These good people are sick and tired of being used by our government—their own government—as slaves. We're all slaves, I tell you, used to produce more tax revenues." He pointed toward the crowd. "Your hard-earned money is squandered. And we can't even trust our own military any more. What was once the greatest military in the world is virtually impotent . . . with low morale and half the defensive and offensive capability that we once had." Mitchem glared at C.D.

UNABLE TO LISTEN to the slanderous insinuations being hurled at his beloved military, C.D. stepped into the center aisle, ready to begin his offensive.

"So, you're an expert on the military, are you? What's your name? I can't place you. Where have you served?" Before the dumfounded man could respond, C.D. continued his attack. "Let me tell you something, *Colonel.*" He deliberately slurred the title, "I am Lieutenant Colonel Lucas Everett Davidson, *active status.* And I'm damned proud of our military's record!" He turned toward the crowd.

"Don't you people remember Desert Storm? Don't you remember our shock and awe campaign?" A panoply of puzzled faces stared at the impressive stranger. "Don't you remember how courageous and effective our fighting men and women were? Don't you remember that we rendered the enemy defenseless in mere hours? Is that a result of an impotent military?"

C.D. decided to get their minds off their misguided anger by telling them a story of his own.

"LET ME TELL YOU MY STORY. A true story about our so-called 'ineffective' arsenal of weaponry and manpower that took place during operation Desert Storm. Do you want to hear it?"

Expectant faces nodded. The crowd was hungry for information.

"So, we have a tank . . . an M1 Abrams. And one of these M1's was on patrol near the Iraqi border. Well, after a violent storm it got caught in a quagmire of mud. The rest of the platoon left the M1 and its crew, but soon three T75's came into view. They were the best tanks in the Iraqi arsenal . . . purchased from the Russians, by the way.

"The first Iraqi tank fired and hit our guys broadside—but you know what? No damage! Our boys just shot back and blew it up. Then the second T75 fired. Again, no damage. But our men fired at them and destroyed that one, too. The third of Iraq's *finest* hightailed it out of there to position themselves out of sight behind a mountain of a sand dune. Well, our visual capabilities *were* state of the art, even during Desert Storm, so our guys were able to 'see' the heat emanating from the hidden enemy tank. We aimed, fired, and darned if our *ineffective* shells didn't blast right through that dune, right into that enemy tank . . . blowing it to Kingdom come. And," he continued, "the story didn't end there! Some of our own soldiers arrived and attempted to help pull our M1 free of the mud. Couldn't do it. So, they blasted it themselves, thinking they didn't want to leave it for the enemy."

C.D. stopped to make sure they were still listening.

"Well, the only damage that M1 sustained was a ding in one piece of the hull and the aiming mechanisms were knocked out of whack. And, to make a long story short, the proper help finally did arrive and they got the thing free and sent it off for repairs. Darned if that *ineffective piece of junk* wasn't made ready for combat again!"

C.D. POINTED TOWARD MITCHEM. "And that, *Sir,* is one of many, many stories you won't hear about . . . because of the bias of the press who, by the way, are supported by ignorant critics like yourself." He turned back toward the crowd.

"He was right about one thing, though. We do have too many irresponsible people running this country and controlling forces they have no business controlling. But you know what? Even George Washington had those problems! Did you know that he was only able to turn things around for the Colonists during the American Revolution because

Congress ran away and he was left with complete control?" C.D. smirked. "Then again that's another whole story!"

He continued. "Look, many of our problems have been corrected, and it breaks my heart to see people continually ignoring the positive changes. And there *are a lot of good things!* In our military and in our government! Desert Storm and the latest war in Iraq are both remarkable examples of how our military has maintained its greatness—and the troubles that followed those conflicts are good examples of the ineptitude of diplomacy. When we pull back, when we try to cater to the lies and rumors of our enemies, that's when we fail. And I might add that, if he was a *real* colonel, on *active* duty, he would know all that." C.D. glared at the podium but Mitchem had disappeared.

Several voices chorused, "Where'd he go?"

Amid the buzz of the crowd, C.D. strode up to the front of the room. He whistled for their attention. "You folks keep saying *the government* did this, and *they* did that. You say the government is to blame for all that's wrong with this country. Well, I say you can't roll all of our problems up in a neat ball and label it government. Yes, there are some bad apples spoiling things—maybe a lot of bad apples. But there are ways to deal with them.

"You don't have to resort to violence because you know what? Those bad apples are afraid of you. Yes, they're afraid of the American citizenry—as a collective whole. And when enough of you care enough to be heard, they do listen. They're too cowardly to do otherwise. But, dammit—you've gotta be sure it's constructive, not destructive, action!

"You do have legitimate concerns. But, before you go on the offensive, you'd better know that you can handle your enemy, and the first step toward handling your enemy is to know who they are. And it's not the whole damned government. Not by a long shot! Your real enemy is comprised of a few cowards who have gained control of the system through default. Yes—default!"

C.D. gave the crowd a good, hard look before he continued.

"To win, you've got to work within the confines of your government . . . the greatest government in the history of the world, I might add. Because if you're really ready to take action, you can let the millions of people who comprise our nation hear your voices. And they'll see it's really their voice! You've gotta find a way to get everyone connected! I swear to you that if you get the right message out with enough voices behind it, you'll scare the pants off your real enemies. And they, my friends, consist of a small number of manipulative, power-hungry cowards and their ignorant accomplices in the mainstream press.

"Yup. Like I said before, the one thing they're afraid of is the American people as a whole—united under the Constitution. You see, over the years, they've been very effective in dismantling the Constitution because they've successfully broken us into bickering factions. Yes, folks, they've been hard at work, turning the American people into *small, dependant, bickering factions!*

"Think about it. The next time you hear a politician speaking, listen to him—or her. Really listen! You'll probably hear about the oppressed blacks. The oppressed women. The poor Latinos. The hungry children. The homeless. The abused. Doesn't their list go on and on? One would think that *that's* all this country is comprised of for crying out loud! But I ask you, if that's true, then how did we get to be so powerful so quickly? If we are *so* oppressed and helpless, then why have we been able to feed one third of the world's population? Why are Americans always the ones to send help and supplies around the world whenever and wherever disaster strikes? And why is 'the American dream' a catchphrase all around the world? Why are people of other cultures flocking here and prospering? You see it all the time, don't you?"

AS HE LOOKED AROUND C.D. saw many astonished faces. They were listening without argument, so he continued. "What I'm trying to say is, there's a lot of good here in America. You've got to take pride in your country.

Take pride in *yourselves!* Take pride in what we've accomplished in such a short amount of time. America is a very young nation, and yet, we've become a very powerful nation. So why can't we Americans take pride in that? Why can't we become a powerful *people* once again?"

One man asked, "So how do we do that? You've done painted a pretty picture, Colonel. But, it ain't gonna be easy. Not easy at all!"

"I didn't say it would be easy, but I do believe it's doable. Now, I've got an idea—does anyone here have any kind of connection with the press?" C.D. saw a number of determined hands shoot into the air. One woman told him about the man who attended their last session. " . . . A fella from a place called French Lick, Indiana, if you can believe that. He was all fired up about seeds and genetics and such. Promised to do some nosin' around." She bobbed her head so many times, C.D. found himself wondering if she'd been a chicken in a past life.

"Good. So can you find him? And others like him?"

C.D. spent several minutes with the audience, eliciting their suggestions and making his own recommendations. Once the discussions began to wind down, he addressed the crowd again.

"Well, folks, if you really want to make a difference, a positive difference, I'll do everything I can to help—if you want me to. But I must warn you, I won't tolerate a mob mentality." The crowd responded with heartwarming, foot-stomping applause. But this time the noise was not jarring.

C.D. responded with equal enthusiasm. "Okay then, I think we've got a deal!"

"I'D WATCH MY BACK if I were you. Mitchem had fire in his eyes before he disappeared."

"I'm sure you're right, John. I didn't like his looks, either . . . or his style." C.D. raised his brows and tilted his head. "I'll do a check on him, see what he's been into. One thing I'm sure of, though . . . he's had training in conditioning. I'd say he's looking for recruits for something and I don't think it's a good cause. At any rate, I'd bet my last dollar he doesn't give a fig about the issues he was talking about."

John agreed. "Thank God you came. This group seems to get bigger . . . and angrier."

"That's for sure," Manny said.

"SO, C.D., WHY DON'T YOU join me and the guys at Manny's apartment? We could make some plans for that next meeting."

"Sounds good, John. But I can only stay for a couple of hours. Gotta catch a flight back to DC."

***

Chapter 31

"Good, nobody's following me."

*M*itchem accelerated with maniacal determination. *Why'd that damned military man have to show up? Things were going so well!* He pounded his steering wheel and glanced at his rearview mirror. *Good, nobody's following me.*

Mitchem's wrath diminished with each mile as he headed toward The Baltimore. The secluded, family-run motel on the outskirts of Anchorage commanded a dazzling view of the Alaskan skyline, but Mitchem had chosen it for another reason—it's airstrip. His line of work occasionally required a fast exit. He scowled when he passed LeRoy's Little Biscuits. He had felt claustrophobic the one time he had eaten there. *Wasn't bad enough the place was like a stuffy little closet . . . their food was lousy, too.*

By the time Mitchem passed The Alaskan Bedding Shop, the last retail store on the strip, he was fully in control again. *Well, I guess it was time for me to get away,* he thought. *I probably couldn't get any more recruits there anyway.* He slammed the car door and swaggered toward the front steps.

Mitchem swaggered even when he did not have an audience.

***

Chapter 32

Missing in French Lick

*A*nnaleigh wrenched uncomfortably in her seat. Normally she loved her job, but tonight it was hard to concentrate during her late-night shift at French Lick's smallest radio station. She grabbed the headphones and her eyes darted from the AM/FM LPB levers up to the computerized digital clock/thermometer. She delivered the time and temperature live, and forced herself to focus on the job at hand. *Pot down the mike,* she reminded herself. *Switch it off and find the next Public Service Announcement on the digicart . . . and for God's sake, remember to hit forward between songs to eliminate the dead air space.* The station manager hated dead air space and never got tired of saying, "Dead heads make dead air space and I don't want any deadheads at this station!" The joke amongst the DJ's was, "Dead air equals dead DJ—if she finds out!"

Annaleigh thought she had a great job. She got paid to play her favorite music for five hours a stretch. A softy at heart, she loved artists like Donny and Marie, the Carpenters, Kenny Rogers, Lionel Ritchie, and Connie Francis. She was even acquiring a taste for country, thanks to the new greats like Clint Black and LeeAnn Grimes. But tonight she was not enjoying the music—there still was no word from her brother, Ben. It had been a week since her sister-in-law first called, her voice quivering with anxiety. Benjamin Frankel had not returned home from The French Lick Express.

The weekly newspaper was Ben's passion. He often worked late, so Joanne had not been worried when he missed dinner. But when nine o-clock came and went and he still had not called, she decided to contact his office. *Not there, darn it! Well, maybe he's on his way home.* Ten o'clock went by, and then eleven and still no word from Ben. Just before Midnight, she called Annaleigh at WFLM.

ANNALEIGH HIT THE PLAY BUTTON and swiped at a tear that spilled from her eye. *Where the heck is that brother of mine?* She wiped the wetness off her fingers and reached for Lee Greenwood's patriotic tribute to America while resolving to contact the police again. She and Joanne had already called every friend and relative and as many of Ben's contacts as possible. Several times. And they had grilled every staff member at the Express. Several times. It was as if Benjamin Frankel had disappeared off the face of the planet.

Annaleigh did not know it, but as she and her sister in law searched for Ben, another family was going through the same ordeal in Germaine, Illinois. Ralph Williams, a well-known print shop owner, had also disappeared without a trace—just like several other hardworking citizens across the country.

THE DISAPPEARANCES orchestrated by Colonel Mitchem, had been so sporadic that no one made the connection. That's why he felt confident enough to add one more name to his list—Colonel Lucas Everett Davidson.

Mitchem had already decided to toss C.D. in with the other troublemakers when Perry Jordan called, asking him to deal with the nosy military man.

When he hung up from that call, Mitchem looked remarkably like the Cheshire cat.

***

Chapter 33

Tommy told Jerry about the shooting

Jerry Johnson was waiting for Tommy Sykes. They had fallen into a routine over the past few weeks. It started when Jerry offered to pay the boy to help organize the garage. A few days later, they painted the patio table, and the list just seemed to grow from there. Jerry had hoped to boost the boy's confidence by teaching him new skills, but he found a serendipitous boost for himself, as well. He enjoyed the boy's company, deriving a great deal of satisfaction each time he taught Tommy something new.

Tommy was always an enthusiastic worker, but he seemed to relish the yard work the most. So today, Jerry was going to teach him how to trim the hedges. He checked his watch when he heard the now-familiar footsteps on the porch. *Right on time,* he thought.

"HEY, DR. J. I'M HERE!"

"Hi there, kiddo. I've got a great job for you today— we need to trim the hedges." He reached for his electric clippers and headed down the steps. He stopped, though, when Tommy failed to follow. "Hey, kiddo, what's up? I thought you'd like to try this."

"Umh, yeah. But, well . . . I gotta ask you somethin'."

"Sure, Tommy. Shoot."

Tommy continued to hesitate, so Jerry put his clippers back on the wicker table and reached for the door. "C'mon, sport. These chores can wait. Let's grab a soda and you can tell me what's bugging you. By the look on your face, it's serious."

"Yeah, it is. Thanks Dr. J."

Tommy dutifully followed the man he had come to trust, and before they reached the kitchen, he plunged into his story.

"Well, I had this dream, and . . . ."

TOMMY TOLD JERRY about the shooting and the man whom he was sure had threatened his friends, and the dream. His voice broke several times when he got to the part where Larry and Benji's car had crashed. Somehow, it was hard to say it out loud—hard to say that they were dead.

Jerry's first response was to call the police, but when he reached for the telephone, Tommy panicked.

"No! No police—they'll never believe me!"

"Okay, Tommy. I'll hold off for now, but you know we can't just ignore this." He gave the boy's shoulder a tight squeeze. "Look, I tell you what . . . why don't we get to work on those hedges—take your mind off things for awhile. Some times it's easier to sort things out if you keep yourself occupied." He searched for a sign of understanding in the boy's eyes. Didn't want to push him. At the boy's nod, he said, "Good. But, don't forget . . . we can stop and talk again—any time you're ready—okay?"

TOMMY FORCED HIMSELF TO LISTEN as Jerry described the box hedge and its ongoing care. He wanted to do a good job, wanted to forget that man's agonizing grab for the sky, wanted to forget that Larry and Benji were dead.

"Okay—but will you watch while I try the first one?"

"Sure," Jerry said as he pointed toward the corner. "Let's go to the back of the house—you can start there." He showed Tommy how to set up the guide string and within minutes, the top of one hedge was as smooth as a table-top and Tommy was beaming triumphantly.

Jerry peered at the hedge and offered a supportive pat. "Good work, Tommy."

"Thanks!"

"So are you okay with it—or do you want me to watch you do the next one?"

"I'm okay, Dr. J. I'll yell if I need help."

"Great. I'll be in my office, okay?"

"Yup."

Tommy decided to do the tops of all the hedges first, then backtrack to do the sides. The buzz of the machine soon droned out the rest of the world. Its power was hypnotic. *This is better than Nintendo,* he decided with a slim grin, and suddenly, he was Power Man and the hedge was his arch enemy, Zortak!

"Okay, Zortak," he cried above the buzz. "I'm gonna cut you down to size!" His eyes blazed and he attacked the hedge with vigor. When his arms grew tired, he stopped to admire his work. He looked around, thinking, *Boy, I wish Mom could have a house like this.*

Neat and tidy with large gray shutters, the two-story Queen Anne was surrounded by the hedges that formed a continual living shelf just below the windows. Rose bushes dominated the back yard patio, and there were tall, flowering shrubs on the front corners of the lot.

TOMMY HAD JUST completed the back hedges when Jerry reappeared. "Hey, that's a great job, kiddo! Looks like you're already a pro. Look, Tommy, I have to pick Steve up at the station—want to come along? It'd be a good time for you to meet him."

"No thanks, Dr. J. I'd rather just keep working."

"Sure. Look, there's more root beer in the fridge if you get thirsty. Help yourself." He headed toward the car, then looked back. "I'll be back in a jiff. But Tommy . . ."

"Yeah?"

"We've gotta talk some more."

"I know, Dr. J. I know."

***

Chapter 34

*A*fter calling Jerry, Brick boarded the train. He was still searching for a seat when it snapped forward, forcing the passenger cars to clank noisily into each other. Seconds later, the engineer's warning toot sounded. *Just a tad too late, friend,* Brick thought as he retrieved an elderly woman's pocketbook. A skinny teenager cursed and Brick suspected he wasn't as mad about the sudden jolt as he was about the lost opportunity. From the way the boy glared at him, Brick guessed he probably wanted to retrieve the purse—*for himself.* He shot a warning look toward the boy then settled into the nearest vacant seat.

Brick became oblivious to his surroundings and visions of honey blonde hair invaded his thoughts. *Evie!* He had never believed in love at first sight—until now. He absentmindedly picked at a wiry tuft of stuffing that protruded from his leathery cushion and wondered what it would be like to stroke her hair. He was sure it would be silky. *Real silky.*

The train's thick windows rattled as it thundered along the tracks, but Brick did not notice. He drifted in and out of a dreamlike state until they finally chugged to a slower speed and the conductor announced their arrival.

Suddenly alert, Brick knew he would have to be very careful, but when he saw Jerry, a pang of guilt pinched his conscience. He had taken off without a clue as to where, why, or how long he would be gone. He knew the astute psychologist would sense that he was deeply troubled, but he still was not ready to talk.

"THANKS FOR COMING, JER . . . sorry for the short notice."

"No problem."

Brick was glad that Jerry was not asking questions and as his friend maneuvered the car into the slowly moving traffic, his mind wandered back to their college days. When they met, they were sophomores who had transferred to Manhattan College during the spring semester. Brick had seen Jerry sitting alone at a corner table in an otherwise crowded cafeteria and asked to join him. The two quickly formed a hard and fast friendship.

Once the hassle of the Beltway was behind them, Jerry asked, "Why the train, Brick? What happened to your car?"

"I . . . it's . . . it's in the shop." *That was a great comeback,* Brick chided. *I've gotta do better than this or he'll suspect something's up. I can't get him involved in this!* Then he had a fearful thought. *Good Lord! If they trace me, Jerry's gonna be in danger too—after all we live in the same house. Why didn't I think of that before? Damn! I've gotta tell him.* Brick suddenly found himself wondering how he could have been so foolish.

"LOOK, JERRY . . . THERE'S SOMETHING I need to tell you." He cast his eyes downward and took a deep breath.

"Well, sure, Brick. Go ahead."

"I just don't know where to begin. It all seems so un-believable now that I'm back." He squeezed his eyes shut and rubbed his temples.

This was the opening Jerry had been waiting for. He eased his voice into the soothing tone of an experienced counselor. "Okay, fella. Take your time. Whatever it is, I'm listening—you know I'll help if I can."

Brick glanced at his friend's concerned face, grateful that he was not being grilled with a thousand questions.

"Well, okay. Here goes . . ." *Yeah, here goes,* he thought. *I'll give him the short and sweet version.*

Brick swallowed hard.

"I inadvertently learned about a plot to control the country's food crop production with unethical biotechnology and I was a witness to a murder and we both may be in danger because of it all." He was suddenly out of breath and clenched his mouth shut, not yet willing to admit the rest of his thoughts. *And I've fallen in love with an incredible woman who probably hates me because I almost killed her.*

Stunned by Brick's revelations, Jerry forgot to concentrate on the road. The car made an alarming swerve. Pandemonium reigned as tires screeched, brakes squealed and horns blared. Jerry clutched the steering wheel in a frantic effort to regain control. The relentless centrifugal forced slammed Brick against the door as the car careened across the four-lane highway.

Irate drivers shook their fists at the unpredictable Buick. The tires were still screeching at the edge of the road when Jerry finally regained control of the car. And then, the harrowing experience ended as quickly as it began, leaving both men breathless in its wake.

"Boy oh boy, Brick—when you say unbelievable, you mean *unbelievable!* What have you been doing since then? Where did you go? Why didn't you call the police?" Jerry's professional demeanor was gone. His voice squeaked. "And what do you mean danger for both of us? What kind of danger?"

Here I go again, Brick thought before telling his story for a second time. He still left out the part about meeting Evie Victor and how he had revised his theory of love at first sight.

"THANK GOD YOU'RE OKAY, Brick. I can't believe one of your colleagues was murdered and I didn't even

116

know it! But, then again, I have to admit I haven't been watching the news. Too busy with my work, I guess."

"I'm glad you didn't hear it—you might have put two and two together and gone to the police when I didn't show up." Jerry's stricken face told him his hunch was right.

"I know I sound paranoid, Jer, but I'm just not sure who's involved in this. I have a hunch they're powerful enough to own a few cops, too. But the worst part is, I'm afraid that it's only a matter of time before they track me down." He suddenly sat up. "Which reminds me—have any unexpected repair men appeared on the doorstep?"

"Just the meter man for the electric."

"Isn't it early for a reading? Did he go inside?"

"No. Well, maybe. I mean, I guess he could have. Look, I didn't have any reason to question him!" Jerry made a white-knuckled turn off the highway as he admitted, "I was out back spraying the roses. I really don't even know how long he was there."

"You can be sure he was no meter man . . . not at this time of the month. I'll bet he's bugged the house. My God. They must have quite a network to act that fast!"

Jerry clenched the wheel even tighter and concentrated on his driving until he had to brake for a traffic light. The engine idled softly. He murmured, "So now what do we do?"

"We'll have to search for a bug. And then we'll have to come up with a plan. But I'm glad about one thing—I'm glad I didn't tell you any of this on the phone."

After several awkward moments of silence, Brick offered his long-time friend a heartsick apology. "My God, Jer. I'm so sorry to have gotten you into this."

"Hey, guy—it wasn't your fault. You couldn't help what happened, so let's just do what we can to get through this—okay?"

"You're a good friend, Jerry."

Brick felt buoyed by Jerry's steadfast loyalty.

"Okay, so here's what we do. We go home and act natural—I need a shower anyway. Then we quietly search for bugs. Then we go to Peggy Sue's—my treat—and we decide what to do. I should be hearing from Dr. Bascomb before too long." His eyes opened wide. "I'm glad he's got my cell number—and not the house!"

They both gulped.

Moments later, Jerry parked in front of the pristine, two-story Queen Anne home that they shared. The boxwood hedges created a symmetry that softened the look of the white clapboards and charcoal gray shutters. The overall effect was simple, understated and perfect for the home's two male occupants.

"Why don't you take your shower? I'll check on Tommy, then we can meet in the study."

"Who's Tommy?"

"Oh, that's right! I was about to tell you about him when you dropped your little bombshell back there. He's a teenager I've hired to do odd jobs around the house."

When he saw Brick's troubled look, he added, "He's been coming around for a couple of weeks now. You know, we haven't had much time to catch up lately, with you working on your report for Feeday and me on my grant. I just never got around to telling you about him."

"Yeah, we have been busy at that."

"Well, I'll tell you about him at Peggy Sue's."

"Okay. But Jerry . . ."

"What?"

"Remember—when we get into the house, act natural. Don't let on that we suspect anything. We don't want a bunch of high-paid thugs breaking the door down." At Jerry's shocked expression, Brick quickly added, "It's just a precaution. I'm probably paranoid."

"Bob Jette wasn't paranoid, and look how he ended up. Be paranoid, my friend. Be very paranoid." Jerry's eyes looked owlish as he rendered his advice.

***

Chapter 35

What if we've been bugged?

---

*A*fter his shower, Brick forced himself to act normal. "Hey Jer—here I am, all squeaky clean—but who's turn was it to do the shopping? I just used up the shampoo."

"Well, Bud, it was your turn—a week ago."

"S-o-r-r-y! I guess I better make a list—huh?"

"Yes. Please do."

BRICK HAD JUST STARTED to search for bugs when Jerry suddenly caught his attention. With wide, crazed eyes, he was jamming his finger toward the door.

Brick realized he had something important to say, but did not want to be heard—in case they really were being bugged.

"Okay, I started the list, but I'm getting really hungry. Why don't we head for Peggy Sue's?"

Jerry could have kissed him. "Good idea! Let's go." He grabbed his sport coat and led the way to the front door, but once they were outside, he stopped so abruptly Brick's chin slammed into his head. The impact didn't phase Jerry, but a shocking pain shot up Brick's jawbone. He thought, *Now I know what they mean when they say they see stars.* He rubbed his chin and followed Jerry down the steps.

"Brick! I didn't dare say anything in there . . . in case we *are* bugged. But I just realized that Tommy could be involved in all this!"

"What? How? I thought you met him before it all happened!"

"God. I can't believe I was so rattled I forgot his story. You said two teenage boys were in the car when Bob Jette was murdered, right?"

"Right."

"And, you wouldn't know this because you were away, but apparently those boys were killed soon after that. In a crash! Tommy told me about it this morning. He saw the shooting. The two boys were his friends. What if we *have* been bugged? What if somebody was listening when Tommy told me about it?"

"Damn! Let's go back inside so I can finish checking your den. If I find something, we've got a bigger problem than I thought. But Jerry, we've gotta talk about needing to get something ready for the mail or something . . . anything that'll explain our sudden return—just in case somebody *is* listening."

Brick's jaw was still throbbing. He rubbed it and thought, *If I find one, there may be more in the same room—they usually have a backup.* He waited, ready to follow Jerry again—at a safe distance.

TOMMY WAS ADJUSTING the guideline on a nearby hedge when Jerry's agitated voice caught his attention. He realized Dr. J. was talking about Benji and Larry so he dropped his clippers and crept closer. He wanted to hear more.

"Okay, you guys, so who was the shooter?" When neither man spoke, he took a menacing step forward. Although Jerry didn't feel threatened by the movement, Brick wasn't going to take any chances. He grabbed Tommy's arm.

"You must be Tommy, right?" The boy didn't an-swer—he just scowled. "Listen to me. I don't know who it was. I didn't even see his face, just a glimpse of the sleeve of a white linen suit, and I'm sure your friends don't dress in expensive linen. All I know is, it had to be connected with something that I overheard that morning. The guy who was gunned down was ready to expose a very powerful organization." Brick looked straight into Tommy's eyes. "I swear to you, that's all I know. It's really all that I know."

Brick realized the boy was in pain. He released his grip. "Sorry. I didn't mean to hurt you."

Tommy rubbed the angry red mark on his arm and growled, "That's okay—wasn't nuthin'." He was *not* going to admit how much the man's grip had hurt him.

Jerry cleared his throat and asked, "What should we do now?"

Tommy answered, "We're gonna catch that guy, that's what we're gonna do."

"No, *we* aren't. Jerry and I will handle this—you are going to stay out of it."

"Oh yeah?"

Brick towered over the boy. "You don't have a clue about who he is, or who he works with, or where to find him. And I'm not going to tell you."

"Oh yeah? I thought you didn't know anything about the guy."

"Well, I don't. I've got a hunch about how to find him—but I'm certainly not going to let you get half cocked on us. That's a fact."

Brick turned toward Jerry. "Right now we should check the house for bugs."

Tommy's eyes opened wide. "Hey, maybe one of the guys saw something. I'll ask them tonight."

"You've got to be careful. You can't be too obvious."

"What do you think I am—stupid? It'll be cool. We're all really mad about what they said about the guys in the news—you know?"

"Well, I guess it'll be okay."

"As if I need your permission to talk to my friends. Besides, you couldn't get to first base with them."

"Okay. Fine. Do what you want. In the meantime, I think we'd better see if we can find any evidence of surveillance." Brick reached for the doorknob and turned with a warning. "For God's sake, you guys . . . don't let on that we suspect anything!"

BRICK HEADED STRAIGHT for the telephone in Jerry's study. Sure enough, a tiny surveillance device had been installed. He held it up for Tommy and Jerry to see. Then he resumed his search. He had learned the process at the FDA when he shadowed a security expert who routinely sweeps through the offices. He never dreamed he'd have to use his newfound skill in his own home.

Brick's suspicions were confirmed. A little plastic strip about the size of a postage stamp was attached to the rim of Jerry's desk lamp. He did not want to tip them off by disturbing either bug.

"Okay Jerry . . . here's that contract."

Jerry winked. "Good. We can drop it in the mail on our way to the diner."

"Okay, so let's get going—I'm starving!"

ON THEIR WAY to Peggy Sue's, Jerry encouraged Brick to review his conversation with Bob Jette. "Maybe you'll remember something important."

Brick did his best to repeat every word. Jerry listened quietly until he got to the point when Bob mentioned *Snow White*. Then he perked up.

"Doesn't it strike you as odd that he'd expect you to have an interest in a *Snow White* video?"

"Well, yes. But I really didn't dwell on it. So, what are you getting at?"

"Maybe it was some kind of clue? A coded message or something?"

"A code? How would he be sure I'd pick up on it? Like you said, it's not likely that I'd be interested in a Disney cartoon."

"Well—there you go—that's my point! So maybe he was afraid somebody was listening and he couldn't think of anything else. After all, it was a pretty strange, yet innocuous kind of thing to say to a grown man—don't you think?"

"Yes. But, if you're right—about it being a code of some sort—what could it possibly mean?"

Jerry zigzagged across the sidewalk with increased animation as he developed his theory. "He could have added something to it. A tape, I mean. It's just a guess, but I'm sure Bob's family has Disney tapes. His kids are teenagers, right? So he probably figured that nobody'd touch it."

Brick increased his own pace. "Who knows what could be on it. It could have names, faces, schedules even. Who knows!" He snapped his fingers. "Well, I guess I'll have to pay my respects to Mrs. Jette . . . see if I can visit and nose around a bit."

"Good idea."

Brick was already reaching for his cell phone. Mrs. Jette answered on the second ring. She said she was leaving the next day for Florida. She said, "I'm sorry, Brick, but now is not a good time for a visit. Maybe we could get together when I get back?"

Brick said again how sorry he was for her loss and that he would call at the end of the month. After he hung up, he asked Jerry, "Do you know how to pick a lock?"

Jerry stared with raised brow.

Tommy thought, *Fingers can pick a lock—he's really good at it.*

If Jerry had seen the gleam in Tommy's eyes, he'd have been forewarned. But, he had not.

"We'll go tomorrow night, around 2 am. They live about four miles outside the city. A nice secluded house." Brick grinned. He'd been a guest at their cocktail parties a few times. His grin disappeared, though, when he saw Tommy's eager face.

"Sorry, Tommy, but I just wouldn't feel comfortable including you on this caper."

"That's okay. Anyhow, I'm gonna be with the guys. I'll let you know what I find out, though." He hesitated before asking, "But how can I reach you guys? You ain't gonna go back to your house are you?"

"Right. Here's my cell."

123

Brick pulled a slip of paper out of his pocket and scribbled his number while he spoke. "Well, I don't think you'll be in any danger, Tommy, as long as you stay away from our house. But, still—you should be careful, okay? If you get the slightest idea you're being followed, let us know, okay?"

"Sure."

Tommy gave a thumbs up, then sauntered across the street. He was already making his own plans for the "heist". He thought, *Sam and the guys won't want to miss this. I hope Rob's car is still running.*

JERRY WATCHED WITH suspicious eyes as Tommy sprinted across the street. The boy gave up too easily.

He thought, *What's he up to?*

***

Chapter 36

Ah . . . Maria!

---

*W*hile Brick and Jerry were planning their 'Snow White Heist' Martin Bascomb was tactfully questioning past associates. His first step was to call Maria Charbonneau at the University of Vermont. He welcomed every chance to talk with her and despite the gravity of the situation, this was no exception, but he had decided not to tell her about Brick Little's fantastic story . . . unless he had to.

"Hello . . . Maria? Martin here. How are you?"

"Martin! How wonderful to hear from you . . . it's been *too long! Way too long!* So, what's up hon? Are you planning to come this way anytime soon?"

Martin was glad to hear the pleasure in her voice.

"Well, Maria, I may just do that. Think you can spare an evening for an old codger like me?"

"You know better than to ask, you rascal," she admonished. "Besides—don't give me that old codger bit— we're close to the same age *and you know it!"*

"Oops. I'd say that faux pas is worth a dozen roses or two . . ."

"At least! So—what's on your mind, besides me?"

"Well, as much as I love my work here at the shop, I'm feeling out of touch—haven't seen any of the old gang for quite a while. Do you know where I can reach William Tafft? Is he still in Detroit?" As he spoke, Martin wrote three names across the top of a sheet of paper and drew vertical lines between them.

"Yes. As a matter of fact, I saw William about a month ago. He came back to attend the funeral of one of his cousins—you remember Jimmy Dunne? From English Lit?"

"Yes. Of course! I was sorry to miss his service."

"Yes. Well, you know what? William's the same stodgy old coot he always was."

Despite the disparaging remark, there was no malice in Maria's voice. Martin visualized the deep laugh lines and ever-present mischievous sparkle in her eyes. "I'm not surprised." He chuckled. Maria had always joked that the starch in William's impeccable suits had somehow found its way onto his body.

"But I do miss him, Martin. I miss you all." She sighed with the satisfaction that only fond memories can evoke. "He was an excellent teacher, despite it all—a real character, that one. Do you remember, Martin, how everyone would straighten up and look alert whenever William marched down the corridor? Like a storm trooper, he was."

"Yes, the students said they hated him while they were in his classes, but I believe they did respect him."

"We all did . . . despite the jokes. Well, at any rate, he hasn't moved for ten years. Want his number and address?"

Martin could hear a series of crisp *thwaps* and pictured her rosy nails flipping through her Rolodex. "Thanks, but I've got that one." He put a big X across William's name. "But how about Sam Aaronson and Julia Mahoney?"

"Well, Julia still lives in Vermont, in the Burlington area; but from what I've heard, she's got a project in Tennessee. Still as close mouthed as ever . . . and defensive, too."

Again, despite the harsh words, Martin detected no malice in Maria's voice.

Her tone softened. "It's too bad she didn't get the recognition she deserved. Although I never got very close to her, I felt bad about the way they treated her around here."

"Yes. I could never understand why the administration could not get beyond her personality." Martin's brows plunged toward the bridge of his nose. "A scientist should be

judged by his or her credentials . . . not by personality!"
Surprised by his own vehemence, Martin softened his tone.
"Sorry for the outburst, Maria, but I'm afraid things are often
reduced to a popularity contest—*even in the academic
world!* It just baffles me." His brows sprang back up.

Maria exhaled with a gusty laugh. "No need to
apologize, Martin. It makes my blood boil, too. And
speaking of personalities . . . we've had some beauts—don't
you think?"

"Now Maria . . ."

"Okay. Okay. I stand corrected! We've had some
unique and memorable personalities here at UVM." Hearty
guffaws and unladylike snorts belied her angelic observation.

"So, Martin. As I was saying, Sam is on sabbatical in
New York. Wait a minute while I pull out their numbers."

Martin heard her shuffle through the Rolodex once
again. Moments later, she was back on the telephone. "Okay,
here we go—got a pen handy?"

Maria dictated the phone numbers and addresses
slowly so he could keep up. "That's it, hon. Now, when can I
expect my roses?"

THE TWO OLD FRIENDS chitchatted for awhile
and then agreed to meet as soon as Martin could make the
trip. He hung up, cheered by pleasant memories of the
vivacious Maria and her flaming red hair. He thought, *Those
auburn tones may be long gone, but she's still got that quick
rhetorical wit and that wonderful penchant for laughter.*

Laughter permeated the very air when Maria was
around and deep, crevice-like crows feet framed her
sparkling blue eyes as proof.

***

Chapter 37

Oh Lord, not Julia!

Martin looked at his list. He had contacted all three of his old colleagues and had taken his usual meticulous notes.

William Tafft was working on a longer seed viability for carrots. The man seemed enthusiastic about his theories and welcomed Martin's thoughts and comments. He had even extended an invitation for Martin to see his work. Martin was impressed and said he'd be delighted to visit when his schedule would permit. *Strike that one,* he mused. *He's not a likely suspect.*

Martin learned that Sam Aaronson was hoping to increase production per foot of pole beans. Martin knew the current rate was between fifteen and twenty pounds from each ten-foot row and that by increasing production, more precious space could be utilized for another crop without having to increase one's acreage. *Or,* Martin mused, *a farmer could simply increase his yield of beans significantly.* Like William, Sam had extended an invitation. *He's not a suspect, either. He wouldn't want me there if he were.*

That left Julia Mahoney. Martin had heard that she was trying to develop a new variety of winter rye that would increase the concentration of nitrates in the soil. There was nothing sinister about that project, but he was not happy to learn that she was heading for Tennessee and was too busy to talk. *Tennessee? That's where Alexander brings his people.*

The notion that Julia could be a prime suspect put Martin in a somber mood.

***

Chapter 38

A momentary shock of recognition

Shortly after finishing his first day of research at the Library of Congress, John Victor entered the front door of Peggy Sue's Diner. It had been recommended by a clerk in the archives.

"It's clean," she had said, "and inexpensive." But most importantly—in John's estimation—it had home-style food, including several, ". . . thick, mouth-watering pies with *absolutely* the flakiest crust in the East."

John definitely wanted to check out those pies. He was famished and emotionally drained after reviewing countless documents and personal accounts of the soldiers who won the battle at Fort Donelson. As he waited to be seated, he thought about the men who had fought in the Civil War. Despite unimaginable hardships, they prevailed. He wondered if that kind of courage could be found today.

AFTER TWO SERVINGS of a wonderfully hearty beef stew with perfect crusty rolls, John was ready to order his pie; but the choices were just too great—so, he ordered three.

"I'll have a slice of the peach pie," he said. A concoction that he had never seen before, it was smothered with a mouth-watering cheese custard that he could not resist. "And a slice of chocolate cream pie. And raspberry crumb, too . . . it was my mother's favorite."

The incredulous waitress had to comment. "It's so good of you to think of your mother—but are you sure that's all you want?"

Her sarcasm went unnoticed.

"Oh, yeah! More coffee, please. With extra cream?"

She shuffled back to the counter, muttering about bottomless pits as she fetched the pot.

AFTER JOHN HAD DOWNED the first two slices of pie, the waitress returned with more coffee and a glimmer of respect. "I've gotta hand it to you, Sir. I thought you were in over your head with all that pie—and after two servings of stew, too!" She held up the coffeepot. "Ready for a refill?"

"Thanks." John held his cup and explained, "Heck, when I was a kid, I'd eat a whole pie without blinking an eye. I have to admit I am a bit stuffed now, though."

"I hate you," she said with a grin. "Not an ounce of fat on you. I bet I put on a pound just from carrying them."

DAMO WAS FINISHING his first cup of coffee when he saw Brick Little on the corner of the street with a teenager and a man who was probably the schmucko psychologist, Jerry Johnson. Damo's eyes narrowed as he watched them talk to the boy. He wondered if the kid was connected to the boys in the wreck—if so, he might be a loose end.

Damo ducked behind the dessert menu when Brick and his friend entered the restaurant.

The chubby shrink looks even dumber than he sounds, Damo thought. He called to the waitress, ordered a refill and congratulated himself on his choice of seats. He had a view of the street and he could watch most of the diners without looking obvious. There was one guy hogging down several slices of pie at a booth near the back. Half a dozen couples and other groups were scattered amongst the remaining seats.

WHILE JOHN WAS SAVORING the peach pie, two men entered the restaurant. Before they took the seat behind him, he had the odd feeling that the tall man experienced a momentary shock of recognition when their eyes met. It was so fleeting he decided he had probably imagined it.

ALTHOUGH BRICK FAILED to see Damo, he did notice John. *That guy looks awfully familiar,* he mused as he and Jerry took their seat, but the thought was quickly forgotten when the waitress approached with the menus.

JOHN HAD NOT INTENDED to eavesdrop, but he could not ignore the muffled conversation behind him after he heard something about C.D. being missing. *That couldn't be C.D.,* he thought. *Maybe they mean 'C.D.'s' as in music.* Feeling slightly foolish, he eased himself back in his seat and strained to listen. When he tilted his head slightly to the left, he could hear almost every word.

"I'M REALLY WORRIED, JERRY. Bascomb suggested that I call Tom Monroe—you know the senator that helped me last month? Well, it's not like him to disappear without a word. And Helen said his friend, Colonel Davidson, is also nowhere to be found. And, she said the colonel—they call him C.D.—insisted upon talking with the senator a few days ago but wouldn't say what it was about. I think it's just too much of a coincidence for both of them to be out of touch all of a sudden." Brick leaned forward. "Especially since we know that Monroe was spearheading the opposition to the GoMO Bill."

"A senator . . . and a colonel? Missing? And no big waves in DC?" Jerry glanced around nervously. His voice dropped. "How powerful are these people, anyway?"

JOHN DID NOT BOTHER to listen for the whispered response. He was too busy thinking.

132

C.D. AWOL? But I just talked to him a couple days ago! He decided he'd have to follow these guys and learn more, so he slurped down the rest of his coffee and pulled out his money clip. He left a generous tip for the waitress, then quickly slipped out of the diner.

DAMO WAS ON HIS THIRD cup of coffee when the Pie Pig paid the waitress. Her smile told him the guy was a big tipper. *Well, I won't haf'ta leave much then!* he reasoned. A few minutes later, when Little and Johnson ordered their dessert, he decided it was time to go. *Oh well, I better get out of here and wait for them someplace outside. They might notice me if I follow them from here.* His orders were to make Brick Little talk. Perry Jordan had said to find out what he knows and who he's been talking to . . . and then to deal with the situation.

JOHN NOTICED AN INTERESTING book store across the street. He figured he'd have a good view of the restaurant from inside. A break in the staggered lanes of traffic allowed him to hurry toward the store's lively display of enticing tomes. A poster of Mary Higgins Clark's latest bestseller dominated the window on the left. When John entered the shop, a courteous young sales clerk appeared out of nowhere, undoubtedly summoned by the clatter of bells on the door. She waited patiently as he perused the front shelves.

John loved the smell of bookstores, from the toxic, inky odor of the latest editions, to the dry, dusty familiarity of old leather-bound volumes. He stopped and took a deep breath, luxuriating in the pungent blend of ink and incense. Knowing that he had a few minutes to spare before the two men finished their meal, he asked if there were any books on treasure hunting.

"Yes, Sir. We have a few right over there." The young woman was still pointing toward the wall on the left when the bells announced the arrival of another shopper. She offered a brief welcome to a tall man in linen before turning back to John.

"The books you want are about halfway down the aisle, to the left—about shoulder level."

"Thanks. I'll check 'em out." John paused long enough to pluck the Mary Higgins Clark book off the shelf, then rushed down the aisle toward the section devoted to treasure hunting. He was happy to see a paperback that he had been hoping for. It included precious metals conversion charts in the back. John carried both of his finds to the front of the store and pretended to thumb through them while keeping an eye on the restaurant across the street. Soon the two whisperers emerged. They headed west on foot.

John tossed thirty dollars at the clerk and said, "Keep the change." When he turned back toward the door, he was surprised to see the other shopper staring intently toward his own two quarries. *What's up?* he wondered. Instinct told him, 'nothing good' when the man stepped into his path. They collided and John's books flew out of his hands to skid across the linoleum. Cold eyes bore into his own eyes and he was rudely shoved aside.

Killer's eyes, John thought with a chill. As he scooped up his books, the clatter of the bells muffled the man's angry curse. John realized that he now had three men to follow. *This is ridiculous,* he thought. *I feel like I'm in a cheap spy novel.*

INSIDE THE BOOKSTORE, the grateful clerk was still beaming at the biggest tip she had ever received. She watched curiously as John dodged back and forth amongst four lanes of slowly moving traffic. When he disappeared from view, she happily returned to her afternoon chores with thoughts of the skimpy blue bathing suit that she'd finally be able to purchase.

JOHN'S FIRST TWO SUSPECTS stopped at a stand to buy some fruit. The heavyset one scurried like a chipmonk, so he called them Chip & Dale. And as the stranger followed them onto a side street, John dubbed him

Sylvester. *I don't know if those two are as mischievous as my favorite cartoon duo, but the dude from the bookstore is definitely a rude cat.*

John lost sight of his three suspects at one point, but he sprinted up to the corner just in time to see Chip and Dale enter an attractive, two-story home. Sylvester was not far behind, and when he hesitated, John stopped to watch.

Moments later, John sighed with morbid apprehension. Sylvester had pulled out a gun.

Oh geeeez, he thought. *This doesn't look good.*

***

Chapter 39

*B*rick and Jerry were stunned. An intruder had burst into the study gripping a 9mm Walther revolver. Brick realized that it was the linen-clad finger shooter. But now, the ugly glint in his eyes was reinforced with a very real, very deadly gun. Brick found himself wishing he and Jerry had not decided to return to pack overnight bags.

DAMO'S COLD EYES NARROWED and his equally cold voice ordered, "Okay you, get over there next to your buddy." When Brick did not move, he shouted, "Do it now! I don't mind usin' this. And keep your hands where I can see them." He shook the gun then settled his aim upon Jerry. That was all the urging Brick needed. With hands in the air, he sidled toward the hapless psychologist.

Struggling to keep his voice steady, Brick stopped and asked, "Who are you? What do you want?"

Damo took a lanky step forward. "Don't play dumb with me, Little." He shook his gun again. "My friend here . . . says I'll be the one to ask the questions. For starters, what were you doin' in Boston?"

"Boston? How did . . . ?" Brick's eyes widened when Damo tightened his aim on Jerry. "Hold it! I'll tell you. I was, umh . . . visiting a friend."

"Yeah, right. *What* friend?"

Brick hesitated, trying to buy time. For one thing, he needed a weapon. His mind raced for options while his eyes darted across the shelving behind Jerry. There were several heavy wrought iron dogs that would be within reach if he could position himself near the wall. He took a few more steps, thinking, *Thank God for Jerry's passion for canine doorstops . . . they're heavy enough to give this guy a good whack.* He could see that Damo was becoming increasingly impatient so he scurried closer to Jerry—and the dogs."

"So, I'm waitin', Little. What friend?"

"Well . . . " Brick nonchalantly rested his elbow next to Jerry's favorite Yorky. At the same time, he noticed a flash of movement. He was astonished to see the familiar-looking stranger from the restaurant creeping toward the intruder. The stranger held his finger to his lips and prepared to pounce, but fearing that the gun might go off and hit Jerry, Brick ignored the warning.

"So, who's that behind you?" he asked.

Damo smirked. "Yeah, like I'm gonna fall for that one." Despite himself, Damo turned to look. Amazement etched a row of crevices into his wide, suntanned forehead when he saw John, and his gun whirled toward him. Brick took advantage of the moment and hurled one of the statues.

There was a sickening thud as iron met scalp. Damo uttered a high-pitched moan before dropping into an unconscious heap next to the wrought iron Yorky. At the same time, the gun skittered across the highly polished floor.

John stared at Brick and whispered, "That was quick thinking!

"How'd you know we were in trouble? Who are you? Say, didn't we just see you at the restaurant?"

"Don't worry. I'm a friend of C.D. By the way, why did you think you recognized me back there—I know we've never met before."

"Pretty observant, aren't you? You just reminded me of someone, that's all. It's something about your eyes, I guess. Look, I think we'd better get away from here, real quick. Somebody might be listening and I don't want to have to face any of his buddies." He pointed toward the prostrate figure on the floor.

"Listening?" John asked.

"Yes. We found two bugs in Jerry's office."

John bent down to take a closer look. "He's gonna have one heck of a headache when he comes to." He turned to Brick and said, "Let's get moving. I'll tell you who I am later."

ONCE THEY WERE SAFELY in John's motel room, the three men compared notes. John admitted that he had overheard bits of Brick and Jerry's conversation at Peggy Sue's.

"So, come on, guys, tell me what this is all about. I just saw C.D. less than a week ago and I can't believe he's missing, along with a senator at that! By the way, why haven't you gone to the police? And who bugged you?"

"Slow down! One at a time."

"Look, something is going on and I'm gonna find my old colonel one way or another. And by the way, who is this Bascomb guy you spoke about. Did you mean that famous botanist in Massachusetts?"

Brick's eyes narrowed and as he straightened his tall frame to its full height, he felt like a wolf towering over a suicidal banty rooster.

Without backing down, John explained, "Look, I asked C.D. to help me with something . . . and the next thing I know, two strangers are saying he's AWOL." John continued to look up at Brick. His voice hardened. "And now, I want to know about your reference to Bascomb—was it the plant guy from Massachusetts?"

"Why do you care?"

John grabbed Brick's lapel. "Listen, you. I told you my story and now I want yours. My sister's with Bascomb and I'll make mincemeat out of anybody that gets her hurt."

"That's it! You look like Evie!"

"What do you know about Evie?"

"Not as much as I'd like."

That one wistful statement spoke volumes to John Victor. Evie always attracted men, and the guy's sad tone told him that she had been her usual feisty self. He wasn't surprised.

BRICK PEELED JOHN'S HANDS off from his crumpled lapels and as he smoothed the fabric with his fingers he decided to trust Evie's brother with his tale.

"Okay, here's our story. Very powerful people seem to be pulling some nasty strings to get their pet legislation passed . . . it has to do with patents for genetically modified foods. I believe the thug you followed to our house already killed someone, and several people have come up missing, including your buddy, C.D." Brick sat on the bed. His eyes followed his finger as it skied across the puffy blue coverlet.

"Their first step, I think, was to attempt to gain control of the supply of hybrid seeds on a national scale. They haven't succeeded yet, but I'm afraid it's only a matter of time. Then they've been trying to slant legislation in their favor . . . and some officials from the FDA are probably in their pocket. That's where I work, by the way."

Brick looked up at John then, and said, "We call it Feeday . . . the FDA, that is. Anyhow, the worst thing is, Bob Jette, one of my co-workers, was gunned down. I didn't get a clear view of the shooter, but I'm pretty sure it was our intruder."

Brick sprang from the bed. "And it has to be related to the GoMO Bill! That's the connection between Senator Monroe and Bob Jette! Bob's department was reviewing it for FDA approval, and the senator has been leading the fight against it! But I wonder where C.D. fits into it all?"

"It's that food thing again," John said. "Our would-be vigilantes were talking about scientists messing around with foods. Something about genetics, I think. At the time I figured it was just a bunch of liberals whining against big business."

"It doesn't have anything to do with political ideologies, necessarily. This is about controlling the very sustenance of life. Controlling food. At the very least, there's billions of dollars at stake . . . maybe trillions!"

"Heck—that's a good motive for murder . . . and more, if I ever heard one. But, what's this GoMO Bill you mentioned?"

"It's been proposed to give extensive patent rights to the creators of genetically altered food crops. But it has a much broader scope than most patent bills. Monroe wanted . . . wants . . . more time to study it." Brick suddenly changed topics. "By the way, what's your name?"

"John. John Victor."

"Well, John . . . I'm Brickford Little—Brick to my friends—and this is Jerry Johnson. We're going to have some fun tomorrow night to see what we can find out about this mess. Want to join us?"

Fun? Through narrowed lids, John studied them both. Brick's eyes were sparkling with mischief and Jerry had shrugged a little too innocently. He finally said, "That depends—I guess—on what we're going to do . . . "

"We're going to watch *'Snow White'* . . . .

***

Chapter 40

"Cleverness is not wisdom."
EURIPEDES

*A*lexander thumbed through his Rolodex. It was time to call Senator Miller. He wanted a progress report on support for the GoMO.

Miller picked up the phone on the fourth ring.

"Oh, good, you're still there," Alexander said.

Miller wrinkled his brow and thought, *That arrogant man always seems surprised to find me where I say I'll be.*

"Of course, Alexander, I've been waiting for your call . . . and before you ask, I can assure you that we already have the support we need. My people have done a good job."

"Excellent. That legislation has to go through. If they don't pass it, we'll lose our patent. The whole operation could receive a big setback—and I hate setbacks."

"There's no problem, Alexander. According to our latest round of calls, we have a majority. Sixty-four percent!"

Alexander grunted with satisfaction. "That's fine, Miller. Fine. Keep it up. And, keep me posted." He hung up.

Miller winced. He knew all about Alexander's reaction to setbacks. A year ago, investigators found the dismembered hand of one of Senator Gottreid's aides. The poor kid had allegedly been trying to get Gottreid to change his mind on one of Rossweild's pet projects. Obviously he had failed. Rumors flew, implicating Alexander, but no one ever found any proof of the allegations—or the rest of the body for that matter—but Miller knew what had happened.

The kid had failed to prevent a setback. *Well, I'm not going to make that mistake,* he thought. *Especially with the GoMO!*

AFTER ALEXANDER HUNG UP on Miller, he took a sip of juice and placed a call to Ricardo.

"So, Ricardo. Did you find the—ahhh, *personnel*— that we talked about the last time I called?"

"Of course, Mr. Rossweild. Everything is already in motion. We have a man who has had experience around small airports."

"Shut up, you fool. Not on the telephone! Never! Do you hear? *Never* discuss the exact nature of our business." He pictured Ricardo slithering deeper into his seat. It always gave him a small degree of satisfaction to know he had that effect on people. He was tempted to stretch it out with an awkward silence, make him squirm even more, but not this time. He wanted some answers. *Now!*

"Never mind that now, Ricardo. Just tell me how many—shall we say . . . *deposits*—have been made?"

"Two of them. And Perry Jordan has been on top of it. He said that Miss Mahoney's assistant has analyzed the . . . err . . . deposits. They're working."

"Splendid! Then we should see some results soon!"

With glazed eyes, Alexander visualized the effects of those "deposits." If the jet fuel experiment was, indeed, successful, they would be able to proceed with regional applications. He couldn't wait to hear the news reports about the invisible "blight" affecting the targeted crops. The farmers could be ruined—unless, of course, they got some help. And he, Alexander Graham Rossweild, would step in and see to it that they got the necessary funds to help get them through the tough year ahead. He'd be a hero. And all they had to do in return was to sign SanFidel's contract.

Alexander grinned with Grinchy glee.

"That's all for now, Ricardo, but, keep me informed."

"Yes, Mr. Rossweild."

***

142

Chapter 41

Sure, Tommy . . . we'll go

---

*A*fter leaving Brick and Dr. J. at the diner, Tommy went home to wait until it was time to meet his friends. He found a note clipped to the fridge. *Oh, good,* he thought. *Mom and Jimmy will be gone 'til late tonight. That means she won't have a chance to ask about my day. She'd know somethin' was up.* He poured a glass of milk and made a sandwich. *Nuthin' to do 'cept watch TV.* He flipped to the Discovery Channel and stayed glued to the screen until it was time to meet his friends, Sam, Rob and Fingers.

THE FOUR TEENS MET at their usual spot—a gritty lot near Sam's apartment building. Abandoned playground equipment, rusted and misshapen, stood like prehistoric skeletons in a sea of dusty soil and spindly weeds. It was hard to imagine that young children had once played with unfettered abandon in this neglected park.

Rob, Fingers and Sam the Can were already hanging out when Tommy arrived. He admired Sam, the leader of the group, who predictably popped the top off a can of beer and noisily sipped the froth. Sam always had a beer on hand— that was how he acquired his nickname. Yet he never seemed to drink an entire can. Tommy appreciated the fact that Sam never got drunk. He wondered if Sam's weird fascination with beer was somehow symbolic. And now, as he watched his friend sip the froth, he decided he'd ask Dr. J. That kind of stuff was right up his alley.

Tommy liked Fingers—a talented pickpocket who was always kind hearted, and he was glad that Rob was big. *Real big.* His size and strength often deterred violent encounters—much to Tommy's relief. He figured they'd all want to help find Larry and Benji's killer and to clear their names, so he was not surprised to hear that they were willing to follow Brick Little and Dr. J.

SAM AGREED WITHOUT HESITATION.

"Sure, why not? We gotta find out who wasted our guys—so, count us in. Where and when, Tommy?"

Sam's dark features intensified to reveal his Hispanic heritage whenever he became excited, and the thought of avenging the death of his friends excited him. As tough as he was, Sam was a pushover for a good cause. That was another reason why Tommy admired him.

"Tomorrow night, about one or two a.m. They wouldn't tell me where, so we'll need to follow them."

Sam looked up. "Hey, Rob . . . can we use your wheels?"

***

Chapter 42

---

*M*idnight had already come and gone when two cars cut through a series of intersections in Washington, DC. They appeared to be just two more additions to the late-night revelry, but they were not. Brick drove the first car. He and his passengers, John and Jerry, were completely unaware of the teens following them.

When Brick stopped at a red light, John spied a group of partygoers. They reminded him of a pack of wolves with their sporadic bursts of laughter and inebriated howls of delight from dimly lit parking lots. *All we need is a full moon and some fog,* John thought ruefully, *and maybe some fangs.* After hearing Brick's story about genetics and murder, he felt like he was in a Dean Koontz novel. He suddenly yearned for the tranquility of Alaska. He wondered what Betty was doing. *Probably watching the night-time news and wondering what I'm doing,* he thought..

FROM A SHORT DISTANCE BEHIND, Tommy and his friends peered at the taillights of Brick's metallic blue Buick. "They'll probably turn sometime soon, Rob."

"I know. I'm watchin'em. I just don't want to get too close. Maybe I should drive past 'em when they turn, do you think?" Rob glanced at Sam with questioning eyes.

"Yeah. Good idea, but don't go too far. We don't wanna lose 'em—you know?"

***

Chapter 43

At the Jette's back door, Brick brushed his eyes with the back of his hand and spoke without realizing it. "I've gotta concentrate on this."

"Good idea. I like to be focused when I'm breaking and entering, too," Jerry quipped. Just seconds later, he was astonished to see his friend push the door wide open. "Would you look at this, John? He's picked that lock like a pro. Something in your past you haven't told me about, Fella? Like say, a rap sheet, or B&E 101?"

"Very funny. My cousin and I used to play private eye as kids and lock picking became our specialty. Actually, she was better than me." Brick slipped inside with a whisper. "Come on, you two . . . I'll lead you to the family room."

The large room featured a brick fireplace that was centered on one wall. Floor-to-ceiling bookcases lined either side of the hearth. At the far end of the room, plump, flowery cushions perched on the overstuffed sofa and chairs that faced an entertainment center. Brick imagined the happy hours that Bob and his family must have spent cocooned in this cozy space—happy family times that could never be repeated. He wondered if they had ever owned a big floppy-eared dog, and pictured himself and Evie happily nestled together in a room just like this on a Saturday night. But the vision faded, suddenly replaced by Evie's angry glare. He winced. He knew he should not have sped away.

John's whisper soon interrupted Brick's thoughts.

"Over here, guys. You *did* say to look for *Snow White*, right?."

Brick and Jerry scurried to his side. "Looky here," he whispered. He pulled the video from the shelf and examined it. "And the wrapper doesn't fit right."

Brick shook his head.

"He took quite a risk, leaving it on this shelf, I mean. What if his kids or their friends decided to watch it? I can't believe he'd leave it here if it's really an incriminating piece of evidence."

"You're probably right, Brick, but we might as well check it out since we're here. You never know—people do strange things when they're under stress. And maybe he figured his kids had outgrown Disney movies and wouldn't touch it. He might have intended to leave it here only for a few hours. I guess we'll never really know."

"Okay. Let's see what we've got." John slipped the tape into the VCR and was studying the remote buttons when, as he would tell the story later, all hell broke loose. Fingers had made a sound when his leg went numb and Brick sprang into action. He lounged toward the intruders and knocked one of them to the floor.

THE CRUMPLED FIGURE HOWLED, "Ouch! Wait . . . it's just me!"

A wave of fury brought Brick to his feet. He dragged the startled boy with him. "Tommy! What the hell are you doing here? I thought you were going to talk to your friends." Brick looked around and saw two guys holding Jerry up against the wall, while a fourth teen towered behind John who was struggling to breathe within his vice-like grip.

Tommy gasped, "I did. That's why we're here. You're not the only one who lost a friend, you know." He broke himself free of Brick's clutches and declared, "We don't wanna hurt nobody. We just want to see the evidence, too." Tommy looked at Sam and Fingers who still had Jerry pinned to the wall. "He's okay, you guys . . . Dr. J. won't give you any trouble."

"Thanks Tommy," Jerry said. Ever the peacemaker, he urged everyone to relax. "Well, since we all came for the same thing, let's not waste any more time. Let's just see what we've got."

Brick gave a disparaging snort but he followed Jerry's lead.

Sam growled a warning, "Just don't try nothin' funny. We got you guys outnumbered, ya know."

"We know . . . we know," John muttered as he crept away from his gargantuan captor. "Believe me . . . I don't want to offend King Kong here." He scuttled backwards when Rob scowled.

***

Chapter 44

Snow White

*T*he seven determined men and boys sat down in Mrs. Jette's family room, unaware that the next few minutes would create a lasting bond between them. They presented a vivid contrast to the silly antics of the comical figures that danced on the screen. When Walt Disney's nephew appeared, Fingers could not hide his dismay. He grumbled, "I always hate this part . . . that guy's a real dork." At Rob's amused chortle he rushed to explain, "Hey. My little sister's always watching this crap. I can't shut it off all the time, you know."

"Sure. Oh, sure. We believe you," gibed Sam. "No wonder you're always snackin' at those burger joints . . . you probably collect *all* the Disney toys." Chortle, snort. "How about 'The Little Mermaid?' I bet she's your favorite!"

Sam's infectious laughter filled the room . . . until the evidence appeared on the screen. It was not a professional taping job—the lighting and sound were both bad. But, despite this, it did not take long for any of them to recognize the grim implications of the mottled footage.

BRICK WAS SURE THAT the vial contained a sample of the terminator formula. They were bragging about using it in military aircraft, bragging about how it could stunt the growth of their competitor's crops. *Could they really do that?* he wondered.

The screen went black for a moment, then it revealed

a map.

John was the first to comment. "That looks like Tennessee. I was just researching that area at the Library of Congress. See up in the top left-hand corner? Between the two rivers? That's where Fort Donelson is." He scrunched forward and squinted at the screen. "Can anybody make out the printing? Looks like Dominion, or something . . ."

The image suddenly fluttered and the screen was filled with black snow. Brick said, "I've gotta hand it to you, Jer—I don't think I would have picked up on Bob's *Snow White* clue without you." The scheme was even bigger than he had imagined. *Using the military? Stunting entire crops? No wonder Bob was gunned down.*

John spoke softly. "You know, I've heard a lot of rumors about jet fumes containing poison. Most of the tests have come out negative, but people still claim it's some kind of plot. You guys know what I'm talking about? Those grids of jet fumes that crisscross the sky? They're called contrails. There's been a lot of controversy about what they are and whether they have a purpose. Some people believe the things are making them sick. There's even been reports about hospital emergency departments being swamped with people after the skies were filled with contrails. Makes you wonder, you know?"

"Yeah. I heard about 'em, too," Sam said. "There's a cool guy on late night radio who talked about it—somewhere in Arizona, I think. People called him from all over the country claiming that sometimes there's this stuff that falls outta' the sky, kinda like cobwebs. And people get real sick, just like you said." He looked at John. "Ain't nobody been able to prove it, though—the stuff just disappears. Art Bell, the radio guy, don't believe the government is doin' it to deliberately hurt people. He even wondered if it's some kind of . . . umh . . . of . . ."

". . . Inoculation." John finished the sentence for him. "I heard his discussion about it, too. I didn't take it seriously at the time, but it looks like *these* clowns are really *doing* it. A regular botanical warfare for crying out loud!"

Jerry hit the rewind button and turned toward John. "Here's the strongest military force in the world, and they're going to be used to sabotage the food supply of their own citizens according to this tape . . . and they don't even know it. So now we know why Bob Jette was killed. And we know that these guys are screwing around with our farmlands. But, I don't get it. Even if they've tried using that formula on a small scale, on a few targeted crops . . . why haven't we heard anything about it in the news? You'd think the farmers would be screaming their lungs out. We haven't heard anything about unexplained crop failures."

Brick had. "Well, actually, Jerry, there was a problem a while back when a large amount of corn crops went down the tubes. I don't think anyone ever figured out the cause. Like everyone else, I just assumed it was some rare blight or something, but I wonder if . . . "

John finished Brick's train of thought, ". . . if it was one of their first attempts? That's possible. Now that you mention it, I remember reading about that, too."

"You realize what this means, don't you? They've probably got it perfected. And it looks like they're about to do it on a large scale, using the military, no less."

Jerry interrupted. "Look guys. I don't think we should stay here and debate this thing any longer. Let's not forget what happened to the owner of this house. I think we should go back to the motel where we don't have to worry about being arrested on a breaking and entering charge . . . or worse."

Brick agreed. "Good thinking, Jer." He directed a suggestion toward Sam. "Okay guys, what do you say we split up . . . one of us with two of you in your car . . . and the other two in our car. Deal?"

"Deal." Sam looked at Rob. "Tommy and I will go with the squares. Why don't you and Fingers take the short one in your car."

Brick and Jerry stared, without comment, as John crowed, "Well, at least I'm not square." He looked at his former captor. "By the way, why do you call your buddy

Fingers . . . or don't I want to know?" His voice faded as he led the way toward the back door.

They all motored back to the city in silence.

AFTER PROMISING TO STAY QUIET the boys drove away in Rob's car. They had agreed to meet the men the next day. Brick watched from the doorway as Rob backed his car onto the street. He turned toward John. "Those guys aren't half bad."

"Yeah. They've got a lotta' spunk and their hearts are in the right place. Amazing don't you think? Considering how much time they've probably spent on the street."

Jerry, who had been uncharacteristically quiet, finally voiced their concerns. "We should get those boys out of town."

"You're right, Jerry. Let's sleep on it, though." Brick glanced at his watch. "After all, it's nearly 4 a.m."

Brick and Jerry shared the full-size bed. John settled himself in the recliner with one eye on the door. He knew he would not be able to sleep—not after that video.

Dean Koontz—here we come!

***

Chapter 45

"Our pesticide sales will more than triple!"

The first voice on the video belonged to Perry Jordan. Tall and imposing, he was comfortably in control of the meeting. "So, people, let's take a look at what we've accomplished. Thanks to the successful experiments of our gifted lady scientist, we've already started manufacturing a whole series of GMO products." A quick glance revealed confused faces. "GMO, gentlemen. GMO is an acronym for genetically modified organisms. It can refer to either plant or animal species, but of course we're interested only in plants for our purposes . . . at this time.

"We have a whole line of products that have been genetically altered. Super plants, if you will. What makes them so special, for us, is that once a farmer plants SanFidel crops, he'll have to use our chemical products as well. The plants have been genetically structured to reject all other known forms of pesticides or growth enhancers. Our pesticide sales will more than triple. And, if they don't believe us and they try to use products from another source . . . " He looked around with a grin, ". . . well, let me just say they'll regret it! And, we'll make a *killing*, if you'll pardon the pun." He welcomed a few malicious chuckles. "And, we've had an added benefit—thanks to a natural phenomenon, called drifting. So, even Mother Nature is helping us to reach our goal of complete crop domination."

"What's drifting?" asked one of the men.

"Drifting. Cross pollination. They're one and the

same, gentlemen. You've heard of pollination, where insects and winds cause a plant's pollen to cross over to the female plant? Well, our researchers have found that because of drifting, neighboring crops acquire the same characteristics as our patented products. And then they reject all other chemical treatments.

"In other words . . . " He paused for effect. "In other words, gentlemen, neighboring farms will experience unexpected crop failure because they're using some other pesticide—and they'll be watching as their neighbor's crops, which happen to be SanFidel products—flourish! So, who do you think they'll turn to?

"Our plan is already working . . . chemical sales are double the original quota. I'd say that our super corn was a huge success. For the long term, what we want is complete domination of the food production market. But drifting is a slow process, and if we remain dependent upon Mother Nature, it could take several years. Probably decades. So, we plan to "help her out" so to speak. Speed things up dramatically—with our terminator technology. To do that, we tried applying the formula to a few isolated pockets of farmlands throughout the country. And get this—it was done with fumes from small jets, and it worked. Wherever those planes flew, the crops have been stifled. And, I'm pleased to report that our friend Rodney here has come up with an ingenious plan to help us speed up that process even more. Why wait for Mother Nature when we have the means to do it ourselves? Go ahead, Rodney . . . go ahead and tell them." Perry's eyes almost registered warmth when he urged Rodney to explain his plan.

Rodney cleared his throat. "As top aide to Brigadier General H. Edward Carrey, I have access to the military purchasing structure. I'll see to it that our base purchases from participating fuel vendors." He clasped his palms together and lowered his voice before telling his audience that the Research & Development Division often scheduled flight tests. He'd see to it, he said, that the flights would occur over targeted farmlands—at Perry's request, of course.

"So, Rodney. When can you arrange it?"

"Well . . . I'll initiate the paper work as soon as you give the word." He tilted his head importantly before adding, "Then it'll take a few days to go through the usual channels." He turned toward Perry with questioning eyes. "If you wish, it could be done right after the big shindig at the Rossweild mansion."

"Sounds good, Rodney. Do it."

~~

GREAT SCOTT. HAVE MERCY on us all.

General Carrey's special agent, Commander Timothy Perkins, had the sudden urge to break out of his hideaway and crush a few skulls. Especially Rodney's.

I never did like the pompous little squirt. God almighty, Harry's gonna blow a fuse when he finds out about this duplicitous little shit..

Perkins realized that a physical attack would be impossible. Besides being totally outnumbered, he'd been tucked into the tiny space for so long that he thought his legs would stay buckled and twisted forever. He crushed the urge, thinking, *I'd burst out of here and fall flat on my face.* He watched with helpless fury, but he did take heart in the knowledge that the meeting would soon end and he'd be able to get out and stretch.

Perkins realized he couldn't send his video to General Carrey through normal channels—*Rodney'd intercept it for sure.* After several minutes of careful consideration, he decided it had to go to someone totally unrelated to his command. *Bob Jette will be good. As a mid-level exec at the FDA, he won't have any contact with these s-o-b's. No risk of raising suspicions. He'll be able to get it to Harry!*

THANK GOD THOSE GOONS are gone. Perkins carefully unfolded himself from his hiding place in the built-in storage unit. Its modern design featured a faux finish full of optical illusions—the perfect camouflage for a hidden camera and its operator. Perkins knew his legs would buckle if he didn't move slowly. *V-e-r-y s-l-o-w-l-y*. He took the time to stretch and knead his cramped muscles before making his way out of the conference room.

***

Chapter 46

"We judge of man's wisdom by his hope."
RALPH WALDO EMERSON

C.D. lurched forward when his driver stomped on the brakes. There was a roadblock ahead. A master gunnery sergeant had planted himself in the middle of the road with a rifle snugged to his shoulder—and it was aimed directly at them. Their jeep crawled until another soldier signaled for them to stop.

"Want me to check it out, Sir?"

"Sure thing, Len."

Four uniformed Pfc.'s stepped forward. Two of them headed for the driver's side and two toward C.D.

"Identify yourself," ordered one of them.

"Captain Leonard Russo, assistant to Colonel Davidson." Lenny pointed toward his passenger. "That's Colonel Davidson."

The master gunnery sergeant stepped forward. "Colonel Davidson, would you step out of your vehicle, please?"

"What's this about, soldier?"

"Just step out, Sir."

C.D. bristled: "Tell me what this is about, first. And that's an order! Then, I *might* step out."

Without warning, Lenny was slammed into the side of the jeep and ordered to, "Spread 'em, kid." To his astonishment, they cuffed his hands behind his back. "You can't do this," he sputtered. The others had already yanked

157

C.D. out of the jeep.

"Sorry, Sir. But we've got orders."

"Orders? Who the hell gave you orders to manhandle a colonel and his staff?"

"Orders came straight from Major General Carrey's office, Sir."

C.D. barked, "General Carrey? For what?"

"I don't know, Sir. We were just told to take you in, any way we have to. That's all we know, Sir. We wasn't told nuthin'. It's a *need-to-know*, Sir, if you know what I mean, Sir."

C.D. could see that the young man did not enjoy carrying out the baffling orders.

"Okay, Len—we'd better do as they say."

"But, Sir!"

"Don't struggle, Len. We'll get it straightened out—pronto. But, with a directive from General Carrey we could be shot for resisting. So, for God's sake, cooperate!"

MUCH LATER, AFTER BOUNCING for miles in a truck and transferring to a small aircraft, C.D. and Lenny were still not aware of the charges against them. They landed in darkness that made it impossible to identify landmarks.

"Where are we?"

"Shut up and get up."

"You can't talk to him like that . . . you're talking to a colonel, you numskull!" Lenny lunged at the offender, but was struck on the back of the head. With a tiny moan, he slumped to the floor of the plane.

C.D. roared, "That wasn't necessary! I'll have your stripes when this is over!"

"Oooh, I'm really scared," chortled his captor. He shoved C.D. hard, slamming him into one of the seats. He was snatched up again—only to be shoved and yanked repeatedly until he reached the open door. Flanked on either side, he was forced through the exit and down the narrow ramp to the ground.

"Will you at least tell me where we are?"

"We're at Domino One."

"What the hell is Domino One?"

"That's for me to know and you to not find out." Derisive laughter filled the air.

C.D. REALIZED THEY were outnumbered—there were ten of them and they seemed to be very well disciplined. *Some sort of special unit*, he guessed. *I probably should feel flattered they think they need so many men to handle me.* C.D. knew that escape was definitely not an option—at least not yet.

C.D. soon found himself in a large gymnasium-like space. He had no idea what became of Lenny—had not seen him since they were dragged off the plane. He looked around. Three walls were flanked with narrow bleacher-like tiers—each level filled with Army cots. He stared with unbelieving eyes.

"Hello friend. Welcome to the United States of Hell," said a quiet voice from a nearby bunk.

***

Chapter 47

Snatched!

Tom Monroe checked his watch. He was early for his meeting and at quarter of five it was still unbearably hot. A bead of sweat slid down his left cheek as he studied the historic brick building in front of him. The Miller building. From the West Wing one could see the Capitol Dome. It was spectacular all lit up at night. Tom had always loved to come here, even if it *was* named after his political nemesis—the man he was about to meet. But today he could not appreciate the site. He approached the steps with a deepening sense of foreboding.

Miller had never made the slightest gesture of friendship in the past, and certainly had never solicited Tom's advice. *So—why now?* he wondered. *The GoMO Bill? My phone calls must have paid off! I wonder if it was the calls to Ricardo and Perry Jordan . . . or the one to my favorite snitch?* Tom clenched his mouth shut. He had decided to widen his net and interrogate Jimmy Dawson, convinced that Jimmy could spread more disinformation than anyone else in the world. The guy had become very wealthy doing just that.

Jimmy's network thrived in DC. After all, knowledge was the key to power and to profit. A snitch's loyalty was forged by zeroes—the more they saw to the left of a decimal point, the better. C.D. called them "Zip Men" because of the number of zeroes they commanded. Tom called them "Six Shooters" because of the six-figure prices they often charged for 'shooting' off their mouths. *Yup,* Tom decided, *somebody must have been talking to Miller.*

Not one to linger, he gave a big sigh and sprinted upwards, careful to avoid the forensic chalk marks that outlined the position of Bob Jette's body after he had been gunned down. Zigzagging grotesquely on the surface of the steps, they were faded by rain—but the sobering effect was still the same.

IN ONE OF THE CHOICE OFFICES in the West Wing, Senator Miller impatiently drummed his fingers on the surface of his ornate mahogany desk. Across the room, a stone replica of Perseus perched on top of a pink marble pillar that was elaborately carved with fig leaves and scallops. Next to the pillar, a 16th century sculpted Greek settee was precisely arranged with velveteen cushions of faded green and burgundy. An ornate brass and gold mantle clock revealed that it was five minutes before five.

Miller thought, *Monroe should be here any minute now—the chump is always on time.* A fleeting smile crossed his face. *This'll be the last obstacle before the party. Then I'll be free!* He was not surprised when Marilyn buzzed to announce Tom Monroe's arrival. *Now all I have to do is wait for her to leave. Then I'll offer the Scotch.*

Miller glanced at his credenza and his face twitched. His whole scheme hinged on Tom Monroe's well-known love of Scotch. *Well, he'll get the best . . . along with a goodly dose of the sedative.* Miller's face twitched again as he reached to answer the buzz.

"HELLO, TOM. COME ON IN and take a seat."

"Thanks." Tom glanced around from his stance at the threshold. His eyes rested momentarily on Perseus and he wondered how the man could afford such expensive furnishings for an auxiliary office. He sauntered toward the chair and asked, "So . . . why the mystery? Reconsidering the GoMO, are you? Why else would you to invite a peon like me here?"

Miller raised his hands. "Now, now, Tom—let's put

our differences aside for once. Okay?" He was rewarded with a tentative nod.

"All right then. Look, Tom: I'm working on a project and it's not the GoMO Bill. That's not the only pie on my plate, you know. Well, this could be of tremendous importance to our great nation, and I want one hundred percent cooperation. As much as we disagree, as much as I'd like to see someone of my own ideology in your seat, Tom—and as brutally frank as we've been toward each other—I do admire your perseverance and your tenacious energy when you commit to something. I also know you've got a loyal following who would turn their back on a good idea just to avoid siding with me. Am I right?"

No, chum, that's the game you and your followers usually play, Tom thought. But before he could respond, Miller forged on.

"So—I just want to take off the gloves for this one. I want to present you with the facts and get your gut reaction. No promises. No commitments now. Just chew on it and get back to me. By the way, I'm waiting for the report that spells it all out. Should be delivered any minute." He raised his brows with a friendly smile. "How about a drink while we wait? I've got a bottle of Black Bush. So, what do you say?" For a moment he was afraid his prey would not take the bait, but to his relief, Tom agreed.

"Sure, why not? I always love a good Scotch."

Miller whirled around to face his credenza. Painted tromp l'oell, the front looked like a shelf full of leather-bound books, but it was actually a sliding panel that concealed a mini wet bar. He silently congratulated himself for having the foresight to put the powder in the glass before his guest arrived. He poured the expensive amber liquid into two crystal vessels and gave them both a quick stir.

He spun around and handed Tom his drink.

Tom took a quick swig and closed his eyes with contentment.

"Mighty good stuff, Senator."

"Glad you like it. Drink up—there's more where that

162

came from. By the way, has your buddy C.D. shown up yet? I heard he was AWOL. Even I find that hard to believe."

Ah hah! He's fishing for information, Monroe thought. His voice hardened. "I don't believe for one minute that he'd disappear of his own volition. I'm beginning to think something happened to him."

"Any ideas?"

"No." *But your friendly attitude makes me suspicious.*

"Too bad." Miller took a sip from his drink. He wondered what was taking Perry Jordan's men so long. He began to perspire. After all, he could not afford to have Tom get suspicious. He suddenly needed another drink, felt compelled to pour one, but instead, he heard his own voice above the nervous ringing in his ears.

"Oh, good. I think I hear the delivery man now. Here, let me pour you another one." His eyes held Tom's attention as his shaking hand poured the glistening alcohol. "Drink up—I'll take care of him and be right back."

DAMO LASALLE and his pal Bender were waiting in Marilyn's office. Perry Jordan had arranged for them to transport Tom Monroe to Domino One. Miller did not know about Domino, had no interest in knowing where Tom would be dumped. He figured the less he knew, the better.

"Where's the patsy?"

"Shut up, you fool," Miller scolded. "He's not *out* yet. It'll take a few minutes. So, do you have everything?"

"Yup—everything you said. We got a wheelchair, a wig, a shawl, and an old lady's pocket book. It's all here. Hell, we even got a nice strand of pearls to round it all off," Damo sniggered.

Miller was too nervous to see the humor. "Good. I'll signal when he's asleep. You know what to do, right?"

"Right. We wheel him/her out the back door and take him/her to the old man's hiding place. But I don't see why we can't just whack him. Be a lot easier." Although Damo thought it would be a hoot to dress the almighty senator up like a sickly old woman, he preferred a more direct approach toward getting rid of a 'problem' like Tom Monroe.

Miller stared with disbelieving eyes. "He's a United States Senator, for crying out loud." Cold eyes stared back as if to say, 'so what?' Without another word, Miller turned his back on the two men and returned to his office. To his relief, Tom was already slumped in his seat.

"Okay, you guys. Come on in. Make sure the wig's on straight and he's totally covered with the shawl and blankets—and get him the hell out of here."

AFTER THE TWO MEN wheeled Tom Monroe away, Miller called Perry Jordan.

"Perry? Miller here." He glanced toward the door and relaxed. "The scotch was well accepted—no interference with the delivery."

"Good work. Now, did you get that report from San-Fidel? It spells everything out, including plausible responses to the opposition's questions. You must see to it that Monroe loses his following. We need that patent—the old man's not going to accept any more delays."

"No problem. We've already got a reliable man taking Jette's position at the FDA, and the USDA is in the bag, too. I've also got a couple of news anchors convinced that we're on the way toward solving world hunger. Hell, those brainless do-gooders on the major networks will believe anything we say as long as it's what they want to hear." He shifted in his seat and glanced once more at the door. "And, according to my sources, you'll be able to get total control of the organic farmers within the next decade."

Perry considered the news, then thought to himself, *I'll have control of all of our farmers, every last one of them, in just a couple of seasons, you fool.* He wanted to tell Miller what he really thought of him, but he did not want to upset him—at least not yet. He might still need him. "That's fine, Miller. Fine," he said.

"So. I've done my part. When can I expect to be rewarded for my hard work?"

"We've already transferred half of the funds to your

new account offshore. You'll get the rest when the GoMO is in effect. And, Miller . . . you'd better be damn sure Rossweild gets what he wants. He's a sore loser."

I'll fool them all, Miller thought, as he poured himself another drink. *Even half of the promised amount is enough to live comfortably on where I'm going. I'm not waiting to see what happens to the damned GoMO bill. I'll be gone right after the big shindig.*

***

Chapter 48

<hr>

Is there a final judgment?

<hr>

*J*ulia lay in the crumpled wreckage. She knew she was dying, yet she felt an unusual sense of calm, taking comfort in the realization that in the end, she had tried to do what was right. *I'm so glad I sent my reports to Martin.* She closed her eyes wearily. *If there is to be a final judgment, perhaps my efforts will account for something?* As a scientist, Julia had always scoffed at religion, only believing in the provable realities of the physical world. But now, as she faced the harsh realization of her own mortality, she was not so sure.

She knew there was a chill in the air, but she wasn't cold. *Aren't you supposed to feel cold? Aren't you supposed to tremble with shock when you are so badly hurt?* It was as if she were no longer attached to her body. There was no pain, no sensation whatsoever. But her mind was alert. *Why didn't I go to the authorities, or at least call Martin back? Why'd I accept that monster's invitation? No! Don't think about that! I've got to focus. Oh please, God—I've got to focus on something else.* She tried to think about better days, happier times, but there were so few of those in her life. It was easier to think about her visit to Alexander's mansion, the visit that ultimately brought her to this painless, but slow and certain death . . . .

JULIA HAD AMBLED up the marble walkway. She had stopped to breathe in the sweet fragrance of the delicate white "Margaret Merrill" roses that bordered the patchwork of stones leading to the front door of Alexander Rossweild's mansion. The door itself was a work of art, with hand-blown, lead-framed windows and a gothic arch. To her left Madame Caroline Testout roses with magnificent deep red petals scaled the wall, seemingly on a quest to burst through the second-story window. Delicate floral drapes added a regal simplicity as they held dominion high above the lively display.

Julia trudged up the wide marble steps that stretched along the entire length of the old gray granite wing, determined to find the truth about Alexander Rossweild's real intentions. She had become increasingly suspicious of the uses to which her research would be employed. She was a botanist. She wanted to increase food production. But she now suspected that Alexander was into food control. *Not just control of our food,* she decided. *He wants to control us all— through our food supply.*

T. Henderson, Rossweild's butler, answered her ring and led her to a parlor before retreating to announce her arrival. Julia was left alone to admire her surroundings. Three walls reached up to a height of at least fourteen feet with long, carved panels of teak wood. On the south wall tall windows allowed the sun's rays to spill into the room. A crystal chandelier sparkled above her head. An enormous humpbacked sofa, flanked by two over-sized stuffed chairs, hugged the expansive oriental carpet and offered a commodious view of the hearth. Mirrored display cabinets on either side of the carved-marble fireplace showed off priceless treasures within. *Trophies,* she thought. *Alexander doesn't collect these things out of a love for them. He doesn't love anything—or anyone. He's not capable!*

JULIA CONTINUED HER quiet speculations until a door opened and two men entered the room. Instantly repelled by the tall man's swagger, she thought, *How transparent.*

"Well, hello," he gushed. "I am Colonel Mitchem and this is Ricardo." Julia quickly pulled her hand away to acknowledge Ricardo's courteous greeting. She suggested that they take a seat, gladdened that she had positioned herself in front of a chair.

"Lovely estate, don't you think, Miss Mahoney?"

"Yes. Magnificent."

Julia guessed from Mitchem's furtive glances that he must have been unexpectedly summoned, too.

T. HENDERSON RETURNED. He said, "Mr. Rossweild is ready to see you all now."

Mitchem offered his arm to Julia and they followed in the wake of Henderson's clattering footsteps. The manservant stopped at the threshold of Alexander's office, his English accent a perfect match for his stern personality. "Miss Mahoney, Colonel Mitchem and Mr. Ricardo are here, Sir. Shall I send Master Timothy in to assist?"

"No. That will be all. I'll ring when we're finished." Alexander turned toward Julia. "Well, well. I'm delighted to see you, Miss Mahoney." He gestured toward the two men. "Come right in gentlemen and make yourselves comfortable. Anyone care for a drink?" He pointed toward a well-stocked bar.

Mitchem responded first. "Thank you. I'd love a Scotch. May I pour for you Mr. Rossweild?" Alexander declined, so Mitchem helped himself and aimed a questioning glance toward his two companions. Julia declined his offer, but Ricardo gratefully accepted a drink and scurried to claim a chair next to her. Mitchem emptied his own glass and swiftly poured another.

Alexander watched his guests. He had not yet explained his reason for summoning them to the mansion. Like a cat toying with its prey, he enjoyed Mitchem's unease immensely. *That man is annoying. If he weren't so good at recruiting, I'd make him squirm like the worm that he is. And Ricardo is just a nervous fool no matter what the circumstance.*

"WELL NOW, MISS MAHONEY. I'm sure you are

wondering why I asked you to come. Actually, I must say I'm quite impressed with your work . . . you've surpassed our expectations." *And you're no longer useful to us,* he thought.

"Thank you, Mr. Rossweild. I do have some concerns about the project, though. Could we talk some time soon? In private? I also have ideas for publishing the results."

"Of course . . . of course, my dear. My secretary will be here in the morning. You may ask her to find an opening in my calendar. In the meantime, I hope you will enjoy being my guest for dinner this evening. We have a lovely room all prepared for your stay." *Yes, enjoy your stay, while you can.*

"Thank you, Mr. Rossweild. I'd be delighted." There was a disturbing glint in his eyes that reminded Julia of her neighbor's cat the first time it spied Sammy, her pet mouse.

Rossweild shifted his attention to the men. "There are a few matters that I would like to discuss with each of you, in private, but it can all wait until later." With exaggerated hospitality he offered, "In the meantime, I hope you will all feel free to entertain yourselves here at my home. I regret that I cannot join you until dinner, but I have both indoor and outdoor pools, a sauna, tennis court, and almost any other amenity you might wish to indulge in. And," he directed his gaze toward Julia, "I have one of the best personal libraries in the country. Please feel free to browse. And, of course, dinner will be served at eight."

Ricardo thanked his host profusely for his 'very, very generous hospitality' and admitted 'pure delight' to have the opportunity to enjoy the magnificent estate, ' . . . in the company of such a delightful, intelligent young woman, of course.'

Mitchem stood up. "I saw her first, my friend. You'll just have to wait your turn."

ALEXANDER GRAHAM Rossweild could be an enchanting host when he chose, and he chose to be at his best when he sat down for dinner with Julia, Mitchem and Ricardo. He regaled them with accounts of his travels and encouraged a lively discussion about politics. Ricardo forgot to be nervous and Julia was able to enjoy the delicious seven-course meal. She enthusiastically answered her host's questions about her research at SanFidel as they waited for dessert, and when he encouraged her to submit a proposal regarding her ideas for future projects, Julia was tempted to change her opinion of him. *He doesn't seem so bad after all,* she thought.

UNFORTUNATELY, JULIA'S RELIEF would be short lived. Later that evening, Colonel Mitchem walked her to her door, then departed, much to her surprise, without a fuss. His eyes narrowed with a sly smirk as Julia eased the bedroom door to a close. She thought it was odd behavior— had thought he looked like the proverbial cat who swallowed a mouse as the bolt click clicked into the lock, but it took a few minutes for the significance of that double click to register in her brain. Halfway across the room, Julia kicked off her shoes and drew her foot across the carpet, sinking her toes into its cushy depth. She flexed her foot and her toes snapped. Twice.

What? Her heart lurched and her brain replayed the sound. *Two snaps,* she thought. *Like the door! Oh no! It can't be!* She whirled around and rushed over to twist the knob. It wouldn't budge. She was locked in!

The sound of her own heartbeat pulsed in Julia's ears. Stiff with fear, she backed across the room and sat heavily on the bed, jiggling the ruffled canopy overhead. Like a helpless mouse in a cage, too frightened to move, she gazed around the room, no longer able to appreciate the plush carpeting or the priceless silver and crystal displayed upon the exquisite mother-of-pearl inlaid vanity.

Fear obliterated all rational thoughts. Softly, she moaned, "I'm trapped. I'm trapped." She lay there for hours, listening to the sounds of the mansion. Footsteps came and went. Whispery voices could be heard outside her door. After hours of drifting in and out of a restless sleep, her mind finally settled upon a vision of her pet mouse, Sammy and pulled her out of the helpless mantra.

SAMMY HAD WON JULIA'S HEART at the onset of an experiment a year ago, and he had saved his own little hide, too, when he stood up with unmouselike defiance. His whiskers twitched, and when his beady eyes issued a bold challenge, she did not have the heart to continue the experiment. She took him home as a pet. Since then, he has lived in luxury, a miniature tyrant squeaking his mousy demands from within his cage on her side table.

Julia silently thanked little Sammy for unwittingly inspiring her to defy her own captors. She was also glad that she had sent her report to Martin Bascomb. The detailed information about her experiments and her recent misgivings would be more than enough to warn him that SanFidel had to be stopped. She was sure that he would know what to do.

Martin and Julia had been on opposite sides during debates on the subject of genetic engineering. She had maintained that all of the sciences within the broad heading of biotechnology were inevitable. ". . . There is so much to learn, so much good that we can do right now," she had insisted with animated naiveté.

FOR YEARS JULIA HAD BEEN snubbed by most of her colleagues at the university and she had been overlooked, time and again losing out on prestigious promotions and the funding that went with them. So, when Alexander's people had approached her with their offer she did not stop to analyze their motivation. She had been wooed by their promise of unlimited funding and scientific recognition. *Wooed and duped,* she now realized.

They said they were looking for ways to stunt the growth of an entire genus of invasive weeds. They said they wanted to free up more land for food production and provide farmers with a safe means of weed control. They said they hoped to eventually produce superior edible plant life and that she would be on the cutting edge of that technology. What she found was entirely the opposite: The technology that she had developed for the weed terminators was secretly being altered with potentially devastating consequences.

JULIA HAD CLIMBED down the fire escape ladder. She had reached her car and she had driven at least half a mile down Alexander's meandering private road before she saw the headlights in her rearview mirror. She knew they would catch her; knew the treacherous cliffs to her left were no worse a fate than being in the clutches of these henchmen. With quiet resolve, Julia slammed her foot to the floor and did her best to stay on the winding road. But her best was not good enough. The huge six-wheeler roared swiftly toward the little red sedan. One bump sent it hurtling over the cliff. Truly terrified, truly helpless this time, Julia screamed as she sailed into oblivion.

***

Chapter 49

*T*om Monroe stretched his stiff limbs and peered at his surroundings with the hesitant confusion of one who has been drugged. He looked around: There were cots everywhere. He wondered, *what are all these people doing here?* But even in his dazed condition, he summed up the serious nature of his situation with sickening disbelief. *A prison camp.* He rubbed his eyes, and as he pressed the knot in his neck, his mind started to clear a bit. *How the hell did I end up here? The last I remember, I was having a scotch with Miller.*

A suspicious thought surfaced: *N-o-o-o-o—no way! He couldn't have stooped that low—could he?* Tom knew there was no other plausible explanation. *Miller must have drugged me!*

Eyes wide open, vision finally clear, Tom busied himself with speculations about the other prisoners. All of them were men. As he continued to scan the room, he was amazed to see a familiar figure on one of the cots. *It can't be!* Still a bit shaky, he managed to stumble down the bleachers without falling. He looked around to see if there were any guards. None were in sight, so he shuffled across the floor for a better look.

My God . . . it is C.D.!

C.D. HAD BEEN LOUNGING on his cot, involved in quiet conversation with his bunkmate, Ben Frankel. As they talked, he busied himself with his shoelace. He'd been practicing his knots, tying and untying half a dozen of them. He held a flawless triple half hitch up for inspection, then asked Ben to repeat his story, one more time.

"C'mon Ben. Maybe there's something that you missed in the telling last night. Even the slightest detail could lead to something important."

Ben inclined his head and said, "I'll tell it a hundred times if it'll help." He rolled onto his back and scrunched his blanket into a thick pillow-like wad. It was scratchy. He longed for his own pillow, and cool, clean sheets. He wondered what Joanne must be thinking—realized she must be going out of her mind by now. He thought, *I bet she's already called my sister.* He knew, though, that these thoughts were not helpful. So, with determination, he forced himself to focus on C.D.'s request.

"I think it all started when I went to visit a friend in Anchorage. I was doing a story on genetically modified foods and she said there were people with more than a passing interest in the subject at some citizen's rally. So I flew up to Alaska to check it out." His stomach growled noisily and he remembered the hot airline meal that he had waved away. He let out a big, hungry sigh before continuing his story.

Half way through the part about the meeting in Anchorage, he noticed a commotion on the floor below. "Hey Colonel, that fellow seems to be awfully interested in you." Ben pointed toward the middle of the room.

C.D. could not believe his eyes. "Good Lord, it's Tom! Tom Monroe! Don't tell me they've got him, too!"

". . . As in Senator Tom Monroe?"

"Yes, he's a good friend of mine."

C.D. was about to climb down to meet Tom when he saw a couple of guards headed toward him. He knew it was too late for a warning, and too foolish to fight them, so he helplessly watched as they led his friend away.

Ben broke the awkward silence with a simple observation. "Well, at least the senator was smart enough to go without a struggle."

"And you know what Ben? As soon as you mentioned your article about the genetically modified foods, I got an idea. And seeing Tom clinched it. I'll bet this is all about the GoMO legislation. Seems like that's the only thing that links the three of us. Maybe these other people were opposing it, too. Maybe we should ask them about that." So far, everyone had vehemently denied any knowledge of anything that could have caused his imprisonment. C.D. decided that a new set of questions might clear things up for a lot of them.

***

Chapter 50

Where's Perkins?

---

*M*ajor Margaret Mary Mackenzie peered through the blinds. A few enlistees were marching in unison, following their leader as she chanted her orders and led them on a tour of the Research and Development headquarters. The scene brought back memories of her first days in the service. Her bunkmate called her Mac. The nickname stuck.

MAC UNCONSCIOUSLY smoothed her unruly hair and replaced her cap. She wondered how many of those raw recruits would stay on as career soldiers. *Not many,* she thought. *Even fewer—in the specialty services.* It was tough enough for men, but much tougher for women. Despite modern attitudes, women were still looked upon as the weaker sex. Many men still harbored the belief that the army was no place for a woman. *That's not true,* she thought. *There's plenty for us to do!*

Mac removed her cap and smoothed her hair again. It was her only habitual nervous gesture and it did not occur very often because she was, according to her peers, as solid as they come. "Nothing bothers Mac," they often said.

But she was bothered now: She had not heard from Perkins for too long. As General Carrey's top undercover man, Commander Timothy Perkins often left with a quick peck on the cheek, saying he'd be 'on assignment for awhile.' She was used to that. And as a professional soldier herself, protocol demanded that she not ask questions; but there was something in his eyes this time. *He didn't even say if he was working for Harry,* she remembered.

Mac scolded herself: "I've got to be patient. Tim always comes back." But positive thoughts could not erase the worry lines that creased her forehead. As she scrunched her hair again, she thought, *Protocol be damned. I'm gonna ask Harry. And,* she scowled, *if I'm lucky, he won't put me in the brig for it!*

MAC LOOKED AT HER WATCH. It was almost time for the weekly staff appraisal. *Okay, enough of these maudlin thoughts. I'd better focus on the job at hand.* For solace, she reached into her M&M jar. It was a familiar sight for everyone at R&D, and it was the source of many amused speculations. "It's no wonder Mac made the rank of major at such a young age," they joked. ". . . she even has enough influence to have candy monogrammed for her."

Major Mac popped a bright red M&M into her mouth and headed toward the conference room. She would call Harry right after the meeting. *Protocol be damned!*

***

Chapter 51

Missing Mac.

*P*erkins missed Mac. He had been away far too long. He missed the curve at the nape of her neck that he was sure had been created just for his kiss. He missed the smell of her freshly shampooed hair and the jaunty way that her beret perched on her auburn tresses. Thoughts of her had helped him through his latest ordeal and he hoped that she missed him, too. Most of all, he regretted the fact that he dared not call her.

There's no way to know if Rodney has snitches at the R&D Center. I don't even know if he's aware that I'm on to him. For all I know he might bug Mac's phone or even her apartment—just watching for me.

Perkins had to remind himself of Rodney's treachery whenever he felt the urge to call Mac. But he took some comfort in knowing that he was on the mend and would soon be back in action. In the meantime, he was enjoying a pleasant interlude as he recuperated at Scott Hamilton's cabin. Scott's dog was a great companion, too.

"What do you think, Lucas? Should I ask her to marry me some day?" He tossed the rawhide bone and grinned as the large German shepherd raced at a gleeful gate across the fragrant, pine-covered lawn. Lucas was a playful five-year-old dog who never tired of chasing his toys— especially the mottled rawhide bones that became sloppier and chewier with each retrieval.

"Okay you big lug, that's it for now—I'm not touching that slimy thing again." The dog gazed at him with the saddest brown eyes that he could muster. "Sorry fella, but that thing's just too gross for me."

Lucas tried his most pathetic expression.

"Okay—I tell you what. I'll take you . . ."

Even before Perkins finished his sentence, the dog danced with joyous anticipation.

"Boy, Scott, I guess you weren't exaggerating about how smart he is. I didn't even have to finish my sentence." Scott chuckled. "Didn't I tell you to be careful with the 'W' word?"

PERKINS REACHED FOR his cane and pointed toward the trail at the southern end of the lawn. "Let's go for a you know what." Obviously the dog understood: He sprang forward and was almost a hundred feet away by the time Perkins reached the bottom step of the rustic wooden porch.

This walk with Lucas would be the wounded man's second foray outside since he had arrived at Scott's door, exhausted and hurting from two broken ribs, multiple lesions and a twisted ankle. As they proceeded along the trail, black-capped chickadees flitted from one branch to another, urging them on with their distinctive little chirps. A chipmunk chattered its haughty challenge and Lucas scurried back and forth in search of the brazen little rodent, sniffing at uprooted trees and inspecting every rocky crevice. As he watched the dog, Perkins remembered the crevice he had slept in during his painful escape from Domino One.

***

Chapter 52

He dared not travel during the light of day.

Commander Perkins was lucky—very lucky—and he knew it. He had healed remarkably well after his escape from Domino One. While the landscape of northwestern Tennessee was not particularly mountainous, the exertion of climbing up and down the rolling hills and swamplands and wading across the many creeks that poured their muddy waters into the Cumberland River, had taken their toll, especially since he dared not travel during the light of day.

Perkins loved history and during his painful journey through the wilderness he occupied his thoughts with the knowledge that he was probably on the same terrain that General Grant's soldiers had trudged across during their descent toward Fort Donelson. He took odd comfort in the realization that possibly—just possibly—he might be reliving some of the anguish that the regiment's wounded soldiers had experienced over a hundred years before him. He tried to picture them as they might have struggled—weary, hurting beyond belief without modern conveniences like antibiotics and painkillers. *Painkillers! God, he could have used some himself.* He knew that he had a broken rib or two among other things, and the pain had been excruciating. He still winced when he thought about one particularly painful morning . . . .

HE HAD STOPPED to study his surroundings. The sun was on the verge of rising and it was time to find a place

to hide until nightfall—he had to assume that a team from
Domino would be searching for him. Just a few feet to his
left he spied a small rocky overhang. Perfect! His thoughts
suddenly switched to a map-making class where he had
learned that parts of Tennessee were included on the list of
only a few places in the country where you had to use an
agonic line to calculate north/south positions because there
was no difference, or declination, between geographic north
which is depicted on maps and charts, and magnetic north,
which is shown by a compass. Most people don't know
there's a difference, he realized. Heck, he admitted, most
people wouldn't care, except maybe Mac. Thoughts of her
took his mind off the pain and got him through the excruciating chore of gathering fresh pine boughs to create a
protective barrier for his hideaway. When he had enough for
that, he laid a few more on the ground for bedding—then
settled into his little den.

Perkins felt lucky to have found this rocky overhang.
And he was glad to see some sticky pine pitch had oozed
from the larger branches. He rubbed some of it on his cuts,
knowing that years ago, the pitch from white pine was used
to heal and protect wounds. He suspected with sudden
satisfaction that General Grant's men may have used it, too.

The exertion had taken its toll. Feverish and exhausted, he slept in fitful spurts, his mind flitting from
comforting thoughts of Mac to inspiring fantasies about his
heroes from the Civil War. At one point, Perkins found
himself gazing at the ledge above his head. It reminded him
of one of his Civil War paintings. Why? His feverish brain
puzzled over the triangular pattern, but sleep came before he
could summon up the memory.

THE WALK WITH Lucas went smoothly and Per-
kins was happy to realize that he was not even out of breath.
He knew then that he could continue his work. He had tried
several times but he still was not able to reach Harry at his
private number. That worried him, but he knew it would not
be wise to call headquarters—or Mac. He also had no idea if

his video had reached Bob Jette, and ultimately, therefore, Harry.

Perkins was grateful to Scott for his assistance and hated to ask more of him, but he needed a car. The elderly recluse had no vehicle of his own, but his neighbor, Thelma, sometimes took him down to the valley for provisions. He was sure she would help if he asked.

Scott was right. Thelma agreed to let Perkins use her late father's sedan. She did not ask any questions—and he was glad.

***

Chapter 53

Soldiers? Not!

---

*B*ack at the cabin Perkins packed a few essentials. Then he spoke to Lucas. "Sorry fella, but I can't play—I gotta make it an early one tonight. Gotta get up with the birds!" He gave a sympathetic shrug as the dog flopped to the floor with a disappointed woof.

ON HIS LUMPY COT Perkins thought about the events that brought him on his painful journey to Scott's out-of-the-way cabin. It all began about two months ago when Harry pulled a few strings and arranged for him to pose as a tough mercenary so he could earn Colonel Mitchem's trust. *Colonel? Ha. If he's a colonel, then I'm Cinderella. And I sure as hell 'ain't' no Cinderella!*

It did not take him long to receive an invitation to join Mitchem's band of soldiers. *Soldiers? Ha. The only cause these guys'll fight for is a paycheck—and maybe the thrill of a kill.* It was a dangerous scheme, but Perkins believed it was his only chance to see just how extensive Mitchem's network had become.

His ribs were still tender on the left side, so Perkins rolled over. While he struggled to get comfortable on the cot, he recalled his 'interview' with the 'colonel' from Alexander Graham Rossweild's private little army . . . .

PERKINS HAD PARKED in the visitor's lot near the front entrance of an abandoned factory. As promised, the front door was unlocked and it did not take him long to find Conference Room B.

He knocked. A gruff voice barked a command to enter, but his mind was racing. *This is too easy,* he had thought. *They're gonna test me sooner or later . . . .*

Perkins gave the knob a twist and jumped to the side—just in time to avoid a deadly blast of bullets. Sweat poured off him and every major muscle tensed, ready for flight; but he was determined to appear unruffled. He casually grunted, ". . . Thought you wanted to *talk,* not decorate the walls with my *entrails.*"

"Very good, Perkins. I'm suitably impressed. You passed the first test. Most men don't *live* through my *entrance exams.* Come on in; no more tests—you have my word on it."

Perkins knew that men like Mitchem had a twisted sense of honor. If he gave his word on something, he'd stick to it, no matter what.

He recognized Mitchem from pictures the general had shown him. Four other men were there, but they definitely were not pleased to see him. Perkins figured they probably were disappointed that their four-gun welcome had not turned him into Swiss cheese. He wondered if they'd be on KP later. *Or worse.*

Mitchem spoke again. "I'll get right to the point, Perkins. I'm a busy man and I can't afford to waste time. You've been recommended as a fine soldier, one who'll do whatever it takes to complete a mission. I need good men like you—so if you're interested, you'll start right away.

"In just fifteen minutes a chopper will arrive here. You'll be taken to your new post. Generous payments will be deposited into a special account for you each month. In return we demand complete loyalty. From now on, you belong to us, but the money will pile up until the end of your service."

Perkins noticed that Mitchem's buddies got glassy eyed when he mentioned the money. *Must be competitive wages, but I wonder how many of them live to get theirs?* He realized that Mitchem was watching him. He saluted. "Thank you, Sir. How long will this assignment take? And, if you don't mind my asking, what am I going to do?"

Mitchem leaned forward, his voice cold, inflexible. His eyes glinting like polished steel. "I *do* mind your asking. You'll be apprised only as needed." He advised softly, "Just do what you are told, when you are told—or we'll have to arrange another 'test'. Understood?"

Perkins understood. "Yessir."

Without taking his eyes off Perkins, Mitchem barked his next order. "Okay, boys, take him to the field. I think I hear the chopper."

BY SIX PM, PERKINS HAD arrived at his new "post" along with two other new recruits. They were stripsearched and given a uniform and a duffel filled with necessities plus two extra changes of clothing. *Just like the Army,* Perkins thought, *but worse. Go AWOL here and you won't go to the brig—you'll be shot.*

A steely-eyed captain addressed the three new men. "I'm Captain Isaakson. For the next couple of weeks you'll be mine. You got that? Mine. You're here because you are good and it's my job to see *how* good. But as far as I'm concerned, right now you're just trainees—freakin' trainees—on probation."

Perkins got the message. Trainees were on a level with earthworms, not much more than scum, until they proved themselves. He wondered how they would have to prove themselves, but it didn't take much imagination to realize what would happen if they failed. Mitchem had already spelled it out for him.

"Do *what* you are told *when* you are told. And don't ask no questions. If you pass the test, you'll get your assignments. Mess up and you're dead."

Perkins thought, *Yup. I was right—dead right.*

Isaakson looked each of them in the eye and Perkins had the feeling that the guy hoped they would mess up, or at the very least, ask a question. When they remained at attention, mute and obedient, Isaakson executed a salute.

"Okay. Mess is being served now, men. Down that

185

hall—big open doorway to your left. Hustle your asses over there pronto. There ain't no room for lagers around here. And don't get nosy, you hear me? You just march those asses right back here afterwards. Then we'll set you up in your new quarters." Three salutes and three 'Yessirs' earned an 'at ease'. Perkins was glad that his fellow trainees knew better than to ask questions. He wondered if they had survived the same entrance exam.

PERKINS THREW HIS DUFFEL onto the empty cot and nodded a curt hello to his roommate. Expressionless eyes stared, then looked away. *Okay*, Perkins thought to himself, *so much for the buddy system. And I was afraid I'd be stuck with a chatterbox.*

THE TRAINING HAD BEEN HARSH, the schedule grueling, but Perkins managed to learn quite a bit about Domino. It was amazing how much people liked to talk.

Domino One, he learned, was a prison camp for Alexander Graham Rossweild's enemies. And there were three others just like it: One in the wilds of Vermont, one in Indiana, and one in the state of Washington. Perkins thought, *boy, he must have quite a list.* There were politicians, newspaper publishers, lawyers and other citizens who had seen what they shouldn't have seen, or had spoken out against Alexander. On his third night of guard duty, Perkins was horrified to see that one of the prisoners was C.D.

Good God!

He waited and watched, but there just wasn't any opportunity to get to him. Perkins realized he would have to get the word out! Some how. . . .

There was more freedom of movement during his night watch: Only three guards on the entire north wing until sunrise. So, at 3:45 AM, Perkins found the opportunity he had been waiting for on a catwalk that encircled the facility. Escape ladders hugged each corner. Rolled up tight until needed, they were only accessible from above.

On clear nights there were spectacular views of the

Tennessee countryside. Its rolling hills, rivers and forests stretched for miles. But tonight, the sky was a murky gray and a blanket of thick, damp fog girdled the compound. *Perfect escape weather.* As he crept toward his unsuspecting victim, Perkins shivered. *Was it the damp night air that seeped through his clothes and into his bones? Or, the knowledge that he'd have to kill—or be killed?*

Afraid that the guy would hear the thunderous beating of his heart, he delivered a debilitating blow. He hoped his aim was not too low, otherwise it could mean a lot of suffering before death. He hated to cause suffering, even when he was killing an enemy. Perkins grimaced at his own twisted logic as he approached his next victim.

This one wouldn't be quite so easy. It was Mr. Congeniality, the roommate from hell. He seemed to sense the approaching threat and spun around, prepared to deliver a powerful kick. A direct hit could cause deep fissures in the liver, followed by peritonitis and death. Perkins knew all about the dangers of a powerful, well placed kick. He rolled away, but not soon enough to avoid a broken rib or two. He did manage to grab the offending foot and yanked his foe off his feet. Mr. Congeniality wrenched away, only to hit his head against the cornerstone before slamming onto the concrete floor. Perkins gave him a final chop as he went down.

Perkins almost hit the rock-hard floor himself, but despite the overwhelming pain, he managed to lower one of the escape ladders and maneuver himself over the wall. Nothing vital had been hit, but he knew he was in for a lot of misery. To make matters worse, he twisted his ankle when he dropped onto the rocky slope. Slowly and painfully, Perkins limped away. He had to make steady progress for the next hour at least. He figured he had that much time before anyone realized what had happened during the night watch. He headed south toward the cabin of his father's old army buddy, Scott Hamilton. He hoped he could make it.

***

Chapter 54

Miller has powerful allies . . .

I *don't like the sound of this.* Senator Josiah Whalon unscrunched his massive frame and perched on the edge of his high-backed leather chair as he listened to his irate colleague, Theodore Steele. He hugged the receiver to his ear. Annoyance wrinkled his face.

"I tell you, Joe—we're going to be hung up to dry on this one. Tom Monroe has not done a thing for two days now and SanFidel's people are all over me. I haven't seen even one new piece of evidence to back up Monroe's claim that the GoMO is bad. Not one! And, apparently, he doesn't care enough to provide me with the information that I asked for. I'm going to side with Miller on this . . . can't afford not to! There's little enough pork coming my way, you know, and next year I'm up for re-election. I've simply got to be able to come through for my state. And we both know that Miller has a reputation for delivering."

"I hear you, Theo. I guess you have to do what you feel is best. So why are you calling me about this?"

"I promised Miller I'd announce my position, but I'd like someone to back me up. So, are you with me? Miller has powerful allies, you know, and as one of the smaller states, you could use a few friends. Say, aren't you working on that new education package? You know how it works, Joe. You scratch Miller's back and he'll scratch yours—or, at least he won't *stab* you in the back."

"Well, I guess you can count me in . . . for now. But

188

if Tom comes through with some solid arguments against the GoMO, I'll have to reconsider."

"That's fair enough, Joe. But you won't be sorry." Senator Theodore Steele poked the speaker button with his pen and slumped into his seat. Relief flooded in. *That wasn't so hard after all.*

***

Chapter 55

The invitation.

*A*lexander was enjoying a pleasant brunch on his patio. His favorite roses had blossomed riotously over the past twenty-four hours and their sweet fragrance filled the air. He was sipping his freshly squeezed orange juice when he heard the familiar footsteps of his butler.

"What is it Henderson?"

"I'm sorry to disturb you, Sir. It's Mr. Jordan. He says you have been expecting this call."

"Yes, Henderson. Yes." Alexander reached his hand high up over his head and yanked the telephone away with a curt dismissal. "That will be all, Henderson."

"Yessir."

Henderson executed a perfect one-heeled wheely and hurried back to his chores. As he slipped through the door, he thought, *One would think the pleasantness of the day could seep into that sour soul of his. Yes, one would think so.*

Rossweild barked into the telephone. "Have you extended my special invitation?"

Not much on manners, are you? Perry thought. "Yes. He's already filled out his, umh, menu for the big party. And our special recipe promises to be a big success. Huge, I'd say."

"Splendid!" Without another word he punched the off button and took another sip of his juice.

Perry jerked the receiver away from his ear. *What a Neanderthal. I'd like to feed him some of that 'recipe'. The wrinkled little man already looks like he's had a sample. But, then again, nothing could stunt that ego of his.*

WHEN HE GOT OFF the telephone with Perry Jordan, Alexander called Senator Miller. For once he was not upset to hear the click of an answering machine as it whirred into action. *I didn't want to speak to that airhead anyway,* he thought. He left a message. "Miller, it's Alexander. Looks like we've perfected that wonderful *recipe* I told you about. It will be the talk of the town after the party. Those who are still riding the fence will come our way after Monroe puts the pressure on. He grinned, *Monroe will have to convince them—or I'll see to it that he'll have a lot of blood on his hands.*

***

Chapter 56

---

*D*amo's head was throbbing. He did not want to open his eyes. *Oh, man. I musta' had a few too many brewskies this time . . . I need just a little more sleep.* He rolled over and reached for a pillow, but instead of his soft bed he felt a hard, scratchy carpet—no blankets, no pillows. *What the heck?*

He tried to sit up. *Big mistake!*

He gripped his head and dropped back to the floor as raging pain and a wave of nausea overwhelmed him. *Okay, Damo. Think. Where am I?* Through painful slits he peered at his surroundings. Straight ahead was the shelving that housed Jerry Johnson's professional journals and an assortment of heavy canine doorstops. One of them was on the floor next to him. "Now I remember. That creep musta got me with the dog." Anger and a thirst for revenge blocked the thunderstorm in his head and with an explosive curse, Damo leapt to his feet.

"What the hell time is it—I gotta check in with Perry—then I'm gonna find those twerps." But the relentless pounding resumed its attack. He thought, "I better find some aspirin first, then maybe I'll search this dump for clues." On his way to the bathroom, Damo decided the couch would be a very good place to use as a base of operations—after he checked in with Perry. He took a step, but stopped to hold his head, then shuffled, v-e-r-y slowly, toward the medicine cabinet. *That airhead better have lots of aspirin!*

***

192

Chapter 57

*M*elvin stood in front of a telephone booth near a busy street corner, just beyond his favorite liquor store. With his right hand tightly clutching a brown paper sack filled with two six-packs and a bag of corn chips, he groped for Perry Jordan's private number.

"Darn thing's gotta be here—it's just gotta!"

He balanced the bag on top of his ample belly before reaching into his other pocket. "Yayyy—here it is!" he exclaimed with glee—until he tried to yank it free. Unfortunately, he knocked himself off balance and careened into an elderly woman who was waiting to cross the street. Unbelievably, he managed to save his precious parcel. Still trying to yank his hand out of his tight right pocket, he slurred, "Sorrrry, maaam. You *okayyy?*"

The woman wrinkled her nose and backed away from Melvin's fowl breath. Her brows shot up with renewed distaste when she noticed the lumpy belly that was bouncing its way out of Melvin's tee shirt. With a wide-eyed gasp, she scurried away.

Melvin blinked as the woman split in two before his eyes. He blinked again as the two of her drifted out of sight amongst a sea of doubles. "Jeeeez! There's twins all over the plaaaase today.*"

When Melvin returned to the job of freeing his hand, he gave a final mighty yank. "Yayyy! I got my hand back—and the note, too!"

He swung the wrinkled slip of paper back and forth in front of his eyes until it came into focus. "My writin' ain't toooo goodddd," he admitted before gently placing his purchases on the floor of the telephone booth. He dialed, waited, then said, "Hi—It's meeee. Ain't seen 'm taday neither. Heard hizzz secretary sayin' he wuzzz away on family bisnissss. I'll report again, tomorrow."

***

Chapter 58

*M*ajor General H. Edward Carrey stormed through his front door and tossed his briefcase onto the plush settee. It popped open and he glared at the contents as they spilled onto the floor. The fastidious general knelt on his good knee and shuffled through the half-dozen folders—luckily the loose papers had not spilled as well.

"Well, thank you God, for something good today." His relief was not exaggerated. It would truly have been a tedious job to sort through the papers and return them to their respective folders. "I know. It serves me right for losing my temper."

Harry's temper was legendary at the R&D command center, and he knew it. *Poor Rodney,* he thought. His aide, Major Rodney Carrousel, would blush like a scarlet tanager if he knew that the infamous HarryCarrey was aware of the office scuttlebutt. Sometimes his staff even took bets to see who could predict how many times the "old man" would lose his temper on a given day. Harry heard that Rodney had been dead-on this month.

Rodney's a good man, Harry thought. *Disciplined— and quick on his feet.* Harry believed that Rodney was an excellent soldier. But the poor lad was cursed with a fair complexion and the most incredible tendency to blush. He liked to glare at him now and then just to see how red he would get.

Harry looked upward once more and lamented, "I know, it's mean, but there's something to be said for comic relief. After all, you did bless us with a sense of humor!" The brief waggish interlude helped Harry to get his composure back.

Harry often talked to his Creator when he was alone. It helped him to stay in control. He placed the folders back into his briefcase and strode toward his home office with the confident resolve that was his trademark. That was all that Harry had to do to perk up the morale of his troops—just look confident and in control. The men would follow him anywhere without question.

As Harry entered his office, he realized that it was time to take action. He had not heard from Commander Perkins for far too long. And today was the last straw: He heard that Senator Monroe was totally unavailable and C.D. was in danger of being pronounced AWOL, which he knew was a crock. He'd had several men on the lookout for C.D., to no avail. That was definitely worrisome.

C.D. and Tom Monroe were the ones he had decided to confide in, and Harry was not naive enough to think it a coincidence that two of the most honest men in town were out of reach at this point in time.

"Confound it all, now who can I trust?"

Harry decided that he needed a little fortification before determining his strategy and fixed his usual Scotch and soda, on the rocks. *Lots of rocks.* Then he slipped into the kitchen and rummaged through the fridge for a bite to eat. As usual Mandallah, his part-time cook and household "girl Friday," had left him a platter full of her delectable cooking. He was happy to see a plate of beef stew—his favorite. Mandallah had to be one of the best cooks he had ever known. *Good old-fashioned meat and potatoes that a man can sink his teeth into.*

As he ate, Harry's attention wandered toward the framed photographs on the wall. His favorite was a portrait of himself with the wild boar he bagged during last fall's boar hunt in Vermont. The photo reminded him of the state representative he had bunked with. He thought, *Now there's a gutsy guy with a common-sense approach toward life and toward his work in the Vermont State Legislature. Now, what was his name? Fred. Yes—Fred Hanson.* Harry figured that Hanson was too honest and too far removed from the beltway to become involved in Rossweild's unlawful scheme. *He might have some good contacts, too,* Harry thought. *Outside the loop.*

AN IDEA TOOK SHAPE as Harry gobbled down the last few bites of his stew. "Okay," he said. "Now I'm ready to kick ass." He looked upwards. "God willing, of course!" As an avid student of American history, Harry liked the idea of teaming up with a Vermonter. *Kind of like getting hitched up with Ethan Allen and his Green Mountain Boys during the American Revolution.* He decided to give Fred a call from his private line.

Commander Perkins was the only other person, besides the installer, who knew the line existed. It was the latest in technology, with a scrambler built in so that no one could eavesdrop. *More secure than Fort Knox* he often told Perkins. Harry dialed Hanson's number, thinking, *Commander Perkins! I hope he calls soon—I surely do.* He was not surprised to hear his friend pick up on the second ring. He figured they probably weren't very busy in up there in the boondocks.

"REPRESENTATIVE HANSON. May I help you?"

Good, solid voice, Harry thought with approval. *Just like I remember him.* "Hello, Hanson? This is Major General Carrey—we bunked at the boar hunt last year . . ?" He waited for a response.

"Yes. Why, yes, of course. How are you General? And to what do I owe this pleasant surprise?"

"Actually, I'm taking a few days off, starting tomorrow. Unexpected, but much needed. I'll be heading through your neck of the woods. Think you could get free for a few drinks—or dinner? Maybe we could plan another hunt."

"Count me in. But I insist that you be my guest here at Shady Pines. Can you spare a night or two? We just got out of session and to tell you the truth, I'm ready for a diversion."

"By George, I'm already looking forward to it myself. Hoped you'd be able to find some time. I'll be stopping in Rhode Island tomorrow for a bit, first. My sister's there, you see. How does Thursday sound to you?"

The two men completed their plans and Fred promised to e-mail directions to his home.

Next, Harry called his sister.

"SO, HARRY—HOW CAN you tear yourself away from Mandallah's cooking? Is something wrong? You're not sick are you?"

"No, no, Regina. Nothing's wrong. But, you're right about Mandalla. It's not easy to live without that famous stew of hers."

"Oh, Harry—it'll be good to see you. George is away, so it will be just the two of us. We can do lots of catching up. Well, I'd better go so I can get your room ready."

". . . Until tomorrow, then, Regina." He hung up and busied himself with packing. Then he dialed Mandallah's number to let her know he would be gone for a while. "But do not tell anyone that I'm gone," he emphasized before hanging up.

***

Chapter 59

Let's not play games—or shall we?

"Senator Monroe, don't look so forlorn! Things aren't that bad—really they're not."

Perry Jordan's condescending voice grated against Tom's nerves. "You have a lot more power than you might think, Senator. Oh, by the way, I'm sorry about that lumpy cot. But not to worry—you'll be sleeping in your own comfy little bed tonight."

"Never mind my nightly accommodations, Jordan. Why'd you bring me here? What do you want?" The shrewd senator knew that he would be expected to give something in return for the implied freedom. *Probably something unthinkable.*

"It's rather simple, really. And you'll be a hero, too, with a chance to save lives!"

Perry watched as Tom surreptitiously scanned the room. "Forget it, friend. There's no way to escape from here."

Tom shrugged. "I guess you're right. So, Jordan, let's quit the games. What do you want from me?"

"Just your cooperation and your support." Perry offered his own nonchalant shrug.

"Support? Of what?"

"The GoMO."

"No!" Tom exploded. "I won't do it. I'd rather die first."

Perry did not doubt his sincerity. "Perhaps. But

199

would you like to see Colonel Davidson die? And the other people in that room downstairs, too?"

"You're bluffing!"

"I knew you'd react that way, so I came prepared." He raised his voice. "Bring him in."

The door opened and an elderly man was shoved into the room. Tom could see he was already in pain. *Animals!* He thought. *The poor guy can barely walk.*

Without uttering a word, Perry picked up a revolver and removed three bullets. The old man held his breath, ready for death. Perry sang, "Fifty, fifty," softly, sadistically, before giving the barrel a spin and pulling the trigger.

Tom watched with horror until the hammer delivered a barren click. He burst out of his chair and tried to grab his murderous captor before rough hands shoved him back. He shouted, "You're insane, Jordan—insane!"

"Aren't we all?" Perry searched Tom's face with calculating eyes. "So—here's how it goes. Each time you say no, we'll bring somebody else in. I'll spin the barrel and shoot. Sooner or later somebody's going to be a gonner and Jimmy here'll just keep bringing me more targets. We can play 'til they're all dead."

An expectant glint emanated from Perry's eager eyes as he spelled out his chilling plan. "And I have lots of bullets—wanna say 'no' again, Tom?"

"My God! You're talking about these people as if they are worthless possessions to be traded or tossed aside. They're thinking, feeling human beings!" Tom knew that his protest was futile. Perry was already reaching to give the barrel another spin. *I can't let this continue!* He thought with a chill.

"Okay. Tell me what to do. I'll cooperate . . . if you promise not to hurt anyone." Tom saw disappointment flitter across Perry's face before his eyes held the glimmer of victory.

Tom glowered.

Perry smiled. "See? Everybody's happy now and you've just saved a life." He bent forward, his face so close that Tom could feel the warmth of his breath and smell his spicy aftershave. He tried to pull away but Perry yanked him back. "Don't cross me, Monroe. As you can see, I don't bluff." He straightened up then and took a seat behind the desk.

TOM SLUMPED WITH RELIEF when the old man was led away, unhurt. He noticed that the insane glint had disappeared from Perry's eyes. Without the scent of a fresh kill in sight, Perry easily regained the persona of a decisive businessman.

"Okay. Here is what you need to do." Perry explained to the astonished senator that Alexander Graham Rossweild was going to host an important party to rally support for the GoMO legislation. All Tom had to do, he said, was attend the party and urge the other legislators to support it.

"What happens to these prisoners after I do that?"

"That remains to be seen. But as long as you cooperate, they won't be shot." He pressed his mouth into an ugly line. "Think of it this way, Monroe . . . at least you'll be buying these people some time." With a sadistic snicker, Perry gave Senator Tom Monroe a thumbs up.

"Okay men. Take him upstairs. Let him get cleaned up before we send him home." As Tom was led away, Perry could not resist hurling another warning: "And don't tell anyone about last night's little pajama party, if you want these people to stay alive. Next time, I might not take *any* bullets out of the gun." He laughed at the shocked look on Tom's face.

"Oh, by the way, Senator, it's black tie. See you there!"

Tom trudged away, flanked by two strong young guards, with Perry's demented laughter echoing through his ears until the hum of the elevator blocked it out.

***

Chapter 60

Evie was poised for a fight

---

*T*he morning after the *Snow White* heist, Brick called Martin Bascomb from a pay phone. He described the astonishing tape—without mentioning how they got it—and urged the botanist to continue checking on his old colleagues, ". . . especially if one of them is named Julia."

Martin almost dropped the phone. "Did you say Julia?"

"Yes. They talked about her work on the tape. They've changed her formula, whatever it is, and they want to destroy farm crops with it."

"My Lord in heaven. I was afraid it was her. I just didn't want to believe it." Martin's voice faded. "I surely did not want to believe it."

"I'm afraid it's true, Dr. Bascomb. I'm sorry."

Brick scuffed his feet on the floor of the tiny booth. He knew the old man was disenchanted, so he decided to get his mind off Julia. "By the way, could you put Evie on the phone? I'm with someone who wants to talk to her."

"Evie? Why certainly, she's right here." Martin raised his bushy eyebrows as he beckoned for her to come to the telephone. He blocked the receiver and whispered that Brick Little was on the line and had asked for her.

Evie grabbed the telephone.

WHILE MARTIN WAS WHISPERING to Evie, Brick asked John to take the receiver, but he did not give up

202

his space in the tiny booth. John thought of the old joke, 'How many elephants can you fit in a telephone booth?' As he squeezed in beside Brick, he decided it couldn't be very many. He expected a friendly greeting. Instead, Evie's angry demands blasted his ear.

"Ready to apologize? Don't you know it's danger-ous—driving that fast?"

John stared at Brick and pretended to hang himself as he listened to his feisty sister. Brick understood and slashed his own throat with his finger. That did it for John. He had to whip the receiver high over his head as they both chortled uncontrollably.

Evie thought she heard birds chirping in the back-ground. She stopped yelling and waited for Brick to render his excuse. But it was the opportunity John was waiting for. He croaked, "What the heck are you talking about, Sis? When did you see me driving?"

"John?"

He winked at Brick, thoroughly enjoying his sister's breathless confusion.

Evie whirled around and stared at Martin who shrugged with equal bafflement. "John? What are you doing on the telephone? Dr. B. said it was that awful Brickford Little!"

"Well, Brick *was* on the phone, but I asked to talk to you. Look, Sis, it's a long story—I'll explain later. By the way, are you all right?"

Brick poked him and shook his head violently. He wanted John to know that Evie did not know anything yet.

"Yes, of course I'm fine. Why wouldn't I be? Wait a minute, does it have something to do with *him?*"

Without skipping a beat, John continued, "Oh, just wondering—you sounded upset is all. By the way, what's this about fast driving and why should Brick apologize?"

"Oh, never mind. It was nothing." She was *not* about to talk to her brother about *that* man. Instead she asked, "But—where *are* you? How do you know *him*? When are you coming *here*?" She punctuated each question with raised brows and voice.

"Washington. We met by accident. In a couple of days, probably. Okay?"

"Well, I guess so." She wanted to put Brick out of her mind so she focused on her brother, excited at the thought of seeing him so soon. "Can you really come in a few days? Dr. B. is looking forward to meeting you—he thinks treasure hunting is fascinating."

"Well, it is! Why do you think I got hooked?" A movement suddenly caught his eye. It was Brick. John nodded at both Brick's gestures and Evie's excited plans before jumping in to end the conversation. "So, Sis—I gotta go, but we'll see you real soon."

"What do you mean, *we*? Is Betty coming?"

"No. I mean we, as in Brick and me."

Wide-eyed and tight-fisted, Evie shouted, "Him!"

"Don't get your truffles ruffled, Sis—he's a pretty neat guy. Oh," he added, "Can you put Dr. Bascomb back on? Brick wants to talk to him again."

Evie whipped the telephone away from her ear. With exaggerated distaste she handed it back to Martin.

Brick explained about the boys and said he did not feel comfortable leaving them behind in Washington. He added that his house had been bugged.

As he had hoped, Martin extended his invitation to them all.

EVIE, MILLICENT AND MARTIN prepared enough sleeping quarters to accommodate their oncoming guests. Later that day, while Millicent shopped for groceries, Evie exclaimed, "I'm so glad John is coming! I'm sure you'll like him, Dr. B." She put her hand on his arm. "But, I want to know what's going on. I'm not blind, you know. There's been a change in you ever since Brick Little was here. I've heard you at night—I know you're not sleeping well. Isn't there something I can do?"

"Oh, don't you worry about me, my dear. And you'll learn about this business all too soon, I'm afraid.

But, please . . . wait until your brother and his friends come.

"By the way I'm only too happy to meet any member of the Victor clan. I've grown quite fond of you, you know, Miss Victor." He proved it by giving her a fatherly hug.

WHILE EVIE AND MARTIN BASCOMB were talking about him, John was packing his bags. After stuffing his oversized duffel, he called Betty.

"John, I've got a message for you," Betty said in her cute Southern drawl. "Manny called. He wants you to know the next meeting was postponed for awhile. He's hoping you'll be able to get to it after all, if you finish your business in the lower forty-nine in time. He was pretty upset, too, though. Seems several people are missing. He said something about a hell hole called Domino One. He asked me to get your number if you have one, so he can get it from me. He knows you usually keep your cell phone turned off."

John demanded, "Who's missing?"

"They all were at those meetings, he said, or they're connected to them somehow. Let me see . . . "

JOHN PICTURED HER in his mind. *Let's see, her eyes'll be raised toward the ceiling about now—deep in thought with pursed lips twitching back and forth. Then she'll tap her chin with her pointer finger.* He knew she'd tap her chin seven times—it was always seven—then her eyes would light up and she'd respond.

John had just enough time to count to seven.

"There's a publisher from a little weekly paper called The French Lick Express, and a man from a print shop in one of the Southern states, too. Seems they were both working for the group. Those are the only two that he specifically mentioned, but he said there were more."

"Well, I'll be darned! C.D.'s gone, too. And apparently so is a friend of his . . . a senator named Monroe. Our culprits are getting desperate, hon, or they're just awfully sure of themselves. A United States senator and a colonel for Pete's sake!"

BETTY'S HEART JUMPED. *Oh, God. He's gotten himself into another dangerous mess!* She knew it would be useless to discourage him from getting involved. *Heck,* she thought, *he's already involved.*

"Sounds like you already know what's going on."

"We don't have all the answers yet, but at least this time I've got some help."

"Well, at least I'm glad you're not alone on this one."

"Nope. Got lotsa good guys with me on this caper—so don't worry." He knew she would, though. "Look, Betty, I have to go now but I'll call you again soon. We're gonna visit Evie and her boss, that highfalutin botanist. Here's the number, by the way, so you can give it to Manny the next time you hear from him."

"I hope you aren't getting into anything too dangerous! I'm still trembling over your encounter with those convicts." She tried to control the tremor in her voice. "So, when do you think you'll be coming home? Soon, I hope!"

"I'm not sure. I'll call after I get to Evie's." He added smugly, "Her boss thinks treasure hunters are fascinating. Love ya, gotta go. And don't worry!"

"Love you, too, and don't forget to *call,*" she reminded before the inevitable click.

JOHN SCOWLED at the receiver. *I wonder how many people have actually disappeared? I think we need to find out what we can about this Domino One place. Boy, I hope Manny calls—real soon!*

***

206

Chapter 61

*M*ajor Rodney Carrousel strode proudly toward his Mercedes. He had just left a meeting at SanFidel's private executive retreat. He was on top of the world. He had been given the okay to initiate his plan. *His plan!* Perry Jordan had given him credit for his idea *right in front of the others.*

He unlocked the car door, thinking, *I'm playing in the big leagues now and soon I'll be able to see some justice.* He burned with the desire to avenge his father's death. *I promise you, Dad, I'll get even with them for abandoning you. They'll pay. They'll all pay. They should have done more for you and all the other MIA's.* Confident that he would soon quench his thirst for revenge, Rodney gunned the engine and sped onto the highway. He felt invincible.

THE NEXT MORNING Rodney peered into Harry's office. He was ready for their usual morning update, but Harry wasn't there.

"Damn! Where is the old coot. He didn't tell me he'd be away." He flipped through the calendar.

"Nothing! Well, maybe he left a message at my desk." Across the hall, his own desktop revealed nothing, but the red eye on his machine was blinking. He slapped the play button and bounced irritably from toe to toe as he listened to the mechanical voice that announced, "You have two messages." Finally Harry's voice boomed out of the slotted speaker. He would not be in for a few days, he said, because of a 'family thing'.

Rodney could not believe his luck. "Great! I'll be free to put through the changes once I get the daily crap out of the way!" For the first time since he enlisted, Rodney dove into his paper work with pleasure. He finished in record time and after a short lunch break, he called the procurement office.

"Hello, get me Hank Schuyler, please."

Moments later, Hank's nasal greeting broke into the dull void called elevator music.

"Hi, Hank? This is Major Carrousel. Remember that little fuel deal I told you about earlier? Well, it's time. You should have received all the stats already."

After Hank confirmed that it was all there, Rodney continued his orders. "Remember, no one is to know about this until I say so." Rodney envisioned the pale young man at the other end of the line. *Like a damned zombie—he doesn't even question a big change like this.* Rodney grinned with derision. *If I cared, I could have his stripes for it. Lucky for him I don't. Anyway, by the time the general hears that we have a new fuel vendor, it won't matter.*

RODNEY COULD NOT FORGIVE the government or the military for leaving his father in Viet Nam. *They should have tried harder. Well, this is for you Dad—for you and for all of your buddies who were lost or captured in Nam.* Then he thought about his unwed, broken-hearted birth mother who had given him up for adoption. *This is for her, too. And for all those empty years.*

Rodney was an impressionable teenager when he had learned the truth about his birth parents. That was when he vowed to find his mother and make the government pay for abandoning his father. He had almost given up ten months ago, after years of searching, when a solid piece of evidence literally fell into his hands. It was easy to follow the lead that had ultimately brought him to his mother . . . and he had been surprised and pleased to learn that she lived in Washington.

Afraid of the ultimate rejection, Rodney had watched her from a distance for several days before finally building enough nerve to introduce himself. But she welcomed him with an embrace that seemed to melt the empty years away. Rodney felt an instant bond with this elegant woman who, without hesitation, shed tears of sadness and joy upon meeting her long lost son. Rodney was amazed that she had been in such close proximity to him for so long, and he was proud of the life that she had built for herself. He also thought it extremely fortuitous, too. As the top aide to a respected senator, she was privy to a lot of useful information.

But the joyful reunion did not quell the rage he felt over the loss of his father. *Well, enough of this reminiscing. I've got to adjust these flight orders to make sure that those test planes fly where I want them.*

THERE WERE THREE MISSIONS coming up where the pilots would be testing new surveillance equipment and Rodney wanted to be sure that they flew over certain corn fields.

***

Chapter 62

A parcel from Julia!

Millicent peered through the doorway with the eye of a seasoned housekeeper. Martin had announced that he would be spending the entire morning in the laboratory so she decided it was the ideal time to give his study a thorough cleaning.

After nudging the heavy table far enough to make room for the vacuum, Millicent exclaimed, "Glory be, some mail has fallen behind there—I hope it's not important." She tossed one letter on top of the desk without much notice, but the bulky manila envelope was another story. She read the return address: J. Mahoney, Burlington, Vermont.

"*Hmmm.*" Millicent squinted and pursed her lips. The name seemed familiar. Several faces ran through her mind before it came to her. "Of course, Julia Mahoney—that mousy assistant professor that Martin had worked with a few years back!"

Millicent thought that Julia could take a few pointers from Evie. She decided, *oh, well, it's not mine to judge.* Her soft round body followed her shoulders in a bouncy, philosophical shrug as she placed Julia's package on top of the pile. She made a mental note to tell Martin about the recovered mail when she served his lunch. That done, she attacked the room with gusto.

When she finished dusting, polishing and vacuuming, Millicent stood back to survey her work.

"There we go! It fairly sparkles!" With a satisfied

sigh, she aimed her portly frame toward the kitchen.

"Time to prepare lunch," she stated matter of factly, but in the hustle and bustle of fixing sandwiches, tidying up the kitchen and preparing treats for their oncoming visitors, Millicent forgot to tell Martin about the thick manila envelope that she had found in the den.

**

Chapter 63

*E*vie flung Martin Bascomb's front door wide open and ran to give her brother a welcoming hug. She also gave Jerry a friendly hello and graciously welcomed the boys who hovered like big, friendly puppy dogs at the sight of her. There was no mistaking the fiery challenge in her eyes, though, when she gave Brick Little a curt nod and her most judgmental glare.

Boy, I remember that look! John thought. He had learned long ago to avoid his sister's wrath. A polite cough lured his eyes toward the elderly man on the steps. *That must be the highfalutin botanist. From that shrewd grin, I think he's got those two figured out, too.*

Evie stopped glaring at Brick long enough to make the introductions. "This is Doctor Martin Bascomb. Dr. B., this is my brother, John."

John opened his mouth to speak, but Evie continued the introductions, then said, "Come on in, you guys. We figured you'd be hungry, so we fixed some sandwiches. And Millicent made a couple scrumptious strawberry rhubarb pies, too. Hope you like them!" She turned toward her brother. "I know *you* will—just save some for the rest of us, okay?"

John produced his most angelic smile.

Tommy exclaimed, "Awesome! Are you really John's sister? Do you really do scientific stuff with plants? That's really neat."

"Yes, really!" Evie was charmed by Tommy's unfettered excitement. "Actually I haven't done much research yet." She raised one perfectly arched brow toward her mentor. "I've been learning the ropes down in the shop. But if you're *really* interested, I'd love to show you around." The brow wriggled toward Martin once again. "That is, if Dr. B. says it's okay."

Martin smiled warmly. "Certainly, Evie. I'm always glad to encourage interest in our work. Perhaps we have a soul-mate here in Mr.—now what is your name again, son? I'm sorry, it must be my age. I simply don't remember names anymore."

"Heck, Sir. I don't remember names too good myself. I'm Tommy Sykes."

"Well, Tommy Sykes, you may call me Dr. B. I've been playing with plant life for fifty years and I must admit that I'm rather proud of my work. I'll be delighted to have Evie show you around."

Martin turned toward his morose guest.

"Welcome back, Mr. Little. I can't say that I'm happy about the circumstances that have brought us together, but I'll do what I can."

"What circumstances, Dr. B.? And, now that you're all here, I want to know what's going on." Evie demanded, "Who the heck *are* you, Brickford Little, and how did you meet my brother?" Then she turned an accusing eye toward John, "And why are you traveling with a dangerous man like him?"

BRICK HAD HEARD ENOUGH. "I am not *dangerous!*"

"Yes you are . . . you, you . . . *lunatic!* You almost ran me down! Don't you know any better than to go speeding down a winding driveway like that?"

"And don't *you* know enough to stay out of the road? That's pretty reckless if you ask me." Brick's eyes blazed with emotion—from the sting of her accusations and from the reminder of the fright he had experienced during their harrowing encounter.

"For your information, it's not a *thoroughfare*," she roared. "It's a *private driveway* which is rarely driven on, except for the inhabitants, of which I-am-now-one."

"That doesn't excuse your recklessness. For God's sake, I could have los . . . " He faltered. ". . . I could have run you down!"

Embarrassed by the slip, Brick turned away.

Everyone watched the heated exchange with awkward fascination until Brick glared at the boys. "Come on you guys—let's get the luggage."

Sam and Fingers exchanged amused shrugs and agreed to help.

Brick stormed toward the car, his chest heaving as he plunged his key into the trunk lock.

Surprised by the heated exchange between Brick and Evie, Jerry pumped his host's hand a little too heartily. "Well, Dr. Bascomb, I've heard a lot of wonderful things about you. Brick and I have been friends for years. Actually, we're old college buddies." He finally released Martin's hand before adding, "This is an awful mess, and I'm sure glad we've got someone with your credentials on our side. I just hope it's not too late."

"NOT TOO LATE FOR WHAT? For crying out loud, will someone *please* tell me what is going on? What "awful mess" are you talking about? John, what have you gotten yourself into? Or more appropriately, what has *he* gotten you all into?" Evie glared at her brother, then at Brick who was approaching with the luggage.

"Evie. Evie. You can't blame Brick for this—he's one of the good guys. Believe me, this isn't his fault. He stumbled into a real nightmare, and we're all here to try to figure out what to do. I'm talking about murder, kidnapping, conspiracy; and powerful people who will do just about anything to anyone to get what they want." He turned toward his host. "Dr. Bascomb, haven't you told her anything?"

Before Martin could speak, Evie parried, "No he

hasn't. But he's been a nervous wreck ever since *his visit*." Her stormy eyes shifted back toward Brick and her voice faltered, ". . . and Dr. B. hasn't slept well, either."

Martin squeezed Evie's shoulders and admitted that he had not explained anything. He noticed Brick's gloomy shrug. "As I told you before, Brick, there are only a few who would be capable of the scientific end of this. I already suspected it was Julia—and your call quite well confirmed it. Now the question is, how can we check on her and see how far along she is. I still can't believe it of her—but they say you never truly know anyone . . ." Martin's voice faded, but he shook off the sadness and continued. "However, fellows—and my most gracious young lady—why don't we enjoy Millicent's delectable repast right now. Then we can compare notes and inform Evie of the entire devious plot?"

John gushed with relief. "Thank God! I was beginning to think I'd have to devise my own devious plot to get some of that pie!" Laughter broke the awkward spell as Martin led the way to the kitchen.

EVIE WATCHED WITH AMUSEMENT as the boys virtually inhaled their sandwiches. She was glad that, despite their rough exteriors, they were pleasant and even waited, albeit somewhat anxiously, for the others to finish. She could not say the same for her brother. He was the first to reach for the pies. *Some things never change,* she thought.

MARTIN WATCHED with amusement when John wolfed down his second slice of pie, but when he turned toward Brick, his eyes and voice were somber.

"Well, Brick, since you were apparently the first one to stumble onto all of this, let's start with your story. Then I'll tell you what I have found. But first—let's move to the parlor. It's more comfortable."

BRICK PERCHED on the edge of a leather settee and glanced at Evie. She had snugged herself into an overstuffed chair. *Like a kitten,* he thought. But as their eyes met he changed his mind. *No. More like a tiger, ready to defend her cubs . . . against me, dammit.* He reluctantly turned his gaze toward Martin.

"Thank you. Well, for me it all started four days ago. I was working on a special project in my office building—I'm a regional manager. I oversee dry, packaged goods at the Food and Drug Administration—when I overheard one of my colleagues, Bob Jette, in the next room. Bob was on the farm crop end . . . you know, soy, corn, wheat, that sort of thing. He was very upset—yelling, actually—about a conspiracy involving biotechnology. He was making some pretty incredible accusations.

"I didn't get a chance to see who he was with in that room, but I *do* believe the person had to also be associated with the FDA." Brick's voice deepened. ". . . but I did see two other guys and I'd bet my mothers' son that one of them was a well paid henchman. I saw him pretend to shoot Bob in the back."

Brick's eyes glazed. The memory sent a chill right through him. "I called Bob later that morning. Wanted to warn him. When he answered, I could tell that he was still upset. He didn't even ask me why I called, but he suggested that we meet that same afternoon." He stopped, immersed in his memories.

PAIN FLASHED ACROSS Brick's face. "I saw him get shot down on the steps of the Miller. He was on his way to see me." His voice cracked with emotion. "I was slouched in my rental car, waiting to see if he was being followed." His eyes scoured the room for reactions before he exclaimed, "My God, I figured they'd be a ruthless bunch, but I am *so* sorry—I just *didn't* see it coming! As soon as the gun fired all hell broke loose, and I *couldn't move.*"

EVIE COULD SEE HIS HORROR. She was over-whelmed by the desire to lay a comforting hand on his shoulder, to reassure him, but she knew that he did not want sympathy. Instead, she clasped white-knuckled hands around

216

one knee and waited for him to resume his story.

"BUT I DID SEE THE SHOOTER—he was in a car with two teen age boys. I could see that they were frightened, but then the car sped off and apparently crashed soon later, killing both of them. Everyone wrote it off as reckless driving and those poor boys were identified as the killers." He gave Tommy and his friends a sympathetic nod. "But, I think the killer was one of the men I saw at the Miller that morning.

"I thought I was the only one to see the guy in the back seat with the boys. None of the witnesses who stepped forward mentioned him—so the police took the easy way out—assuming the boys had taken on a dare to shoot someone in order to get into a gang."

Brick's voice dropped to an angry growl. "I know they were scared. I know they had no choice." He punched the arm of his seat in a feeble attempt to ease his anger. "I don't know how extensive their power is, but if these people could infiltrate the FDA, it stands to reason they could have moles in the police department, too . . . so I didn't come forward . . . ."

Brick peered at Martin. And then at Evie. His voice became hushed, incredulous. ". . . and now we know they even have help within the military."

Martin's eyes widened but his voice remained small. "Good Lord in Heaven."

"Well, I didn't know it at the time, but Bob had given me one clue on the telephone. He mentioned a video. It was actually Jerry who figured it out. Anyway, Jerry and I decided to get our hands on it and *that's* where these other guys got involved."

JOHN DECIDED IT WAS TIME to add his own spirited rendition. "I was in DC, researching the Civil War for some clients when the next thing I know I'm meeting Brick and Jerry and they're inviting me to see a *Snow White* movie."

Evie's brows wriggled skeptically. "*Snow White?*"

Brick jumped at the chance to talk to her. "Yes. *Snow White*. Well, as it turned out, it was a surveillance tape of a meeting. They were talking about a botanist." He turned apologetically toward his host. "Her name is Julia. They said that her work to isolate the growth genes of weeds was successful. *Too* successful, though, because instead of using her research on *weeds*, they hatched the scheme to stunt the growth of their competitors' *crops*."

When he saw the pained expression on Martin's face, Brick added kindly, "If it's any consolation, Dr. Bascomb, I'm sure she never suspected what they were capable of." He turned toward Evie. "Obviously you know about hybrids. Well, this bunch already has much of the control of the hybrid seed market, and now we know they intend to stunt the major competitive agricultural crops in the country. They might even create a shortage of seeds, and by that time, the non-hybrids will be pretty much under their control, too.

"Then these guys—who have also been getting control of *distribution* by buying up the major supermarkets—will have control over food *production*, too. Just think of the power they'd be able to wield over us—not to mention the billions and billions of dollars they'll be able to reap if potatoes, which now cost about four dollars for a five-pound bag suddenly cost five dollars . . . or six or ten dollars, even. And corn now costs about eighty cents a can. Just think if it suddenly costs two dollars? And with the terminator, they'll be able to wipe out all their competitors. Think of the deprivation. Who's going to be able to afford those prices? In the process, they just get richer and more powerful."

"Their arrogance is shocking!"

Brick gave Martin a knowing look. "Thank God for that. In the video, they explain how they intend to transmit the terminator. They're going to use contrails. You know, those trails of smoke we see in the wake of airplanes? One of the men in the video said he had a way to do it, using the military. After all, since the President has waged his war on terrorism, no one will ever question the presence of military aircraft. All these monkeys have to do is control the flight schedules—then they'll be able to target any area they want."

"The military? I don't believe it!" Evie exclaimed. "How could they control the military?"

"Well, they don't have to control the military, per se. Just some of the tools 'n resources, like airplanes and fuel. They already own several pharmaceutical companies. Is it so hard to figure that they could own fuel companies, too? Or the plants that build aircraft? Is it that hard to accept that they might have their own manpower in these places?"

Evie relented. "I guess you're right. But that would take an incredible amount of money—not to mention power."

"Yes. And we don't know yet who's the anchor within that power chain. They were smart enough not to mention any names. They kept referring to someone as, "the old man." And you can bet your boots we'll be doing some digging to try to see if any names pop up. We can start with SanFidel. That's the chemical conglomerate that *was* mentioned."

"SanFidel? That makes sense. They *are* on the cutting edge of GMO's—both plant and animal related. And they control a large portion of the seed market *and* they create pesticides as well. The "old man" you heard them talk about would be Alexander Rossweild. I would not be surprised to find that he is behind all of this. He certainly has enough power and wealth, and I've never trusted him." Martin's eyes blazed with anger. "My word. As surreal as this all seems to be, it actually is beginning to make sense . . . with no one being the wiser, until now."

Martin raised his brows and leaned toward Brick. "And it all, I am sure, started out so innocently, with unsuspecting scientists like Julia. But everything is going down a central path, you know. Seed companies have been bought up by chemical companies. The number of independent suppliers continues to dwindle as the buyers snowball into mega corporations. To think they're using the study of botany as a weapon! My own field. My own colleagues! There are many things we've been looking into, but it was supposed to *help* mankind—not *enslave* us!

"We've been working on those growth regulators for some time now. Terminator technology they call it. But it was developed to be useful. In orchards, it may help to stem the growth of grass—for less mowing and fewer expenses! But think of the devastation of this technology if it got into the wrong hands. Think of an entire crop of corn that refuses to grow to its maturity!" Martin's tirade came to an abrupt end but his chest continued to heave with the momentum of his fury. When he stopped to clear his throat, Evie sensed a lecture coming on and snuggled deeper into her chair.

"ON THE CELLULAR LEVEL so much has been done. Plant breeders have made major contributions— increasing the yields of crops and diminishing their susceptibility to hazards that limit their productivity. Why with corn alone, it has been estimated that the annual production in the United States has been increased by 750,000,000 Bu's (that's 26 by 16 to the sixth m third)"

When Martin saw the puzzled looks, he exclaimed, "Oh, if I only had my flip chart out, I could demonstrate."

John rendered his own interpretation. "I think it translates to, 'a hell of a lot of corn.' Am I right Dr. Bascomb?"

". . . Err, yes. Multiply them out and the sums are staggering. And we've helped in Western Europe as well. The yields of wheat and barley have been increased by approximately 1% per annum since the late 1940s. I myself have been working on developing the ability to restore pollen fertility with so-called restorer lines. Perhaps the restorer line is the way to go to undue some of this. It's fascinating work!" Martin's eyes glazed as he thought about it, but the polite clearing of throats brought him back from his self-induced trance.

"I'm sorry. I do go on sometimes." He stood up and stared at the roses in the side yard. Without addressing anyone in particular, he asked, "So, now, what do we do?"

John offered a suggestion. "Well, for starters, I got a lead about a place called Domino something. I'm expecting a phone call anytime now that might shed some light on the situation. It might even be where they're holding C.D.—if they really did get their hands on him." To himself John thought, *I hope Manny calls soon—real soon.*

Martin's head bobbed with approval. "I'm afraid we'll all have to do our part to outfox these devils. In the meantime, I suggest that we try to get a good night's rest. Perhaps tomorrow we can come up with a plan." He stretched his legs and his knees cracked noisily. "But before we head upstairs, is anyone ready for more pie?"

Evie jumped up, ready to fetch a tray. Tommy and Brick both catapulted off their seats with offers to help, but much to Brick's chagrin, she took Tommy's arm, flashed him a big smile and said, "I'd love your help." Then she announced to the others, "Tommy and I will be right back with the goods." When they left the room, Brick said in a gruff voice, "By the way you guys, we have to assume that we are being watched, even if there is no sign of it. There could be eyes peering over any ridge, or ears parked behind any corner. We have to act as though we are marked men— and woman." On the last word, he glanced wistfully toward the door.

John put a hand on his shoulder. "Don't worry Brick . . . she likes you. A brother knows these things."

"Am I that obvious?"

Rob, Fingers, Sam, Jerry, and Martin all chorused John's one word response. "Yes," they said, and snickered at his red-faced groan.

***

Chapter 64

A pasty robot . . . with a tick!

Perry Jordan would have preferred to be in his gleaming office at SanFidel. Instead he was a quarter mile underground in a damp, botanic environment with a scrawny plant freak who probably had not seen the light of day for the past six months, *and* who probably did not even care. But Perry wanted to see the results of the terminator experiment for himself; so here he was, standing in front of rows and rows of potted plants at the Dixonville Laboratory.

As a group, all of the specimens appeared to be perfectly healthy seedlings at various stages of growth. In each row, half of the plants were tagged with red labels, the other half, blue. The tall plants with the blue tags looked as though they were at least a month or more ahead of the others. However, the shorter plants had been sewn at the same time but had received applications of the terminator formula.

"So, Lawrence. They still look healthy."

"Yessir. They've remained sturdy, with bright green foliage and strong roots."

Perry noticed that as he spoke, the pale young man dipped his head with a mechanical movement that left the collar of his turtleneck permanently misshapen. *Good grief,* he thought, *he's like a pasty robot with a tick.*

Lawrence continued talking and dipping. "They present all of the characteristics of healthy, disease-free plant life. We've monitored them very closely. Do you see the stunted ones on the bottom shelf? They've passed their maturity date, yet, no one could ever guess there is anything wrong—until it's too late." He dipped extra deep for emphasis.

"Perfect. Lawrence, you're a genius." Perry watched with little emotion as the botanist basked happily in the light of praise. "And how about the samples from the fields near the airports?"

"Well, Mr. Jordan. If you'll come this way, I'll show you." Lawrence dipped through a narrow doorway. "It's too soon, of course, to see anything with the naked eye," dip, "but under the microscope, well, it's conclusive. The growth regulator has been shut off. Terminated!" Dip, dip.

"Miss Mahoney's theory can be applied to any genus, and with my formula it retains its effectiveness even when it's disbursed into jet fuel." He led the way up a narrow staircase, into the sterile laboratory. "Would you like to see for yourself?" Lawrence dipped toward one of the microscopes.

"No, thanks. I'll take your word for it."

LAWRENCE WAS TRULY DISMAYED. He had hoped to have more time to impress Mr. Jordan with his vast knowledge of the subject. But the curt response was a signal that the interview was ending. He thought, *perhaps I won't be interested, either, after my vacation.* He was scheduled to take a break the next day. He wondered if there were any laboratories in the Bahamas.

"Thank you, Sir. I'm glad you are pleased." He remained in low dip as the powerful man left the room.

***

Chapter 65

The Tin Man

*P*erkins looked down from the cockpit of The Tin Man. He thought, *Boy, it's good to be back in the air.* He glanced appreciatively at the interior of his plane, loving every dial, switch, clamp, and lever. With its 150-horsepower piston engine, the four-seat Cessna was reputed to be the Honda Civic of the air. *You're one good little shuttle,* he reflected, before returning his gaze to the panoramic scene below.

It was a cloudless day and Perkins had a clear view of the snakelike rivers that cut through the lush forests and rich green farmlands, which, from 5,000 feet, looked like lumpy, velveteen pillows. Roads, from four-lane highways, to narrow, string-like country trails, stretched across the terrain, sometimes crossing rivers, sometimes winding their way alongside them. But his momentary preoccupation with the scenery and the thrill of flying did not take his mind off the purpose of this flight for long. Perkins was on his way to Alaska to see his old friend, Manny, and to get his help.

THOUGHTS OF MANNY brought Perkins back through time, to his first days at the Research and Development Division of the Office of Strategic Service. The history of the OSS was colorful and could be traced back to the establishment of the American Academy of Sciences, commissioned by President Abraham Lincoln, during the Civil War to, "establish a partnership between scientists and the military."

The project changed names and focus throughout the years that followed Lincoln's initial directive. Limited funding and varying degrees of presidential support forced the programs to come and go with sporadic operations until the 1940's, when the National Defense Research Committee (NDRC) was formed. At that time President Roosevelt arranged for a branch in London. They flourished throughout the war, then quietly gained prestige and momentum through the decades of the cold war years.

Perkins had been proud to become a part of the current Division of Research and Development. Everyone called it R&D. Right from the start he was stationed under Major General H. Edward Carrey and had wasted no time in his efforts to earn the man's respect. Harry trusted Perkins to lead many of his special missions. *Lead? That's a laugh,* he grumbled good naturedly. *Most of the time I'm the whole mission.* And he had been working alone on this assignment, too. But he'd decided that SanFidel was too big. Its outreach, too encompassing. And now he did not dare even to contact Harry, so he'd decided to enlist the aid of an old friend—a guy who was truly out of the loop—his old buddy, Manny, who now lived in Alaska, of all places. *Well, he's certainly out of the loop up there,* Perkins thought. He decided that he'd rather take a good old-fashioned communist plot or a military coup over this, any day.

Perkins realized that the two biggest threats to American citizens were, their own lethargy and the greed of unethical politicians and the businessmen who paid them. *Not all of them, for sure, but all it takes is one bad apple.* After witnessing the secret meeting, Perkins decided that SanFidel was definitely the most rotten of them all.

As it bucked and trembled in a patch of turbulence, the Cessna forced Perkins to focus on his flying. He gripped the throttle with a steady hand to guide the craft through the gusty sky. It did not last long, however, and his thoughts returned to their own journey through time. Memories of his special missions, some pleasant, some not, occupied most of his thoughts throughout the remainder of the flight.

BEEP. BEEP. The honing device that Harry's flight team had developed worked like a charm. He had just entered the air space of the city's landing strip. Perkins reported his position to the local unicorn and asked for clearance to land. When he received the go ahead, he circled once, then eased The Tin Man into its final descent.

MANNY WATCHED AS Perkins taxied onto a designated parking area. He thought, *I don't know how anyone can stand to fly a little bucket of bolts like that.* He called out, "Hi there!" and was rewarded with a salute.

Perkins climbed out of the cockpit and stretched. Bouncing from leg to leg, he admitted ". . . Not as young as I used to be—muscles seem to get tighter every year."

"Yeah, I know what you mean." Manny waited as Perkins retrieved his overnight bag. "Good to see you, Perk. Been too long. What *has* it been? Two, three years?"

"Too long, for sure."

"So—tell me about Scott. How's he doin'?"

"Married to his whisky. I give him credit, though. He hung in there and nursed me back to health." Perkins gave a sketchy account of his escape from guard duty at Domino One. He also described the video that he had taken at SanFidel.

Manny whistled. "Sounds like you've hit the tip of an ice berg. A big one at that!"

"Yeah. A really big one."

Manny could see that Perkins was tired and hungry. "Why don't we get on our way? We can stop for something to eat on the way to my apartment if you want. LeRoy's Little Biscuits is just ten minutes from here." When Scott agreed, Manny suggested, ". . . Tell you what. I'll wait in my truck—it's the red Comanche over there—while you arrange to park that bird of yours.

Perkins agreed and picked up his bag.

"Here, make yourself useful." He shoved it into Manny's arms without waiting for a reply.

With a sardonic grin, Manny swung the leather strap over his shoulder. He thought, *He hasn't changed much—still thinks I'm his freaking pack mule.*

AT THE RESTAURANT, Perkins devoured a heaping plate of Hungarian goulash. "You were hungry all right. By the way, I saw you eyeballing that chocolate cake over there." Manny gestured toward the glassed-in display. "Forget it. LeRoy's cakes look good, but they're about as tasty as a cardboard carton."

"That's okay. I'm stuffed anyway." Perkins stopped to mop up the last bit of tomato with a crusty roll. "So, you mentioned something about missing people and genetically altered foods? I'm not surprised—they talked about the same stuff at that meeting I taped. Maybe there's a link there—between SanFidel and your missing people." Perkins shoved at his plate and took a sip of his coffee before continuing.

"Well, guess what? I'm pretty sure I saw C.D. at Domino. If they could get at *him* without anybody noticing, God only knows how far they've gone. That's why I can't risk calling anybody. Like I said, I can't even reach *Harry* now. So, why don't you tell me what *you* know?"

"Well, I think you're right—there has to be a connection. Too many coincidences. By the way, a meeting has been set up for tonight. Same group I was talking about. Want to go?"

"Yeah. I think we should." Perkins reached for his wallet.

"When does it start?"

"Seven thirty. C'mon—we can drop your bags at my place first. It's right on the way."

***

227

Chapter 66

"We've gotta get that map!"

Perkins and Manny arrived at the meeting room early, hoping to get seats in the back where they could observe everyone who entered. The empty meeting hall was dimly lit much to Perkins' delight. He took a seat next to Manny. Moments later, two men appeared on the stage.

"SO RICARDO. WHAT'S THIS about the old man's party?"

"He's throwing a gala event to celebrate a victory with the GoMO bill. All the top people from SanFidel will be there. And senators, too. A real big deal. Black tie!"

"So how come I wasn't invited?"

Ricardo reminded his companion, "I have a very important position with the FDA and as such I've had to deal directly with people from SanFidel. Top people. And I've also been doing some work directly for Mr. Rossweild."

"Hah! I'll bet you do real *special* jobs, too, like kidnappin 'n stuff. Arranged any hits yet?"

"Don't even say such a thing! I don't go that far. He's a powerful man, you know. He has a lot of things that need to be done quietly. It's as simple as that. And that's why I'm here today: I have a special job for you and your crew."

"It's about time. My guys've been champing at the bit, waitin' for some work. We wasn't too happy when Mitchem took off. He promised us some good money."

"Well. I'm here to see that you get it. We want extra

228

men stationed at Domino and at the factory." He hoisted his briefcase onto the table and gave it a pat. "I have a map that shows the two locations and the details of our plan."

Ricardo's companion checked his watch. "Okay, whatever. So, we still got a few minutes before the meetin' starts. Let's go outside for a smoke before the people get here. You c'n give me the details later.

PERKINS STARED AT MANNY. He whispered, "Talk about luck! He left his briefcase on the table. We've gotta get that map!"

Manny whispered, "Why don't I go out back and strike up a conversation with our mouthy friends. I can keep 'em occupied while you check it out—then I think we'd better arrange to crash that party."

They scurried soundlessly to the front of the room. Manny looked at the cheap leather case and whispered, "What if it's locked?"

Perkins grinned and fluttered his fingers. "No problem."

"I should have known. Well, I'll start whistling Dixie if I think our friends are headed back too soon."

"Okay. Sure." Perkins was already inspecting the lock. In no time he was rifling through the contents. *Hmm. It's gotta be here somewhere.* The map was spread out on the bottom of the case, underneath a loosely fastened divider. He realized the factory they mentioned was the same where he had met Mitchem. A quick perusal showed nothing else of obvious importance, so he grabbed the map and snapped the case shut, then sauntered back to his seat.

MOMENTS LATER, six people entered the room and settled themselves near the front row. Manny returned in the company of the two men as a second group arrived. By the time he made his way to his seat next to Perkins, the room was nearly full. He said, "They told me what's on the agenda for tonight. I don't think it's worth staying for, so why don't we make a quiet exit before they realize the map's missing? From that smug look on your face, I figure you got it."

"Yup."

A noisy group entered the room, providing the perfect opportunity to slip away.

PERKINS SUGGESTED THAT their first job should be to get the map to John and his friends. "Since those guys are connected to Dr. Bascomb, I think that's our best bet. He's highly respected in his field." He confided, "I don't want to let this thing out of our sight—we should bring it ourselves. Can you come?"

Manny nodded.

"Good."

Perkins pointed toward a circle that someone had drawn on the map. "I know this place. This is the factory where I met that weasel Mitchem and this is Domino—practically in Scott's back yard, as the crow flies." He thought dryly, *but I wasn't a crow when I made that trip.* The memory of his exhausting escape through the hilly terrain and swampy wetlands made him wince. It was a treacherous journey for an injured man.

Manny tipped his chair back and took a sip of beer. "Arrogant creatures, aren't they Perk?"

"Yup, but that's good." He nodded with confidence. "Arrogance breeds sloppiness."

"SO PERK, HOW ABOUT a thermos of coffee? I don't want you falling asleep at the wheel in that bucket of bolts."

"Hey—airplanes don't have steering wheels. And The Tin Man isn't a bucket of bolts!"

While Manny busied himself with the coffee, Perkins pulled out his charts and found a small airport in Williamstown, Massachusetts. He figured it was fairly close to Dr. Bascomb's residence, *as the crow flies—or the Tin Man—that is!*

***

230

Chapter 67

*P*erry Jordan gave his final instructions before ordering one of his men to drive Tom Monroe back to Washington. "Make sure you keep an eye on him all the time—I wanna know if he sneezes. Got that?"

"Yeah. We got it. He ain't gonna go nowhere without a tail. You c'n count on it."

"OK, then. He's all yours. But remember—no rough stuff unless it's absolutely necessary. We need him at his best at Rossweild's shindig. Got that?"

"Yeah. We got it."

TOM'S MIND RACED as fast as the car, but Perry Jordan's chilling coercion dominated his thoughts. Mile after mile of changing countryside went unnoticed by the reluctant passenger as his mind continued its own relentless pursuit, until he lurched from a sudden slowdown. The driver was making a right-hand turn.

Tom thought, *So, we're finally getting off the blasted highway. Should be in downtown Washington soon.* He blinked, finally aware of the scenery. The buildings seemed to sway like amorphous blocks of jello with the abrupt change in speed and his mind grabbed the blurry image and spun toward a new direction.

Hmm. The power of speed . . . it can change your

perception of things. Why can't I just harness the power of speed to fight these devils? He jammed his fist into the armrest and asked himself, *Why do I have to feel so powerless? Hmm, power. That's one of the terms that motivational guru uses. What's his name? Tony something. Yes, Tony Robbins. Always carrying on about asking questions—the right questions—then taking action to empower yourself.* Tom realized he had been asking negative questions. *Definitely the wrong ones. According to Robbins that'll just bring negative answers.* His outlook brightened. *I've gotta ask 'how can I' instead of 'why can't I'. It's a long shot, but what the hell? I'll give it a try. Heck, if this works, I'll tell Robbins about it. Heck, I feel better already.* He settled back in his seat and focused on positive thoughts for the rest of the trip. He smiled at the first positive image that flooded his brain—the image of Perry Jordan behind bars.

TOM WAS GLAD THAT Perry's men did not follow him into his townhouse, but he still did not feel safe. *It's like someone was in here.* He looked around. *I can feel it.* He decided that someone probably had been there, and they probably bugged the place. He peered through the front blinds, not surprised to see the car still hugging the curb. He knew they'd watch him. Even if the car eventually disappeared, they'd be out there somewhere. *They'll be watching all right.* He looked at his telephone. *And listening.*

The living room with its russet draperies, plush velveteen sofa and chunky end tables no longer held its cozy appeal. 'The harvest effect,' Tom's decorator had gushed. The rusty, bronzy, lemony colors of fall were, "Colors of comfort . . . " she said, ". . . reminiscent of the fall harvest." But now it just seemed cold and abandoned, as if he had been gone for weeks. *Just my nerves,* he decided, but he could not shake the uneasy feeling.

Tom decided he was exhausted. Too tired even, to search for bugs. *No point in removing them, anyhow,* he mused. *Jordan's men wouldn't like it.*

The blinking light on his answering machine finally

caught his attention. He removed the tape and stuck it in his pocket. *Maybe there's something important here. Maybe even a message that came before all this began.* If that was the case, he was not about to give Perry's goons a chance to hear it.

"Darn! I guess I can't risk going anywhere or talking to anyone." He kicked off his shoes and marched into his bedroom. He had to get some sleep.

"YOU GUESSED THAT RIGHT, MONROE." Damo leaned back in his seat and muttered, "This'll be another boring night. I'm gettin' sick of babysittin' these chumps." Damo thought that Perry Jordan was wasting his talent with the surveillance jobs. He preferred action. He turned on the radio and settled in to listen to his favorite talk show host. "I hope he doesn't get another stupid shrink on." As he waited for the show to start, Damo thought about the conk on the head he got at that shrink Johnson's house. *I'm gonna keep my eyes on that place, too. Maybe they'll get stupid and go back home.*

***

Chapter 68

Evie slipped out the back door.

The sun was almost due to make its appearance, but Evie was still tossing and turning. Last night's revelations had been too much for her nerves. *Now I know why Dr. B. has been so distracted,* she thought. Giving up all hope of sleep, she shrugged into her favorite robe and gathered the plush fabric around her slim waist with a determined tug. She peered into her bedroom mirror and raked her hair into place before tiptoeing down the stairs and heading toward the kitchen.

With a hot cup of tea in hand, Evie slipped out the back door and eased herself onto the swinging bench. The view was breathtaking. Mt. Greylock's stately profile was illuminated by a faint golden glow that foreshadowed the splendor of the rising sun.

As Evie sipped her tea she heard the raspy call of a crow that challenged the musical chirps and trills of the songbirds that she loved. She always enjoyed listening to the songbirds. Smaller and less powerful, they were not as brazen as the crows, but they would not be outdone. *Like me,* she thought.

As she reflected upon the bold maneuvers of the birds, Evie decided there were lots of human crows—noisy, ill-mannered, ready to steal from those whom they perceived as weak.

Something spooked the bawdy birds. They disappeared with a rush of fluttering wings and angry squawks. *I wish we could get rid of their human counterparts that easily,* she mused.

EVIE CONSUMED HER TEA with a purposeful gulp, as if to drink in the courage she knew would be needed in the days to come. *They may have a head start on us,* she thought, *but we're not outdone yet!* She prayed that she and her friends would prevail—*like the songbirds.* She swung her legs to the floor, ready to contribute her all to the fight; but she suddenly realized that she was not alone. Even before Brick Little stepped out of the shadows, she felt his eyes on her; and that familiar, unbidden heat stirred within.

Evie spoke first. Awkward. Contrite. "Looks like you're an early bird, too." Before she lost her courage, she turned toward him. "You've been through a lot, Brick. I'm truly sorry. I know I've been terribly rude . . . and, well, it's really not like me."

"It's okay. You had no way of knowing." Encouraged by her friendly tone, he looked down at the empty cushion. "May I?"

"Yes. Of course." Her heart beat irratically as he settled in beside her. She was glad she had finished her tea—she'd have spilled it for sure.

Brick flexed his long legs and gently pushed them into motion. They remained silent for a long time, lulled by the soothing, hypnotic rhythm of the swing.

He finally spoke. "Evie . . . when this is all over, do you think we could be friends?"

"Why, yes, I . . . I think I'd like that." *Talk about the understatement of the year!* Her heart raced even faster.

"Good. I . . . " His voice faltered. He did not know what more to say.

"I know."

Brick realized that her reply—a mere whisper—sealed an unspoken promise. He shifted closer, setting the swing into motion once again. The bulky chains squeaked softly and Evie nestled comfortably at his side. He lifted one hand and toyed with a stray lock of her hair. Just as he had

235

expected, it slid through his fingers. *Soft and silky.* With a little moan, he pulled her into the circle of his arms and placed soft kisses on her hair. Her forehead. Her chin. And then his lips brushed against hers, softly, gently, again and again, in synch with the rhythm of the swing, his urgent need gaining momentum with each movement. He drew her deeper into their kiss, then, unaware of the groan that rose from his throat.

Evie responded with her own rising passion, her soft whimper urging him to continue his pursuit. She felt breathless. But a primitive longing soon drove *her* to satisfy *his* need and she instinctively knew how to do it. Gently pulling away, she gazed into his eyes and dragged her fingers down his cheek, into the crevice of his neck and across the expanse of his wide shoulders. She felt his muscles ripple in response and she reveled in her newfound power.

The pursued had become the pursuer.

She kissed him again then, hungrily and deliberately, but her desperate fervency was abruptly shattered by a cacophony of laughter from within the kitchen. Her eyes fluttered open. Her desire dissolved and a wave of self-conscious awareness set in. She jumped to her feet and tucked her robe back into place. Desperate to regain her composure, Evie lurched toward the screen door. She looked back and whispered, "I'm sorry. I—I have to go," before bursting through it.

Crushed by the unexpected turn of events, Brick sprawled back in his seat. No longer soothing, the swinging bench jerked backwards with a cold, rusty clank.

IN THE KITCHEN, the boys were howling with mirth at the antics of one very creative chef at the grill. Jerry was entertaining his audience with his "amazing flapjack flipping." Evie had entered the room just in time to see a huge pancake hurtle within inches of the ceiling, only to drop ceremoniously onto his griddle, behind his back, no less.

The boys roared with laughter and encouraged John Victor who held his own spatula, microphone fashion. In his best announcer's voice he addressed them. "Thank you. Thank you, Lady and Gentlemen. You have just witnessed the incredible, the unstoppable Famous Freddie the Fearless Flapjack Flipper. Stay tuned for the Disappearing Flapjacks, Featuring the Fabulous Four Famished Friends."

Sam stomped his feet and howled while Tommy played the helpful servant, wiping away the tears of laughter that were streaming down his face.

The chuckles continued as Evie took on the role of interviewer. She picked up a wooden spoon and interviewed the chef. "Tell us, Famous Freddie—how on God's Good Earth did you become such an in-*fallible* flapjack flipper?"

After deftly flipping another one, Jerry spoke into her spoon. "Oh, my mother's favorite movie was *"Christmas in Connecticut."* Have you seen it? The one with Barbara Stanwick? She was a writer for a woman's magazine and was supposed to be this fabulous cook when really, she couldn't even boil an egg. Well, to make a long story short, she got put on the spot and had to flip a flapjack for her bossy publisher, so she closed her eyes and prayed. Well, it fell right onto her spatula." He leaned closer to the spoon. "I loved that scene. After that my sister and I started a flapjack flipping competition. And here I am today, Freddie the Fabulous Flapjack Flipper." With that brash statement, he hurled one into the air.

Sam fell to the floor, engulfed in his infectious laughter once more, and Jerry sheepishly promised to scrub the ceiling fixture.

***

Chapter 69

On the last leg of their flight to Massachusetts, Perkins gave Manny a nudge to wake him up. "Hey, guy, we're almost there . . . you should buckle up."

Manny rubbed his eyes and grumbled about bossy captains as he struggled to snug up his shoulder strap. "Why didn't you just let me sleep through this? You know how much I hate landings."

Perkins snickered, "I know. I'm still laughing since our stop in Chicago." He glanced at the wet stain on Manny's lap.

"I couldn't help it. They don't make Styrofoam the way they used to!" Manny winced at the memory of the jet that had roared over their heads. Startled by the sudden deafening sound, he had crushed his cup and spilled scalding hot coffee onto his lap.

"I told you to put that cup away."

"I thought it would help ease the tension."

"It did, Manny. It did. You can't be tense when you're laughing, and I definitely was laughing." He gave his friend a reassuring pat on the shoulder. "Okay, look. The sky is clear, there are no gargantuan jets in the neighborhood and we have a clean runway. We'll be down in two shakes. So go ahead and close your eyes until it's over." He beamed with pride and bragged, "The Tin Man hasn't failed me yet!"

True to his word, Perkins performed a flawless landing, but when the Cessna's engines hummed to a stop,

238

Manny still had to pry his fingers off the seat cushion. With a grunt of relief, he jumped to the ground and fumbled for his cell phone.

A LILTING FEMININE VOICE answered the third ring. "Bascomb residence, Evie Victor speaking."

"Hello. Evie—you're John Victor's sister, right? Can I speak to him, please? Tell him it's Manny."

"Sure thing, Manny. He's been expecting your call. Hold on." She waved to her brother. "Your friend, Manny's on the line!"

"Thanks Sis. Hey, Manny—what's up?"

"An old friend flew me down to Massachusetts and I'm pretty sure we're only a few miles away from you. Look John, we've got some information for you. Can you pick us up?"

"Sure! But what do you have?"

"I'll tell you all about it in the car. We're at a little air strip in Williamstown."

"Okay. Hold on for a minute, will ya?" John called to Evie, "Hey, Sis. Do you know where the airport is in Williamstown?"

"Sure, why?"

"Well, Manny and a friend of his just flew in. They want us to pick them up."

"It's about a fifteen or twenty-minute drive from here."

John spoke into the receiver. "Be there in half an hour or so." After he hung up Evie offered to get Brick.

EVIE FELT HER THROAT TIGHTEN when she entered the library where Brick and Tommy were playing a tense game of Sequence, by Jax, Ltd. Brick's eyes bore into hers for a split second and then returned to the game. She could see that a fierce competition was in progress, yet she could not help but feel rejected by his apparent disinterest. *I guess I deserve the cold shoulder after running out on him this morning,* she thought.

Martin looked up with kindly eyes. "Come watch the game, Evie." He gave an empty cushion a pat. "They're neck-and-neck in the final round with three wins each. We'll be declaring a champion any minute now."

"I'd love to, Dr. B., but I came to get Brick."

At the mention of his name, Brick's eyes bore into hers once more. "Yes?" he crooned. Craggy brows, raised in question, only seemed to enhance his masculine appeal.

The half-whispered question felt like a caress. Evie tried to speak. "I, umh . . . " Like a school girl in front of the handsome captain of the football team, she felt awkward, aware only of *him. Stop being such a dolt,* she chastised. *You're not a schoolgirl anymore.* Evie finally took a deep breath and declared, "Actually, John wants you to drive us to the airport. His friend Manny is there with someone—a Commander Perkins I think he said. Anyway, he said they have some important information for us."

Brick slammed his cards onto the table with a challenge for a rematch. ". . . but, I'm afraid it'll have to wait, sport," he said. "Looks like we've got some other action to concentrate on right now."

EVIE, JOHN AND BRICK crowded into the front of Martin's spotless Buick and she settled in close to Brick. She stared at the bluejeaned thigh that seemed to set her own on fire. No one spoke as the car hummed across ten miles of winding country road, but when the intersection came within sight, Evie's breathless voice broke the silence. "Okay. The town common is just a little farther. You have to bear right at the fork, John, but keep to the left lane when you get there. Then it'll be a sharp left onto 7 North and an almost immediate right onto 2 East, then the airport's a couple of miles or so past the village. Got it?"

"Got it! Right, right but left, then left, but right."

"Right."

"Right."

Brick laughed. "You two sound like that old comedy team, Stan and Olli. Do you always bandy about like that?"

"It's hard to stay serious when John's around. Everyone in our family calls him the walking laugh machine. Everyone except Aunt Glenna, of course."

John gave his sister a haughty stare. "That's enough out of you."

"Oh? And what *does* your Aunt call him?" Brick demanded.

"The family *scoundrel*."

Evie grinned wickedly. Her thigh, still pressed against Brick's muscular leg, burned even hotter as their eyes met.

John retorted with brotherly logic, "It's your word against mine, Sis. And you . . !" He glanced at Brick, "You shouldn't listen to slanderous gossip. After all, I did save your life, you know. That shouldda' bought *some* loyalty, I would think."

Evie sat up straight. "You *what*? You saved his life? When? Where? How?"

John let out a big sigh. "Me and my big mouth. Well, it wasn't much, actually. It was how we met. I guess we forgot that part of the story, huh Brick?"

"I guess we did."

Evie whirled an accusing eye from one to the other. "Yes you did. So tell me . . . what happened?"

Brick answered first. "Actually, one of the guys that bugged our telephone followed me and Jerry home and your brother followed him. It was right after he eavesdropped in the restaurant."

"Darned lucky for you I did eavesdrop."

"Yup. I can't argue that one."

"So what happened to him? Who was he? Where is he now? I take it you didn't call the police?"

John said, "Well, he was sort of napping when we left. I bet he was one angry dude with a vicious headache when he woke up, too."

"I get it. You clobbered him."

"Well, actually, I can't claim credit for the hit—Brick did it with a wrought iron dog. But I created the diversion."

He beamed across his sister's head. "That was good aiming, by the way."

"Thank you." Brick was ready to change the subject. "So. What do you think these two guys have for us anyway?"

"Beats me. But it must be damned important for them to fly it all the way here from Alaska."

"Yeah. That's what I was thinking."

Evie poked her brother. "We don't have much farther to go, John, the road to the airport is just ahead. Actually it's more like a long driveway. There it is—see it up on the right?"

"Yes—I see it."

Evie scooted closer to the dashboard. As the Buick ground its way across the pebbly lot and eased to a stop, she saw two figures stride forward. John put the car in park and jumped out to greet them.

"Hey, Manny. Good to see you."

"Hey, fella! This is my friend, Perkins."

"Hello." As he greeted the newcomer, John noticed that Brick and Evie had fallen behind. "Oh. Guys. This is my sister, Evie, and our friend, Brick Little. Brick and Evie, you heard Manny's introduction, right?"

"Yes. Hi guys," Evie reached for Manny's hand first. "Any friend of my brother's is a friend of mine." Brick nodded his welcome and sized them up.

Manny glanced at John. "I bet you're wondering why we flew here unannounced."

"A question or two did cross my mind," John quipped. "But look, why don't we get you guys back to the house, then you can tell us all at once."

***

242

Chapter 70

Brick was right.

---

*M*artin decided to occupy his time with his houseplants while he waited for Evie and the men to return. He hoped the information would be useful. *Why else would they fly all the way down from Alaska? Oh well,* he reasoned, *it's time to stop worrying.* He knew Millicent was on a campaign to improve his outlook—she had become relentless in her quest to cheer him up—checking in on him several times a day with offers of refreshments and assistance. *She must have opened and closed the drapes in my study at least three times yesterday morning alone,* he thought. *Perhaps if she sees that I'm busy with the house plants she'll ease up a little.*

As he watered the potted plants in the entryway, Martin thought back to the day that Brickford Little had come to him. "What do you think, Fancy? Would you like to have your growth stunted? I should say not . . . your oversized leaves are such a treat to behold! And I'll just bet you're ready for another long drink." He happily inspected the Fancyleaf caladium before sticking his finger gently into the soil. "I was right, you are thirsty. Here you go, little lady."

Martin turned around to admire the display next to the large window. "Brick was right—this is a pleasing sight." He squinted at the Velvetplant before exclaiming, "Oh, oh, I see Millicent has been at it again. I've tried to explain to her how you prefer to be next to the window, but she thinks your beautiful pot should be displayed in front." He could not resist touching the soft leaves that resembled thick velveteen cutouts as he returned the pot to its rightful position. "There you go, back home where you belong."

When he finished doting on his plants, Martin sauntered into the den—it was time to tackle the mail. As he looked at the stacks of envelopes, he admitted, "Millicent was right. It has been piling up." *Hmm. The best thing, I guess, is to separate these into four workable piles: Junk mail, reading material, bills, and personal.* He pulled himself tight to his desk and peered at the large manila envelope.

"Good Lord, this is from Julia!" He tore it open. A quick perusal confirmed that Julia had been working for SanFidel and she had decided to confide in him. He rushed to the doorway and called out. "Jerry! Millicent, everyone! Come quickly! I've heard from Julia!" The front door slammed and footsteps clattered toward him.

Martin addressed Evie, first. "Thank goodness you're back. Look! Look here! Julia Mahoney has sent me some of her research. She thinks her work is being misused." His eyes glowed with satisfaction. "I knew she was ethical—I just knew it!" But the light in his eyes quickly dimmed. He exclaimed, "I'm going to call her at once!" He reached for his Rolodex and fumbled for her number. While he listened to an endless string of rings, he looked at Brick.

"Julia discovered that her intern, Lawrence, has been working with combustibles. That could mean the fuel those men spoke of in your tape. And see here? She tells where the experiments are taking place. This must be what they were talking about on that video!"

Brick beamed. "Now that we know where they are doing their dirty work we'll be able to stop them!"

MANNY STEPPED FORWARD and introduced himself. "Dr. Bascomb—I'm Manny Atkinson and this is my friend Commander Perkins. We're sorry to intrude, but we just weren't sure where else to go. It looks like Julia's information will support what we've got."

"To start with—you're not intruding at all. Actually,

I have the feeling that we'll be needing your help." Without hesitation, Manny unfolded the map that brought him to New England.

John recognized the markings right away. "Hey guys! That's the map that we saw on Bob Jette's video!"

Perkins was surprised. "You saw my video? How the hell did you see it? Bob was supposed to get it straight to General Carrey!"

"So you're the one who sent it." Brick shot a quick glance toward Jerry and the wise psychologist nodded, urging him to break the news to the commander.

"So you don't know what happened." Brick closed his eyes and took a deep breath. "It was by pure chance that I, that is we . . ." He gestured toward the men and boys. ". . . we, umh, found the tape. We didn't know what to do with it or who to trust, but we knew we had to get out of Washington until we could sort it all out." He took a faltering breath before explaining, "Perkins, I'm sorry, but Bob Jette was murdered."

Perkins appeared to collapse into the nearest seat. "Damn." He shook his head slowly, looked up to ask, "Was it because of the tape?"

"Not exactly. Well . . ." Brick hesitated, searching for the right words to ease the man's conscience. ". . ..maybe. But I don't believe anyone else knows anything about the video. Even if they did, I doubt that they knew he had it. To the best of my knowledge, his home wasn't even searched. But I do think it caused him to confront one of his colleagues within the FDA. And I think *that's* what got him killed." His voice tapered to a raspy whisper. "I'm sorry."

"Damn." Perkins leaned back and rubbed his eyes. "Damn," he repeated. "Damn them."

THE BASCOMB RESIDENCE remained brightly lit deep into the night. After all of the stories were exchanged, it was clear that Perkins was a capable leader, so they urged him to develop a strategy.

"After all, Perkins, you don't know if you'll even be

able to find General Carrey. For all we know he's a guest at Domino now, too." John tried not to think the worst. "And we don't have much time. We think they're ready to use the terminator on a huge scale. And if they've actually taken Senator Monroe, they must have something up their sleeve regarding the GoMO bill. I really think we gotta act fast."

"I know you're right, but you're civilians!" Perkins waved his arm in a sweeping gesture toward the boys. " . . . And you guys—hell, you're just kids!"

Sam and Rob catapulted off their seats to protest, but Perkins barked, "Sit down!" They obeyed without a sound.

"Now, as I started to say, you guys are still wet behind the ears as far as I'm concerned." He held up his hand to ward off another objection, "But you're what I've got . . . and I can tell that at least you've got street smarts." He grinned despite his exasperation. "So I'm not gonna let you off the hook, either." The boys were elated. Sam gave Rob a hi-five.

"Look, guys—it's late. What is it Evie? Midnight?"

She looked at her watch. "It's 12:17, actually."

"Okay. So let's get some shut eye. I'm sure we can come up with a strategy first thing in the morning." He turned to Martin apologetically. "It looks like you've already got a full house, so . . ."

Martin raised his hand. "You won't be any trouble at all. There's still a spare room upstairs that just happens to have twin beds. And Millicent will be back in the kitchen tomorrow." He turned with a grin. "You'll love her cooking."

John chimed in, "Especially her pies. I bet she bakes more if we have two newcomers!"

Evie shook her finger at her brother. "We wouldn't *need* more if we didn't have a glutton like you around."

"Hey. I resemble that remark."

Ten voices chorused, "You sure do!"

Laughter rang through the front hall as Perkins and Manny followed their kindly host up the stairs. Their unlikely crew followed close behind.

FROM A DISTANT TREE TOP a curious owl blinked as he watched the lights switch off, one by one, in the Bascomb residence. He punctuated the ensuing silence with a series of distinctive hoots and waited for a response. None forthcoming, he spread his wings with owlish dignity and left his perch to glide across an open field in search of a tasty nocturnal snack.

TUCKED IN HER BED, Evie listened to the owl's hoots before drifting into a fitful sleep where giant feathered airplanes swooped down upon the land to scoop up acres and acres of corn crops with enormous steel talons.

***

Chapter 71

Here's a plan!

*P*erkins slept the deep sleep of a disciplined soldier until five a.m. Fully refreshed he dropped to the floor for his usual sixty pushups. He counted softly and effortlessly, pleased that he was back in shape. When he got to fifty, Manny sat up, still groggy from sleep.

"My God, man, are the birds even up yet?" Manny raked his wavy black hair with his finger tips, stretched, and softly joined the count. ". . . Fifty-eight, fifty-nine, sixty. There! We're done!"

Perkins rolled onto his back. "You wish—now it's time for a few sit ups. Wanna help count them, too?"

"No thanks, I'm exhausted." Manny jumped off the bed and reached for his pants. "I think I'll see if there's any other early birds in this house. Maybe I can rustle up some coffee while I'm at it."

WITHIN FIFTEEN MINUTES everyone was up. Millicent insisted they start with a hearty breakfast, and as she and Evie busied themselves with its preparation, Perkins set up a strategy session at the table. He taped the map to the wall and borrowed one of Martin's flip charts. On the first page he listed their major areas of concern.

"Okay, let's eat up. Then I'll tell you what I think we can do." He looked around then and noticed that John was not there. "Hey, Evie, where's your brother? Don't tell me he's a late sleeper?"

"Not a chance, Perkins. He's on the back porch. I think he's using the view."

Brick, who had been listening to the exchange, gave her an odd look. "Using the view?"

"It's his balance theory." Evie laughed. "Why don't you go out and tell him it's almost time to eat. You can ask him about his theory while you're at it." Her eyes smoldered mysteriously.

"Now I'm intrigued. I think I will."

JOHN WAS PERCHED on the steps, deep in thought.

"Sorry to intrude, but they sent me out to get you. Breakfast is almost ready." Brick took a moment to admire the view before speaking again. "This is quite the place, don't you think—with the mountain for a backdrop and all?" He took a deep breath. "And smell those flowers!"

The two men sat in companionable silence for a few minutes before Brick spoke again. "So, John . . . Evie said you were out here 'using the view' . . . something about a balance theory?"

Brick had finally won John's full attention. "It's just something I learned from an old prospector. You see, Alfie believed there's an almost mystical balance within nature, maybe even the Universe. He said all needs can be fulfilled when everything is in its place."

John's eyes returned to the view as he thought of his crusty old friend. "But if you disturb that balance, things can come undone." He stood up then, and stretched. "It's hard to explain. I just seem to see things a little more clearly when I'm outside. You know, there are so many people in the world today who paint everything black and white. No compromise at all, like for instance, the gun control fanatics." He looked up at Brick. "They mindlessly link all guns with the death of innocent people, but they've gone too far. They exaggerate, twist the facts to get people to see things their way. There's no balance!" He saw Brick's puzzled expression and struggled to continue his explanation.

"Look. We live in a physical, material world, right?"

"Okay, I'll give you that."

"Well, for every action there's a reaction: Up/down. Hot/cold. Fast/slow. You follow?"

"So, far, but . . . ."

"Well, between the two poles there's a lot of space. The temperature is a good example. You got *extreme* cold. Then there's *very* cold. And then *really* cold. And just *cold.* Then there's luke warm. Warmer. Hot. *Too* hot." John's words came faster as his thoughts gelled. "Let's say it's too cold. So, you take action! But you can go overboard and make it too hot, right?"

"You got that right. Take my Aunt Margie—she cranks up the thermostat until the rest of us are sweating bullets."

"Well, there you go, she goes too far." He looked at Brick. "See what I mean? No balance."

"Yeah. But how does that help us here?"

John looked contrite. "I'm still working on it."

"BUT YOU'RE RIGHT, John."

Both men jumped when Perkins appeared. His mouth slid into a friendly smirk. "Sorry—didn't mean to startle you."

He sat on one of the steps. "I think you're right on track, John. As soon as you spoke my wheels started to turn. Balance *is* what we need. And balance is what we'll get!"

Before John or Brick could ask how, the screen door swung open and Evie popped her head out to announce that breakfast was getting cold.

Perkins whispered mysteriously, "I'll tell you all about it after we eat."

***

250

Chapter 72

*P*erkins rallied his unlikely band of comrades together and said, "Now—here's what we got. The way I see it, we have four major problems." He pointed at the flip chart. "Number one—in Washington there's the GoMO and the legislative shenanigans." He circled Washington. "Number two and three are Domino One in Tennessee, and the factory and formula." His marker skated around Tennessee. "And finally, we've got Rossweild's party." Perkins took a deep breath.

"Look, people. We've got a tough fight on our hands but it's not hopeless—especially if we put John's balance theory to work.

Evie's eyes popped open. She gave her brother a high five. "Way to go, big bro!"

Perkins ignored the playful interruption. "So Brick, you've got a good head on your shoulders and you're more than capable of taking care of yourself. I think you gotta go back to Washington. Do some sniffing around—see what you can find. And Evie should go, too."

Evie gasped. "Me? Go to Washington? What can I possibly do in DC?"

Tiny crows feet framed the eyes that shifted her way. "I've been watching and listening. You've got a head full of knowledge, you're an expert in your field and you're working with one of the most respected men in the world of botany. So you can establish yourself with Senator Monroe's people and start lobbying—lobbying hard—against the GoMO." He spread his hands. "Get some balance back on our side."

Evie hoped she would be able to live up to his expectations.

"Yes, of course. I'll do whatever I can."

"Good then. It's settled. I'll fly you and Brick down to DC right away." He put a big check mark next to Washington.

"So okay, people, the next thing is to get John and Manny down to that factory. Manny—you still got what it takes with fireworks?"

"Yup: Like riding a bicycle. Besides, I've done a little bit of explosives for the fire team. Right John?"

Perkins did not wait for John's reply. "Good. So, I'll fly you guys down there."

Perkins soon had Jerry and Tommy established at "home base" to watch the shop and keep the lines of communication open. "This way, Jerry, you'll be able to stay in touch with your clients. I'm sure you'll want to do that—and you certainly can't go back to your home until we're sure it's safe."

"Thanks, Perkins. I really *do* need to get in touch with some of them, although my practice isn't what it used to be because of my grant project. But I can definitely work from here, if it's okay with Dr. Bascomb, that is."

Martin nodded agreeably. "Of course. Of course."

Perkins continued. "And Tommy—I'm counting on you to help out around here. You and Jerry can fill in while Dr. Bascomb and Evie are away."

"Sure! This place is awesome."

Perkins continued with his plan. "And now, Dr. Bascomb. Didn't you say that Rossweild had funded your work once? I'm thinking we should get you down to the mansion. I bet the egotistical sonofabitch would drool at the thought of having you at his little shindig."

"Of course! Wonderful! And I could see if I can find Julia! She wrote that she was going to meet with him."

Perkins was already focused on the next item on the chart and barely heard him. "That leaves the guys, here." He made eye contact with Rob, Sam and Fingers. "How about joining me for a little shoot out at the O.K. corral?"

"Right on, man!" Sam was ready for action.

"But first, you'll have to pass the CTP Boot Camp."

Sam demanded, "What the hell is that?"

"It's the Commander Timothy Perkins' Boot Camp for Civilians."

"What?" Their faces fell.

"Listen guys, I'm not trying to insult you. I'm sure you'll be able to help, but I won't have you with me until I can see what you can do." His eyes skated over Rob and Fingers and settled upon Sam.

"Look, it's not an insult—I've been in this business for ten years and General Carrey still stops to test *me* every now and then. I hope it won't come to it, but people's lives might be in your hands at some point. I have to know if there's any question about your fitness for duty—and I have to know now."

"Sure thing, man. Test us all you want—no sweat."

"Oh, you're gonna sweat, my friend. You're gonna sweat."

Sam peered at Fingers and Rob through thoughtful slits. He knew they were in good shape. *After all,* he thought, *we haf'ta cope with dealers and thugs all the time.* He tried to reassure himself. *Nuthin' could be worse than that.* But when he shifted his gaze toward the commander's face, he wondered, *Or could it?*

BY 8 AM, PERKINS WAS ready to transport Brick and Evie to Washington. He planned to return to the Berkshires to pick up John after he and Manny got supplies for their mission in Tennessee.

"Okay, guys. If you need me, call Dr. Bascomb's house but ask for Barry. For God's sake, don't use my real name, okay?" They both agreed. "Good! In the meantime, I'll be teaching our street urchins how to handle themselves."

"I think you've got some good soldier material there, Perkins. Especially Sam and Rob. After all, they've probably already had a lifetime of survival lessons on the streets of DC."

"Yes I know. Well, I'll turn them into fighting men, instead of oversized juvenile delinquents." Perkins busied himself with the gauges on his instrument panel. Satisfied with the levels, he eased forward.

The Tin Man taxied onto the tarmac and Perkins spoke again as if there had been no break in the conversation. "I'm not sure about the kid with the dimples, though. He looked a little disappointed, but he's too young, and he's not as tough."

"Don't worry about Tommy," Brick replied. "He's attached himself to Dr. Bascomb, and I'm sure he'll be happily occupied. And I've noticed that Fingers will do just about anything for Sam. He's a lot brighter than he lets on."

"I noticed." Perkins focused on his take off procedures while his passengers settled in for the ride. He did not even have to look to know that Manny was clutching his seat. He did glance back at Evie who was staring out the window. *Boy,* he thought, *she's got it all. Guts, brains and looks. Just like Mac.* He suddenly missed Major Margaret Mary Mackenzie more than ever.

***

Chapter 73

*B*rick sprinted up the steps of Helen's office building with the ease of an athlete, but he forced himself to saunter through the corridors at a slower pace. He stopped to compliment a young aide on her new hairstyle and he congratulated a colleague on his recent successful presentation on environmentally correct packaging, but he sped past Stanley Mason's office. *That guy's always ready to give a dissertation on the pros and cons of anything! I can't deal with him today.*

Brick burst into Helen's suite of offices and asked the startled receptionist if she was available, then pushed through her inner door without waiting for a response.

"I'm sorry to intrude, Helen, but have you heard from the senator today?"

"Well, hello Brick. This is a surprise! I'm sorry, but Tom can't be reached at all today—you know how busy he can be this time of year." *I still don't want to let on that I'm concerned,* she thought. "Is there anything that *I* can do for you?" She leaned forward, urged him to sit down.

"Thanks, but no, Helen. I really need to see him in person." As he pulled up a seat, Brick put his finger to his lips and placed a slip of paper in front of her. She took his cue, read the note and nodded in the affirmative. *Great!* He thought. *She'll meet me later.*

Helen then made small talk as she scribbled her own note, suggesting they use her cousin's home. She was sure it would be a safe place that no curious eyes or ears would find. After all, she would be watering the plants and feeding the parakeet for another week while her cousin was enjoying the Bahamas. Helen suddenly wished that she had gone on the cruise, too.

Brick shrugged. "Well, I'll just have to keep checking in with you, 'til I can see him. I hope you don't mind."

"Of, course not, Brick."

"Thanks. Well, I'd better run." Brick's chair scraped against the floor when he stood up. He pushed it closer to the desk and tapped two fingers against the notes before staring pointedly at the shredder.

With a wink and a nod Helen snatched them up and fed them into the machine. She stared, transfixed, as it whirred into action. She continued to stare at the strips of paper long after Brick left and the machine fell silent. She was beginning to feel as if her life was in shreds.

HELEN FINALLY TORE HERSELF AWAY from the shredder, but her heart was not in her work. She fussed for almost an hour after Brick left, then picked up her purse and buzzed her secretary.

"Susan, it's almost four o'clock and my head is pounding. I think I'll cancel my 5:30 and call it a day. Would you please call George with my apologies? And there's a list of committee members here on my desk—you know, the Community Relations Committee? Would you please call them and see how many will be able to attend the meeting next week? And don't worry about the report you're working on—I'll help you with it in the morning. There's still plenty of time.

"Oh, good. To be honest, I've been at the keyboard for so long with this thing I'm afraid my fingers will grow roots and I'll be permanently attached. Stopping to make those calls will be a relief!"

Susan suddenly blushed and stumbled through an impassioned apology. "But, I love the work, really I do! I hope that didn't sound like a complaint . . . ."

"Susan! I know you weren't complaining, and actually, I was thinking you were due for a break. And, just for the record, I feel *so lucky* to have found you."

"Thanks!" The young girl blushed even more, but the pink of embarrassment deepened to crimson pride. ". . . I hope your head feels better real soon!"

***

Chapter 74

"**S**o Commander—what'cha think? Are we doin' okay, or what—Sir?"

"Your doing fine, Sam. You know—you guys should become career men. I think you'd both make the grade. And I tell you what, when we get out of this situation, I'd be happy to give you letters of recommendation."

"Cool. We thought about enlisting—you know, for special services or something, but we didn't wanna get stuck with grunt-work, you know? I heard it's who you know—not what you know or what you can do."

"Well, everybody has to start at the bottom—but I could pull a few strings to make sure you have a chance to show what you can do. Can't make any promises, mind you—but I'll do what I can."

Sam and Rob chorused their appreciation as they jogged in place. Rob's T-shirt was dark with sweat but his face showed no strain as he wound down to a slower heartbeat. Sam was smaller and wiry, but it had been a strain to keep up with Rob's long, sturdy gate. After their two-mile jog, beads of sweat rolled down his cheek.

Fingers was another story. He had fallen behind and still had not returned. Perkins guessed that he was napping under a tree somewhere. He sat down on the porch swing and offered the final verdict.

"Okay. You both passed. You're in."

He gave them both a steely stare. "But this is no

258

game, you guys—and I won't hesitate to kick either one of you in the ass the minute I think you're not following orders. I can't be distracted by worrying about you guys." His brows squeezed together and he added emphatically, "You listen to me. You do what I say. No second guessing. Is that understood?"

"Yup. I mean, Yessir! We won't let you down, Commander." Sam gave his word with a solemn nod.

Perkins knew he meant it. He could not help but wonder, though, about their buddy, Fingers. *Where's that cagey little rascal? I wonder if he got stuck down at the big hill?*

***

Chapter 75

"The years teach much which the days never know."
RALPH WALDO EMERSON

*O*n Thursday, Major General H. Edward Carrey turned his car into Fred Hanson's driveway. His face wore a frown. He wasn't sure how to broach the subject. *I can't just say, by the way Fred, I think some funny business is going on in Washington and there's a sinister plot involving biotechnology.* As he climbed out of the car he looked heavenward and asked, "Well? I need your help more than ever—I don't want to sound like a paranoid old crackbrain!"

When Harry knocked on the door he heard Fred's deep voice call from within. "Come on in, General. I'll be off the phone in a jiffy."

Harry entered the rustic foyer and was relieved to hear Fred end his telephone conversation in the adjoining room.

"WELCOME TO SHADY PINES, General. I'd offer you a seat but something tells me you'd like to stretch your legs after that drive. How about a drink, though?" He gestured toward his bar. "Scotch? Bourbon? Help yourself while I add this note to my calendar."

"Thank you, Fred—don't mind if I do." Harry strode across the oriental carpet that was bordered with a navy and wine-colored geometric design. He admired his host's alcoholic stash as he thought, *A bit of scotch might be just the thing.* He poured a drink and looked around, liking the rustic ambiance. He sniffed with appreciation—the scent of cedar filled the air.

"You've got quite a spread here, Fred. Interesting blend of wood and stone."

Fred proudly followed Harry's eyes around the room. "It's custom built—by a Vermont-based firm, of course—and I'm quite pleased with their work. Been here about six years, now. Want a quick tour? I still love to show it off." He sprang from his chair despite Harry's lukewarm response.

"People thought an old bachelor like myself would rattle around in over 3400 square feet, but it suits me fine . . ." His grin reached his eyes, ". . . especially when the nieces and nephews visit. But, wait until you see the study upstairs. It's a marvel, and this fireplace looks to be dry stacked—can't see a speck of the mortar in it!"

Fred looked dreamily toward the expansive hearth, remembering Howie Randall, the stone mason who had supervised the project. *Howie's a true artist,* he thought. Howie and his crew canvassed the property for the stones, then rinsed and scrubbed them before painstakingly chipping each one until it fit perfectly into place.

Harry thought, *I might as well humor him until I can broach the real purpose of my visit.* He poured a quick refill and reluctantly followed his host, but he perked up when they entered Fred's favorite room. "I see what you mean about this study, Fred. Almost too good to work in."

"You're right on that one, General. If you look up at the ceiling, you'll see some of the beams are hand painted. I got the idea from that oil mogul out west. What's his name?" Fred's forehead crinkled. "I know—It's Phillips! Anyhow, he left an incredibly stately home to the Boy Scouts of America decades ago. They give tours of it, you know." His thoughts drifted back to his own private tour. "It's what sparked my interest in interior design—and it was the inspiration for this room. You know, Harry, when I come in here it seems to soothe my soul. It's a great place to mull over the problems I encounter at the legislature. You'd think it would be easy, being a state rep in little old Vermont.

Quite the opposite, actually."

"I'm sure. So, Fred—anything of interest lately? In the legislature, I mean? I imagine you've got your finger on the pulse of your electorate out here. Pressure to be accessible, and all that."

"You're right again, General. I was just on the telephone about one of the muddiest issues, yet. We're stymied with the current technical maze of GMO legislation. Affects a lot of my constituents, you know."

"I've heard some grumbling, even within the beltway." Harry's mind slammed into gear. *Bingo—what a perfect segue for the real reason for my visit! This won't be so hard after all.* "By the way, let's forget the general crap. It's Harry to you."

"Honored."

"So what's it all about—this GMO stuff? I've heard a few disjointed rumblings in Washington. Anything to do with that chemical conglomerate? You know, SanFidel?"

"Yes, they're definitely in the middle of it. God . . . the biotech industry is pumping millions of dollars into campaign contributions to both the Democrats and the Republicans. They're also putting massive effort into advertising campaigns. They're pushing real hard for patent control and the path they're leading us down is not one that I'm comfortable with. The more I learn, the less I like it. I'd rather focus on taking care of our family farmers, and demand support for sustainable and organic agriculture and secure the mandatory labeling and long-term testing of genetically engineered foods."

"You don't say."

"Yes. And many of my constituents don't like it one bit either. But while some biotech opponents are insisting on an immediate moratorium on all G.E. foods, I'm not sure I'm ready to go that far."

"G.E.? I thought they were GMO's?"

"Sorry. G.E. stands for genetically engineered. Some refer to them as G.M. foods, genetically modified, that is. It doesn't matter what you call it, though: A rose is a rose, as they say. But I can't help but think that *this* rose has sharp thorns. *Very* sharp thorns."

"Quite right."

"And then, there's the issue of drifting."

Harry looked confused so Fred explained, "Drifting. Umh, pollen drift."

Harry continued to stare blankly.

"Pollen drift—when insects or the wind cause pollen to move to another plant. You know, pollination."

"Well, of course. But why would the lawmakers stick their noses . . . " Harry paused mid-sentence, "Sorry, I didn't mean to be offensive—it's just . . . "

Fred laughed. "No offense taken."

Harry tried again. "So, why would politicians get involved with this drifting if it's just about pollination?"

"Well. It's because drifting from genetically devised plants can affect neighboring organic plants. So get this, Harry—because the genetic characteristics are patented, the big corporations believe that the organic farmers should compensate them for the drift-altered crops. *Crops that have been contaminated through an act of nature for God's sake!* And the farmers—rightly so, I might add—are saying, 'Wait a minute—you've tainted our crops, so maybe you should compensate *us!*' It's just a mess, Harry. It's a *very* messy issue and we don't have any answers yet. At least, none that I'm happy with.

"And there are other legislative issues at stake with GMOs. Some come under the auspices of the Ag Committee, some under Natural Resources, and of course, some under Commerce. Then there are some issues that overlap. There are four or five bills up for review in the Vermont Senate alone that deal with genetically modified seeds and foods. And liability is another thing, and it's a Judiciary Committee issue, too. Like I said, Harry, it's a mess—a real mess—with high-power conglomerates using the almighty dollar to get in our faces."

"Damnation! I thought it was a federal issue, but it's at the state level, too." Harry did not envy any politician the job of sorting it all out.

"I'm glad to say, though, that many of these issues are "stuck on the wall" at the moment, so there's no pressure to take a stand or take action, yet."

"Stuck on the wall?"

"In Appropriations. Without enough support, the bills're left indefinitely—until someone musters up enough interest."

"But, you're already feeling at least some of that pressure to deal with them. Am I right?"

"Unfortunately, yes. It's hard to know what to believe, or who to believe. There's a grassroots group who claim that within the next five to ten years, the biotech industry plans to genetically engineer all of the food in the world. I place them out in left field with the environmental wackos, myself." He added, "On the fringe, they are. Wackos!"

"That would have sounded a bit excessive to me, too, just a few days ago, but, I'm glad you brought it up, Fred, because I don't think they are so wacko."

Fred gave Harry a piercing look. "So, what do *you* know?"

"Actually, it's related to my real reason for coming."

"What? Now why would a military man like you get involved in this issue? And, if you don't mind my asking, Harry, why me? What brought you to my doorstep?"

"Quite frankly, my friend—your integrity—my belief in your integrity. I needed to get away from the city, because, confoundit, I don't know who I can trust on this one. It's insidious!"

FRED GESTURED toward a pair of comfortable red leather arm chairs. "C'mon, let's sit down. So, give me the facts, Harry, and tell me what you want me to do." Fred was a shrewd man and he knew that the stakes had to be high for a man like the general to be so cautious. He listened quietly until Harry finished his story.

"So, we've got the murder of an official from the FDA. A senator is unaccounted for, a colonel is missing and

264

an undercover agent has failed to surface. They're tied together because all four have been checking on—or working to block—the GoMO Bill in one way or another."

He stopped abruptly. "But Harry, how could men of that caliber be missing without the whole world hearing about it? Can you tell me that? Where's the press when there's a real story?"

"Well, the murder was written off as a random, gang-related drive-by, and the others haven't been listed as 'officially' missing—not yet, anyway. So no one in the press is suspicious yet. It's just as well until we sort it all out." He lowered his voice to a raspy rumble, "If we can."

"Let me ask you this, Harry. Are you thinking you may be next on their list?"

"It's a possibility I suppose, but highly unlikely. I haven't done any snooping, myself, I just sent Perkins. But thunder and tarnation, I wish I knew what *happened* to him!"

"What do you know about Senator Monroe? Have you spoken to Helen?"

Harry shook his head. "It's only a hunch. The woman just didn't sound like herself. She said he was unavailable." Harry pulled a speck of lint from his sleeve. "Monroe has *never* been unavailable to me. Never. He knows better."

FRED THOUGHT, *He probably does know better, and so does everyone else who deals with you, I'll bet.*

"Monroe and I go way back, Harry. Classmates at Yale, you know, but, I'm a simple country man at heart, set on being a state rep here in Vermont. Wanted to come back and help my friends and neighbors. Needed to. Monroe, on the other hand, went on to bigger and better things—he'd had his sights set on Washington for as long as I can remember." Fred slid forward and slapped his knees. "So why don't I give Helen a call? See what she might tell me?"

"Good idea, man. Give it a shot."

* * *

265

Chapter 76

Not safe in my own home?

---

*B*rick had a feeling of deja-vous on the streets of Washington. He scowled and chastised himself for being such a worrywart, but the vision of Bob Jette's body on cold, hard concrete steps suggested that his precautions were justified. He waited until he was satisfied that no one was following, then took a few brisk steps toward the address that Helen had provided.

MOMENTS LATER Helen ushered him toward the kitchen table. It smelled like a bake shop, with tantalizing aromas. He wondered how she had found time to bake, but he was not surprised. Helen's pastries were legendary within the belt way—as legendary as her boss's eloquence on the senate floor. Some people even joked that her turnovers may have won a few votes.

"Help yourself, Brick—I've got a few munchies left from last night's dinner party. This one over here," she swept her hand to the far end of the old porcelain table, ". . . is filled with chicken salad. Something tells me you haven't eaten much today. And now, *please*, tell me what you know. Why the clandestine notes and gestures in my office? Why did I get the distinct feeling that it might not be safe to talk in my own home?"

"I'm sorry, Helen. We believe that both C.D. and the senator have been kidnapped. And they're not the only ones."

She sagged like a deflated balloon. "I was afraid something awful had happened. But I wanted to give it at least another day before sounding the alarm." She looked into his eyes. "How do you know? Who is the we you spoke of? Do you think they are all right?"

"It's a long story, Helen. But first—yes, I'm sure they are both alive. I came here to see if you know anything that might be helpful, and to see if anyone has approached you about Tom—or—the GoMO bill."

"No. Not a word. But, what's this about the GoMO?"

After taking one last bite of the delectable pastry, Brick pulled a photograph out of his pocket. "Do you recognize any of these men?"

She slipped her reading glasses on and studied the photo.

"Why, yes."

Her face seemed to whiten with the shock of recognition. He thought, *what's that about?*

"This one here," she gestured with a shaking finger toward the young man with the blond hair. "It's Rodney Carrousel. He's Major General Carrey's top aide. And that one on the end there is Perry Jordan. He's CEO of SanFidel. And if this has anything to do with the GoMO, I'm not surprised to see *his* face. But I'm afraid I don't know who the tall one is and the other faces are too blurred to make out. A couple of them do look like people who are often with Mr. Jordan, but I can't be sure."

Brick was disappointed to learn that Helen did not recognize the finger shooter, but he kept that piece of news to himself. *No sense in frightening her if I can help it.*

Helen straightened her elegant frame and pushed a stray hair away from her eyes. "You must be familiar with SanFidel, Brick—they've been the driving force behind Senator Miller and the push to get support for the GoMO. I'm sure you realize we're against it. We believe that their work with GMOs has not been properly tested, and we want to stop them from releasing any more products until they've taken the time to test the results." She squinted in Brick's direction. "Do you think they're behind the disappearances?"

"Well, it's certainly starting to look that way. These men are ruthless, Helen, and lately they've become bold. Makes me wonder if they've got the resources to pull it all off."

"Pull all what off?"

When he saw Helen's puzzled expression, Brick asked, "Did you know Bob Jette?"

"Why, yes! I was so sorry to hear about his death. Such a terrible tragedy! And he was a family man, too. I don't mean to sound heartless, Brick, but I think those hoodlums reaped what they deserved."

"Helen. They didn't kill Bob! I know it for a fact because I was a witness."

She gasped.

"As a matter of fact, Bob was on his way to meet me when he got shot. I saw the whole thing, and I'm sure that those boys were just pawns. There was a third person in the car with them . . . and after Bob went down, the gun was aimed at *them*. It was only a split second, but I saw their faces and those two boys were frightened. They were not willing participants—I'd stake my life on it!"

"Oh—the poor things! And here I was, judging them because of what I heard in the news. But how does Bob's death tie in to the disappearance of Tom and C.D? And how do Rodney and the bunch from SanFidel fit into the equation?"

Brick made a mental note of her familiar use of Rodney's name before answering.

"Well, Bob went haywire when he found out what they were doing and he was foolish enough to let them know he was going to "blow the lid". I heard the whole thing from the adjoining room. I didn't see who he was talking to, but I did see Jordan and that tall guy waiting in the hall. I was lucky to go unnoticed, then and later when Bob was gunned down."

"Oh Brick, how dreadful for you."

"Well, it appears that this guy . . ." He pointed toward

Rodney, ". . . is about to use his influence to have certain fuel companies fill military aircraft with tampered fuel."

"WHAT?" HELEN SPRANG from her chair and Brick wondered once again about her connection to Rodney.

"Now that's absurd! Rodney's such a polite young man. He's always been so *thoughtful*. And General Carrey is as upright as they come. He would never allow . . . ."

Brick interrupted her. "Helen, we know Harry's not involved. One of his agents, the man who took this photo, will attest to that. But, Rodney *is* involved. We have it on video. I'm sorry, Helen—I don't know what your connection to him is, but we've got him bragging about it. On tape. There's no doubt about it.

"You see . . . the fuel that they talked about will contain a chemical compound that SanFidel's people had developed. It's a biodegradable compound that affects specific plant life—it actually stunts the growth cycle—and then, apparently, it can't be traced in the environment. It's biodegradable."

Brick saw that Helen was struggling to keep her composure, yet he continued to hammer her with the information. "We believe SanFidel has plans for wiping out their competitors and then coming to the rescue—so to speak—with their so-called super chemicals and seeds. Genetically engineered, patented seeds. God only knows what that stuff will do to us in the long run, not to mention the power they'll render over all of us."

"Oh, my God."

"And SanFidel has gained most of the control of the seed market. They could, and probably will at some time, dry up the availability of all produce seeds. It could become virtually impossible for the average person, or small farmer for that matter, to have their own vegetable garden. Then we'll all *have* to purchase food from these scoundrels."

"Oh Brick. That can't possibly be true! How can they do that? There *has* to be enough opposition to stop them." Helen's conflicting emotions drained the color from her face.

Brick looked at her, long and hard. "Like Senator Monroe? And C.D.? And the hundreds of other people who might yet be held at Domino One?"

"Domino?"

Brick was surprised by her swift reaction.

Helen demanded, "Tell me what you know about Domino! It's got to be the missing link on the senator's note pad!" She sprang to her feet. "Just a minute, Brick. I'll be right back."

BRICK WAS ALREADY REACHING FOR another pastry when she called from the other room. "Help yourself to more food, Brick!" He grinned and took two more. As he munched on the delectable chicken-filled triangles, he wondered about the inner turmoil that he was sure he'd seen on Helen's face. He suspected she was hiding something. *Oh well, she's obviously trying to be helpful now. Maybe she's just worried about the senator.*

HELEN REAPPEARED with the patchwork of paper shreds that she had painstakingly pieced together. "I pulled these out of Tom's waste basket yesterday." She looked sheepish. "I've done this before to figure out what he was up to. See? It's a cryptic list that didn't make much sense—until now. Right here it says, Where's Domino. So, why don't you tell me what you know about it?"

"It's where we believe the senator is being held, along with several other people. Apparently, it's a modern Auschwitz, right here on American soil. God only knows what they'll eventually do to the people they're holding there.

White faced, she fell into her seat.

"I'm sorry, Helen. I shouldn't have said that." *Damn! If she wasn't worried sick about the senator before, she is now.*

"It's all right, Brick. I'm a big girl and I don't need to be pampered." She shook her head. "Please. Tell me everything."

He took a deep breath.

"There isn't much else. So, now you know why I was so secretive in your office. They seem to have people in the FDA and in the military. God only knows what other government agencies they've managed to infiltrate. I don't know who to trust. And I don't know who might be listening. One thing's for sure, though . . . Senator Monroe is about the only person with enough clout to stop the Miller Machine. And now he's gone."

Brick shot Helen a warning glance. "So, it stands to reason that they might be watching and listening to you, too."

Helen accepted his warning. Then, as if calling from some unseen source of inner strength, she raised her diminutive frame to its full height of five foot two.

"WHAT CAN I DO TO HELP, Brick? I can't just sit here doing nothing." Her mind raced, *I've got to stop this, somehow. Maybe I can reason with Rodney.*

"I'm glad you asked, Helen. Because one thing I believe you can do is start telephoning everyone that the senator has been talking to about the legislation. I really don't think our "friends" are going to be put on the alert because you would just be appearing to do your job. As a matter of fact, I have a friend—a botanist—who's willing to help you with a telephone blitz. And if anyone could sway them to your side, Evie could. I'm sure of it."

Helen brightened at the thought. "That would be wonderful! I must admit, I *am* lost when it comes to the *technical* end of the subject. So tell me all about her."

Brick's eyes took on a dreamy quality. He was remembering Evie's hungry kisses, but he snapped out of it under Helen's quizzical stare. He cleared his throat. "So, her name is Evie Victor. She's got a lot on the ball—landed an internship with Martin Bascomb, the botanist from Massachusetts."

"Oh! She's with Dr. Bascomb? She *must* be a whiz to be working with him."

Brick beamed. "Yes, she's amazing. And she's a fast learner, too, so I'm sure you'll have her up to speed on the GoMO in no time."

"Where is she? When can she start?"

"She's right here in Washington and she can start tomorrow, if you like."

"Wonderful! Yes! Why don't you send her to my office first thing in the morning!"

"But Helen . . . " Brick felt the need to provide another warning. ". . . please be careful about what you say when you make your calls. Don't let on that you know about any unethical business. We really don't know who might owe them a favor."

Helen exhaled loudly.

Brick had the uncomfortable feeling that she was holding something back. Something important. Probably something about the young man in the photo.

"THANK YOU SO MUCH for filling me in, Brick. So now, what are you going to do next? She stood up then and pointed toward the coffee pot. "How about another coffee before you go?"

"Don't mind if I do." He took a sip and the phone rang.

Helen jumped. Admitted, "I guess I'm on edge," before she answered the third ring.

"Hello?" She paused, then exclaimed, "Of course! Representative Hanson! Of course I remember you—you're Tom's friend, from Vermont. What can I do for you?"

Brick sipped his coffee, content to wait and think about Evie. But a sudden change in Helen's voice caught his attention. She was suddenly too careful, too controlled.

"I'm sorry, but I didn't have the opportunity to speak to the senator today. We were quite busy." There was a long pause as she listened, and then Brick saw her eyes open wide.

"He is? He is? My that's interesting!"

Another pause . . . .

"Are you completely sure? Oh, I'm so glad to hear that. Please, give me your phone number. I promise I'll call as soon as I learn something!"

She closed her phone and exclaimed, "Oh Brick, this is great news! General Carrey is in Vermont. He's with State Representative Fred Hanson. They appear to be suspicious about the people involved with the GoMO and they are just as worried about Tom and C.D. as we are!"

"What did he say? Why did he call you?"

"Brick! You're beginning to sound like me with all those questions. Fred is an old friend of Tom's. It seems that the general became alarmed when I told him that Tom was unavailable. I guess that was stupid of me—Tom's *never* been too busy to see General Carrey. He's chairman of the Senate Committee that oversees Harry's R&D projects, you know. And, of course Harry knows C.D. would never go AWOL. Apparently, he first became suspicious when some expected information did not surface—one of his men who was supposed to have videotaped the evidence has disappeared." She looked at Brick. "Well, of course—that must be . . . ."

"Perkins! No wonder he couldn't reach the general— the old devil's "AWOL" himself! Thank God I was here when Hanson called. I really should call Perkins and let him know! Then I'd like to speak to the general myself. I did hear you say he's still with Hanson, didn't I? You got the number, right?"

"Yes. Go ahead and call now. Use my cousin's phone, though."

They looked at each other. She turned white. He looked stormy. They both hoped no one had been listening.

WHILE BRICK WAS MEETING with Helen, Evie was pacing back and forth in her hotel room. *I hope the senator's people want me to help them.* She stopped. A frightening question flashed through her mind. *What if they catch Brick?* She shook her head. *No, I won't go there—I've got to think positive.*

Evie decided a diversion was in order, so she turned on the television. Like a robot, she clicked through the available stations. When she realized that she had clicked onto *Seventh Heaven* for the third time, she spoke to herself.

"Oh, this is hopeless, I can't concentrate."

Too keyed up to watch anything, she clicked it off and decided to walk down to the gift shop for some hand creme.

Evie grabbed her purse, picked up the key card and headed toward the door. She stopped suddenly and decided to leave a note. *Just in case he comes back while I'm out.* She left the note in a conspicuous place and hurried out the door.

***

Chapter 77

. . . Come on man—speak!

*F*red Hanson's telephone rang. He answered and handed it to Harry. "It's for you, General. Some guy named Brick Little. Says he's with Helen—you know, Tom Monroe's assistant."

"Hello, Mr. Little? Major General Carrey here. I understand you're with Helen? What can I do for you?"

"Well, General, I think we can help each other. I'm not sure where to begin. But, for starters, I'm sure you'd like to know that Commander Perkins is okay. He's . . . ."

"Great Scott, man! That's the best news I've heard in a very long time. So, where is he? Why hasn't he contacted me? Come on man, speak!"

"Yessir! Of course, Sir! But I think the commander should talk to you, himself. If you want, I'll give him Mr. Hanson's number."

"Good enough. Is that all?"

"Well, no, Sir. Perkins . . . umh, the commander, said to tell you there's a video, but he couldn't send it to you. He mailed it to Bob Jette at the FDA."

"Bob Jette? But he's dead, man!" Harry's voice boomed so loud, Brick thought it would leave a mark on his eardrum. He yanked the phone away from his ear.

"Yes. I know he's dead. I saw it happen."

Brick held the receiver at arm's length until Harry's long list of expletives faded.

"It's a long story, General. But the important thing is

we've got a lot of evidence against SanFidel, including the tape. And we know where Colonel Davidson is." He thrust the receiver away again, but there were no more ear splitting explosions.

"Well, Mr. Little—is that all?"

"Actually, no Sir. We've got a plan. The commander has us all in place, but I think he should tell you himself."

Harry did not want to wait, but he decided that it *would* be best to talk with Perkins, rather than a civilian. "Okay, Mr. Little. But can you tell me one thing? *Where on God's Green Earth have you people been?"*

BRICK WAS NOT FAST ENOUGH to save his eardrum this time. He had the feeling that if Harry could have jumped through the phone wires, he would. He envisioned the man's bulky frame whizzing along the wires from state to state, with thousands of telephone poles toppling in his wake. When Harry finally fell silent, he answered.

"Well, Sir, after Bob Jette was killed—I knew it had to do with the GoMO bill by the way—I contacted Martin Bascomb. He's a respected botanist . . . ."

"Yes. Yes. I know who he is. Go on."

"Well, we've all been at *his* place in Massachusetts." Brick did his best to tell his story, including Bob Jette's meeting and murder, the finger shooter, Tommy's friends, and the attack at his home when he met John. He managed to placate Harry, but he suddenly remembered that Rodney was involved. He thought, *Oh, God, he's not gonna like this—I'll be lucky if I have any ears left.*

"There is one other thing you *definitely* need to know. It's your aide, Sir—I'm afraid that Rodney Carrousel is a major player in this plot. A major player."

Harry exploded, *"Rodney?* There must be some mistake. Surely you're wrong."

"I'm sorry General. There's no question about it— he's right there on the tape, contributing to the scheme. That's why commander Perkins didn't send it directly to you—afraid that Rodney would get his hands on it."

Harry whispered, more to himself than to anyone, "Right under my nose."

"I don't think Rodney and his friends are aware that we have enlisted Dr. Bascomb's aid. I don't think they know they were taped, either. So, Rodney should be relatively easy to pick up." Brick heard a grunt and figured it was Harry's way of agreeing.

"Certainly. Certainly." Brick was relieved to hear that Harry had made up his mind. He gave Helen a thumbs up. But when Harry suggested, "Let's cut this call right now and I'll hitail it to Bascomb's," he knew he'd have to disagree.

"Well, Sir: I'm afraid nobody's going to be there for long. Don't forget—Perkins didn't know where you were, and he didn't know who he could trust, so he drew up his plan. But, Sir . . . ?"

"Yes? Spit it out."

"Well. Is there anybody *you* can count on?"

"I think so. Yes, by George, I'm sure of it. As a matter of fact, I'll be doing some planning myself."

BRICK POKED THE OFF BUTTON and handed the phone back to Helen. With a mixture of fear and excitement he predicted, "Well, I guess we'll be seeing some action, one way or another, real soon. But I'm afraid if they find out how much we know, they'll be even more desperate." He gave Helen a pleading look. "Now, look, Helen, you be careful—I don't want to find you on our missing list, too."

"Of course. But don't you worry, Brick, I'll be fine. After all, I'm sure most of the people I'll be calling will be *expecting* to hear from our office. We'll just stick to the issues of the legislation. It's part of what I do for Tom, and enlisting the aid of a professional, like your friend Evie, is an obvious strategy. I'm sure they wouldn't read anything into that, either."

Brick gave Helen a hug for good luck and said he'd stay in touch, but, as he reached the door a thought occurred to him. "Helen, one thing I don't understand about all this is the silence of the press. I would think they'd be all over you over Tom's disappearance. Wouldn't they smell a hot story like this?"

"Not really. They've known the senator for a long time. They've seen him go off without warning in the past." She suppressed a grin. "They're used to it, having him disappear when he's working on delicate legislation, that is. Not a single one of them suspects that I'm worried, and that's the way I'll keep it for as long as possible. After all, it hasn't been long enough for *them* to become suspicious; but if he doesn't show up soon, I'm afraid I will have to prepare a statement."

"I tell you what, Helen—why don't you hold off on that until we hear from the general again. Maybe we can put our heads together and help you with it."

"Thank's Brick. That's one monkey off my back."

HELEN EXCLAIMED, "I'm so glad you came to me, and I look forward to meeting your Miss Victor in the morning." With her pleasant blue eyes riveted to his, she pleaded, ". . . And please, Brick, you be careful yourself."

"I will." He dashed down the walkway, closed the gate and turned to give her a salute.

Helen held her hand up with a single wave. *Such a nice young man*, she thought. *It's too bad Rodney had not grown up to be more like him.* She sadly turned away. She was certain that Rodney's desire for revenge was fueling his actions and she reasoned that he must be so consumed by it that he simply did not know what he was doing. She felt she just had to warn him. It was the least she could do to appease the guilt and the ache that remained in her heart since her decision to give him up for adoption so many years ago.

***

Chapter 78

*F*red watched as Harry's fury grew. Like the Incredible Hulk, Harry transformed into a ferocious, bear of a man. He shook. He quivered. And his usually tanned, leathery complexion flushed from chalk-white incredulity to a bright red. *Boy, he looks like he could pop,* Fred thought as Harry's face became engorged with rage.

Finally, the indignant general sputtered, "Rodney! Rodney Carrousel a traitor? Damn him!"

Like an engine letting off steam, gathering momentum, Harry increased his verbal vehemence. "How could he? That red-faced little squirt—how could he do this? He won't get away with it I'll crush him like a bug and then I'll annihilate the lot of them!"

Harry grabbed the telephone and dialed. As he listened to the ringing at the other end of the line, he looked at Fred and explained, "Now that I know Rodney is the one, I know who I can trust. And, most importantly, who I *cannot.*" His thick brows lunged toward each other as he waited for someone to answer his call. Finally, an operator put him through to Danny Roberts, a special unit captain.

"Hello, General Carrey? Captain Roberts here, Sir. How can I help you, Sir?"

"I've got a special job for you, Captain. And I want you to listen closely. Very closely!"

"Yessir."

"I want you to *arrest* Major Carrousel."

"You want me to what?"

"I'm sure you heard me the first time, Captain—I want you to put that little scoundrel in the brig." Harry bellowed, *"And do it right away—I want Major Carrousel in the sonofabitchen brig!"*

"Yes, *Sir*! But what are the charges, Sir?"

"Conspiracy, for one. Misuse of military property, for another, and I can assure you this is only the beginning. And keep a heavy guard on him at all times until I return."

"Consider it done, Sir! And when can I expect you to return to base, Sir?"

"I'm not sure yet, Captain, but I'll be calling again. That will be all for now."

Harry hung up. His eyes glowed with satisfaction as he told Fred, "One down, more to go!" Then he picked up the receiver and with vigor, he dialed again.

***

Chapter 79

Maybe Alexander will help?

*H*elen was heartbroken. Her guilt grew like a raging malignancy, devouring all clarity of thought, making her desperate to find a way to atone for Rodney's unhappy life. *Rodney! My poor, handsome, misguided son!*

Helen knew that Alexander Graham Rossweild was the power behind SanFidel. *Tom always says to go to the source,* she remembered, *so I've got to find a way to talk to Alexander.* She hoped she could persuade him to release her son from whatever obligation he had with SanFidel's people. *Alexander is the only one who could get Rodney away from those monsters.* Feverish with desperation, ready to place Rodney's welfare above all else, Helen now believed that Alexander Graham Rossweild was her only hope.

As God is my witness, I'll even help him with the GoMO if he agrees to help my son.

***

Chapter 80

Eerie. That was the only word that Brick could now conjure up to describe the pleasant home that he and Jerry Johnson shared. He crouched near the bushes, compelled to watch and listen before he dared to enter through the back door. The soft hum of an airplane, hidden by expansive sheets of rippled gray clouds, droned above. At his feet, a large black ant laboriously dragged a dead insect, twice its size, across mountainous piles of twigs and leaves. He watched as it struggled with its single-minded mission of serving its Queen and her colony. He thought, *Alexander Rossweild would love to turn us all into two-legged ants, to serve him.*

When the hard-working insect stopped and wriggled its antennae Brick wondered if ants ever questioned the order of things. He decided, *probably not . . . but that's the difference between us.*

BRICK SHRUGGED OFF his contemplative interlude and focused once more on the surveillance of his home. Finally satisfied there was no one else about, he went inside and crept through the kitchen and dining room. He stopped and took a deep breath before continuing toward the study. He told himself, *of course, there won't be a body on the floor now.* He knew the dapper thug would have regained consciousness and left the premises, but he felt a chill scurry up his spine when he saw the statue that he had hurled at the man. It was now perched on Jerry's desk. Just knowing the intruder had picked it up and had consciously placed it there was unsettling.

Brick pictured the man wandering through the house, touching his things, snooping for clues to his identity—to his life! But he shook off his trepidation and turned away. Then he tiptoed up the stairs and entered his bedroom. He needed a change of clothes.

Family photos, some framed, some not, now seemed to be mocking him. His favorite striped shirt remained slouched on his bed where he had carelessly tossed it, one sleeve reaching grotesquely across the pillows. The rocking chair that once graced his Aunt Margie's front porch stood solid and mute.

Eerie, be damned! He fought to control the pounding of his heart. *This is my home. These are my things, reminders of my family.* He craved the comfort that they once had given, angry that now somehow, they had become ghostly reminders that evil had crept through his home.

Or was it still lurking?

Brick's eyes popped wide open at the thought and he sucked in a gallon of air. *Nah—that only happens in the movies!* Exhaling slowly, he stepped forward. He decided to hum a few bars from his favorite McCartney tune. *"Yesterday, all my troubles seemed so far away—now I need a place to hide . . ."* He stopped. Were the prickles on the back of his neck the result of some sixth sense? He glanced around, scanning the room once more. Could inanimate objects send some sort of indecipherable aura of warning? Or was he, as he decided, just reacting to his own song? "Great choice of lyrics, dork," he muttered. *"That* didn't help."

Brick reached for the closet door but stopped. If he opened it, he'd remove the barrier. *Barrier? Between me and what? The Bogeyman? Nothing's out of place,* he reasoned. And he had almost convinced himself there was no tangible indication that anything was wrong—until he heard the soft squeak of shoe leather behind him.

And then it was too late. A debilitating whack on the

back of the head sent Brickford Little spinning into darkness.

Damo chortled as his victim collapsed to the floor, but he was annoyed to realize that he had dropped him in a room with a soft carpet. *Wouldda' been better to hit 'em downstairs so he could smack himself on the wood floor,* he thought. *Like he did to me.*

Damo shrugged. *Oh well, I can hit him again, later . . . .*

***

Chapter 81

We can't find Rodney!

*C*aptain Roberts gave his crew a tilted look and let the air blow out of his lungs before admitting, "Damn, but I hate to make this call." Throats cleared and five heads nodded. Harry reacted badly to bad news. They all knew it.

Danny reached for his cell phone. As he punched in the number he asked, "Eight-oh-two, what area code is that?" No one knew. After a few rings an unfamiliar male voice—sturdy, but expectant—answered.

"Representative Hanson, may I help you?"

Roberts thought, *A state rep, huh? I don't recognize the name, though.* "Yessir, this is Captain Roberts. Major General Carrey gave me your number, Sir. Is he with you, Sir?"

"Yes, he is, Captain." Harry was already hovering, eager to grab it out of his hand.

"Hello, Roberts—what have you got?"

"Bad news, Sir. We can't find Rodney."

Harry bellowed, "You can't *find* him?"

"No, Sir. He was already off base when you called and hasn't come back. I put out an alert, on the q.t. of course. We'll pull him in as soon as he shows." Roberts waited for the general to bellow again. Nothing happened, so he continued nervously. "We got no clue where he is, but, don't worry, Sir—we'll get him. Sooner or later, we'll get him."

"Yes, I expect you will find him—you *must*! But just a moment, Captain, hold the line."

Harry stopped to consider his options. *Now where would that traitorous little swine be?* He pictured Rodney, thought about his habits, his friends. It did not take long to picture him preening in his uniform. *"That's it!"* Harry jammed the receiver into his ear and yelled, "I think he's probably headed to the party, Roberts. Check it out."

"Party, Sir?"

"Yes. This whole thing has to do with a company called SanFidel, and they're being honored at a big dinner party at Alexander Graham Rossweild's estate in Tennessee."

"Yeah? Aren't they the ones pushing the genetics? Big splash in the news about it a few months ago wasn't there? Seems like they're always in the news—donating money to charity and building educational centers and all."

"Yes, Captain, they're the ones. They do have a knack for getting favorable publicity at that! But they won't have such a benevolent reputation when I get through with them."

"So, General—what do you want me to do?"

"Crash that party, Captain. I want Rodney and the CEO of SanFidel—Perry Jordan is his name—in the brig. And I want Senator Miller, too.

"Oh, and Captain? Turn the place upside down and find me some proof that Rossweild is dirty. And don't worry about probable cause—we have proof that Jordan and Rodney are guilty of conspiracy to misuse Army property. That's enough for me."

***

Chapter 82

Evie's eyes sparkled.

Evie looked approvingly at the newly refurbished reception room before introducing herself to Helen Aaronsen and her secretary, Susan Griswale. She was pleased with their friendly welcome and assured them that she was eager to get started.

"So—Ms. Aaronsen, what do you want me to do?"

"Well, for starters, stop calling me Ms. Aaronsen! Everyone calls me Helen."

"Of course. Thank's—Helen."

"That's better. Now, I'm going to have Susan get you settled into one of our spare offices. I'm afraid it isn't much more than a closet, but it *is* pleasant and it has everything you'll need, including a private telephone line, a rolling file cart and a desk . . . with a *very comfortable* chair. There's no computer, but I don't think you'll need one."

"You're right there—I prefer to rely on my own hand writing." Evie shrugged, ". . . After all, I've spent hundreds of hours logging my experiments in the laboratory."

"Brick said you're a brilliant scientist."

"He did?"

"Well," Helen insisted, "I'm sure that if you're working with Dr. Bascomb you'll go far in your field."

Evie's eyes sparkled with pleasure.

HELEN ASKED SUSAN to show Evie her space.

"Be glad to. Oh, by the way, I left three phone messages on your desk—none of them urgent. And I'm afraid no one has responded yet to your calls about GoMO." Susan turned toward Evie. "So, let's get you set up! It's right through this door." She stood at the threshold of the tiny office. "There's a carton behind the desk that's full of note pads, pens, paper clips, and such. Why don't you settle in while I get us some coffee? Then we can put in a request if you need anything else."

EVIE ARRANGED EVERYTHING to her satisfaction before Susan placed a tray before her.

"Here you go, Evie. I never did ask how you like it, so I brought the creme and sugar. Help yourself." As Evie added two sugars and a splash of creamer to the steaming cup, Susan sipped her own and asked, "Do you need any other supplies?"

"I don't think so. Thanks, Susan—you've done a great job. Now all I need . . . is to know what I'm supposed to do!"

They both giggled.

"C'mon then. Helen said to join her once you're all set up." As an afterthought, she said, "You should probably bring a note pad and your coffee." As Susan led the way, she thought, *I'm glad Evie's here. I'll bet we'll be able to stop the GoMO bill with her help!*

HELEN WELCOMED EVIE INTO her office, but it was obvious she wanted to get right to work. Evie placed her pad and mug at one end of the conference table, then pulled up a chair. Susan poured another round of coffee before retreating.

"Well, Evie—Susan made a list of the senators and their colleagues, with cryptic notes about their stance on the GoMO. And I've jotted down a few personal tips to help you get into their heads," Her eyes sparkled with mischief. ". . . and believe me, some of them have very big heads. We can spend a few minutes reviewing these notes, and then we'll each take half and start calling."

"I hope I can make a difference with this."

"I'm sure you will, Evie. Brick said you'd be able to explain it all in simple layman's terms. The dangers of unrestricted biotechnology must be understood!" Concern wrinkled her brow.

"Well, that *should* be easy enough, I guess. After all, Dr. B. and I have spent hours discussing the issue."

"Good then." Helen held up one of the pages. "Here's where I think you should start . . . "

TWENTY MINUTES LATER, Evie sat at her desk. Two pads were in front of her. One listed the senators that she would be calling. The other was blank. She had thought about writing a little script, but decided it just wasn't her style. *I don't want to sound rehearsed,* she thought. *Besides, each call will be different, depending upon who I talk to.* She took a deep breath, and picked up the receiver.

Her first call was to Senator Thornton from Massachusetts. He had originally opposed the GoMO, but somewhere down the line he had been persuaded to change his position. Helen thought he would be a good one to start with because he had already demonstrated some sympathy for their cause, and he was a pleasant man. *I'm glad Helen thinks he'll be willing to speak to me,* Evie thought as she dialed his number.

"Senator Thornton's office, may I help you?"

It was a male voice. *Quite young,* Evie thought.

"Hello. My name is Evie Victor and I'm calling from Thomas Monroe's office. May I speak with the senator?"

He cleared his throat. "Can you to tell me the nature of your business? Then I'll see what I can do."

"Of course. I'm calling about the GoMO legislation on behalf of Senator Monroe and Dr. Martin Bascomb—and it's very important that I talk with Senator Thornton as soon as possible."

"The GoMO? Yes, I'm sure he'll talk with you. You did say you're associated with Dr. Bascomb, right?"

"Yes."

"Okay. Please hold while I see if he's available."

Evie heard a soft click. *Well, at least he didn't brush me off with a lame promise to have someone call me,* she thought. She stared at her list until the pleasant voice returned. "Miss Victor? If you can hold for just a few minutes, the senator will be free to speak to you. But he does have an appointment soon, so I can't promise how much time you'll have."

"Thanks! Thank you, so much!"

Moments later, the senator's deep baritone boomed, "Hello, Senator Thornton here—may I help you?"

"Hello, Senator Thornton. My name is Evie Victor. Umh, first off, thanks so much for taking my call."

"Part of my job, young lady—glad to be available when I can."

"Well, I'm sure you're very busy so I'll get right to the point. I'm calling about the GoMO legislation. I'm a botanist and I work with Dr. Martin Bascomb."

"Yes, Nick told me. I'm quite familiar with his work. Good man, that Bascomb. I respect his work ethics, too."

Evie smiled. *That's one point in our favor!*

"Yes. He's a brilliant scientist. Well, to make a long story short, Dr. Bascomb and I have been working with some of Senator Monroe's associates. *A little white lie won't hurt,* she thought. "We're very concerned about the GoMO legislation. We firmly oppose it, and I would like to have the opportunity to explain why, and I just wouldn't be able to do it justice on the phone, so I'm hoping you'll agree to meet with me—I promise it will be time well spent."

"Well my dear, I've always believed in looking at an issue from all sides, and since the GoMO is important legislation, I probably should hear you out. Have to admit it's a confusing issue."

"Yessir, it is. And that's why I need more than a few minutes on the telephone. What I'd like to do is have our assistant, Susan, make the arrangements with your staff—if you'll let them know that she'll be calling, that is."

"Yes. Yes, of course. I'll tell my staff right away."

"Thank you, Senator Thornton."

"Thank you, Miss Victor. It is Miss? I'm looking forward to hearing what you have to say."

Evie took a deep breath, then exhaled slowly. She closed her eyes and concentrated on releasing all of her muscles before punching in the next number.

TWO HOURS LATER, Evie sat back with a satisfied sigh. She had made eleven appointments. And each call had ended on a positive note. *My association with Dr. B. sure has been helpful,* she acknowledged. She was not willing to credit herself with her good luck.

Moments later, Helen poked her head through the doorway.

"How's it going?"

Evie revealed an enormous grin. "Oh, Helen. I've spoken to seven aides and six senators . . ." She pulled herself tight to the desk, planting her elbows on the blotter. ". . . and they've all agreed to talk." She rested her chin on her hands. "Two senators actually said they would vote according to Dr. B's recommendations!"

"Wonderful!" Helen gave a delighted clap. "You know what? I'm famished—so how about taking a well deserved brake for lunch? It'll be my treat."

Evie whirled around in her chair and threw her arms wide. "I say, olay!" She laughed and explained as she reached for her purse, "I feel like I've been slaying bulls all morning." But when her eyes met Helen's, a tingle surged up through the back of her neck. There was a fleeting glint, like that of a frightened deer caught in the headlights of an oncoming eighteen-wheeler. *Now what's that about?*

Determined not to let a case of nerves spoil the excitement of the moment, she said, "I'd love to go." With a dismissive shrug, she decided she had imagined the frightened deer look.

***

Chapter 83

Maybe there's news about Tim!

---

*M*ac was trying to enjoy an evening of relaxation when the telephone rang. She looked up from her latest Carol Higgins Clark mystery and frowned. *Do I really want to answer that?* She did not. Instead, she poured herself another glass of Cabernet Sauvignon and took a quick sip before returning to her favorite PI character, Regan Reilly. Regan was about to meet her best friend, Kit, in Aspen where, unbeknownst to the two of them, a baffling mystery would require Regan's super deductive skills. Mac had been looking forward to reading about Regan's adventure. She needed the diversion—anything, really, to take her mind off Perkins—and she did not want to be interrupted.

On the fifth ring, the machine whirred into action and she heard her own voice utter her latest recorded greeting. But her eyes opened wide when Major General Carrey's thunderous voice boomed from the little black box.

Maybe he has news about Tim! She rolled off the couch and lurched across the room. But while the general was unnecessarily identifying himself, she came to an abrupt stop. *Oh, God. It can't be good—he wouldn't call me at home just to give me good news.* Her hand froze on the receiver, but then, Harry's voice boomed again.

"Call Captain Daniel Roberts as soon as you can." He had started to say, 'and that's an order, Major,' when Mac grabbed the phone and gushed, "Hello, Sir. I'm here, Sir. What is it, Sir?" She held her breath waiting for the worst, mentally urging, p*lease, tell me now. Don't make me get the news from some guy I hardly even know!*

"So you are there. Well, Major, it's about your inquiry as to the whereabouts of your, umh—friend—Commander Perkins? Please forgive me for taking so long to respond, but he has been undercover, under the strictest code of silence."

Mac wanted to shout, *C'mon, you old curmudgeon, out with it!* Instead she managed to say, "Yes, General. I realize that." He paused again, and her adrenaline gushed. She wanted to shake him. *C'mon, c'mon!* She raked her fingers through her hair. Twenty seconds later—an ungodly amount of time in Mac's estimation—Harry spoke again.

"I'm not calling to apologize, Major. We've simply been doing what we must do. As you know R&D has more on the plate each year, even as our enemies and competition become more and more unscrupulous."

Good God! She thought. *Just tell me about Tim, Harry . . . just tell me about Tim!*

"I can assure you however, that I have just received word that the commander is in great shape, and he sends his regards to you, through me."

Mac squeezed her lids shut but tears of relief still spilled onto her cheeks. She wanted to shout "Hallelujah!"

Harry cleared his throat with a guttural harrumph before adding, "Under normal circumstances, I would not run relay with personal messages, you understand."

Mac's eyes sparkled with tears and excitement. *It's a good thing the old coot isn't here,* she thought. *I wouldn't know whether to smack him or kiss him.*

"But these are *not* normal circumstances and at this point in time, I need your assistance."

Mac's relief suddenly dissolved. *What does he mean, not normal circumstances?* She abruptly ceased to be the worried girlfriend. She was a career soldier. Alert. Capable. Waiting for orders from a commanding officer.

"What can I do, Sir?"

"You are to check in with Captain Daniel Roberts at

once. He will have the necessary information. I want you to do whatever he asks of you, Major. That's an order. And, Major . . . ?"

"Yes . . . ?"

"Not a word to anyone. Not a word about Commander Perkins. Not a word about your meeting with the captain, and not a word about this conversation with me. Not with anyone, except, of course, Captain Roberts. Not even your own mother, Major Mackenzie! Is that understood?"

"Yessir! Understood, Sir. I'm only to talk to Captain Roberts, Sir—about this, whatever it is, Sir!"

Harry broke the connection before she could ask a single question about the situation.

"This must be big if he needs *my* help," she reasoned. She called the captain and was out the door in minutes, stopping only to erase her answering machine, grab her emergency pack and strap on her gun.

"Only God and HarryCarrey know where I'll end up tonight," she muttered as she sprinted out the door toward her brand new emerald green Jeep Cherokee.

The long-anticipated mystery novel remained forgotten on the floor with Mac's gold filigree bookmark sticking out to hold her place as she embarked on her own real-life adventure.

MAC MET CAPTAIN ROBERTS at a tiny cafe that she and Perkins frequented. The heady scent of freshly ground coffee beans and yeasty sweetbuns filled the air, reaching the dimly lit corners of the room where extra tables were sandwiched between tall wooden benches. Roberts was already waiting in the farthest booth at the back. Mac remembered with a pang that she and Tim had sat there the night before he left for his mission. She took comfort in the knowledge that he was still okay as she walked past several happy couples and slid into the seat across from the captain.

He spoke first. "Good choice, Major. We've got plenty of privacy here."

"The waitresses are efficient, too," she told him. A

young redhead had already appeared with order pad in hand. Mac ordered a coffee with lots of cream. Roberts asked for the same.

Mac was in no mood for small talk. "So, Captain, why the cloak and dagger? What has Harry dug up?"

"I don't know much myself, Major. I'm afraid we're all on a 'need to know' basis. But I can tell you that Harry has ordered me to toss Rodney Carrousel in the brig under heavy guard—and that you and I are going to a party."

Mac did not know which piece of news was more astounding. "Rodney in the brig? Us at a party? Is this some kind of joke?"

"No. To start with, Harry's charging Rodney with conspiracy to misuse Army property. And the party? Well, it's a big shindig—black tie—at Alexander Rossweild's. He's that billionaire that's always in the news. We've gotta crash the party as quietly as possible, and keep our eyes and ears open. And get this . . ." He leaned closer. " . . . we're gonna pick up a real heavy weight along with Rossweild's men, too—Senator Miller!" He clenched his lips into a stubborn line, then slid back into his seat.

"Miller? My God, what's going *on*, Roberts? Why us and not the police? Or the FBI or the CIA or whomever it should be? And where does Tim fit in?"

"Tim? You mean Commander Perkins? I don't know. I'm afraid Harry's not talking much—just bellowing his orders." Roberts lifted his hands to emphasize his own bewilderment as he whispered. "He says he can't trust anybody except us. He wants you to hand pick a couple of your best women to attend that shindig, too.

"No other person should know about this, Major. Not a soul. We don't know how many people Rodney has on his side. And apparently they've got insiders at the FDA, and God only knows where else, so we just can't go through regular channels. You gotta be creative when you sign your girls—I mean women—on, too, if you get my drift."

Mac and Captain Roberts spent the next few minutes

brainstorming, deciding upon their approach to the party, and settling on the size and scope of the crew that they would need.

***

Chapter 84

*M*artin Bascomb took one last look at the plants in his solarium and jotted down a new item on his list of things for Jerry and Tommy to do while he was at Alexander Rossweild's mansion in Tennessee.

"Okay Tommy. Why don't you take a look at this list and see if you can read my notes."

Tommy took the clipboard and used his finger as a pointer. His eyes widened at how neatly and perfectly the elderly man had printed his extensive list.

"Gee, Dr. Bascomb, this is the best handwriting I've ever seen. How do you make all your letters so perfect? Nobody c'n read my writin'."

"Discipline, Tommy. And many years of practice. Once you've ruined a complicated experiment because you misread your own notes, you develop tidy penmanship. Very tidy. Otherwise, it can take hours, sometimes weeks, to make up for lost time and unnecessary errors."

"Yeah. I guess so." Tommy's face puckered at the memory of an incident at school. "I had to rewrite a 500-word composition last semester, just because my teacher said it was too messy. I guess I just wanted to get it done and over with."

"But you had to work twice as hard in the end, didn't you?"

"But, it's so hard to slow down! I hate writing and I just want to get it over with—fast."

Martin persisted. "But it *isn't* faster, is it?"

Tommy sighed, "No."

"So, why don't you employ a bit of discipline the next time, Tommy. You won't work nearly as hard or as long."

"Sure, I guess."

"Well, young man, I believe we've touched on everything you'll need to know in here. I trust that you and Doctor Johnson will keep things in order while I'm gone."

As they approached the lengthy hallway that connected the hot house to the kitchen, Tommy smelled the welcoming aroma of Millicent's raspberry pies. He gushed, "Boy that smells good," and quickened his steps. "Come on Dr. B. Let's go before Evie's brother gets his hands on Millicent's pie!"

Tommy rushed toward the source of the tantalizing aroma in awkward spurts, keenly aware of the elderly man's slower gait. *Like a thoroughbred in training,* Martin thought. *Eager for the race—but still mindful of his rider's commands.*

Martin chuckled. "Go on ahead, Tommy. You'd better hurry—John will probably be there any minute." He knew that his housekeeper's culinary magic would conjure up a kitchen full of hungry men.

As Tommy bolted toward the kitchen, Martin imagined the opening gates at Saratoga. He had the feeling that Tommy had changed somehow, for the better. *An important gate has just been opened,* he thought, and he decided that Tommy Sykes would not be spending much more time on the streets. Not if he could help it.

MARTIN SHOT HIS LONG-TIME friend and homemaker a playful jibe. "Now Millicent. You *are* going to be kind, aren't you—and allow me to sample some of that delectable pie before I depart?"

"Martin Bascomb. I'll have no such nonsense. What will these fine young people think of me? You know *perfectly well* that I have never stopped you from sampling my pies." She paused long enough to reach for a tray that had been hidden by her plump frame, and offered it with a flourish. "But, before you do, why don't you eat a hearty lunch? I've prepared your favorite, chicken 'n biscuits. And, there's a cold asparagus dish that I finally got the courage to try." She feigned fearful apprehension as she offered the sumptuous entrees.

"Millicent, my dear, you spoil me. And we all know that your cooking skills are superb, so I *know* that the asparagus will be delicious. And *you* know it, too." Without further hesitation, Martin sat down and helped himself to a generous portion of the savory chicken.

"Come now! Are you all going to stand around watching me eat?" Chairs creaked and utensils clattered as Martin's guests sprang into action. "Millicent, that includes you, too." He was happy to see that John had already pulled up a seat for her.

Millicent held up her hand and spun around toward the oven. "Don't mind if I do, Martin, but I just need to check on this last pie." After slipping on a pair of quilted oven mitts sporting dozens of tiny crowing roosters, she peered into the oven. "There we go . . . done to perfection if I do say so, myself!" When she carried the steaming pastry to the marble pie bench, Millicent was rewarded with noisy applause. Pink with embarrassment, she hung her mitts next to a rooster-bedecked dishtowel, then happily accepted her seat. But Millicent was not hungry for her own cooking—she had an appetite for news. She hoped she would finally find out what was going on.

When Millicent heard Jerry's story, she grew silent, but she made up for it when she cleared the kitchen table. Pans clattered and cabinet doors slammed as the red-faced woman took her anger out on the dirty dishes.

MILLICENT WAS STILL angrily scrubbing when Fingers tipped his head toward Martin. "I was thinkin', Doc. Could I drive you? To Tennessee, I mean? I'm a good driver, an' I . . . ." He hesitated, then gushed, ". . . well, I just don't trust that freakin' guy! You shouldn't go there alone!" Not only did he feel protective toward the elderly scholar, Fingers was also hoping to escape Perkins' Boot Camp. He did not appreciate the lessons in self-defense, or the running—or the situps. *Please God. No more situps!* He crossed his fingers under the table.

Fingers glowed with excitement when Perkins agreed. "You know—I think that's a great idea." He turned toward Martin. "I'm sure he'd be helpful, Dr. Bascomb."

***

Chapter 85

*T*o celebrate their success with the senators, Helen took Evie to LaFiesta al Greca, her favorite lunchtime restaurant. From the moment they entered the dining room until they left, the two women, easily mistaken for mother and daughter, attracted admiring glances.

BACK AT HER OFFICE, Helen thought about Evie. *She's a wonderful young woman—so smart and helpful. She'll make someone a wonderful wife one day.*

"Oh well, it's time to stop daydreaming and get some work done." Helen sat down and flipped her daybook open to see if Susan had penciled in any new entries. As her finger slid down the page, thoughts of Evie mingled with worries about Rodney. *Evie would be good for him,* she concluded. *If only . . .*

She shook off her fears. "Well, I only have a few calls to make. Then I'll have the rest of the afternoon free."

The time whizzed along as Helen completed the arrangements for a series of informational "No to GoMO" meetings. But when she came to the final entry on her calendar, her heart lurched. Even the initials AGR, hastily jotted down in her own handwriting, looked menacing. But she resolutely took a deep breath and made the call.

Alexander Graham Rossweild was surprisingly agreeable. *What'll he want in return?* she wondered nervously after she hung up.

***

Chapter 86

Brick was shoved through the doorway and when his knee hit the hardwood floor, he felt a shocking wave of pain.

I won't cry out, I won't, he resolved, even though the goon behind him had just slammed a fist into one of the swollen welts on his shoulder blade. Motionless and mute, he forced his focus away from the grueling ordeal. From a half squat on the floor, he could see several dozen people lounging along cot-lined walls.

My God, this must be Domino. I wonder if Colonel Davidson is here. Or—Senator Monroe? Brick tried to stand up. He heard feet shuffle behind him and braced himself for yet another jolting whack, but the man just grunted and slammed the door shut. Despite the mind-numbing pain, Brick was alert enough to realize a heavy iron bar was grinding against metal casings as it slid into place. He turned, stared at the door, wondering why Damo LaSalle had not killed him. *He's one sick puppy,* he thought. *He probably wanted to . . .umh . . .* Brick lost his train of thought because the room started to spin. *What the . . . ?*

C.D. REALIZED that the young man was going to fall, so he leapt across the floor and grabbed his shoulders. Another strong pair of hands lifted Brick's feet.

"Okay, Ben. Let's get him over to that cot over there." C.D. noticed that blood was seeping through the back of his shirt. "God. Look at his back—they must have whipped him. Let's try to ease him onto his stomach so we can take a look."

They carefully lowered Brick onto the cot. Ben said, "Okay, that's good. Boy, he took quite a beating—did you see his eye? Swollen shut. And there's a gash on his head, too!"

C.D. winced as memories of combat—memories that he never spoke about—came rushing back to mind, but he shrugged them off.

"I'll bet he's got quite a story to tell."

"We'll know soon enough—I think he's coming-to already."

***

Chapter 87

Gotta be prepared for the big party!

---

*P*erkins, Rob and Sam flew to a small landing strip in Tennessee where they called a taxi for a ride to the nearest town. Their first stop was a rundown second-hand shop. Perkins told Rob and Sam to wait while he conducted business with the owner.

"I wonder what they're gonna do back there."

Sam watched as the shopkeeper pulled the cheap vinyl door to a close. Its pleated plastic sagged at the top.

"I don't know—ain't nothin' in this dump but junk," Rob replied. He was standing in front of an old porch table with chipped paint and brittle spikes of wicker. A thick layer of grime covered most of the tabletop. Rob thought, *and that's the best piece he's got.*

MOMENTS LATER PERKINS reappeared, flashing a fake press pass. He told the boys that he was going to set up an "interview" session with Rossweild. *This'll get me in for sure,* he thought as he looked at the little plastic card. It was common knowledge that Alexander Graham Rossweild could never turn down favorable press coverage.

After they left the dingy shop, Perkins bought a new outfit and a tuxedo. He thought, *I gotta be prepared for the big party.* He also rented a mid-level luxury car for the last leg of the trip, thinking it would help to promote the image of a talented, but not-yet-well-known journalist.

***

Chapter 88

But I am at war . . .

*F*red Hansen could see that Harry needed to think, so he made his way toward the kitchen. It was time to brew up a pot of coffee.

HARRY DID NOT EVEN NOTICE that Fred had left the room. He sat, silent and still, for a very long time. He thought about Perkins and how he had persevered over the past two years, sometimes risking life and limb as he gathered evidence against SanFidel. *SanFidel,* he thought. *A great example of our new enemy! There's been no formal declaration. I cannot plead my case to the president, the chiefs of staff, or even to the people. But I am at war.* Harry thought about his enemy and how warfare has changed. *Sly and insidious, they infiltrate the armed forces and other agencies to manipulate the government as they bend and twist the constitution with new legislation to suit their own purposes.*

"We are dealing with the worst kind of enemy—the enemy within," he often warned Perkins. "An enemy who can contribute millions of dollars to charitable projects and spend even more millions on public relations programs to honor themselves while they slyly devise ways to gain more power."

Harry believed that the American people, for the most part, bought it, often fighting *for* the scoundrels, and unknowingly against themselves *and* the well being of future

305

generations. He longed for the old days, when war was openly waged—when you knew your enemy. He thought of Pearl Harbor and the Japanese. Of Hitler and Mussolini. *During those wars your own countrymen were on your side.*

Harry stared at the stonework in the fireplace, marveling at the simplicity of it. *Simple—like the good old days.* And once again, as was his habit, he found himself wishing he had been around during the American Revolution, but, as he pondered the plight of the founding fathers, he found himself wondering how they felt. *After all, most of them were Englishmen and were forced to fight against their own countrymen and soldiers from their homeland—and then, during the Civil War it was sometimes brother against brother!*

Harry was forced to admit that maybe things haven't changed much after all. He shook his head. *Haven't we learned anything?* He drummed his fingers on the arm of the chair. *But, at least back then you knew when someone was shooting at you, and you could hear the canons and artillery as they blasted away on the front lines.*

Not so anymore, he reckoned. *Not so anymore.*

FRED RETURNED WITH COFFEE and Harry gratefully accepted a steaming mug.

"I just don't understand it, Fred. Rodney had so much going for him. Why would he do this? Why would anyone?"

"Well, it usually comes down to just one or, a combination of, three things. Money, power, and revenge. Doesn't seem to matter what the crime and circumstance. You've got to understand—these mega-corporations are operating on a global basis. Do you realize what just a few pennies of profit could mean when it's multiplied on a daily basis by every living person, and every pet or herd of livestock that must eat? And they're so *clever* about hiding their real motivation. So very clever!

"They claim that the only sustainable way to feed a growing world population is by having farmers throughout the world grow gene-altered crops. They suggest that these crops will produce better yields, and therefore solve a world hunger problem being caused by a food shortage. And that's the rub, Harry. There's no *real* food shortage!"

"But, what about the starving populations?" Harry wriggled his eyebrows reprovingly. "Hunger *is* a real phenomenon, Fred! I've *seen* it myself!"

"Harry, Harry!" It was Hanson's turn to become impassioned with anger. "Yes. Hunger exists. No doubt about it! But do you know that it has been documented that 78% of all malnourished children under the age of five live in countries with food surpluses? Food surpluses, Harry! Hunger is not about food *shortages*—it's about *poverty* and *poor distribution* practices. Which leads us back to the money, Harry. And power. And control. Like the saying goes, 'follow the money, honey . . .'"

Fred's feet were planted firmly on the carpet when he leaned his lanky frame forward, and with elbows on his thighs he clasped his hands, steeple style to support his chin. When he blinked, Harry decided he looked like an oversized praying mantis.

"Genetically-engineered food is not a sustainable solution, either, Harry. It'll hurt our farmers."

"How so?"

"When gene-altered seeds are purchased, farmers sign a contract. The contract makes it illegal for them to save seed from their own crops for next year's planting. That's because, according to our already existing patent laws, the seed companies own the product and its, umh, its, progeny, if you will. And did you know that at least 1.4 billion people depend on farm-saved seed for their survival? Real sustainable farming practices will be eliminated because the farmers bound by this contract will be forced to purchase their seed supply each year. It turns small farmers into hi-tech indentured servants!"

Fred stopped talking long enough to take an angry gulp of coffee. "Hunger could be eliminated right now. It could have been eliminated last year or even fifty years ago, Harry! The same corporations—and Third World governments, I might add—whose profits have risen over the same years have thus far done nothing to end hunger. And on top of it, they're encouraging the downfall of small, sustainable farms."

Fred looked up sheepishly. "I'm sorry for this pleonastic ranting, Harry, but I get so darned fired up when I think about this. There is just so much that could be done. But it isn't!"

"I'm sure you're right, Fred." Harry found himself wondering what pleonastic meant. He resolved to look it up.

Fred closed his eyes, slowly shook his head, and whispered, "We could end the hunger! We *really* could if we could just overcome the greed." He gulped the last few drops of his coffee and grimaced at the bitter taste from a couple of stray grounds.

***

Chapter 89

*M*ac scowled at the telephone. *It's just like Harry to come up with a near impossible task. Putting through the paper work for my own sudden leave is one thing, but how am I going to pull it off for two more people from our small division without raising suspicions, and whose suspicions am I supposed to be worried about raising, anyhow? But I am glad he was thoughtful enough to let me know about Perkins.*

Mac drummed the surface of her desk and broke a nail. "Darn!" She continued her thoughts as she clipped the chipped edge. *Now—who can I pick for this escapade?* She studied the names on the duty roster. "Of course! Sadie-Lee Jarvis and Hannah Dick!"

Lieutenant Dick was a mastermind at chemistry and mechanics. *No wonder we call her Handy—she can create anything out of nothing. And both she and Sadie-Lee are masters of the martial arts.* Mac believed that both women had impeccable moral standards as well. She knew she could stake her life on their abilities and their integrity, but she hoped she wouldn't have to.

MAC DECIDED THAT luck was on her side for this one. She had easily reached both women. Sadie-Lee was already on leave and happened to have her cell phone with her. She had even planned a camping trip and was already packed. Handy was on duty, but was overdue, she said, for a few days off. She confided that her leave officer owed her a favor. Just minutes later Handy called Mac to report that her paperwork would be processed within the hour. *Must have been a big favor,* Mac thought.

The two women met Mac at 10 p.m. that evening. She repeated what Captain Roberts had told her about their mission.

"Just how dangerous is this going to be, anyway?"

"I really don't know, Handy. But if Harry is right, they've already killed and the stakes are high. Very high."

"I guess it doesn't matter that much. I've been training for the worst for a long time." Handy did not bring up the fact that she always had scored at the top of her class.

"For now we just have to get invited to that party. Handy, I hope you can fit us up with some of your toys."

"Sure thing, Major. I've been working on some new stuff that is state-of-the-art, and it sounds like they're gonna be perfect for this assignment, too." She grinned mysteriously. "Worthy of Calvin Klein."

"Great! I'd love to see what you've got, but right now, why don't you two go change your clothes. The Captain's sources say those guys frequent the Ducklebee Club. I'll pick you up in an hour."

Sadie-Lee looked askance. "The Ducklebee? The Ducklebee, as in exotic dancers and hookers?"

"Yup. So, dress accordingly. Got anything that will fit in at a place like that?" Both women reluctantly admitted that they did. Mac was glad they did not question her own wardrobe. *There are some perks at holding rank,* she thought with relief.

As soon as she returned to her apartment, Mac jumped into the shower and then chose the little backless dress that Perkins had bought for her a year ago. She had never worn it in public. She'd told him that she was saving it for a masquerade party. She still blushed with excitement as she remembered the provocative look in his eyes when he softly replied, "Then I can't wait for Halloween."

As she struggled to get into her dress, Mac cursed at his picture. "What the hell were you thinking, you sex-craved maniac?" But when she finally got it on she had to admit that it fit perfectly. She felt out of character in the form-fitting spandex, but as she inspected her reflection in front of the full-length mirror, the only flaw was the sour expression on her face. The tight bodice revealed a tantalizing hint of cleavage that swelled and heaved with each indignant breath. Despite her annoyance, Mac had to admit the overall effect of the dress was exactly what she was aiming for. *Dress? This isn't a dress! It's a giant Band-Aid with a zipper. The things I do for my country—and for Major Generals!* She resigned herself to the inevitable lusty stares and smarmy glances that were sure to come her way at the Ducklebee. *Charlie's Angels, eat your hearts out.*

Mac reminded her reflection, "Now remember—all you have to do is gain the confidence of one of these thugs. Make him want you. Get an invitation to Rossweild's party. And then—find a reason to make this a short night!" She knew she would have to turn on the charm big time to pull it off.

After a final inspection, Mac picked up her purse and keys and headed toward the door. Her hand froze on the knob when inspiration struck. She whirled around and grabbed her trench coat out of the closet. *At least I don't have to feel naked while I'm picking up the girls.* Mac grinned mischievously as she envisioned them in front of their own mirrors, then experienced a brief twinge of penitence, knowing they'd be feeling like cheap hookers, too.

JUST AS MAC EXPECTED, the two women had little to say until they were safely seated in the car. And then predictably, Handy let loose with a three-minute tirade. Once finished, she offered an embarrassed apology. "Sorry, Mac, umh, Sir. I know you don't like this assignment any more than we do. I guess I just needed to vent."

"No apology necessary, Lieutenant. I know exactly how you feel—believe me! Let's just put our feelings aside and get this job done. All we need to do is ingratiate ourselves to these men and get them to invite us to Rossweild's party. They'll never suspect three floozies." She pointed toward a manila envelope that was wedged above the visor.

"Take a look at their profiles."

Sadie-Lee gave an amused snort as she snatched the first photograph away from her partner. "I'll take this one, he's kinda' cute!" She laughed and settled down to study the profiles. Moments later, Mac eased the car toward the red-suited attendant who was leaning against a pillar in front of the Duckelbee.

Mac slid to the sidewalk and handed her keys to the young man before turning toward her reluctant companions. "Okay, ladies. Let's go have some fun." With a deep sigh, she snatched the ticket and sauntered seductively toward the front door.

It did not take the three women long to locate their targets who were watching the entertainment—a blond who possessed questionable vocal talent. She crooned enticingly and the men loved it.

Mac thought, *If she can turn them on, they'll notice us for sure.* She glanced at Perry with encouraging eyes. He squared his shoulders and flashed her a confident smile. *Jerk,* she thought as she claimed a seat that afforded a clear view. *A few more smarmy glances and he's mine. Lucky me.*

A scantily clad waitress with enormous breasts approached with an order pad. Mac found herself staring at a peek-a-boo bodice that must have been made from two lace doilies. *Tiny lace doilies.* She wondered how they stayed in place, but Sadie-Lee and Handy seemed oblivious to the marvel of physics that was thrust before them. They both nonchalantly ordered a vodka and tonic.

"I'll have the same," she said, her unblinking eyes still on the doilies.

"Okay. That's three v-t's." With a quick nod the waitress turned and jiggled past Perry Jordan's table, but he did not notice. His eyes were still on Mac.

The thrill of the hunt was on. Her target was hooked.

Perry and his companions all responded to the inviting smiles and a waiter soon brought an invitation asking the three women to join the men at their table. The adrenaline pumped through Mac's veins, creating an alluring flush. She noticed that Sadie-Lee and Handy were also blushing—with embarrassment. She also noticed, with satisfaction, that the scantily clad crooner was frowning. At the bar. Alone.

THE MEN THOROUGHLY ENJOYED Sadie-Lee's infectious laughter, and her quick wit. Thanks to the ongoing diversion, Mac was able to make tactful observations that steered the conversation toward their work and it did not take long for Sadie-Lee's sleazy companion to start bragging about the upcoming party at Rossweild's mansion.

Once the topic came up, it was easy to procure the coveted invitations.

***

Chapter 90

Now that's an ego trip for you!

---

*I*n Tennessee, Perkins was receiving his own invitation, thanks to Alexander's vanity.

"How kind of you, Mr. Perkins. And, the timing couldn't be better—I'm hosting a magnificent party this weekend. We're celebrating what we know will be an historic vote in the legislature. Please come as my guest and feel free to capture it all on film. It's black tie, of course. Does that pose a problem?"

That's it, you sleaze. Take the bait. "Not at all, Mr. Rossweild. I'm always prepared for black tie."

Rossweild's vainglorious pleasure was evident. "Good then. Do you have directions?"

"Yes, of course. Everyone knows how to find your fabulous estate, Mr. Rossweild." *Must give you wet dreams, you piece of shit.*

"Then come right along as soon as you like. My staff will be expecting you."

"Thank you, Sir. I'm delighted." *But, I'll be ecstatic when I can put you away, you skumbucket!*

PERKINS SHOWED HIS ID at the gate and drove up the winding drive toward the mansion. *Now that's an ego trip for you—he's got a permanent parking slot for the press.* He popped the hatchback wide open and pulled out his luggage. He hoped no one was watching as Sam and Rob climbed out of the back seat.

"Now, keep your eyes open, you two, and stay out of sight. You know the signal if I need you, right?" Sam gave a thumbs up before he disappeared behind a nearby tree. Rob was already out of sight. Perkins wondered how such a big guy could be so fast on his feet.

Perkins openly admired the surroundings as he strolled toward the front door. He knocked—then continued to stare at the marble steps, the enormous pair of Italian urns, the ornate fountain with twin cherubs, and the riotous roses that climbed up toward the second story window. Finally an aged butler showed him to the foyer and left him alone. Henderson quickly returned, saying Mr. Rossweild was unexpectedly detained, but hoped that Mr. Perkins would be willing to stay for the entire dinner party—if he was prepared."

"Yes. I'd be delighted."

Henderson bowed slightly before gesturing, "If you come this way, James will show you to your room."

"Sure. By the way—what's the dress code here?"

"Black tie. *Always*."

"Good. I just didn't want to be overdressed."

The butler pumped his eyebrows—his only reaction before changing the subject. "And by the way, Sir, Mr. Rossweild says you should feel free to roam about and use whatever amenities you wish while you are his guest. There's a swimming pool in the back. The pool house has bathing trunks, Sir, and there's a wonderful library—as well as a media room."

"Thank you very much. And please extend my appreciation to Mr. Rossweild."

"Yessir. Very well, Sir." Henderson vanished just as James made his own silent appearance.

Perkins thought, *What a spooky bunch this is.*

James led him up the stairs and waved him through an open doorway, then backed away without a word. Perkins shifted his gaze all around, thinking, *This isn't a room . . . it's an apartment.* He hung his tux in the closet then flopped on the bed.

***

315

Chapter 91

We're on location, General!

Mac flipped her cell phone open and punched Major General Carrey's number. She glanced around to be sure that she would not be overheard. *God,* she thought. *This place has more servants and guests lurking about than The Grand Hotel!* She listened to eleven nerve-wracking rings before Harry finally answered.

"General Carrey, here."

"Hello, Sir. Major Mackenzie reporting."

"Major! How goes the good fight?"

"We're on location, ready for the big party. No new developments from our end."

"No news is good news at this point, Major."

"Yessir. I'll report again as you directed.."

"I'll be expecting that call. But Major . . .

"Yessir?"

"Watch your back. Rossweild is a slippery little weasel and Perry Jordan is a veritable snake. A very dangerous snake."

"Yessir. I will, Sir. We all will."

***

Chapter 92

A night in DC . . . with Brick!

---

*E*vie's first day on the job as a lobbyist had passed like a dream. *Has it only been one day?* The morning had been filled with phone calls, short ones with aides and secretaries, long ones with some of the senators themselves. And after a pleasant lunch with Helen, it had begun again. It had been tremendously rewarding. Four senators who had been on the fence had agreed to block the GoMO, simply because Evie had convinced them that Martin Bascomb was against it. Seven had agreed to meet with her privately over the next week, and almost fifteen other fence sitters were scheduled to attend Helen's presentation on Thursday.

Evie beamed with pleasure when she recalled Helen's praise. "This is wonderful, Evie! I am so pleased with your efforts. You're a *natural*. Have you thought about becoming a lobbyist? We could use someone like you in Washington on a full time basis, you know."

Evie's lashes had dropped demurely. "Helen, please! *Any* botanist could do what I've done."

"Not really, Evie. We've had several experts present our views over the past year . . . and none of them got these results." Helen pointed toward the list. "We'll have a majority, judging from today's results." Helen smiled with her eyes, before adding, "And Tom will be so pleased!" But the smile faded abruptly, replaced by something unfathomable.

BACK IN HER HOTEL ROOM, Evie scowled at the mirror. *Look at me—I'm a wreck! I can't let Brick see me like this.* She headed straight for the shower, then spent the next hour trying on outfits. It would be her first night in Washington with Brick and she wanted to look her best.

***

Chapter 93

The factory.

John peered at the abandoned factory complex. "There it is, Manny—it's right where Perkins said it would be."

"Looks like it."

"Okay, now. According to him there are two security guards on SanFidel's payroll and they're pretty lax. We'll have to take care of them first—then we can get this show on the road." After that declaration, Manny unlocked the trunk and pulled out three leather cases. "Here, John. You take these so I can be free to deal with our friends in there."

"Sure. Whatever you say." John lifted one shoulder strap across his head. The weight tugged at his shoulder. "This isn't too bad," he said. Then he swung the smaller straps across his other shoulder. "Okay, your mule's ready—so let's go."

"Mule? For Pete's sake, you've only got thirty pounds or so!"

"Thirty pounds too many for an old geezer like me."

"Just remember, you said the 'g' word, not me." Manny chuckled as he headed toward the old factory. It was about two hundred feet away. He turned around. "Think you can make it without whimping out on me?"

"Just lead the way and keep your ears open. If the wheezing stops, you'll know I died."

The two men approached a rundown little trailer that had once housed the office staff for an onsite construction crew. It had been abandoned for years and the door

319

grudgingly opened to reveal foul air, redolent with mildew and rotting debris.

A regular breeding ground for asthma, John thought. On one wall three yellow slickers, now dusty and slightly cracked after years of fluctuating temperatures, hung on wooden pegs. B-O-C-A was spelled out in large black letters on a poster that outlined details of the National Building Code. Faded foundation plans were stacked on top of a makeshift plywood work surface. Dust was everywhere, damp and rank with nasty rodent feces, even on the counter next to an old coffee maker.

Manny couldn't resist. "Yum! How about a nice cup of coffee?" He was rewarded with a deep scowl.

"Not right now, thanks. I'd rather kiss a monkey's Dutch uncle." Still carrying the bags, John stiffly looked around. "They haven't been in here—nobody has—for a long time." He jumped to the ground and moaned from the strain of his burden. "My shoulders already have half-inch welts on them. Now I know what it feels like to wear a bra strap. Betty has big welts from hers."

Manny gave him a squinty look and shook his head. The trailer was only about fifty feet away from the factory, near a side entrance. "Okay, let's go. Stay as quiet as you can, and follow me. And remember, my hand up means stop. Hand down means retreat—*slowly and quietly.*"

"Right. Up, stop. Down, retreat. Gotcha!" John repeated with a gravelly whisper.

They crept through the administrative halls of the old factory until they found what appeared to be the "home base" of the guards.

***

Chapter 94

Oops—wrong room!

---

*M*ac had asked Sadie-Lee to scope the place out, so once she was fully dressed, she wandered in an apparently aimless manner. Servants seemed to be everywhere, busy with last-minute preparations. She saw two familiar faces and wondered if they were Captain Roberts' men.

On the second floor, she systematically rushed into bedrooms and then apologized profusely, claiming to have entered by mistake. The first four rooms were either empty or occupied by innocent couples. But she hit pay dirt just two doors down from her own. She was sure she caught a glimpse of Senator Monroe before an inner door slammed shut. Damo and his friend Bender were seated at a small round table.

"Oops! Oh, hello boys—I guess I wasn't watching where I was going!" Bender's stare was unnerving, but Damo gave her a wink. "Not a good time, honey."

Sadie-Lee offered a seductive glance. "Hi there, Damo. Guess I stumbled into the boy's room, huh?" She faltered just enough, then backed out, but not before she could give Damo an encouraging smile.

"I'm looking forward to the party tonight—you know what I mean?" She squeezed her lids seductively, smoothed one hand down her hip and let out a breathless giggle. As she pulled the door shut, she heard Damo's response. *Yuck!* She thought and decided she'd better get back to Mac and Handy.

***

321

Chapter 95

Brick's gone, Jerry! He's gone!

---

*E*vie was worried. It was 9:30 PM, and Brick had not checked in with her yet. *Brick!* She could not stop thinking about him—his intense eyes that brightened when he smiled at her; his strong arms that held her just yesterday on the swing, his sharp wit—he had been such fun at breakfast this morning—and his caressing voice. *So, where is he now?*

By quarter of ten, Evie decided she had to do something. With shaking fingers she dialed Martin's number. Hours seemed to pass with each ring. *Come on, Jerry! Hurry up and answer the darned telephone!*

Jerry's light contralto finally broke the monotonous string of rings. "Hello, Bascomb residence, may I help you?"

"Hi, Jerry, it's Evie! Is, umh, Barry still there?"

"Evie? Hello! No he isn't. What's the matter?"

"Brick's gone, Jerry, he's gone!"

"BRICK'S GONE?"

Jerry's eyes opened wide, but he forced his voice into its professional, soothing tone. "Okay, calm down, Sweetie. Start at the beginning and tell me everything." When she hesitated, he gave her time to collect her thoughts.

"I'm sorry, Jerry, but I don't think there's anything important that I could tell you."

"It's okay, Evie—but please try. Sometimes in the re-telling things come up that we don't even realize we know."

She looked up at the ceiling and pursed her lips, her

322

mind rushing through the day's events.

"Okay. Well, we had breakfast at the cafe downstairs. Umh, I'm at the Alexander Hotel, by the way. And, well—he was going to check on a few things, but he didn't say what." She squeezed her eyes shut and rested her forehead on her fist. "Wait! He did say something about clothes . . ."

"Clothes?" Jerry groaned. "Did he say anything about returning to our house?"

"Oh, Jerry, I didn't think about that. I don't know."

"Well. I've got General Carrey's number. I think I'll give him a call. Maybe he can send someone to the house to check it out. In the meantime, I want you to stay put and get some rest. I'll call you if I hear anything. Don't worry, Evie. I'm sure he's okay."

"Thanks Jerry. I feel better just talking to you."

"Good. I'm glad you called."

"But Jerry . . . ?"

"What?"

"Helen already made arrangements for a cab for me in the morning. I'll be at her office for most of the day tomorrow, so will you call me there?"

"Of course. What's the number?"

EVIE HUNG UP AND STARED at the telephone. *Please ring and be Brick. Or be Jerry with good news!*

JERRY HUNG UP THEN DIALED the general's number. As he hoped, Harry agreed to send someone out to search for Brick.

***

323

Chapter 96

*A*lexander's mansion was the scene of lively activity. Servants had been at work for days, scrubbing every inch of every room, and the caterers were now bustling about importantly, wanting everything perfect for their wealthiest client's big party. In the front entry the crystal chandelier sparkled more brilliantly than ever and the teak walls gleamed with a fresh application of scented oil and tireless buffing.

Alexander was in his glory as he surveyed the grand dining room. *Yes, this will do. This will do, indeed.* He was pleased, but he did not intend to compliment his staff. *Mustn't spoil them, they'd just slack off.* He hoped there was enough crystal and silver to impress his guests. Satisfied with the results, Alexander returned to his office for another hour of paperwork before retiring to his suite to prepare for the party. He reviewed the latest quarterly report from SanFidel and dictated half a dozen letters for Martha to transcribe the next day. Then he paged Henderson.

Henderson knocked at the open door. "You called, Sir?"

"Yes, Henderson. I'll be in my rooms shortly to dress. See that Isaac has everything ready."

"Yessir. I'll call him at once, Sir." The flapless servant turned on his heal and returned to his own duties, inwardly bemoaning, *Now why did he have to bother me with that? He could just as easily have called Isaac himself.*

But once he was seated at his own desk, he obediently made the call.

PERRY JORDAN PACED impatiently in his room. *Just three hours 'til the big event. I should be happy, but something just doesn't feel right.* Perry decided to check in on Monroe to reinforce the need to be persuasive. *Gotta be sure he believes I'll follow through.*

Perry need not have worried. Tom Monroe was very much convinced that he was willing and able—and perhaps even eager—to kill every single person at Domino One to achieve his goal.

When Perry was convinced that the senator would remain cooperative, he decided to fill the rest of his time in Alexander's private gym. While he was no muscular dynamo, he was weight conscious and spent countless hours at the treadmill. He found that he could think better during physical activity. He believed that the extra hard pumping of the blood enhanced his thought process.

SADIE-LEE WAS TELLING Mac and Handy about her find.

"I'm sure I saw Senator Monroe before the adjoining door slammed shut."

"Good work, Sadie. God, it's a relief to know he's alive, but I wonder why he's here with them? I can't believe he'd be involved with their scheme. Are you sure he was dressed for the party?"

"Yes. He was in a tux."

Mac puckered her lips and scrunched her brows, not knowing what to make of it.

"Well, I guess we'll find out soon enough." She turned her attention back to the items on the bed. "Handy, you're amazing." Handy had made her own special preparations for the party, including one of her favorite inventions called the Bug Buster. It created a magnetic resonance designed to inhibit all known surveillance equipment.

325

Handy said, "It'll create a 'bug free zone' of about thirty square feet—enough for our purposes here." She turned toward her friend. "So, Sadie—it's time to choose your weapon."

There was an arsenal of state-of-the-art tools for self defense and criminal apprehension to choose from, each piece designed for use with formal attire. Mac's belt, a beautiful golden cord that encircled her slim waistline several times, doubled as a French garrote or a simple rope to tie up her victims, and its unusual buckles concealed a set of handcuffs. The bangles on her matching bracelet contained tiny syringes. One quick jab would render an opponent unconscious. Her choker held spare bullets for the Walther revolver that was built into her golden zippered purse.

Mac watched with satisfaction as Sadie-Lee wrapped a silver garrote around her own slim waistline. She grinned devilishly and thought, *those guys won't know what hit them.*

***

Chapter 97

Alexander felt a prickly sensation.

A lexander fussed and fidgeted, causing Henderson to lose his grip on his employer's black tie. *Crochity little man. I don't know why he insists on having me tie this thing—Isaac could have done it. I can't wait until I'm free of his incessant orders. After all these years of faithful service, he still treats me like a slave.* Henderson clamped his jaw tight and tried again. This time Alexander remained still.

"There, Sir, it's done." Despite his relief, Henderson's jaw returned to its clench. *These next few hours are going to feel like an eternity, even longer than the decades I've spent looking out for him.*

Henderson's thoughts switched to Alexander's kind father, James Rossweild. He asked the spirit of James to forgive him. *I know I have failed your son, somehow. But I must help them to stop him this time. I must.*

"Is there anything more, Mr. Rossweild?"

"No, Henderson. You may go."

Alexander watched as Henderson spun around on one heel and left. *I don't understand how he can do that. Like a damned dancer, always pirouetting about.*

AT THE FRONT ENTRY the guests had already started to arrive. Scientists, musicians, business leaders, politicians and their supporters, and other members of society's elite flowed into the mansion, each of them eager to see and be seen. Mozart's 'Princess Rose Garden' wafted from unseen speakers to lend an air of elegance to the occasion. The caterer's staff, impeccable in their starched white shirts, waltzed silently through dozens of small groups of guests, offering hors d'oeuvres and aperitifs.

The party was going without a hitch. The guests were enjoying themselves and the service was impeccable. But still, Alexander felt a prickly sensation at the nape of his neck. He glanced about—Damo was oblivious to all else as he attempted to charm Senator Thornton's wife, and Ricardo was nodding with exaggerated animation as a group of women chattered around him. Alexander saw that his security team was interspersed throughout the room. *At least they seem to be alert,* he grumbled. But the prickly feeling would not go away, and to make matters worse, he was annoyed to see Senator Greesley's wife wave for his attention. He expelled an angry puff of air when he saw her launch herself in his direction. He thought, *Good Lord, that wretched woman knows I saw her.*

Like a ship destined for battle, Mrs. Greesley cruised across the crowded room leaving small clusters of people to regroup in her wake. *The old battle-ax! Well, I won't let her hold me up for too long. I'll just have to get rid of her.*

***

Chapter 98

"I gotta get away!"

*M*elvin was frantic. Ritchie had just called to say he overheard Ricardo on the telephone. The sneaky little twinkie was bragging that if he got caught, he could pin it all on Melvin—even a kidnapping! Melvin believed every word, because his buddy Ritchie, who knew everything that went on at the Miller Building, was totally reliable. *Totally!*

"What kidnappin'?" Melvin asked.

Ritchie had lowered his voice, "Word's out Miller got wunna them other senators upta his office an' had 'em taken away, an'he ain't been seen since. I think it was Monroe. Yeah, Senator Monroe."

Melvin squeaked, "I ain't done no kidnappin'!"

"Yeah. Well, that ain't what Ricardo's gonna say. An' if it comes down ta your word against his, I think we know who their gonna believe. And it ain't gonna be *you!*"

Melvin knew that Ritchie was right. Ritchie was always right.

I ain't involved in no kidnappin', Melvin thought when he hung up. *I gotta get away!* He collapsed onto his couch, slapped his palms together prayer fashion, and tried to think. Sometimes, when he squeezed his eyes shut real tight, it helped.

He tried, but no thoughts came.

"Okay, maybe I gotta move around a little. Was I movin' the last time I got a' idea?" He decided to give it a try. He lifted his corpulent torso off the couch and started to pace. With squinty eyes and bouncing belly he thumped back and forth across the room, hoping to come up with something. After several passes he was dizzy and gave up. *Nope. Nothing, darnit!*

Then he remembered. "Oh yeah! I was eating! I think better when I eat!" He raced toward the kitchen, tugged at the refrigerator door and foraged behind the bottles and slimy lumps that once had been tomatoes. The only edible thing he could find was a chunk of cheese. He decided that it would be okay to eat it—as long as he avoided the fuzzy blue spots.

Melvin searched for the best angle to get a good bite and wondered if cheese was brain food. *Prob'ly not—mice ain't too swift.* He carefully sunk his teeth into the good edge. "Gee, this ain't too bad." He decided it was worth the effort to stop and eat even if cheese was not brain food. He reached for a beer to wash it down.

After the hasty feast, Melvin was ready to try and think.

"Okay. I gotta get outta here, but I need a place to go." His fleshy facial muscles puckered with the effort, but this time it did not take long.

"I know, I could visit Uncle Todd!" His brows shot up as he thought, *Hey, the cheese worked! I got a' idea!*

MELVIN DID NOT HAVE much family left. His father walked out on them twenty years ago and his mother died ten years after that. His father was an only child and his mother had only one elder brother, Todd, who had remained childless. There were no siblings, cousins, or happy family get-togethers in Melvin Marshall's life.

Uncle Todd had left the east coast long ago. Although he had been disappointed in her choice of a husband, he had faithfully kept in touch with his sister while she was alive and had always inquired about his nephew's well-being. For a few years after her funeral he continued to send Christmas cards.

Melvin met with his uncle only once after his mother

died. That was when Uncle Todd had told him about a spa that he and a friend had just purchased. *That would'a been about five years ago, when Uncle Todd come ta' Washin'tin.*

Melvin smiled as he remembered the lovely lunch that they shared together. He had gone all out and purchased extra tomatoes and cheese to add to the pizza, but for some reason Uncle Todd did not eat much and he had stopped sending Christmas cards after that. Melvin figured he had become too busy with his spa. The last card was postmarked Tucson, Arizona. Crusted and discolored from the spills and stains of beers and tears, it still dangled on the door of the fridge—Melvin's only memento of current family ties. Uncle Todd's handwritten message had faded away during one particularly poignant beer-induced crying session, but Melvin remembered it word for word, like a poem. He mouthed the comforting words now as he quivered with fear and anticipation. *"Best regards for this holiday season. Fondly Yours, Uncle Todd."* Melvin particularly liked the 'fondly yours' part.

Melvin hoped that Uncle Todd was still in the Tucson area. He tried to remember the spa as his uncle had described it, and shivered with distaste as he pictured scant portions of celery, tiny lumps of cottage cheese and—*yuck!*—fruit on his dinner plate. *That's how people ate at them places. No beer or munchies allowed.*

"Spa, schmahh," he mumbled. *That's just a fancy name for a fat farm for rich people.* He almost changed his mind about going, but fuzzy visions of prison and kidnappers with knives and guns filled his head. *Well,* he decided, *I'll just keep some beer and corn chips some place outta sight.*

MELVIN SEARCHED UNDER his bed for his mother's suitcase and tossed all of his clean clothing into it. Then he scraped last week's dirty clothes off the floor and tossed them in before reverently wrapping his most prized possession—a framed photograph of his mother, taken on her fortieth birthday. He never failed to get misty eyed when he thought about that day. He missed her terribly.

Melvin got stuffed up and his nose turned redder than ever as he choked back the tears; but he felt better as he envisioned her smiling with delight, all dressed in white, as she watched him from above. *If she's watchin' frub heaven I bet she's happy I'm gonna get tageder wid Ungle Todd.* Melvin wiped his nose on one of his dirty T-shirts. Moments later, his eyes glowed with excitement as he pawed through the trash bin under the kitchen sink. It was the perfect hiding place for his money—he knew that no one would *ever* search there.

Good thing that little twinkie paid me, he thought. But the anger quickly faded when his fingers came into contact with the bundles of bills. He still had almost all of the ten thousand dollars from Ricardo. He held up the greasy money in triumph as he whispered excitedly, "Tucson, here I come!" He felt giddy as he reverently fingered each greasy bundle.

***

Chapter 99

Manny delivered a well-placed chop.

"*O*kay, here's where they watch the grounds." John saw that one wall housed a series of surveillance screens. Across the room, a Mr. Coffee machine and a box of crackers shared a countertop with two mugs and a sprinkling of salty crumbs. He felt the mugs.

"They've still got warm coffee in them. Must'a just started their rounds." He thought, *I can't believe they're stupid enough to both be out at the same time.* "Let's watch the screens—maybe we'll get lucky and they won't come back together." He grimaced, "Boy, it'll be good to drop these bags for awhile." He slid the straps off his shoulders and carefully settled the bags down onto the floor, afraid the contents would go boom—*real loud, real hard*—if they were not handled with care.

Manny's eyes were already riveted toward the surveillance screens. He sat up suddenly and pointed. "Hey, look at that—it must be the shipping dock."

"Yeah. Thank God it's empty. Man . . . I'm glad we got here before they were scheduled to go into production. Can you imagine what'll happen to our food supply if that stuff gets spread around?" He looked at Manny and shook his head, then settled in to wait until the guards came into view.

"WELL, FINALLY," JOHN BREATHED as one of the guards appeared. "It looks like he's headed this way.

See? The front door is behind him." He studied the man, tried to estimate his size and strength.

Manny whispered, "Why don't you stay right here in full sight of him and I'll hide behind the door. Just pretend you've been waiting for him, then I'll grab him when I get the chance."

"What do you suggest I say?"

"Say whatever you want. Umh, you could tell him you've got a message for him. Then pretend you can't find it. Search your pockets or something. You know—just keep his attention on you."

"Whatever you say. But when he shoots me first and asks questions later, I hope you'll call my wife. Tell her I was a valiant hero, okay?" His whisper was more of a tight-throated squeak.

Manny just grinned.

A FEW MINUTES LATER the wide stride of a large man's footsteps echoed in the hallway. John heard something jingle. *Probably keys on the guy's belt.* The latch jerked upwards. John almost jumped with it and Manny flattened himself tighter against the wall. With a soft pfft and a squeak, the door swung open to reveal a sour-faced guard. When he saw John he drew his gun.

John whipped his hands high overhead. "For God's sake, don't shoot. I just have a message for you."

"Oh yeah? I'm not expectin' no message."

"Well, I have one. You *are* the security guard here, aren't you?"

"Maybe."

"Then look at this."

John reached into his pocket and the guard adjusted the aim of his gun and barked, "Hold it, bud!" He lowered his voice to a menacing growl. "Go real slow."

John pretended to fumble for a note. "Yessir. Yessir," he prattled. "I'm gonna check my pants pocket now, okay?"

"Ya know what? I don't believe you. We don't put nothin' in writin' here. So, you're gonna tell me who the hell you are an' what yer doin' here, or I'll blow you to kingdom come, one piece at a time. You got three seconds." He shook his Glock.

"I get your point." John yanked a fistful of things from his pocket and managed to drop several pieces, including a folded slip of paper, onto the floor. He wondered why Manny was taking so long to reveal himself. *Any time now Manny—let's not wait for me to die . . . !*

He pointed at the paper. "See? There it is."

The guard stepped closer toward the mess on the floor and puckered his lips. John could see that he was trying to decide whether he should pick up the alleged message, or not.

The distraction was what Manny had been waiting for. He delivered a well placed chop on the back of the startled guard's neck. There was a dull thud as he hit the floor.

"One down, one to go," John announced. "Boy, I'm glad you're on my team."

Manny kicked at the prostrate figure. "We'd better hide the big lug before the other guy comes."

Movement on the video screen caught his attention. "Quick, help me get him behind the desk. Then we'll try the same routine on his buddy—if you're up to it."

They dragged their victim around the desk, tucking his arms and legs out of sight, before resuming their positions.

The second guard was even easier. He walked right up to John and hadn't even drawn his weapon when Manny jumped out and knocked him unconscious. Manny pulled a length of rope out of one of the bags and tied them up as he explained, "I'm pretty sure they'll be out for awhile, but I don't want to take any chances." When he finished tying them up, he headed toward the door.

"Wait a minute," John pleaded. "I need to get these straps so the bags don't bump each other, or me."

"Okay, but hurry up. We gotta get down to the lower level within ten minutes and get these babies set, if we want to get outta here before our two friends here wake up. I'm sure they're gonna be itchin' for revenge."

"Yeah, I bet they'll be downright cranky." John tugged at one of the straps and shrugged his shoulders up and down. "Okay, I'm ready."

JOHN AND MANNY DASHED through the old factory. In one room, huge spools of colored wires were stacked like blocks and galvanized tanks filled the three-story expanse like giant funnels. A metal staircase wound its way to the top of the tanks. John hoped the golden concoction would never flow through the system. To his left, he spied an opening to a stairway.

"Hey, let's see if this is the way down to the lab."

"Okay."

Manny took the lead. At the first landing, he stopped to listen before proceeding to the next level. As they continued their descent, John took advantage of each stop to rest his load on the handrail.

At the third landing, Manny whispered, "We shouldn't have too much farther to go."

"Good."

Much to John's relief, the next landing was the last one.

The heavy metal door beckoned, but before he cracked it open, Manny drew his gun. He cautiously peered through the narrow opening.

"Nothing yet. Just an empty hallway."

John gave a nod then followed quietly. The air was hot and thick with moisture that clung to everything. Several doors flanked the hallway. Manny peered into one of them and saw a series of shelves that lined the far wall. They looked like miniature bleachers loaded with potted plants. He glanced upwards. On the ceiling a grid of lighting fixtures glowed softly.

"Look at at this setup, John—they must be testing the germination process. I think those are grow lights."

John peered upwards. "Looks like it."

Manny closed the door, then crept toward the end of the hallway. He peeked into another room that brought back memories of his high school chemistry class. He immediately turned and gestured toward John. "This's gotta be it. See that vial over there? It's full of liquid, a *golden* liquid."

"It's just like the stuff in the commander's video.

"Okay, then. Let's set up our little surprise. Go ahead and open up the two small bags. They carry the battery units that'll make these babies work."

John winced when Manny ripped open the big bag and pawed through its contents. With deft fingers he built two explosive units and quickly attached one to the far wall of the laboratory and programmed the clock.

"There." He nodded with satisfaction. "C'mon, let's find a good spot for the other one. I can't wait to blow this place to smithereens."

John nodded and wondered why no one was on site.

"Hey, Manny. Don't you think there'd be a scientist here or something?"

"Yeah. I've been wondering about it. But, maybe they're taking the weekend off."

"Well, just to be sure, I'm gonna check the other rooms while you plant your next toy. I don't want to hurt anybody—even if they do work for these creeps."

"Okay. Go to it. But make it quick."

John peered into three other rooms. Finally satisfied that they were alone, except for the murderous guards. He experienced a momentary twinge of guilt, then remembered what Perkins had said about these men. They were all killers. He shrugged and returned to watch as Manny finished his work.

WHEN THE SECOND BOMB WAS IN PLACE, Manny whispered, "Let's get the hell out of here. They're set to go off in fifteen minutes." He looked at John and said, "Now it's fourteen minutes forty-nine seconds." John gulped and snatched up one of the bags. They raced up the stairwell and through the corridors until they found an exit, but when they burst through the door they found themselves in the path of a very large man. John thought, *I guess there were more than two after all.*

The stranger demanded, "Who are you? What were you doin' in there?"

John looked at his watch. They had eleven minutes to get at least a hundred feet clear of the building. He decided to play innocent. "Boy, am I glad to see you. We were just following a couple of snoops. They headed toward that van over there." He pointed to his left.

Without another word, the guy raced toward the vehicle.

Manny whispered, "I can't believe he fell for that."

MANNY RACED toward the nearby hillside—then gestured for John to follow. Sweat trickled down John's face as he struggled to keep up. He was only a few feet behind and not far from the crest of the hill when he stopped to catch his breath. He was glad to see there was no sign of the dolt who went after the fictitious intruders. He gasped, "Keep going, Manny! Don't wait for me—I'll be right behind you."

Manny had already reached the top when John yelled to keep going. On his way down the other side, he tripped on a gnarly root and tumbled to the ground. *Damn!* He sat up to inspect his ankle when a deafening roar shook the earth. His eyes scoured the hilltop, but John did not appear. He shrieked, "Sonofabitch!" And with ragged voice, he exclaimed, "John, you old fart—you better be okay! You hear me!"

*   *   *

Chapter 100

John tried to stand up.

---

*I*t felt like a war zone to John. In a matter of seconds the explosion turned the starless black of night into a brightly lit stage where red-hot metal fragments, fiery wooden splinters and a myriad of deadly projectiles flew toward their hapless targets. Secondary explosions created a cacophony that reverberated so forcefully he thought his skull might explode.

The first blast sent John sprawling to the ground. He had been close to the top of the hill and thought he was out of danger, but stinging sparks had singed the backs of his hands as he clasped them over his neck and head. A trickle of blood oozed from his nose as he cuddled the craggy ground, waiting for the sky to stop throwing shrapnel his way. It felt like an eternity—lying there, not knowing if a razor-sharp piece of metal was going to slice its way into his body, not knowing if Manny was okay.

And then it was over. Blissful silence replaced the roars of the explosions. The pulsating balls of flame stopped filling the sky with their too-bright ventures into the night.

Dammit, my fingers are stuck. John slowly spread them apart. Even more slowly, he craned his neck to look toward the building he and Manny had just vacated. *Was it only a few minutes ago?* It was ablaze.

AT FIRST, JOHN WAS confused by the silence. But then he realized he probably had been temporarily deafened by the explosions. Flames seemed to be everywhere as the buildings and debris continued to burn.

John tried to stand up, then mumbled, "Oh, crap," as he slumped into an unconscious heap.

***

Chapter 101

"Fingers, you look impeccable!"

---

*I*n his delight to have the world-renowned botanist at his party, Alexander had arranged for Martin and Fingers to rent tuxedos at Rembrandt's Rentals, Inc. They arrived in plenty of time to get fittings and have lunch.

WHEN THEY RETURNED to Rembrant's, Martin and Fingers were asked to try the suits on, ". . . just to be sure they are perfect for Mr. Rossweild's party."

Martin stood back to admire his companion. "Well, young man, you look *impeccable*. That tux appears to have been made just for you."

"You think so?"

"Yes, I do. Go ahead, look for yourself!"

Fingers strode up to the full-length mirror.

"Wow, whaddaya know—I never looked so good!" He put one hand on his hip, grabbed his old shirt and danced. Martin watched with father-like pride and then turned to the amused rental clerk.

"I would say that's a yes. And mine, too, please—we need them for tonight, so we'll take them with us."

***

Chapter 102

*M*ac was satisfied with her outfit. Handy's inventions blended perfectly and would not arouse suspicion. She felt ready to handle the unexpected, and as she stared at her image in the mirror, she heard Sadie-Lee snidely ask, "I thought you hated to dress up, Major . . ."

Mac scowled. "I do. Just checking the equipment."

"We could *see* that."

"*Handy's* equipment, you dip stick." Mac blushed and shook her fist at the two chortling women.

"Okay, ladies, move—and that's an order! But remember, just scout out the perimeters, entertain your marks, and reconvene at the punch bowls every twenty minutes, or so. We're not to move until we get the captain's signal." She took a deep breath and forcefully exhaled before adding, "And remember, we have orders to keep our eyes on Perry Jordan and Damo, but I think we need to watch their buddy Bender, too. I'll keep an eye on Perry. Handy, you seem to have caught Bender's eye so you can have him."

"Oh, thanks," Handy gushed with a sloppy salute.

Mac ignored her. "And Sadie-Lee, you can have Damo. After all, you *did* tell him you were excited about tonight!" She could not stifle a grin. "Just think, you've got the easiest mark—he'll be so busy talking about himself, he won't have time to be suspicious of you."

"Yup." Sadie-Lee muttered. "Lucky me."

"Okay, let's go." Mac patted her buckle with a determined grin. She thought, *It'll feel good to send Perry Jordan off in shackles.*

WHEN MAC AND HER CREW entered the main ballroom, most of the other guests were already there. She saw several familiar faces, including senators, scientists and some of the most highly visible stars of the Fortune 500 realm. As she continued to scan the room, she recognized one of Captain Robert's men who was weaving in and out of the crowd as he deftly balanced a tray. He paused next to her and she accepted a martini with an appreciative nod. He gave no indication that he recognized her. *Good man,* she thought. But she wondered wryly if he even *could* recognize her out of uniform.

Mac was still speculating about how Roberts got the guy a position on the caterer's staff on such short notice when she spied Perry Jordan. She forced a seductive grin of recognition onto her lips and hurried toward him.

Perry was talking with Senator Miller, but he was not too busy to notice Mac. *What a honey,* he thought. He held up his hands with a warm welcome.

"Margaret . . . you are more beautiful than I remembered." He turned toward the senator and uttered a hasty introduction. "Senator Miller, may I present Margaret MacVain?" He took Mac's hand and explained, "Margaret, this is Senator Miller—a very important man in Washington, you know."

Mac smiled and accepted Miller's hand. "Of course. Hello, Senator. We're so lucky to have you in Washington. Aren't you the one who fought so hard for more money for the orphans in your state? Inspiring. Truly inspiring." *God, I'm making myself sick with all this sweetness,* she thought, *but he's lapping it up.*

Perry tugged gently at her hand. "I'm sure the senator is itching to make his rounds. Let's let him go, and get you a fresh drink." Miller bowed politely and expressed his thanks before escaping into the crowd. Perry followed him with his eyes before admitting, "He's such a dullard." He quickly altered his voice to a seductive croon to ask, "So how can I properly thank you for rescuing me?"

"How about starting with that refill?" Mac pulled her hand free and hurried in the direction of the bar. *Oops, that's not very friendly—I should be a little more encouraging.* She turned and winked at him. He parried with a lascivious grin and she thought, *In your dreams.* As they wove their way through the crowd, Mac looked for Handy and Sadie-Lee. She was happy to see that they had found Damo and Bender. *I hope their targets are as easy as mine. And I hope Captain Roberts does his thing real soon.* Perry was busy with the bartender so she felt safe to scan her surroundings once more. What she saw stunned her.

A FAMILIAR FIGURE crossed the expansive hall-way to Mac's right and her heart jumped to her throat. *It can't be!*

She had to get away from Perry, free to investigate without arousing suspicion.

Mac put her hand on Perry's shoulder and excused herself.

"I hope you don't mind holding that for me, Perry. I need to powder my nose." She took a few steps before turning back with a dazzling smile. "Why don't you find us a nice cozy spot on the terrace?" *What a Romeo,* she thought, instantly regretting the suggestion. But she had to get him away from the bar, and she had to do it quickly.

***

Chapter 103

*W*hen the musicians began their first session, Perkins figured it was safe to wander through the mansion in search of likely hiding spots for Rossweild's secret safe. He reasoned that he could always say he was looking for photogenic backgrounds. *While the metal detector's in the case, I can say it's photo equipment—nobody'll know the difference.* He hoped to find evidence that would link Rossweild to the unethical use of Julia Mahoney's formula.

The metal detector that John had given him was the most highly developed model in existence. It was not even on the market. The Still-Life MEG-X-200 had a small screen that would show a silhouette of the object to be unearthed. And it could be programmed to ignore up to forty metal items, including nails, bottle caps, and even pipes, steel girders, wires and keys. Its creators bragged that it was light years beyond other models. Supposedly, it could reveal the safe even if it was hidden behind concrete walls or under several layers of flooring material.

After poking his nose through a half dozen doors, Perkins finally found Rossweild's study. *So far, so good,* he thought as he closed the door behind him. *I hope no one walks in on me.*

***

Chapter 104

*A*lexander's surveillance system had been deactivated and Sam The Can and Rob were set up in a pair of oak trees on the Eastern perimeter of the grounds. They each had a pair of binoculars with night vision.

Sam watched the party from his perch high upon the largest gnarly oak tree. He could see the entire east end of the mansion, including the patio off the ballroom. Two pairs of French doors were wide open, offering a great view of the scene within. Snugged in the fork of two enormous branches, Sam was able to watch the people as they milled about. When he saw Fingers in his tux, he thought, W*ay ta go guy—you never looked so good!*

Sam's left foot felt numb so he juggled his beer can and eye gear and shifted to a more comfortable position. *Good thing this perch is wide enough,* he thought. *Boy, I wish I had a tree like this when I was a kid.* As he studied the guests, a light popped on in a room far to the left. When he swung his binoculars in that direction, he saw Perkins. *Way ta go, Commander! I wonder how long it'll take before you find somethin'?* But he nearly dropped his beer when he saw a beautiful woman appear behind Perkins. *Oh, oh. He's got trouble now.* He almost fell off his perch, though, when he saw the two of them join in a romantic clinch. He thought, *Holy smokes, he works fast!*

PERKINS WAS OBLIVIOUS to the beautiful

woman in gold when she slid through the door, but the familiar scent of her perfume caught his attention. He dared not move. *It can't be,* his brain screamed. *No way Mac would be here. Who the hell is it? Should I spin around and rush her? No. Pretend to be looking for my lighter or something? Maybe. No—that's not good either. I could extol on the virtues of mid-Edwardian antiquities . . .?* He turned to get a glimpse of the feminine intruder and the relief almost knocked him of his feet. It *was* her.

PERKINS AND MAC melded comfortably into a long-awaited embrace. When they finally broke apart, he kept a tight grip on her hand and asked softly, "So, Major Mackenzie—what brings you to this den of iniquity? Or should I ask, *who* brought you?"

"Harry, of course. And concern about you." Her whispered reply sent a shiver of pleasure though him.

"I should have known. Thank God the old bird is okay. I haven't been able to reach him." Perkins pushed her at arms length. "But don't tell him I said that." Before she could answer, he clasped her tightly to him once more.

She nuzzled her cheek into the breast of his elegant tuxedo, breathed the familiar scent of him, before quietly taunting, "Scout's honor. I won't say a word—but you'll owe me."

"Good. I've got lots of ideas about how I can pay you back. God, Mac. I've missed you."

Mac allowed waves of pleasure to run through her as he held her, but she knew it had to end. She pulled away.

"Oh, Tim. I was so worried about you."

"I know. I'm sorry, but I discovered Rodney was on the take and I couldn't risk a call."

"Yes, Harry told me. And he's more furious than I've ever seen him. I don't envy that poor little rascal."

"Little *rascal*? Your *poor little rascal* is a very mean, very rich little *rat*. And he deserves anything Harry can dish out, and then some."

"Oh, I know. And I agree, but it was just such a

shock. Who would ever have suspected baby-faced Rodney? I mean he looks like such a *cherub*!"

"Right. He's a real choir boy." Perkins had had enough of that conversation and he did not want to waste any more time on Rodney.

"OKAY. I'VE GOT TO work fast here, Mac. I've been searching for a secret safe. Apparently Rossweild keeps a tight reign on everyone in his organization. No one else has the total picture. So . . ."

She interrupted. ". . . So, that means he must have records somewhere. Probably here?"

"Exactly. I'm sure we'll be able to nail him and his cohorts to the wall when we find those records. If they exist."

"I sure hope so." She leaned toward the metal detector. "That's quite a toy. What is it?"

"It's the latest version of metal detectors. Space age technology. Not even on the market yet. I borrowed it from a treasure hunter."

"A treasure hunter?"

"It's a long story. I'll tell you all about him later."

"Okay. I hate to leave you now that I've found you, but I think I had better return to the shindig." She offered a seductive grin before adding, "Before my date misses me."

"Your date, huh? Should I be worried?"

"Always. They say it keeps the interest going you know. But seriously, he's one of our suspects, a regular *charmer*."

"Oh. Well, sure, as long as he's charming . . ."

Perkins could feel her scowl, but he kept his eyes glued to the dials of his space age metal detector as Mac slipped out of the room.

***

348

Chapter 105

*W*hen Fingers and Martin reached the mansion, they were astonished to see the number of people already milling about. "Now remember, use that magnificent memory of yours, and see if you can find the senator or my friend, Julia."

"Sure thing, Dr. B." Fingers strode proudly into the crowded room. It did not take long to locate Senator Thomas Monroe who was chatting with an elderly couple.

Fingers noticed that he clenched his martini with white knuckles and his eyes continually darted about. *Boy, this guy's as tight as a penny in Sam's hip pocket,* he thought. As soon as he had the opportunity, Fingers edged his way behind Senator Monroe. When the conversation turned to music he decided it was his chance to join in.

"Hey, Mr. Senator, Sir. I've got a great *C.D.* you should listen to. It was, umh, stuck away for a while, but we *found* it. Not a scratch or anything." Fingers tried to wink, but both brows dipped awkwardly.

Tom peered at the earnest young man. He whispered, "A *C.D.* you say, son?" He thought, *If I didn't know better, I'd think he was talking in code! But it can't be. He's just a boy—how could he be involved in this nightmare.*

Fingers tried again. "Could I get you somethin' ta eat, Sir? The mincemeat is pretty good." Fingers searched the senator's eyes with his own, virtually willing the man to listen between the lines. He gratefully accepted the canapés from the waiter and as he offered them to the astonished man, he whispered, "We're gonna make mincemeat outta these guys, Sir. Please come out on the terrace as soon as you can."

After delivering his cryptic message, Fingers disappeared into the crowd.

Tom scanned the room with renewed interest. *If I can believe that kid, C.D.'s been found and someone is going to end this happy charade.* He searched for possible allies. His eyes focused on Sadie-Lee. *There's the young blond who stumbled into our room earlier. I wonder?* As he considered the possibility, he decided, *No, she couldn't be involved— she's too fragile looking.*

Oh, it's probably just wishful thinking. How could I think that boy was trying to give me a secret message? My imagination's running overtime—I'm seeing a boy and a fragile blonde as super heroes. Talk about positive thinking! He tried to shrug off the feeling, but as he continued to scan the room he noticed that the mysterious boy stared back with even greater intensity from the patio door. *What the hell is wrong with that kid's eyes? Either he's trying to communicate something or he's just plain weird.*

Tom decided it would not hurt to check it out. *Oh well. I guess I will step out onto the terrace for a few minutes. I don't think Jordan's men will stop me—I'm not scheduled to give my little pep talk for another hour or so.* He casually made his way across the room. He spied the boy when he reached the terrace. He was talking earnestly with an elderly gentleman. *Hmmm—he looks familiar.*

AS HE TALKED, THE ELDERLY MAN bobbed his head. He seemed to be shifting his focus between the boy and something on the patio floor. Tom caught the boy's eye as he observed, "So, I find you again. Quite a shindig Rossweild's cooked up, isn't it?"

Fingers nodded as he struggled to swallow a succulent stuffed mushroom. Meanwhile the elderly man's eyes continued to drift toward his feet.

Tom could not help but ask, "Are you all right, Sir? Have you lost something?"

Martin looked up. "What? Thank you, but I'm fine. Oh, you're Senator Monroe, aren't you? I'm so glad you're all right!" Martin stepped closer and dropped his voice. "A lot of people have been worried about you." As he spoke, Martin finally stooped to retrieve something that was wedged between the stones. Tom saw that it was an opal button.

"WHO ARE YOU? HOW DID YOU . . ?"

"I'm Martin Bascomb, Senator Monroe. I spoke before your committee a few years ago on the importance of long range testing within the realm of biotechnology. And I know that SanFidel has been involved in some terrible business."

"Of course! But, I'm surprised to see you *here*."

"Believe me, Senator—I am not here to support Alexander's latest political machinations. No! But, of course, he does not know this."

"So, why *are* you here?"

"I'm searching for someone, Senator. A fellow botanist, actually. And I do believe this is one of her buttons. If I'm right, it proves she was here."

Martin held the button up for Tom to see. "Julia was quite fond of opals—she often wore clothing with opal buttons. And this . . ." he paused and clutched it tightly, ". . . was nestled between the patio stones. I'm afraid it's not a good sign. Not a good sign, at all."

Tom felt as if he would burst. So much had happened over the past twenty-four hours and here was this boy talking in circles with a world-renowned botanist who was preoccupied with a button.

Tom tugged on Martin's arm and invited him and Fingers to sit down at a nearby bench.

***

Chapter 106

No news is good news!

---

*E*vie was more exhausted than she had ever been. She had spent the entire day on the telephone describing the dangers of unregulated biotechnology, but her concern for Brick's safety heightened with each hour. And the memory of his kiss lingered in her mind like a ghostly presence. *God, this is awful,* she thought.

She arranged the papers neatly on her desk—then looked at the clock. *It's almost 4. I'm going to go crazy if I don't hear something soon!* She had just decided to call it a day and go back to her hotel room when Susan buzzed.

"Evie, there's a Jerry Johnson on the phone for you. He's on line two."

"Oh, thanks Susan! I'll take it right away."

"Hello, Jerry! Thank God you've called. Any news?"

"I'm afraid not, Evie." He tried to cheer her up. "But, then, you know the old saying—no news might be good news."

Silence hung between them.

"Evie. Are you there? Say something."

"I'm sorry, Jerry. I'm just so worried."

"I know, Sweetie, I know. But look. Harry's men will find him. You'll see."

A new wave of exhaustion swept over her. With quivering voice, she tried to speak. "Jerry . . . ?"

"Yes?"

"I'm going back to my hotel now. You've got the

number, right? Please call me as soon as you hear something."

"Of course." He heard the disconcerting drone of a disconnected line after she hung up.

***

Chapter 107

They know! Somehow they know!

---

*A*lexander saw Tom Monroe on the terrace with Martin Bascomb. *I don't like the looks of that. I don't like it one bit,* he muttered. His eyes swept quickly around the room and he saw too many unfamiliar faces. *Hell and damnation, they know. Somehow they know!* But he did not panic. He was prepared. Alexander Graham Rossweild was always prepared. And he saw the perfect excuse to leave the party.

"Jonathan! And Candice! How are you?" Alexander rushed forward to greet the Jensens with his most exuberant welcome. "I'm so glad you were able to come. I have something that I simply must show you—something you'll love!"

Candice gushed with pleasure. "Well, *thank* you Alexander. You are *so* kind. And now I'm *burning* with *curiosity*, my dear. So *do* tell me—what *is* it that you want us to *see*?" She emphasized at least one word in each sentence like an adolescent schoolgirl; but when she giggled and clapped her hands, Alexander thought she looked more like a seal begging for a fish. *And that ridiculous black dress emphasizes the fact, the way it snugs in at her thick ankles,* he thought.

"Oh, but it will spoil the fun if I reveal the surprise."

She giggled again as Alexander swept his arm theatrically and stepped forward to lead the way. "Just follow me, my lovely Madame." He felt like tossing Candice a ball to balance on her nose as he ushered her across the room.

CANDICE CLUNG to her host with giddy anticipation as her husband followed behind them. She wondered if he was finally going to show them the magnificent Edwardian desk that he had recently purchased at auction. She was prepared to offer him twice the price.

***

Chapter 108

"You won't find it here, Sir."

---

*P*erkins had not found any evidence in Alexander's study. His next search was in the library that overlooked the lawn at one end of the wing. Through the window he could see, and smell, a magnificent collection of lilies in muted oranges and brilliant yellows that billowed high above clumps of spear-like leaves.

He was adjusting the metal detector when Henderson walked in. *Oh, oh. He's a sharp old bird. How am I gonna stop him from tattling?*

He needn't have worried.

"You won't find it in here, Sir, but I can show you where it is."

"Is that so? And just what am I looking for?"

"Alexander's safe."

"Now why would I want his safe? I'm a journalist."

"No, you're not. Please trust me—I've been in touch with a man from Major General Carrey's office, Sir— Captain Roberts. He told me about you. You are Commander Perkins, are you not?"

Perkins was not ready to accept the man's word.

"Can you prove what you are saying?"

"Well, no, Sir. I can only beg you to listen to me." Henderson looked pained as he explained, "I have over-looked Alexander's faults for many, many years—I was trying to keep a promise, you see, to his father, James. But I cannot . . ." His voice cracked and dropped to a mere whisper. "He has gone too far this time and he must be stopped." With a faraway look in his eyes, Henderson's raspy whisper revealed a startling piece of information. ". . . And there was that scientist, Miss Mahoney. I heard Alexander order her demise."

It wasn't the words. It was Henderson's demeanor. Perkins believed the guilt and shame that he saw in the man's eyes.

"Okay," he said. "Show me the way . . ."

***

Chapter 109

Something's not right! It's just not right!

---

*I*mmaculate in his dress whites, Rodney spent the first hour of the evening dazzling young women—rich young women. And his current conquest was Jillian, the beautiful daughter of one of the wealthiest men in Alexander's circle of friends. He knew he could command a lot of respect with a woman like that clinging to his arm. He looked around, nodded at Senator Miller and Perry Jordan. He swelled with pride because they knew and responded to him, but he did not see Alexander Rossweild and that bothered him.

Rodney made a promise to call Jillian the next day and then set out to find his host. He looked around with a wary eye, and just like Alexander, he sensed danger. He thought, *Something's not right here. I'd better find Alexander right away. Maybe I'll earn a few brownie points in the process.*

IN ANOTHER WING, Perkins and Henderson peered at an image on the metal detector.

"Looks like you were right, Henderson. He's got a second safe here—right behind this one. Now all we need is to figure out how to get to it. Got any ideas?"

Before Henderson could respond Perkins heard the unmistakable click of the hammer of a gun. *Oh, Lord, we've been caught.* With hands high over his head, he turned to see who it was.

Alexander Rossweild stood in the doorway, his gun

aimed at Henderson. His eyes were cold. His voice, soft. Menacing.

"Yes, Henderson. Do tell us."

As Rossweild focused on his traitorous servant, Perkins considered his options. He realized he was too far away to pounce on the man. *The maniac would probably pull the trigger before I move an inch.* The only thing he could do was wait, but it was not easy when the adrenaline was pumping and the enemy was so close at hand.

When Henderson met Alexander's stare, his eyes were shiny with emotion. His Adams apple bobbed up and down as he swallowed, and Perkins wondered if the old man had any influence over Alexander Graham Rossweild. *Probably not,* he thought.

Henderson finally answered. "No, Sir. I cannot." His voice sounded tinny, almost robotic.

Perkins suspected that Alexander was capable of pulling the trigger and he realized the old manservant felt he deserved to die this way. After all, he did say he was responsible for the man's shortcomings and that he was ready to accept the consequences.

EVERYTHING SEEMED TO HAPPEN at once. The barrel of the gun shifted slightly and Alexander's gnarly finger squeezed the trigger. The small revolver exploded, sending its first bullet straight into Henderson's heart. The old man was already dead when a second bullet whizzed past Perkins who dove through the terrace door. His shoulder slammed onto the hard surface of the patio. Remarkably, there were no more shots, so he was able to roll out of view without further injury.

ALEXANDER RUSHED to the safe and pressed what Perkins had thought was the head of a screw. A localized conveyor dropped the front compartment below floor level and a second, hidden safe slid forward. Keeping one eye on the doorway, Alexander clumsily pressed his thumb against three knobs that, to the untrained eye, looked like simple lug-bolts. He was relieved to see that Perkins did not reappear. *Good,* he thought, *he's too scared to stop me.*

The internal mechanism whirred slowly. Alexander knew that the safe would open precisely forty-five seconds after he pressed the last knob, but that now seemed far too long. He shook the gun with annoyance. His voice gurgled with impatience. "Come on! *Come on—I* have to get out of here." His feverish eyes glistened when he heard the metallic click and saw the door pop open. "Finally!"

Alexander snatched bunches of papers and several bundles of money. He clutched them possessively, making a mental note to keep the contents of his safe enclosed in clear vinyl pouches in the future for quick retrieval. Then he reached out to press the intercom button on his telephone.

"Helen, tell our fly boy to start the engines. We'll be there in five minutes." *The stupid woman thinks I'll bring her precious son and fly them both to the Bahamas.*

Seconds later, Rodney rushed into the room. "Are you all right, Mr. Rossweild? He stared into the barrel of the gun with disbelief. "Hey, whoa! I'm on your side." He raised his hands and prattled. "I heard you talking on the telephone. It sounded like my mother, Helen. She talked about you the other day. Was that her?"

Alexander could not believe his luck. *So, another fly has crept up to my web.* "Of course that was your mother, who do you think arranged the connection between you?"

Rodney stared stupidly.

"Well, don't just stand there, boy. If you want to see your mama follow me now."

As he headed out the door, Rossweild shouted, "Hurry! We've got to get to the hanger." He shook his gun toward a large brick building that stood in a distant field. Rodney rushed across the room. He stepped over Henderson's body and like a wick, the cuff of his immaculate uniform sucked up a bright red bloodstain.

THE EXCHANGE BETWEEN Rossweild and Rodney gave Perkins enough time to dart around the corner and up the expansive western side of the mansion. *Jeez, they could use the perimeter of this place for a marathon—it's huge!* He was hoping to find help, but what he found when he stumbled around the next corner was shear pandemonium. After Fingers and Martin Bascomb maneuvered Senator Monroe out of the building and into the hands of Captain Robert's men, Mac, Sadie-Lee and Handy had used their special equipment to drop Damo, Bender and some of the other unsuspecting conspirators.

***

Chapter 110

Damo scuttled from bush to bush.

*W*hen that meddlesome Jenson woman screamed it gave Damo the opportunity he was waiting for. She had peeked through the door, hoping to see another spectacular antique—only to find the captain's unconscious prisoners.

Damo regained consciousness at the screams. He had been caught when he followed one of the waiters. *I knew there was somethin' funny about that guy,* he thought, still not realizing that Sadie-Lee had drugged him. Luckily he was near a sliding door that opened onto the garden. There were plenty of bushes to hide behind until he could reach the gnarly elms at the edge of the lawn. Damo figured that he could dodge behind them and then slip into the forest beyond.

From across the room Bender groaned and tried to stand up. That was just the diversion that Damo needed. He eased the door open and slipped out and hid behind the closest bush, then waited to see if he was missed. He was not, his captors were struggling with the curious crowd of people who were drawn by the screams.

Damo crouched low and scuttled from bush to bush, stopping at each until he was sure it was safe to continue. At the outermost bush he decided it was all or nothing and he raced toward freedom.

For once Damo did not worry about the crease in his pants.

***

Chapter 111

It's like the Red Sea—parting for Moses!

*T*he information that Alexander clutched so tightly would destroy him if it fell into the hands of the authorities, but if he could get away, he knew that the long arm of the law would not be able to reach him.

RODNEY WAS SURPRISED to see how agile Alexander was when they sprinted away from the mansion. He winced when Alexander expressed a growl of annoyance because he was trampling across a clump of blue flowers. *Awe come on,* he thought. *He won't be seeing them again anyhow!*

The helicopter's blades were already spinning. They jumped into the rear seats, with Alexander behind the pilot and Rodney behind his mother, just as the massive roof slid open.

Helen and Rodney both watched, mesmerized by the scenes above and below them as their aircraft lifted up into the cloudless sky and as the roof slid back into place far below.

"Look at that!" Rodney's shout could barely be heard above the whirl of the blades. "It's like the Red Sea parting for Moses!" He twisted around to speak to Alexander and was amazed to see that he was not there. "Hey!" He wrenched himself forward to question the pilot, but no one was there, either. Helen was already staring at the empty pilot's seat. Rodney shouted, "Who's flying this thing?"

"I don't know. But don't worry, dear, it must be on some kind of automatic pilot. I'm sure someone is controlling it from the ground. He must have thought it safer to fly separately."

Helen did not know how right she was—Alexander did feel safe. He watched with satisfaction as the helicopter sped toward the distant mountains and he chortled with glee as it burst into thousands of flaming fragments. "Okay, Jeffrey. Take me to the other hanger. No one will be watching for us now."

***

Chapter 112

Sam's aim was perfect.

Damo raced toward the protective canopy of the gnarly elms at the far end of the lawn. He did not see Sam or the colorful can of beer that was hurtling toward his head.

Sam's aim was perfect—his can had hit its mark. He grinned and jumped from his perch shouting, "We got one of 'em Robby! We really got him!"

Sam and Rob hauled Damo off the ground and made their way toward the mansion with their still-dazed prisoner in tow. Perkins greeted them and ordered Captain Robert's men to take Damo off their hands.

Grinning like a proud father, he introduced his two recruits to the other men.

AFTER HE HEARD HOW SAM had bagged the lanky killer, Perkins thumped him on the back and said, sotto voice, "Pretty effective weapon you have there, kid." He took the can that Sam was still holding and stared at the red and gold message that was printed on its side:

Warning: This product may contain
genetically modified ingredients
and it may be hazardous to your health.

Epilogue

A strange swishing sound brought John Victor out of a deep sleep. Cold fingers clamped onto his wrist.

A stick-thin nurse had opened the drapery that encircled his bed and she was now checking his pulse. He was in a hospital. Through squinty lids, John watched the woman as she checked his vital signs. He instantly liked her voice when she spoke. *Soft—and soothing,* he thought.

"Hello Mr. Victor. I'm glad to see you're finally returning to us. Do you remember what happened?"

He remembered all right. How could he forget?

"Hell yes. Explosion." He tried to sit up but changed his mind.

"THANK GOD YOU'RE OKAY!"

John turned toward the familiar feminine voice.

"Welcome back to the conscious world, dear heart, but I think you'd better stay still for awhile and let those bruises heal." Betty aimed her razor sharp gaze straight into his eyes as she uttered a wifely warning. "You are lucky to be alive, Johnny Victor, and when you get all better, I'm going to kill you!" She shook her finger at him before offering a careful hug.

John accepted her embrace then groaned again, but mainly for effect. "Ohhhh. I guess you're right, Bet. I'll just stay put for awhile."

The nurse smiled. "I'm glad you're cooperating, Mr.

Victor, because I'll have to inject a sleeping aid if you don't. Dr. Sheppard said you must have complete bed rest for another 24 hours." She shot him a warning look that was almost as fierce as Betty's. "And I've never let a patient disobey his orders yet." She adjusted his bedding and updated his chart, then announced that she'd be at the nurse's station if he should need her. She stopped at the door to remind Betty that even the morning visiting hours were limited in the intensive care unit and she only had fifteen minutes.

Satisfied that John was behaving himself, Betty gave a smug smile and offered him a sip from a cup of ice chips. He was still happily crunching when Evie, Brick and Perkins arrived.

"HEY GUYS! COME ON IN!" John called in welcome, then remembered to groan just enough to elicit a sympathetic gasp from his sister. She rushed to his side with Brick in tow.

"My God, John—you had us so worried!"

"Awe, don't worry about me, Sis. I've been worse. Remember the hole that boat drilled into my chest?"

"Who could forget?"

Betty stood up then and exclaimed, "A boat in your chest? You never told me about that one." But she quickly shook her head and said, "My God, I don't even *want* to hear about it. Here Evie, take my seat—I've gotta stretch. I think I'll say a little prayer of thanks, too, for there not being any *boats* at that old factory." She looked at John. "Otherwise, one probably would have drilled your head." She touched Evie's arm. "By the way, guys, we have less than fifteen minutes before visiting hours are over."

"We know. The nurse told us."

JOHN NOTICED THAT BRICK was clutching a briefcase with the hand that was not attached to Evie's hand. "So, Brick, is that my stuff you got there?"

"Yes—it's all here, John. Actually, that's why Perkins is here. He noticed some of the symbols you traced and he's sure he's seen them before. He wants to tell you about it."

"Oh yeah? What's on your mind, Perk?"

Perkins took one of the notebooks and thumbed through it. He held up a page headed 'Illinois 6th' and used his finger to circle a patch of wheat that filled the bottom of a small fat triangle.

"This triangle's just like one I saw after I left Domino. I'm pretty sure it's the insignia of a regiment from the Civil War." He tapped it for emphasis. "Whatcha' think?"

"That's what it is all right—I copied it from a Civil War reference book. It matches a sketch I got from one of my clients."

"Well, somebody etched one just like it into some rocks in the hills not too far from here. I'm thinking it might have been carved by a soldier during the *Civil War!*"

John grabbed the notebook. His eyes blazed with excitement. "You saw *this* etched in a rock near here? Right here in Tennessee?"

"Yes—right near here."

"Perkins—I love you! I've gotta get out of this place! Where's my pants?" He swung his legs over the side of the bed, then clutched his head with a groan—a real one this time.

Betty rushed to his side. "Oh no you don't Johnny Victor. You're staying put. You heard that nurse!"

"But . . . "

"No buts, Mr.—except, maybe, for a needle in your *own* cute little butt!"

"You wouldn't!"

"You're right, *I* wouldn't. But *she* would!" She waved a hand toward the nurse who was hurtling toward them like a thin white missile—with needle in hand.

"You're a cruel woman, Betty Victor."

"Yes I am—and I'm mighty proud of it."

Betty gave him a quick hug and made way for the nurse. Then she ushered Evie and friends out of the room.

Perkins called from the doorway. "I'll show you where that etching is as soon as you're able to make the trip." He grinned at John's slurred response. The sedative was already sending the reluctant patient on his own quick trip—into dreamland.

TEN DAYS LATER, John was clambering up a lush hillside a half dozen steps behind Perkins, Brick and Manny. He turned around, gasped for breath and shouted downward. "Hey, you slowpokes! We're almost there!"

Evie shouted back. "Good! I was about to go on strike." By the time she and Betty caught up to them, John and Perkins were already scrunched under a rocky overhang. All she could see was their feet, but she could hear them talking.

"There it is—can you see it?"

"Yup," John grunted. "You were right, Perk . . ..this sure looks like that insignia to me. It's old, too. See? The rock's warn down quite a bit. I'd say from the look of it that it must have been exposed to the elements for a while. I'm thinking it must have tumbled down the hillside. Let's see what we can find higher up."

Evie watched as the two men wriggled their way out of the crevice. When she saw her brother's face she was afraid he was overdoing it—he was beet red and he was breathing too hard. She could see that Betty was worried, too, and decided they'd have to do something. She wondered if her stubborn brother would agree to stop for a lunch break before climbing higher.

"Why don't we stop to eat?" She nodded toward the others, silently willing them to agree. It worked—Perkins winked.

"Good idea, Evie—I'm hungry. And I'm ready for a break. What d'ya say, guys? You hungry too?"

Evie noticed that John was not eating as much as usual. He only gobbled down two sandwiches and three chocolate chip cookies. He then set out to entertain them with colorful stories about his treasure hunting expeditions as they hungrily devoured their own portions, but it did not take long for the excitement of the hunt to lure them back to their search.

At the top of the hill, everyone watched with quiet fascination as John tossed a gold ring and some coins onto the ground. He then turned on his metal detector and tested the response levels. Satisfied with the results, he set to work, swinging his machine with slow, methodical sweeps until he heard the first telltale beep. He shoved a warn leather pouch into Brick's hand.

"Hey Brick, this is full of marker stakes. Why don't you jab one into the dirt at every spot where Betty G here beeps? I'm gonna go through this hillside in a grid like fashion . . ." He gave Perkins and Manny an innocent look before adding, ". . . and when I finish we can all start digging at the markers."

Perkins took the hint.

"Why wait? Why don't the rest of us just start digging while you continue your sweep?"

John winked, "Now why didn't I think of that?"

Betty snorted, ready to hurl a witty retort, when the detector beeped again.

John thought, *saved by the bell!*

The group worked in companionable silence with Brick marking each beep and the other four digging at the markers. Every few minutes someone would whoop with laughter and hold up a find. By the end of the first hour, they had accumulated three nails, two rocks with iron deposits and several unidentified metal objects.

John broke the pattern when he stopped and kneeled to the ground, even though there was no beep.

Brick knelt beside him. "Hey, guy, what's up?"

"I think this is where that etched stone came from." He pointed along a rocky ridge. "See? This is an Ignatius clump and that overhang down there has the same formation. My guess is it broke off right here." He swished the foot of his detector around to underscore his point.

"I'm impressed! You some kind of geologist?"

"No, but when you've been mining gold as long as I have, you learn a lot about rocks 'n metals 'n stuff." He stopped talking and resumed his sweep of the area. Seconds later he was rewarded. *Beep. Beep. Beep.*

"Hey guys! We've got something and I c'n tell from the beeps that it's pretty big. I wish I had my new toy. *It* could tell us what's down there." He gave Perkins a pointed look.

"Sorry—the cops won't give it up yet!"

John looked at their pile of junk. "Coulda' saved us a bunch of digging, too." He needn't have worried, the others did not seem to care—they were too busy staring at the clump.

Manny and Betty dropped to their knees and started to dig. The rest of the group watched expectantly until Betty exclaimed, "Oh, my God—I've hit something!"

Like an exuberant puppy she pawed at the dirt.

"Way to go, sweetheart, dearest, love-of-my-life!" John exclaimed when they unearthed a century-old strong box.

~

INGRID DICKERSON WAS listening to Fox & Friends, the morning talk show on Fox News Channel. She loved E.D. Hill's blunt honesty and the two guys, Steve and Brian, were always entertaining. They were in the middle of a particularly funny segment when the telephone rang.

Ingrid did not want to miss the punch line—she was sure E.D. was about to put one over on Brian. She yelped at her telephone, "Hold your horses, I'm coming." Of course, it just kept ringing. "Okay. Okay. I'm on my way—this better be *good*!" She yanked the receiver off the hook, with one eye and one ear still glued to the television.

"Hello."

A man's voice responded, "Hello, Mrs. Dickerson?"

"Yes. This is she."

"Mrs. Dickerson, this is John Victor. How are you?"

371

Ingrid's heart leaped into warp speed. She forgot the television.

"John Victor? The treasure hunter? How are you? Why are you calling? Have you found something?"

John grinned, "Yes, Mrs. Dickerson. I'm fine. I found your ancestor's stash and I'm pretty darned sure it's everything you've dreamed it was."

He heard a dull thud. *Oh my God,* he thought, *she must have fainted!* He hoped she had a nice soft carpet to land on. He strained to hear the commotion at the other end of the line, glad to realize someone was with her. Several minutes passed before he was able to explain to her excited husband that there was, indeed, a trunk, which according to the papers, held the gold that had reportedly been stolen by one of the Confederate officers during the siege of Fort Donelson.

"Actually," John explained, "I bet there's another family that would love to hear about this—it'll clear their ancestor's reputation. He was accused of stealing the money. General Floyd was his name."

John retold the story of how the Confederate General, John B. Floyd, had been accused of misappropriating $870,000 while he was President Buchanan's Secretary of War. Floyd had demanded a trial, at which point the charges were dropped for lack of evidence. No one ever did find the gold that apparently had been removed from Fort Donelson and hidden during General Grant's advance. But, apparently, he never got over the shame.

John urged the Dickersons to attend a meeting with the local officials regarding the legality of the find.

JOHN MADE ANOTHER telephone call. He told Martin Bascomb that they had found the treasure and Martin told him that he had just returned from a memorial service for Julia Mahoney.

"Poor girl had no family, but we drummed up a re-spectable number of past associates from UVM. Oh, and I heard from Tommy Sykes." He explained that Tommy's mother had agreed to let him work at Pleasant Acres during the summer months. He also reported that Rob and Sam were making plans to sign up for the Army while Fingers was going to stay on at Pleasant Acres as a full-time assistant. "That young man has a good head for business," Martin exclaimed.

John could tell that Martin was pleased to have played a part in getting the boys off the street.

~

HALFWAY ACROSS THE COUNTRY, Melvin was settling in at his uncle's spa in Tucson, Arizona. Despite the strict dietary standards, he was happy—he had a case of twinkies and a six-pack of beer stashed away in the basement.

~

HALFWAY ACROSS THE WORLD, Alexander was drinking a pina colada and throwing darts at pictures of John and Brick. As luck would have it, the story of the Tennessee treasure find had hit all the papers—even in Columbia where a large share of Alexander's assets were hidden.

Alexander had had the brass ring right within his grasp until that damned treasure hunter blew up his factory. Well, he, Alexander Graham Rossweild, had never been beaten. He was going to squeeze the life out of that little nobody! The article said one of John Victor's ongoing projects was in Arizona. Alexander sneered, "Well, Mr. John Victor, treasure investigator—you may have destroyed the formula for my golden liquid and you may have found that trunk full of gold, too, but I've still got treasures beyond your wildest dreams—and I have a few loyal men in Tucson."

The End

THE LIST

ANTHONY ROBBINS. Nationally recognized motivational speaker and consultant and author of several books including my favorite, *Awaken The Giant Within.* ISBN #0-671-72734-6.

MARY HIGGINS CLARK. Often described as America's best-selling Queen of Suspense. Published over two dozen novels, including my favorite, *Loves Music, Loves to Dance.* ISBN #0-671-75889-6.

CAROL HIGGINS CLARK. Daughter of Mary Higgins Clark, author of the Regan Reilly series, including my favorite, *Decked,* ISBN #0-446-51549-3.

DEAN KOONTZ. Nationally known author of thrillers, including my favorite, *Sole Survivor.* ISBN #0-679-42526-8.

JEFFREY M. SMITH. Author of, *Seeds of Deception, Exposing Industry and Government Lies About the Safety of the Genetically Engineered Foods You're Eating.* ISBN # 0-9729665-8-7.

NOFA Vermont. A non profit association of farmers, gardeners and consumers working to promote an economically viable and ecologically sound Vermont food system for the benefit of current and future generations. To contact them, just google Northeast Organic Farming Association of Vermont. Or write to: NOFA Vermont, POB 697, Richmond, Vermont 05477.

MOTHERS FOR NATURAL LAW. Founded in June 1996 to transform the overwhelming problems facing families into simple, practical action steps every mother can take to safeguard the health, well-being and innocence of her children. Greatly focused on genetic engineering. Can be googled on the web. Or write to them at MNL, POB 1177, Fairfield, Iowa 52556.

RURAL VERMONT
A statewide nonprofit, grassroots organization and an advocacy group opposed to corporate industrial agriculture. Just google Rural Vermont, or write to them at 15 Barre Street, Suite 2, Montpelier, VT 05602.